DELPHI FABRICE

THE RED
SORCERER

TRANSLATED AND WITH AN INTRODUCTION BY
BRIAN STABLEFORD

I0591297

THIS IS A SNUGGLY BOOK

Translation and Introduction Copyright © 2022
by Brian Stableford.
All rights reserved.

ISBN: 978-1-64525-093-7

THE RED SORCERER

"DELPHI FABRICE" (the pseudonym of Gaston-Henri-Adhémar Risselin, 1877-1937) began his literary career as an art critic with *Les Peintres de Bretagne* (1898), before becoming involved in the Decadent Movement, under the aesthetic of which he composed a number of works, including *L'Araignée rouge* (1903), the one-act drama *Clair de lune* (1903), which was co-written with Jean Lorrain, Fabrice's mentor, and *La sorcier rouge* (1910). Under the need for money, he gradually turned his attention to romance novels, novels of adventure geared towards a juvenile audience, and "cine-novels" (adaptations of films into photo-novels). In all, he is credited with writing over 120 books.

BRIAN STABLEFORD'S scholarly work includes *New Atlantis: A Narrative History of Scientific Romance* (Wildside Press, 2016), *The Plurality of Imaginary Worlds: The Evolution of French roman scientifique* (Black Coat Press, 2017) and *Tales of Enchantment and Disenchantment: A History of Faerie* (Black Coat Press, 2019). He has translated more than three hundred volumes from the French, mostly in the genres of *roman scientifique*, *contes de fées* and Romantic and Symbolist fiction. His recent fiction includes the visionary science fiction novel *The Revelations of Time and Space* (2020) and its sequel *After the Revelation* (2021); the last in his long series of "Tales of the Genetic Revolution," *The Elusive Shadows* (2020); and the comedy fantasy *Meat on the Bone* (2021), all published by Snuggly Books.

SNUGGLY BOOKS

CONTENTS

INTRODUCTION

Le Sorcier rouge, here translated as *The Red Sorcerer*, signed "Delphi Fabrice," was first published as a 64-part feuilleton serial in *Le Journal* between 31 July 1910 and 3 October 1910, skipping the 2 October issue. There are secondary references to a cheap book with the same title, which appears to be a reprint of the novel, but the Bibliothèque Nationale has no copy and the item is extraordinarily elusive; almost all bibliographic citations of the title relate to the printed version of a five-act melodrama based on the feuilleton, signed "P. de Wattyne," produced at the Théâtre Montparnasse in 1913.[1]

The catalogue of the Bibliothèque Nationale gives Delphi Fabrice's dates as 1877-1937 but offers no further information about him save for the list of his prolific publications. In an introduction to a 2004 reprint of his first and most famous novel *L'Araignée rouge* (1903; tr. as *The Red Spider*), Eric Walbecq states that the author's real name was Gaston-Henri-Adhémar Risselin, and that he was born in Paris, the son of Joseph-Benonie-Adhémar Risselin and Ernestine-Zoé Marchand.

---

1 Pierre de Wattyne is listed by the Bibliothèque Nationale catalogue, along with his publications in book form, as a Belgian journalist born in 1885, who was allegedly on the staff of *La Lanterne*, but internet search engines currently turn up no further information in his regard. The *gallica* archive of *La Lanterne* has mention of a couple of theatrical productions bearing his name, but his by-line does not appear ever to have featured in the newspaper or its *Supplement*.

Many other sources attribute the pseudonym similarly, but it is unclear where the information originated and confirmatory evidence is presently sparse. *Le Figaro* reported in 1934 the death of "Madame Delphi Fabrice, née Fasquelle," but gave no further details. Walbecq notes that although Fabrice had had a son—again giving no further details—his body was unclaimed after his death and public funds had to pay for his burial. A Gaston Risselin born in 1896 is listed among the casualties of the Great War in military records, but there is no way of knowing whether or not that was the son in question. More information about the author can be deduced from his publications, especially the journalistic pieces he contributed to the thrice-weekly *Supplement* of the newspaper *La Lanterne* in the early 1900s, which frequently refer to "Delphi Fabrice," but the reliability of his supposedly-personal reportage, although it is fascinating, has to be reckoned dubious.

What is certain is that Fabrice began his journalistic career in the 1890s working for *La Presse*, where the pieces bearing his by-line consisted of art criticism. The extent of his unsigned reportage is impossible to determine. His signed publications in *La Presse* did not overlap the long series of *Contes rapides* contributed to the paper in 1897-1901 by Jane de La Vaudère (1857-1908), but it is highly probable that the two writers were acquainted at that time, if not via *La Presse* then via the writer and theater impresario Oscar Méténier (1859-1913), with whom both of them collaborated in the late 1890s.[1] In that decade Fabrice formed a close relationship with Jean Lorrain (1855-1906), his literary idol, with whom he also collaborated extensively; for more than a decade his own career effectively rode on the coat-tails of Lorrain and Méténier. The

---

1 Most of the *Contes rapides* were reprinted in the *Supplement* while Fabrice was on its staff, and one or two were embellished, possibly by editorial intrusions, but if Fabrice ever did any ghost-writing for La Vaudère there is no record of it.

suspicion that both of them employed Fabrice as an occasional ghost-writer, in addition to their jointly-signed collaborations, cannot be confirmed, but there is an interesting implication to that effect in Jane de La Vaudére's *roman à clef Les Androgynes* (1903; tr, as "The Androgynes"), in which the famous author Jacques Chozelle—an obvious caricature of Lorrain—exploits and ruinously corrupts a young disciple named André (the protagonist of *L'Araignée rouge* is named Andhré), who is probably based on Fabrice.

Another of Fabrice's acknowledged collaborators was "Liane de Pougy" (Anne-Marie Chassaigne, 1869-1950), to whom he was almost certainly introduced by Jean Lorrain. The precise extent of their collaboration is impossible to determine, but his acquaintance with her had a powerful influence on his work during the early 1900s, which undoubtedly extended as far as *Le Sorcier rouge*. Pougy's ostensible profession was that of actress and singer, but she is usually referred to by historians as a "courtesan," because she made her living as an expensive prostitute; the Parisian stage in the Belle Époque, at all its many levels, was primarily a showcase enabling men ambitious to acquire "trophy mistresses" to fish for prey and permitting young women willing to supply the demand to advertise themselves to suppliers of money, houses, carriages and jewels.

Pougy's first great success at the Folies Bergère was a ballet written for her by Jean Lorrain, who had appointed himself her unpaid publicist. Because she was not a talented dancer, Lorrain wrote a leading part for her in which she hardly had to move, merely exhibiting her notoriously beautiful figure in a gaudily flimsy costume, masquerading as a spider lying in wait in its web while the members of the chorus, playing her prospective prey, did most of the actual dancing. The ballet, *L'Araignée d'or* [The Golden Spider], was staged at the Folies Bergère in 1896 and caused something of a sensation. Its literary influence was extensive; its symbolism is echoed and extrapolated in Fabrice's

L'Araignée rouge, and the staging of an identical ballet by "Jacques Chozelle" is a crucial episode in *Les Androgynes*. Before publishing the novel, Fabrice wrote a short play called *L'Araignée rouge*, which was scheduled for production at La Scala theater in 1900, with another of Lorrain's protégées, "Polaire" (Émilie-Marie Bouchard, 1874-1939) in the lead, before it was banned by the censor—an insult that clearly offended Fabrice and augmented his fervent desire to test and extend the limits of the permissible and the conventional in his fiction and drama: a determination of which *Le Sorcier rouge* was perhaps the most spectacularly peculiar manifestation.

Liane de Pougy's pseudonymous career was planned and guided by the self-styled Comtesse Valtesse de la Bigne, a procuress who had added a touch of class to her own career as a pretentious prostitute by publishing a supposedly autobiographical novel, and Pougy did the same. Pougy would undoubtedly have turned initially to Lorrain for help in that task, but it was probably inevitable that the ever-busy Lorrain would delegate the task to one of his acolytes; Fabrice might well have made a substantial uncredited contribution to Pougy's novels *L'Insaissable* (1898) and *Myrrhille* (1899), the subject-matter of which is echoed in several "courtesan novels" bearing his own signature.

The most successful work bearing Pougy's signature was *Idylle sapphique* (1901), apparently a romanticized account of her seduction by the notorious lesbian Natalie Barney, an American socialite whose salon became the meeting-place of a coterie of talented female poets, including "Renée Vivien" (Pauline Tarn) and Lucie Delarue-Mardrus. The extent of Fabrice's contribution to the novel, if any, is unknown but it is probably no coincidence that he included a markedly different and considerably more scabrous account of a lesbian seduction in a short novel made up of weekly episodes published in the *Lanterne Supplement* between January and June 1903, "Fleurs d'éther et de talus" (tr. as *Flowers of Ether*). The story takes the form of a long conversation between a journalist named "Fabrice" and a courtesan named Nine d'Aubusson, whose anecdotes supply him with copy for his writings. At the time, Fabrice was making extensive contributions to the *Supplement*'s gossip columns, paying close attention to the public appearances of Liane de Pougy and her rival "professional beauties," based on material almost certainly provided by Pougy; the episodes carried a sequence of dedications to the professional beauties of contemporary Paris, and contemporary gossip columns sometimes included letters addressed by Fabrice to Pougy, sometimes calling her by the nickname "Liline" and implying a quasi-intimate acquaintance similar to that between "Fabrice" and Nine d'Aubusson in the story.

The next quasi-autobiographical novel to be published under Pougy's signature was *Ecce homo: d'ici de là* (1903), but it was rapidly followed by "Dix ans de fête: Mémoires d'une demi-mondaine" [Ten Years of Partying: Memoirs of a Demi-Mondaine], which began publication as a feuilleton in the *Lanterne Supplement* in November 1903. The serial was advertised as forthcoming in the "Échos" section of the 28 July edition of the *Supplement* as a novel written in collaboration with Delphi Fabrice, but when it began it only carried Pougy's by-line and readers were encouraged to suppose that it consisted of Pougy's actual memoirs of her early life. In Liane de Pougy's supposed writings, as well as her life, the line between fiction and reportage is very blurred, but no less so than Delphi Fabrice's writings in the *Supplement*, which operate in a murky gray area of unreliable reportage that he had appropriated, lock, stock and barrel, from Jean Lorrain.

When Lorrain had begun writing regularly in 1889 for the "stable" of short story writers assembled by Catulle Mendès to supply *L'Écho de Paris* with material, each on a weekly basis, (stories that were routinely used as the lead items on page one) he soon branched out into the parallel writing of a "diary" column titled "Pall Mall Semaine" and signed "Raitif de la Bretonne" in honor of Nicolas Restif de La Bretonne's largely fictitious accounts of his supposed nocturnal wanderings in Paris, collected as *Nuits de Paris* (1788-94), which Lorrain imitated. The series continued in the pages of *Le Journal* after Lorrain, along with many other members of the Mendès stable, transferred his allegiance to that paper in the mid-1890s. In his turn, Fabrice copied his idol faithfully in his own signed contributions to the *Lanterne Supplement*, which were a regular feature between 1902 and 1909.

Lorrain's writings as "Raitif de la Bretonne" marked a particular phase in his career, when he was approaching the height of his success, and his self-publicization cultivated a notoriety for himself as great or greater than the people he promoted and about whom he related gossip. Cautious at first, his personalized reportage gradually became more reckless, sometimes frankly insulting and marginally slanderous. In one notorious instance, an attack on the dancer Bob Walter (Baptistine Dupré 1856-1907)—who compensated for her advancing age by devising a spectacular novelty act in which she performed a version of Loie Fuller's "serpentine dance" in a cage with four lions held at bay by the tamer Georges Marck—led to his being confronted by Walter at the premiere of one of his plays and struck in the face with a handbag containing a bunch of keys. The account of the parallel incident in *Les Androgynes* has the article in question being reluctantly ghost-written by André, but we can only speculate as to whether La Vaudère knew something about its authorship that was not made public. Whatever the truth of the matter, it certainly left a deep impression on Fabrice, who incorporated caricaturish references to it in "Fleurs d'éther et de talus" and was later sued for slander by one of the dancers with whom Marck replaced Walter in the act, when she took offence at one of his gossip columns.

By the beginning of 1903 Lorrain had thrown discretion to the winds, and had begun representing himself, albeit teasingly, as a flamboyant homosexual with a liking for wrestlers and other circus performers. Fabrice joined in the game with enthusiasm, representing Lorrain in the same fashion in some of his pretended reportage and caricaturing him outrageously, evidently with Lorrain's blessing, in "Fleurs d'éther et de talus" in the character of Jean des Glaïeuls. Fabrice subsequently appropriated "Jean des Glaïeuls" as one of his own pseudonyms and published numerous stories in the *Supplement* under that name. Lorrain's exaggerated characterization of himself probably had some truth in it, although he undoubtedly encouraged Fabrice to add further distortions to it, at least until the summer of 1903,[1] but it is not at all obvious to what extent Fabrice's caricature of himself in "Fleurs d'éther et de talus" had any basis in fact. Exactly how well Jane de La Vaudère knew him is unclear, but the André of *Les Androgynes* is only drawn very reluctantly into a world of homosexual orgies for which he has no natural inclination. In addition to representing himself falsely as a busy socialite, "Fabrice" presumably overstated his intimacy with Nine d'Aubusson; Liane de Pougy appears to have treated him kindly while he was useful to her, but dropped the acquaintance abruptly in 1904, when their literary and theatrical collaborations came to an end.

---

1 The context changed during that year because of a scandal that broke in the Parisian press regarding parties hosted by the writer Jacques Adelswärd-Fersen (1880-1923), an even more notoriously flamboyant homosexual, who was arrested in August 1903 and charged with inciting minors to commit debauchery. The reportage of the trial was exceedingly lurid, and its aftermath forced Adelswärd-Fersen into exile. Lorrain published an article in his defense and volunteered to testify at the trial, but the offer was refused, probably because it was felt that his appearance would do more harm than good; Adelswärd-Fersen thought it wise to return to a more careful diplomacy in his own self-representation, and so did Lorrain. Fabrice soon stopped suggesting publicly that he was homosexual himself, and also ceased repeating the claim that he was a former abuser of ether and morphine, but not until he had published a lurid quasi-journalistic account of *Opium à Paris* (1907), which became his best-selling book.

As to whether Delphi Fabrice really might have been a drug abuser and homosexual poseur, like the Fabrice of "Fleurs d'éther et de talus," it is impossible to tell. Jean Lorrain had certainly given up ether-drinking some time before he wrote his notorious *contes d'un buveur d'éther* (tr. in *Nightmares of an Ether Drinker*) in the 1890s, but he did not want to shake off the marketable reputation that they had cultivated for him. In 1900 he had moved to Nice for health reasons and only visited Paris occasionally, but the gossip column of *Le Supplement* dutifully reported on 28 April 1903 that he had escorted Liane de Pougy to a costume ball, both spectacularly travestied as vagabonds. The change of location did not prevent Lorrain from dying of the after-effects of his ether abuse during one of his trips to Paris in 1906. The immediate cause of his death was peritonitis—the same problem that the Fabrice of "Fleurs d'éther et de talus" claimed to have recently imperiled his life.

Le Sorcier rouge does not feature any character based on Delphi Fabrice or Jean Lorrain, and Liane de Pougy only makes a pseudonymous cameo appearance therein, but it continues his enduring fascination with the shadowy world of Parisian prostitution. Pougy's novels belonged to a thriving subgenre that ostensibly set out to correct the romanticized image of prostitution depicted in such best-selling novels as *La Dame aux camélias* (1848) by Alexandre Dumas fils and only partly-revised by Émile Zola's supposedly-Naturalistic *Nana* (1880). While Pougy and Fabrice—a determined disciple of Naturalism—set out alongside other authors of sensational "exposés" such as Jean-Louis Dubut de Laforest and Jules Hoche to carry that crusade further, it was not until Fabrice penned *Le Sorcier rouge* that he removed his own gloves of discretion completely and set out to depict the world of prostitutes and their pimps with a frank and extreme brutality—so frank and so extreme, in fact, that it required a strange supernaturalization completely at odds with his supposed Naturalism.

The result is odd in more ways than one, and its extremism tests the limits of plausibility far beyond breaking point, but precisely for that reason it is an intriguing exercise in narrative strategy. It is not a good novel, and is certainly very unsavory, but it is quite extraordinary and thus worthy of attention as a specimen. There is a sense in which all writers of feuilleton melodrama were compelled to be "sadistic" in subjecting their heroes and heroines to all kinds of maltreatment as they run the obstacle courses of their rambling plots, but there is a particular extremism in Fabrice's grim and relentless authorial sadism that tempts the suspicion that a complex psychology must lie behind it, although a precise hypothetical analysis is difficult.

By the time Fabrice wrote *Le Sorcier rouge*, his association with *La Lanterne* had ended. He had followed up "Fleurs d'éther et de talus" with the *Supplement* feuilletons "L'Hommme aux treize lits" [The Man with Thirteen Beds] (1905), "Le Crime de l'impasse Rosafin" [The Murder in the Impasse Rosafin] (1908-9), "Souris d'alcove" [Bedroom Mice] (1910) and "La Môme quinze grammes" [The Fifteen-Gram Kid] (1911), which ran alongside several sequences of pesudo-autobiographical articles, stories and character sketches as well as a series of episodes reprinted from *L'Araignée rouge* as "Pages retrouvées" (1906), but his signed contributions concluded in July 1911. He returned to the pages of the *Supplement* in 1920 with a series of "Notes parisiennes" and a brief feuilleton signed "Jean des Glaïeuls," but times had changed and his reassociation did not last long. Following the example of Jean Lorrain, he had attempted to switch his allegiance to *Le Journal*, where his by-line had appeared on a feuilleton jointly signed by Oscar Méténier, "La Dernière aventure du Prince Curaçao" [The Most Recent Adventure of Prince Curaçao] (1908), before the serialization of *Le Sorcier rouge*, and was to be featured again in the sequel to the former, "Curaçao-roi" [King Curaçao] (1912), but it did not reappear there afterwards.[1] His career was, of course deci-

---

1 Fabrice and Méténier are given joint responsibility by some bibliographers

sively interrupted by the war of 1914-18, during which he was presumably in military service, still having been young enough in 1914 to be conscripted.

By 1910, therefore, Fabrice, was an extensively practiced commercial writer who had begun to develop a reputation of his own beyond the shadow of his mentors. He was to go on to write dozens more novels thereafter, but nothing to compare with *Le Sorcier rouge*. Most were routine crime fiction or action-adventure novels, the latter mostly aimed at younger readers, but his belated "courtesan novels" were very weak by comparison with those he had written before the Great War and seemed outdated. The war had undoubtedly changed him, but it had also changed the social milieu[1] and the literary marketplace, and even if he had attempted another narrative experiment akin to the one he had carried out in *Le Sorcier rouge*, the probability is that no one would have published it. Indeed, it is difficult to believe that anyone would have published it in 1910 had it been completed before submission rather than published in daily episodes made up as the author went along.

There is no way of knowing for sure why there was a gap in publication between the penultimate and last episodes of the

---

for ghost-writing a series of more than twenty cheap booklets issued in 1908-10 featuring the *Vie d'aventures et de chasse du dompteur Edmond Pézon* [The Life of Adventures and Hunts of the Lion-Tamer Edmond Pézon]; if that is correct, Fabrice would probably have done the actual writing, although Méténier is likely to have been the intermediary of his contact with Pézon.

1 Prostitution continued unabated, but its habitats were transformed, the entire society of sidewalks, cafés, cheap hotels and the "fortifs" having changed its aspect. The particular species of prostitution of which Liane de Pougy was a superstar had changed too; theaters and cabarets had suffered badly during the war, but the advent of cinema had allowed a fortunate few "professional beauties," including Polaire, to become movie stars; the economics of the new industry only liberated them partly from the need to prostitute themselves in order to make a living, but its existence caused a considerable shift in the pattern of the ambition of young women keen to make a name for themselves. Liane became a princess by marriage and then became a nun, allegedly devoting her later years to good works and piety.

serial, but it is certainly possible that when the editors of *Le Journal* saw the last episode they hesitated before putting it in print, feeling that it was an atrocious violation of their expectations and the expectations of their readers, although they had little alternative but to publish it anyway. The conclusion of the novel is a deliberate challenge to the expectations in question, and many readers probably felt that it was a stark betrayal of an implicit contract between writers of feuilleton serials and their audience, but Fabrice was not wrong to think that his conclusion was an inevitable and entirely appropriate termination of the project that he had set himself and the manner in which he had developed his story. Jean Lorrain would undoubtedly have approved wholeheartedly, had he still been alive, precisely because it would have seemed perverse to do so, but what Liane de Pougy thought of it is not on record. At any rate, it is not entirely surprising that the book version of the novel, if it really exists, is so very elusive. Readers of the present translation can make up their own minds about its propriety.

The translation is made from the *gallica* archive of *Le Journal*. The translation was difficult because of the high density of Parisian and military argot in the text, the terms of which have no precise equivalents in English. I have preserved a few terms in order to retain a little of the flavor of the original, but French terms of abuse are richer and more colorful than English parallel terms printable in 1910, and have a unique tonal quality that does not translate; I have improvised as best I can.

—Brian Stableford, September 2020

THE RED SORCERER

PROLOGUE
The Man of the Heath

The storm continued to rage in the black, opaque and lugubrious night—a night that seemed as sticky as pitch and from which a great rumor was rising, a howling simultaneously menacing and plaintive: the sound of the furious sea hurled in assault against the rocks of the bay of Carnac.

At the door of an isolated small farm against which the squall appeared to be beating a tremulous voice pronounced in the darkness: "Let's go back inside, I'm scared . . . the sea . . ."

"Why are you afraid, Françoise; you know full well that it's the sea that is unleashed . . ."

"Yes, but . . . that Stone down there . . . can't you see it, Father . . . ?"

"The Sorcerer's Stone! We've always seen it. There's no need to be afraid, my daughter. You know full well that the Red Sorcerer, the Pen-Ru,[1] has gone . . . he's quit the heath . . . he won't be seen again . . ."

"Let's go back in; I'm scared . . ."

A gust of wind and a scatter of rain blew into the hut at the same time as Père and Mère Le Goff and their daughter.

---

1 Pen, more usually rendered Penn, means "head" in Breton, so Pen-Ru signifies red-head. Its attachment to a supposed sorcerer reflects the common folk-myth that the Devil has red hair, imported into classic Romantic fiction by Charles Nodier in "La Combe de l'homme mort" (1833; tr. as "Dead Man's Dale"), although in that instance the Devil figures as an administrator of justice, collecting a soul pledged to him by a murderer.

"Since your first communion, you've been frightened of everything," the mother continued when the door was shut. "You imagine all the time that you've seen the Red Sorcerer on the heath. Everyone knows that it's a big Stone . . ."

Mére Le Goff set about preparing to pour the soup into the bowls. Françoise, still pale with fear, sat apart in a corner that was not illuminated by the mantelpiece candle.

The door opened again almost immediately. A man was outlined against the dark background.

"*Ken avo!*" said the fellow as he came in, saluting the masters of the house with the Breton bonsoir.

"*Ken avo,*" replied the farmer and his wife.

Their daughter emerged from the shadows and in her turn, but in a voice less firm, welcomed her fiancé, Mathurin Dagorne.

Agreeable of face, admirably lithe in his short jacket, a hat with long ribbons on his head and a pen-bas in his hand, the Dagorne son was known for ten leagues around for his strength and his skill in wrestling as well as his endurance in labor. He realized the very type of the tenacious, audacious and adventurous Breton, a son of granite and the ocean.

More than one young woman would have accepted with joy to go and join him behind the gable-end to talk amorously, but Mathurin's heart was no longer free; he had given his love to Françoise Le Goff, a fine young woman, in truth, with blonde hair and blue eyes who wore the costume of Auray graciously: a cashmere dress with broad stripes of black velvet, a white chemisette and a bonnet with broad wings. Everything about her respired youth and freshness. She was a true Bretonne, in whom the characteristic features of the race were found, but a perspicacious observer would have perceived that the young woman has something irresolute and weak in her manner, in her appearance and, above all, in her gaze that is rarely encountered among the people of Armorica—and how that debility of character contrasted with the resolute air of the faces and gestures of her parents!

Françoise's mother and father looked kindly upon the marriage of Mathurin and their daughter; he earned a good living; he was passionate about mechanics and directed the locomotive that threshed the grain throughout the region at harvest time.

"You've done well to come and sup with us on this festival eve," said Mère Le Goff to her future son-in-law.

"How is your mother?" asked Françoise.

"She ought to be coming too. It wasn't easy to persuade her; she said that she'd be better all alone by her fireside."

"Good . . . that's good," said Mère Le Goff. "Where is she then, Mère Dagorne?"

"She'll be here. Well, at her age, one no longer walks very rapidly . . . so I came on ahead . . ."

The farmer's wife was still pouring the cabbage soup into the bowls when the aged and stooped Mère Dagorne came in. An old man, tall and thin, was walking behind her.

"Look!" exclaimed Le Goff. "Père Yann!"

"I met him at the edge of the heath and he followed me," explained Mère Dagorne, taking her place beside Madame Le Goff, after having exchanged cordial words with Françoise and her father.

"By Saint Anne, he did well to follow you," replied the farmer's wife, filling another bowl. He can eat soup with us . . . Come here, Père Yann," she said to the old man. "At this hour it's better to be in the house with something warm inside you than on the heath."

Without saying a word, Père Yann approached. The old man was one of those individuals who are known in Bretagne as "innocents"—inoffensive people who live here and there on public charity. For them, as for all the poor, there is always a place by the fireside, a hunk of bread, a bowl of cider and a kind word.

They clustered around the table, therefore, and for five minutes not a word was heard, everyone savoring the good soup that warms the stomach.

Outside, the sea and the rain continued to moan in the black night.

Mère Le Goff was the first to break the silence, after she had replaced her empty bowl on the table. "It doesn't seem to be calming down," she said. "Can you hear the sea?"

"And the rain," added Père Le Goff. "And the wind shaking the house, howling in the chimney and under the doors."

"I can assure you that it's blowing over the heath," said Mathurin. "I could hardly make headway just now."

"You came over the heath!" exclaimed Mère Dagorne, with a hint of fear.

"Of course, Mère," replied the young man, "because it's shorter . . . you're still afraid of the heath, then?"

"By day, no," the old woman declared. By day it's bright, one can see ahead . . . but by night, one only has bad encounters."

The young man was amused. "Bad encounters! Get away! All that is stories. To begin with, what bad encounters could one have? There isn't even a cat!"

But the old Bretonne shook her head. "You know very well what I mean, Mathurin . . . and everyone here knows it as well as you and me . . ."

Père and Mère Le Goff did not breathe a word, any more than the two old women and Père Yann; they limited themselves to exchanging glances.

But Mère Dagorne resumed, lowering her voice slightly, with her elbows on the tabe and her eyes wide with fear: "The heath is full of Stones, big Stones placed upright, no one knows by whom or when: menhirs, dolmens and cromlechs, rocks that serve houses with heaps of little devils, korrigans as people say, which dance all night and if you see them, force you to enter into their round and leap until you die . . ."

Again, Mathurin tried to joke. "Tales of olden times, Mother!"

But his tone was uneasy; his voice rang false, for all of them, men and women alike, felt rising within them in response to Mère

24

Dagorne's words the old ancestral fear, the dead of supernatural beings that persisted deep down in the race. Even Mathurin, in spite of his skepticism—more apparent than real, more in speech than conviction—was subject to the common thought.

"The heath of Carnac is full of korrigans, and all those Stones are their houses. They hide inside during the day, but they come out at night and it's necessary to see them, as small as dwarfs, with big heads. And many a time my late mother heard them singing their infernal round:

> *Di lun!*
> *Di meurs!*
> *Di merc'hers!*

"The names of the first three days of the week, which they're condemned to repeat until the world ends, without being able to recite the rest.

"Ah, Mathurin, you don't believe in the korrigans! Be careful, my son, that what happened to your great uncle Hervé doesn't happen to you. There was no better musician than him in the entire Vannes region, and no man braver. One evening when he had drunk too much cider and eau-de-vie, he declared, as a joke, that he would play the biniou[1] to the korrigans and see how they liked his music . . . and the next morning they found him dead at the foot of a Stone; the korrigans had forced him to play all night and his lungs had collapsed."

Everyone shuddered at that evocation, although it was not new for them; and at that moment a gust of wind battered the house and made the shutters rattle. Mère Le Goff shut her eyes and Françoise shivered in fear. As for the men, they did not say a word; they had gradually become grave.

"Of course there are still korrigans, sorcerers and spell-casters," said Mère Le Goff, speaking in her turn. "People can

---

1 The biniou is the Breton bagpipe.

invent cannons, rifles, railways and machines with which one can talk at a great distance, further than Rennes and Paris, but there'll always be people like that, possessed by the devil, until the end of the world . . ."

They all nodded their heads affirmatively—even Mathurin, gripped again by the ambient fear and the superstitious instincts of the race.

"It's true," said Françoise, speaking in her turn. "Don't they say that one of them is after the horse of Le Meur, the innkeeper? Every night it goes into the stable and beats the poor animal. It appears that in the morning it's so exhausted, near dead with fatigue, that Le Meur finds it on its side, and can't harness it. It can't stand up . . ."

"I've heard it said," approved Père Le Goff. "I've even been told the name of the sorcerer who does it . . ."

"Who is it?" demanded Mathurin, avidly.

"Yes, who is it?" questioned Mère Dagorne, Françoise and the farmer's wife, avidly.

Then Père Le Goff pronounced, in a low voice, as if he feared being overheard: "The Pen-Ru"

"The man with the red head, the bone-setter who lives on the heath!" exclaimed Mère Le Goff.

That name, spoken so brutally, had all the effect of an electric shock. The Pen-Ru! The man with the red head; the bone-setter! They all knew the Sorcerer of the heath! It was him that they went to fetch when someone had dislocated an arm or broken a leg. And in no time, after having brought the fractured parts of the injured limb together, after having ligatured them and muttered over them paternosters that were surely diabolical, the leg or the arm healed. The man had a redoubtable power; more than one person in the vicinity could testify to that.

But woe betide anyone who mocked the Red Sorcerer, woe betide anyone who cast doubt on his science! That person could expect the worst catastrophes. The Pen-Ru unleashed all possible maledictions upon him; it was fatal and inevitable, as implacable as destiny.

"And what has Le Meur done to the Red Sorcerer?" asked Mère Le Goff.

"It's said," the old peasant said, "that six months ago, when the innkeeper broke his leg one night, coming back from the fair, he sent for the Pen-Ru, and the bone-setter reset the leg in no time. But Le Meur, who always wants to be clever, didn't recompense the Sorcerer adequately for his trouble. He only gave him a small coin, and when the man of the health asked for more, he threatened to go and tell the physician everything in order to have him thrown in prison, because only physicians have the right to cure people. The Pen-Ru didn't say anything; he went away without breathing a word. But he surely cast the evil eye upon the innkeeper, because since then, his business has diminished and a heap of misfortunes have fallen upon him."

"That's true," said Mère Dagorne. "Since then, Le Meur has had all kinds of bad luck. First, four cows died in his house in a single night. Four cows out of five! A pregnant mare he had aborted; and in his fields it was the same thing. The harvest didn't yield anything . . . he had no oats, no rye, no luzerne and no wheat. More than that; it appears that less than a month ago he went up to his loft and his reserves had melted away—there was almost nothing left. Some say that it was disease that killed his animals, that it was rats and mice that had eaten his crops, but no! I know what I'm saying . . . it was the Red Sorcerer's evil eye. It cast a spell on Le Meur. You'll see—the innkeeper will come to a bad end."

No one dared to contradict what the old woman said. They all knew the power of sorcerers—even Mathurin, although he tried to deny it—and especially those of Pen-Ru of the heath.

The latter was much more feared than the other bone-setters and spell-casters of the region because of his well-known rancor and also, especially, because of his mysterious origin,

Where, in fact, did the Red Sorcerer come from? No one could say. He had installed himself on the heath of Carnac one morning, about two years before, making a kind of nest in the hollow of a menhir, in which, with the aid of rushes, pieces of wood and earth, he had constructed a dwelling.

A true savage's or primitive's hut, that house of korrigans was soon known throughout the region, especially because its inhabitant, short and thickset, with a large head, a harsh, piercing gaze and brick-red hair, was immediately identified in Breton thought with the little devils with which their imagination populated the heath. Nothing was known about him, of his past or his present. He went to ground in his cabin, sometimes disappearing for entire weeks, and during those intervals the country respired, everyone secretly congratulating themselves on the departure of the sorcerer.

But one evening, someone would arrive and announce the return of Pen-Ru. He had been seen roaming the heath at dusk, his head bowed, surely ruminating some bad turn addressed to those who had spoken ill of him.

Oh, the Red Sorcerer of the heath! It was the thought of him and the idea of his supernatural powers that obsessed the women and men gathered in the remote farm of the Le Goffs, on the edge of the great heath of Carnac on that festival evening.

Outside, the rain increased in strength; a great wind had risen and continual squalls unfurled—and always, in the distance, the lamentations of the sea were howling.

Old Mère Dagorne, most obsessed of all by the fear of the supernatural and magic, repeated: "Yes, the Pen-Ru has cast a spell on Le Meur. The innkeeper will end badly—you'll see . . ." And, shaking her head, looking by turns at her son and the shivering Françoise, who closed her eyes: "May Saint Anne protect us from the evil eye of the sorcerer!"

Abruptly, a cry descended the large chimney: the cry of a seagull landing on the house in the stormy night. And Père

Yann, the innocent who never spoke, started singing an old Breton ballad, his eyes vague:

> *It blows!*
> *It blows!*
> *It's the wind from the sea that torments us!*

At the same moment, there was a knock on the door, which opened brutally, and a man came in, with a blast of wind and rain.

It was the Red Sorcerer!

The fantastic apparition of the Red Sorcerer in the middle of the storm, when the turn of the conversation was entirely toward the mysterious Breton superstitions, cast a veritable stupor upon the Le Goffs and their guests, who were all strangely surprised.

The Pen-Ru advanced at a deliberate pace toward the group installed around the table in front of the hearth, and in a calm voice, he declared: "Excuse me, the company! It's filthy weather outside, and I'm still half a league from home. I've therefore come to ask you for a bowl of warm soup and a place by your fire."

Half amicably and half fearfully, Le Goff replied: "The fact is that it's filthy weather . . ." And he ordered his wife: "Give a bowl of soup to Monsieur the bone-setter."

"Many thanks, Père Le Goff," said the latter, sitting down under the gazes still imprinted with superstitious terror; "I expected no less on your part. You're a worthy man."

"Oh, in Bretagne," the old peasant replied, "a bowl of soup or a glass of cider is never refused."

The Red Sorcerer had taken his place on a little low chair directly opposite the middle of the hearth. He had taken off his broad-brimmed hat and his energetic face, with hard features and sparkling eyes, was brightly lit. His hair, above all, his fiery red hair, formed a fantastic aureole around that face. And everything, in that man of below average height, but with a surprising breadth of the shoulders, explained the species of superstitious terror that he inspired in the naïve Bretons. Thus posed, his two enormous hands with singularly long thumbs splayed before the fire, he positively gave the impression of a gnome.

A silence fell: a heavy silence only troubled by the squalls outside and the plaints of the sea.

"Well, Mother, what about the soup?" Père Le Goff interrogated, brusquely, breaking the uneasy silence.

"Right away," his wife hastened to say. "I've just put a bowl to simmer, on the off chance . . ."

"And it's me who has the luck," said the Pen-Ru, with a loud laugh. "You see, folk like me scent the good odor from afar . . ."

That "folk like me" struck the audience, for all of whom it could only signify korrigans, devils and sorcerers.

"So," the farmer went on, addressing Françoise, "give him a bowl, my daughter." And as the young woman did not budge, he added: "Come on, move! Give him a bowl."

This time, Françoise quit the fireside and the end of the bench on which she had taken refuge next to old Mère Dagorne, and went to the dresser to fetch the bowl that her father was demanding for the stranger.

More than anyone else, doubtless because of her irresolute nature, her absolute lack of will-power and, above all, the superstitions, legends and tales with which her head was stuffed, the appearance of Pen-Ru, the Red Sorcerer, surging forth at the very moment that they were talking about him, like a devil springing from a spring-loaded box, had struck her forcefully. She could not take her eyes off that seemingly-diabolical face; and it was tremulously that she held the wooden bowl out to the man.

"Thank you, Françoise; you're very kind—but why are you trembling like that? Do I frighten you?"

The young woman blushed all the way to the ears, but made no reply.

"I'm not a bad fellow, though," the Red Sorcerer declared, beginning to swallow his soup briskly, "and I do no harm to anyone . . . when they don't do it to me," he added, in a low voice. "Do you, Françoise, who are so genteel . . ."

"How do you know she's genteel?" said Mère Le Goff, while the trembling girl was still standing to the bone-setter's right.

"Don't I know everything?" declared the red-haired man, with a snigger. And he went on, after clocking his tongue. "In the more than six months that I've seen her traversing the heath, I've been able to perceive that she's genteel, as truly as the soup I've just eaten was excellent."

And, turning round, he placed his empty bowl on the edge of the table. Then, before the surprised Françoise was able to retire, he seized her hand with his enormous hands, and examined it attentively.

"Yes, she's genteel . . . and sage. She's a good girl . . . a good character . . ."

He stopped, while the entire audience contemplated him, increasingly astonished.

"Uh oh!" continued the Pen-Ru, examining the young woman's hand more closely. "What's this? That's curious . . ."

Mère Le Goff ventured: "What? What's curious in my daughter's hand?"

"Curious, curious!" repeated the Red Sorcerer, shaking his head. "She's summoned to have a life . . . and she'll see things . . . many, many things."

Then, abandoning the hand of the young woman, who immediately beat a retreat, rejoining her corner of the bench next to Mère Dagorne, he added in a grave voice: "It's me who tells you that. It's written!"

The men and women looked at one another, gripped by a malaise. Mathurin clenched his fists and ground his teeth; it would not have taken much for him to fall upon the Sorcerer and kill him on the spot. But his mother was there, making signals to him.

The bone-setter must have perceived that disturbance of his audience, for he went on, in a joyful tone: "Let's go. I thank you for your good soup. But before departing, I want to cheer you up with a good trick, to amuse you a little. Look at me intently."

He took a hundred-sou coin out of his pocket.

"You see this coin . . . it's a hundred sous, isn't it? And a true coin, a good coin. Look, I'm not afraid of ringing it . . ."

At the same time, he let the silver coin fall to the floor several times; it rendered a metallic sound.

"You see," he went on. "Well, at my command it will disappear from my hand and go to lodge in the pocket of one of you. Hop! You can still see it! Pay attention—hop! It's gone!"

The Bretons opened fearful eyes wide. That facile trick, which would have made a Parisian apprentice shrug his shoulders, appeared to them to be something supernatural and superhuman.

The Red Sorcerer had flipped the coin, launched it into the air, caught it in flight and slipped it into one of his sleeves without any of his audience suspecting the maneuver. Now he agitated his empty hands and paraded his mocking and piercing gaze over his interlocutors. All faces and eyes were turned toward him, fearfully.

Suddenly, his gaze encountered Françoise's. Instinctively, the young woman closed her eyes. It seemed to her that the sorcerer's eyes were piercing her head and drilling into her brain. Her entire body shuddered.

The Pen-Ru perceived that, for he did not take his eyes off her thereafter.

"Now," the Red Sorcerer continued, "I'll find the coin again. Do you know where? In Françoise's pocket. Look!"

He came toward the young woman, who, white with emotion, her heart pounding as if to break in her breast, sketched a small gesture of recoil, quickly mastered by the incisive, affirmative speech and the profound gaze of the bone-setter.

The man leaned over her and made the gesture of rummaging in her pocket; the coin, fallen from the sleeve, was in his hand.

"Look!" he said, brandishing it. "Here it is, back again, the hundred-sou coin, in Françoise's pocket!"

His audience was amazed. The conjuring trick surpassed everything their minds could conceive. Even Mathurin considered the Pen-Ru with astonished eyes, while his aged mother, hunched up beside the fire, recommended herself mentally to all the saints in paradise.

As for Françoise, a little nervous tremor had seized her. Waves of heat were rising to her face, and still the bone-setter's eyes were drilling into hers.

The man grimaced a smile. "Well, does that merit a bowl of cider?" he asked Le Goff.

"Well . . . well, yes!" said the old Breton.

"Pour one, then, so we can clink glasses, and then I'll go . . . I haven't reached my destination yet."

Mère Le Goff served a glass of cider to the Sorcerer urgently, so great was her haste to see him drink and leave.

"You'll excuse us for not clinking," she said, "but these days, we haven't enough . . ."

"Then I'll drink to the health of you all," said Pen-Ru, gallantly. Then, gazing in a particular fashion at Mathurin's fiancée, he added, laughing: "And especially yours, Françoise, to thank you for making the coins you don't have in your pocket."

He emptied his glass in a single draught, set it down noisily on the table, wished the audience bonsoir, pirouetting on his legs, and disappeared briskly, in a manner as abrupt and fantastic as he had come in.

"Oh, I told you so!" pronounced Mère Dagorne, then. "For sure he's a korrigan!"

＊

Françoise slept badly that night, haunted by the strange gaze of the Red Sorcerer, the memory of which pursued her, frightened her and caused her anguish.

That trouble dissipated the next day in the preparations for the fête. Early in the morning she put on her best clothes, although the squall and the downpour continued to sweep the heath. And when Mathurin came to fetch her at ten o'clock in order to go to mass she was very pretty under her white bonnet ornamented with white lace and the little gold cross shining in her cleavage highlighted the whiteness of her plump neck.

Françoise took her fiancé's arm, with whom she formed a charming couple, she incarnating the wild grace of the Breton heath and he handsome, masculine and strong.

The fête was not as successful as in previous years; the weather was too poor and one could scarcely put a foot outside. However, the young folk amused themselves; they danced all afternoon in a barn transformed for the occasion into a ballroom. While they whirled they forgot the Red Sorcerer and his strange predictions.

At about seven o'clock, when it was already pitch dark, they thought about going home. Mère Dagorne's house was on the route that took them to the Le Goff's, and the betrothed couple went in to say bonsoir.

The good woman was sitting by the foreside; her leathery face, ordinarily the color of old ivory, was white—as white as her bonnet . . .

"What's the matter, Mother?" asked the anxious young couple, immediately.

"I don't know what's wrong with me . . . I'm very tired," she said. She dared not admit that the apparition of the Sorcerer of the heath had upset her greatly.

Mathurin loved his mother very much; that sudden pallor affected him so deeply that he said to Françoise: "The old lady is ill, my sweet; suppose we stay with her?"

The young woman agreed.

"No, go on . . . I don't want you to be deprived of amusements because of me. You're young . . . at your age . . ."

Mathurin and Françoise persisted.

"Well," pronounced the aged Bretonne, after having listened to the reiterated propositions of the young couple, "Mathurin can stay with me, since you both insist that I shouldn't be alone. You, my girl, can go on to your home; your mother must be waiting for you to give her a hand with the baking. On the way, since you'll go past Catherine's house, you can ask her to come and keep me company this evening, and that way, Mathurin can go to join you . . ."

"I'd rather stay with you," objected Françoise.

"No, go! I don't want to be a cause of disturbance. I've got that into my head and no one can make me let go!"

Mère Dagorne was stubborn; they could only agree. Mathurin was a little sad to see his good friend depart alone, all the more so because he suddenly remembered the predictions of the Red Sorcerer. He felt his heart swell, suddenly oppressed, without knowing why. He reassured himself, however, thinking that Catherine would be there in a quarter of an hour, twenty minutes at the most, and he would be able to rejoin Françoise in all tranquility.

And the latter, after having embraced Mère Dagorne and wished her a good night, drew away.

A host of thoughts was crowding her head while, well-wrapped up in her large black shawl, walking head down in order to struggle against the wind, which was battering the wings of her bonnet, she headed toward the paternal house. The visit of the Pen-Ru, the Sorcerer of the heath, occupied once again her ignorant and simple mind, endowed with a strong dose of superstition. Now that she was alone, she thought that she could feel the harsh and mocking gaze of the bone-setter upon her, and that gaze pursued her, along with the man's predictions.

She was menaced with seeing many things, then? Very many things, the sorcerer had said. She would not stay in the locale, then? She would leave . . . where? In what near or distant future?

After having informed Catherine, she quit the sunken road to the Dagornes and took a path that led directly to her parents' farm. When she reached the top of the hill it seemed to her that she could still hear the sniggering voice of the red korrigan, still piping.

Yes she would see things . . . many things!

And now the voices multiplied, all howling in the great plaint of the sea, emerging from the hundreds of menhirs and dolmens looking up like phantoms in the menacing plain . . .

Yes, she would see things . . . many things!

She increased her pace further, shivering, enfevered . . .

Suddenly, it seemed to her that out there, in the night, from one of the great black menhirs that were outlined, enormous and titanic, against the night, the Lavandières of legend,[1] the terrible Lavandières of midnight, were rising up invisibly to come to join her . . . Yes, it was them, the horrible Megaeras, clad in linen sheets, who were summoning her into the darkness in order to help them wring out the shrouds of the dead . . .

Oh!

She was no longer walking now. She was running through the puddles of water and mud, which were splashing under her feet.

From the sea, from the heath, from the great Stones, rose a confused and prestigious noise, which made the heavens and

---

1 The Lavandières [literally laundresses] of Celtic legend were three supernatural washerwomen who went to the water's edge at midnight to wash
shrouds for those about to die. The superstition was still current in Bretagne
in the nineteenth century and often figured in Romantic fiction.

the earth shake: an inexplicable mixture of sighs, hoarse groans and plaintive cries, which whistled in the swell . . .

But suddenly, a terrifying Shadow similar to that of a monster or a demon emerged from behind one of the gigantic Stones. Françoise stopped abruptly, panting, dying of fear. A cry choked in her contracted throat. The Shadow headed toward her, and enveloped her entirely. Her ears were buzzing, the blood throbbing in her temples; she felt faint . . .

An invisible caress gripped her waist, conquering her in a supple and authoritarian embrace. She did not have the strength or the courage to pull away; she fell backwards and collapsed on the ground. She was conscious of the Shadow leaning over her; lips were applied to her lips, crushing her mouth with a kiss.

She felt a sharp pain, a tearing in her body. She wanted to scream, but an unfamiliar and indefinable sensation, simultaneously cruel and sweet, invaded her.

A kind of roar resonated in the obscurity; the Shadow got up again, slowly, and a voice rose up in the opaque night—a terribly energetic and willful voice, a voice of command!

"You're mine, now. Mine alone, you hear, Françoise—and it's me alone that you must obey."

The moon split the clouds, and its green-tinted light suddenly illuminated the fantastic apparition. Françoise saw two violet eyes that were attached to her eyes with an incredible persistence. She shivered. Her inconsistent brain became even more flaccid. She felt that she was no longer anything but a thing, an entity forever hypnotized by the terrible gaze of the Red Sorcerer!

For it was him, the bone-setter, who, yielding to a caprice, a curiosity, had attached himself to Françoise's steps when he had seen her coming alone over the health where he was roaming. It was him, the korrigan with the red head, who had just deposited with his frightful kiss an indelible stigma upon that creature devoid of strength.

"You're mine!" he repeated, emphasizing the syllables, "Mine . . . and you must obey me. You will obey me. You will have no other will but mine."

And so saying, he drew nearer to Françoise, his mouth so close to her face that she could feel his warm breath.

"First," he said, in an authoritarian manner, "you're going to quit your house, your family . . . everything! It's necessary that you follow me, because I wish it, you hear! Tomorrow, you'll be alone, at dusk, at the end of the great health, ay the foot of the Quim'Pierr' Stone.[1] And you'll wait for me. You'll be ready to follow me wherever I wish, and to do whatever I wish!"

There was such commandment in the violet eyes and the voice of the Red Sorcerer that those words were engraved on Françoise's soul. She was under the yoke, feeling it, no longer able to resist it.

The Shadow took hold of her again, embraced her ardently, wildly, and repeated: "You're mine! I want it . . ."

---

1 A so-called sacred stone known as La Pierre Quimpierre is situated near Porquéricourt in the Oise, but that is a long way from Carnac and cannot be the one referenced here.

PART ONE

I
Tête-Rouge!

"Do you know him, that brother?"

"I should think so! He's a wonderful specimen, old chap."

"Impossible!"

"Yes, old chap. Can you imagine that when I knew him, he was a ward-attendant at the Salpêtrière . . ."

"At the Salpêtrière? He looked after the women?"

"As I say. And it appeared that the physicians considered him as a phenomenon, because of his gaze . . ."

"What gaze? Shut up—you're mad, or you're trying to put one over on me . . . but I warn you, there's nothing to be done."

"I swear! You haven't noticed that he doesn't have eyes like other people? When he stares at you, it has a funny effect in your head. One doesn't want to look at him, but one is forced to look at him anyway . . ."

"No, you're decidedly a joker. You're telling me stories that don't stand up."

"Take a breath! I swear by the Mec of Mecs that it's the truth I'm telling you. First of all, he only has to look at a woman and he can be sure that she'll fall into his arms . . . he has them all!"

"Good, my friend . . . necessary to beware of that brother, then . . . watch out for our chicks. Whatever happens, he won't touch mine without my passing my blade into his belly. He can use his peepers, but he won't stop me."

While talking thus the two men were walking slowly along the Avenue de La Motte-Piquet near the École Militaire, with their hands in their pockets and their caps pulled down over their noses

"Yes, you can believe me," one of them continued, "he's not an ordinary man A little more than a year ago he took a bad turn . . . I no longer remember what, perhaps he's nicked a wallet from a doctor . . . As there wasn't any proof, there was nothing they could do, but he was thrown out of the hospital. He was on the pavement without a sou when he pulled off a fine coup in the suburbs. Mates vouched for him but as the judges always settle their account they stuck him with six months for vagabondage and two years of convalescence . . . forbidden to remain, if you prefer.

"As soon as he was free he departed for his homeland, in Bretagne. As he had no money and didn't much like work, be-ing a fellow who's always lazy, do you know what he did? The Bretons are superstitious, so he installed himself on the heath in a hut. As he knew a little medicine that he had learned at the Salpêtrière he became a bone-setter, which allowed him to pass for a sorcerer. He did it so well that the folk out there were completely taken in, and they were afraid of him, old chap!"

"No! But it's not a joke, what you're telling me?".

"You're funny! I swear to you that it happened like that. You can ask the mates."

"And his chick, Françoise-la-Bretonne, she's shapely! Where did he dig her up?"

"That's a whole other story, my lad, which isn't in a sack! Open your ears. She was a kind of little peasant, even dafter than the others. She was engaged to a fellow who hadn't yet done his military service. She pleased Tête-Rouge, as people call him since he's returned to the quarter. He had her one evening, and told her that she had to go with him . . . and he looked at her with his funny eyes. The next day, the kid packed her linen and her effects, took her savings . . . a few coppers . . . all that during her parents' absence, who had gone to market early in the morning. Afterwards, she went into town, found two witnesses among the ambulant merchants who went along with it for a bottle, and made her declaration at the Mairie: she was of age, and informed the authorities that she was quitting the region of her own free will . . .

"You'll understand that after that, no one could prevent her from leaving . . . not her relatives, nor her father, nor the pope. In the evening she was at the foot of a stone on the heath, where Tête-Rouge was waiting for her. She didn't know where he was taking her or what he was going to do with her, but it made no difference; she went with him anyway, like a god, ready to do anything he demanded. Tell me after that that he isn't an extraordinary chap."

"Yes, it astonishes me, I confess, what you've told me."

"And you know, his kid, she only knows him. He only has to stare at her and she marches. No danger that she'll flinch! Oh, he doesn't have to fear the straw!"

Their steps had brought the two men back to the dance-hall from which they had departed a little while before in order to talk at their ease. They went in again.

The audience in that local ballroom—a vast wooden shed left over from the last exposition, lost at the end of the Champ-de-Mars—was partly composed of workers of both sexes who came there to distract themselves from the week's hard labor, but most of all by soldiers. The École Militaire and its barracks were close by.

As the two men went into the dance-hall, the orchestra attacked a diabolical polka. The tables were abandoned in haste, shoved aside and even knocked over. Couples formed on the dance-floor and started spinning to the tune, and the racket of brass instruments, in the midst of a cloud of dust that rose from the ground and the mingled odors—cheap perfume, acrid sweat and moist leather—that emanated from the enlaced men and women, excited by the folderols of the ramshackle orchestra.

"Look, there she is, over there, Tête-Rouge's chick, Françoise-la-Bretonne," said one of the two shady individuals when the polka ended and a relative calm reigned in the hall. Dancers of both sexes gathered around the tables arranged around the dance-floor. Others were standing behind the barrier of painted wood.

"Which one is she, Françoise-la-Bretonnne?"

"Over there on the left; she has a red bodice."

"That goes without saying—but she's tasty, the kid!"

"I believe you. She's not yet up to date with the game, but Tête-Rouge takes charge of dressing her. Look at him—he's sitting at a table in front of a cherry. See whether he's keeping an eye on her!"

"Let's get closer, we can have a drink together."

They threaded a path through the tightly-packed ranks of tables and consumers, and were soon shaking the hand of the man they called Tête-Rouge, the former bone-setter and sorcerer, the man who had terrorized the people of the heath.

But how unrecognizable he was! His hair, previously shaggy, was carefully trimmed and pomaded under his English cap; his costume revealed a concern for elegance and it was almost with arrogance and disdain that he welcomed his comrades.

His gray eyes with violet glints never quit Françoise, watching her, commanding her to be seductive, alluring and provocative, to make as many conquests as possible and bring him back a great deal of money.

Suddenly, his eyes took on a strange gleam and his face darkened. His two "mates," having followed the direction of his gaze, perceived that it was fixed on a pompier[1] leaning on the wooden balustrade a few paces away from Françoise. Immediately, Tête-Rouge made an imperceptible sign, with the Bretonne understood.

She quit the dance-hall.

Scarcely had she gone out than her man took his leave of the friends he had just met and left in his turn.

He caught up with her on the Avenue de la Motte-Piquet.

"You saw him. You knew that he was there?" he murmured.

"Who?"

"Mathurin!"

"Mathurin . . . Mathurin . . ." She stammered, going pale. "No, I didn't see him."

"Don't lie," said the man, plunging his gaze into the poor young woman's. He read in her blue irises that she was telling the truth. "He's in Paris; I've just seen him in the dance-hall dressed as a pompier. Pay attention: no stupidities if you ever encounter him; don't forget that you're mine!"

Françoise was trembling with emotion at the thought that she had been within arm's reach of Mathurin, her fiancé, the man she still loved in the depths of her heart and from whom Tête-Rouge had stolen her. Oh, as long as he had not perceived her; as long as he had not divined the métier that Tête-Rouge was making her follow!

She was walking head down, overwhelmed by memories.

"I don't fear him, your Mathurin," Tête-Rouge went on. "You know full well that he can do nothing for you, because you belong to me henceforth . . . you're mine alone, forever. However, I don't want you running into him continually. That would mess with your damned head; your mind would no longer be on your business. And then, on the other hand, I'm

---

1 The *pompiers* [firemen]—or more fully, *sapeurs-pompiers*—were a division of the French military roughly comparable to the British Royal Engineers or the American Construction Battalions.

disgusted with this place; it's full of hooligans and pimps. We're going to decamp. I want to live in Barbès; it's more chic and the clients are richer. You'll earn your crust out there, I assure you. Come on, look at me, kid!"

Françoise obeyed. He divined her disturbance and fixed his violet eyes upon her for a long time, which made her dizzy.

She was no longer thinking about Mathurin.

II
At La Chapelle

"Your deal, Boubouroche . . ."

"There you go, my prince."

And Boubouroche—a stout and sturdy red-head whose friends had nicknamed him thus because of his physical resemblance to Courteline's immortal Hero[1]—swept up the cards scattered on the green baize, which advertised a distillery, with a broad gesture.

"Another round, eh?" he proposed. "While we wait for the mates?"

He started to deal the dirty cards.

"Three, three, two . . . two . . ."

Then, sitting back in his chair he lifted a corner of the coarse curtain and darted a glance outside.

"Damn! It's going to rain. That won't make the job any easier . . . the amateurs are going to go home." Boubouroche paused briefly, and continued: "What I say is for the lads . . . my wife and I have a regular clientele."

"For sure, you're a hard worker," opined Nez-de-Coq, a pale, meager and stiff individual with a little black moustache and a

---

1 Georges Courteline's "Boubouroche" (1882) was originally a short story, which he adapted into a play in 1893, whose protagonist is a naïve colossus who allows himself to be exploited by his friends and deceived by his mistress.

thin hooked nose—hence his nickname. He ground his teeth as he picked up his cards; then, as the rain suddenly began to fall—a spring rain that arrived in gusts against the windows of the bar, anxious as well as curious, he got up and went to the door.

He then appeared in the full lamplight in all his cynical boldness, rather tall, brown-eyed, his voice drawling, an old cigarette at the corner of his lips and a chauffeur's cap pulled down over his eyes; while rocking back and forth he looked outside.

The downpour was making the passers-by flee, splashing through the puddles, seeking refuge under the vault of the Metro.

"After all, Nez-du-Coq," said Boubouroche, sugaring his grenadine absinthe—his "tomato juice"—"the rain's good. The clients, while waiting for the prefect up there to shut his peepers, will lay low for a while . . . then the mates' chicks will take advantage of it . . ."

And Boubouroche, who had come to join his friend by the window, extended his arm and said: "As proof, look; there's Mélie-la-Prune coming to lift a fellow with an aristocratic air."

"Georges-l'Algérien is lucky to have a kid like her!"

"You can say that the brother is a hard worker," Nez-de Coq agreed. "It's at least four times that she's been on the beat until three o'clock . . . and it's now five . . ."

"Yes, five o'clock, in fact. Georges and Tête-Rouge will soon arrive, unless they've run into trouble—one never knows in the métier. They've been told where we'll be; as usual, in the Bar des Amis on the Boulevard de La Chapelle . . ."

Boubouroche and Nez-de-Coq resumed their places at the little table. Darkness had fallen, and the waiter came to light the gas. Nez-de-Coq took advantage of that to order two more drinks.

"Two more tomato juices, eh . . . and be quick!"

Soon, the mechanical organ began to grind out the various pieces in its repertoire, indefatigably.

The successive aperitifs were beginning to take effect; Boubouroche and Nez-de-Coq resumed their card game. Cigarette smoke filled the low-ceilinged room; on the other side of the glazed partition separating the section where the two men were prudently stationed from the bar proper, workmen, employees and coachmen were taking a hasty glass on the zinc.

The organ went on relentlessly, untiringly and methodically, grinding out the new songs consecrated by success...

> *I call her my little bourgeoise,*
> *My tonkiki, ... my tonkiki ...*
> *My tonkinoise ...*

Nez-de-Coq began to hum, stimulated by the music.

"Nail it, old man," Boubourroche said to him. "Don't sing, you'll make it rain harder. Here, I beat your queen."

"You don't say—I'm not blessed. Always bad luck. Another hand lost. How much is the bill?"

"That makes twenty-four darts," said Boubouroche, laughing. "You only have to pay up."

Regally, Nez-de-Coq dropped a louis on to the marble table-top. The waiter hastened to pick up the money, and as the price of his complaisance he received a fifty-centime tip.

"The rain's stopping," remarked Boubouroche. "We can make a tour. Damn! There's Mélie-la-Prune again hooking a fellow. There she goes ... she's taking him to the hotel ..."

"As lucky mecs go, Georges is certainly one ... and that's not all. Well, are we going to take that little tour?"

Bouboroche agreed, but before following his mate he went to strike a match on the next table.

At the same time, Nez-de-Coq, who was already at the door, came back precipitately.

"Damn! Here come the cops; the shepherdesses are going inside. Can you see them coming?"

Hidden behind the curtain they followed with their eyes the two plain-clothes policemen who were advancing, calm and dignified, causing the whores to flee as they approached.

"It's Pied-de-Céleri, the inspector, a malicious cove, in service with an agent. Necessary to watch out. The chicks have tried in the time to bribe him, but nothing doing."

"For sure! He's not accommodating, the brother. The other day . . ."

Boubouroche was getting ready to tell his friend a story, but the door opened brutally and a woman came in like a gust of wind.

"Fançoise-la-Bretonne," said the two men, with a hint of superiority.

"Yes, lads, it's me. I don't want to be thrown in the can by Pied-de-Céleri. Here I am! I'll go out again in a minute—time to let the peg-leg go by . . ."

The two men darted a glance at her in which there was admiration. It is true that Françoise was very pretty and fresh. She was not much older than twenty, with big blue eyes that would have seemed candid without the rings surrounding them, pink cheeks, a thin, blood-red and moist mouth and a slightly turned-up nose. The mass of her blonde hair, twisted into a voluminous helmet above her forehead gave her a rascally air without effrontery. Her black silk bodice molded her taut waist and her opulent bosom, which stood up, young and firm; beneath the fabric the nipples of her proud breasts stood out, as if to make a gap in the embroidery.

Limping, rolling his eyes to the right and the left, Pied-de-Céleri had passed by, followed by his inferior and was lost in the crowd of people waiting for the Metro or the omnibus.

Françoise had posted herself in front of the mirror in order to fix her hair, tousled slightly by her flight, pull her skirt up over her hips and refasten a stocking that had escaped from its garter.

"Now I've put them right I'll return to the fray," she said, casting a final glance into the mirror.

"No, wait," said Boubouroche. "Your man is coming."

"What—he's coming?" said the prostitute, suddenly alarmed. "Then I have to go at the gallop ... I don't want him to see me here; he'll say that I'm idling ..."

She ran to the door. At the same moment, it opened violently, and in a swirl of the curtain, lifted up by a gust of wind, Tête-Rouge appeared, imposing and majestic.

And while Boubouroche and Nez-de-Coq were extending their right hand amicably, Françoise tucked herself up and made herself small in order to pass before her master, whose violet gaze pursued her, full of menace.

The cards abandoned by Boubouoiche and Nez-du-Coq were still lying on the green baize. Tête-Rouge, whose piercing gaze had made a rapid tour of the room, perceived them and said, ironically: "You're always playing cards, what? Better than amour? Lucky fellows! You're lottery-winners, you two!"

The two friends sensed the reproach hidden in those words and, slightly embarrassed by Tête-Rouge's mocking and slightly authoritarian tone, contented themselves with responding: "What do you expect? Necessary to pass the time. One can't always be slaving away."

"Especially when it hasn't stopped raining," added Boubouroche.

"That's good, that's good," said Tête-Rouge, letting himself slide along the moleskin bench. "You're flush! Since that's the case, you can buy me a drink."

The attitude of Boubouroche and Nez-du-Coq had changed completely since Tête-Rouge's arrival. Although they had been at their ease, penetrated by their importance and personal value five minutes before, they now seemed neutered, subjugated, obedient and humble in confrontation with the newcomer.

It was not only on Françoise that the grim Breton exerted

his strange force, his marvelous hypnotic power, but on all those who approached him, saw him for a moment or listened to him for a few seconds. From his entire person, in fact—from his little blue-gray eyes that sometimes had violet gleams, from his thick-lipped mouth and his bushy russet, almost red, hair and his thickset body, a magnetic fluid emanated that inclined all wills to submit and be subjugated by his own.

It was scarcely a fortnight that he had been living in La Chapelle, in a house in the Rue de la Charbonnière, and already, with a tacit accord, all the mates of the boulevard had stood aside before him and had begun, on their own initiative, to consider him as the leader, as the enlightened and powerful consul of whom they had need, obeying him and surrounding him with the immense respect due to the powerful in this world.

So, very honored, the two friends immediately agreed to offer him an aperitif.

The waiter arrived, urgently.

"A large tomato juice," ordered Tête-Rouge.

"Make that two," said Boubouriche.

"Three, even," added Nez-de-Coq, laughing.

"Well, lads, business going well?" asked Tête-Rouge, when the waiter had disappeared behind the glazed door.

"Yes, good, good," affirmed Boubouroche, with his habitual optimism.

"And you, Nez-de-Coq?"

"Oh, you know me. It rolls on, so-so . . ."

"Bah! You're never content, always complaining! Your chick doesn't let you want for anything. You're in commerce . . . you have a display-window, counter, cupboard, chamomile and basin. You're lucky. Whereas I . . ."

"Oh, you, Tête-Rouge," the other two exclaimed, in unison. "You're the mec of mecs."

"That's because I know that it's necessary to keep an eye open with the chicks," said Tête-Rouge sententiously. "If you don't watch them sufficiently, they soon begin to tread water or take breaks. On that side, though, I have no fear. Françoise isn't a kid to short-change me. Since we've been here she plays her four tunes every day, and hasn't yet got habituated to it. She's finally decided apply herself; it's high time, otherwise I'd have been obliged to employ grand means. I haven't brought her from Bretagne for her skin . . . necessary that she work hard, or go hungry. When one thinks that Mélie-la-Prune, who isn't as pretty, in addition to the cash she earns in tolls, makes thirty bullets a day when she goes out, it makes one angry!

And as he moved the curtain aside, out of professional habit, the three men cast a glance outside and perceived, by the faint light of a gas-lamp, Mélie, Georges-l'Algérien's woman, in conversation with a ditch-digger who was vacillating on his legs.

"Well, look at that! What an earner!" opined Nez-de-Coq, with a hint of envy.

"Damn!" said Tête-Rouge. "Your herborist doesn't let you lack for anything. You have your fodder every day, don't you? What do you have to complain about?"

"I'm not complaining. But look at that Mélie; that's at least the ninth type she's been seen to lift since she's been here. Yes, but you see, Tête-Rouge, that one never knows one's good fortune. In the meantime, her man, Georges-l'Algérien, dressed like a gentleman, is probably in the process of plying the magnate or the chichi with chic women . . . gonzesses who have plumed hats and dresses in the latest fashion. If that doesn't make you sick . . . !"

All three laughed.

"Necessary to say," remarked Boubouroche, "that Georges is a true male. He knows how to keep hold of Mélie, and when she plays up, he gives her a good beating. It's necessary to see . . ."

"That's how one makes good fillies," pronounced Tête-Rouge seriously; and, striking his most important pose, his thumbs in his waistcoat, sticking out his torso, he started pacing back and forth in the café.

As he went past the partition of frosted glass that cut the hall in two, he raised himself up on tiptoe in order to cast a glance at the other side. He appeared to be examining someone or something with an immense attention; then he returned slowly to his companions.

"Twenty-two, lads!" he breathed, with a hint of anxiety. "On the other side there's a fellow with a face I don't like. It wouldn't surprise me if he were a spy, a dirty snitch. It would be more prudent to scarper . . . I'm going to do that, because I have an account to settle at the Tour Pointue."

Nez-de-Coq, who had no more wish to attract the eye of the law, paled slightly.

As for Boubouroche, he remained calm. He had little to fear, his situation being more regular, from his viewpoint, than that of his two friends, still young but already old hacks.

"Go and see, Boubouroche," said Nez-de-Coq. "Perhaps it's a client that Tête-Rouge doesn't know yet."

Boubouroche got up and, quite naturally, went to take a look over the partition; then he returned tranquilly to the communal table.

"I don't know him," he said, "but I don't think he's a snitch. I have the habitude of all those in the quarter. That fellow seems to me to be more like a brother."

"You think so?"

"Yes."

"Then go and have a chat with him."

Boubouroche acquitted his delicate mission with a good humor. He opened the small door and went into the drinking-den.

In front of a small table, a thin, pale man with an unhappy expression was sitting facing a girl.

While making a semblance of reading *La Presse*, Boubouroche examined him from the corner of his eye.

At that moment, the mysterious individual turned his head to call the waiter, and beneath the right ear, at the birth of the neck, Boubou perceived a tattooed little blue crescent, the sign of recognition of the brothers of Montparno. Boubou knew that detail, having once been a member himself of that important corporation.

Without fear, therefore, he approached the man and said to him, deliberately: "You're recognized, old chap; have no fear; I'm not one of them." And as the other had gone paler, doubtless not having a very tranquil conscience he added: "The mates call me Boubouroche. Come to the other side and have a chat; there are friends there. But what's your name?"

"The dabs call me Charlot," the other replied, hesitant and nonplussed. "but the mates have baptized me Demi-Sel..."[1]

"Well, Demi-Sel, come and have a glass to celebrate our acquaintance..."

And Boubouroche, pushing him ahead of him, made him go into the room where Tête-Rouge and Nez-de-Coq were waiting for him.

"Nothing to fear," said Boubouroche immediately, to calm their alarm. "He's a mate."

His face beaming, he made the introductions, pointing in turn at his two companions. "Tête-Rouge, Nez-de-Coq, true friends."

Tête-Rouge let a searching gaze weigh upon the newcomer, which searched his consciousness, trying to penetrate the darkness of his soul behind the veil of his thoughts.

"Well, how goes it, mate?" he asked.

"Oh, so-so, but could be better. I've just done six months at Poissy, first division of the sixth... that's bad, old chap. There are supervisors in every corner. They bustle you to work. Oh, the cows! If I ever get caught again, I'll pass them by. They say

1 *Demi-sel* is slightly salted cheese or butter; French dictionaries note that the term was, indeed, employed to refer to part-time pimps in Paris at the end of the nineteenth century, but one suspects that the "mates" might have chosen the nickname in this instance because of its resemblance to "demoiselle."

that it's okay, prison, but it's necessary to have gone that way to know what it's like. You talk as if one's happy there!"

The fellow swayed his head from right to left while talking, clicking his knee, while the others listened to him, their elbows on the table and slightly mocking smiles on their lips.

"There are journalists who tell heaps of stories; they claim that the prisoners are well off: electric lighting, well-served table, nothing to do. Well, I've been there; I know what prison is. There's no one as unlucky as a man who lives in prison!"

"You're right, Demi-Sel; nothing's worth as much as liberty, damn it. Try not to get caught again, now," advised Tête-Rouge

"That wouldn't do. I'm a tricard.¹ I'm on my ninth conviction; one more and I'll be washing my feet. I'll be liable to transportation. Thanks! I don't want to be expatriated: the big blue doesn't tempt me. Only seeing it once, at Trouville, where I'd gone to have a blow-out with a gonzesse on the rebound, made me seasick. Oh no, for sure, this time I've had my fill. For the moment, I'm on leave."

He said that in a tone so naïve that the others, devoid of pity for their new comrade, burst out laughing. Is prison not the risk of the trade, as the mason risks falling every day from his scaffolding and the mariner is incessantly at risk of being buried by the moving waves?

"You're alone, then? You have no woman?" proffered Tête-Rouge again, completing his enquiry.

"Not any more... I'm a widower. I had a chick, in Montparno, when I copped my six months at Passy, but I didn't find her again when I came back. I don't know what's become of her. Anyway, it's not a great loss for me, that woman was a camel, nasty, and bone idle. She didn't even send me a dart while I was fattening the government's lice. That's not surprising, though—I've never been lucky with women."

---

1 The argot term *tricard* has several meanings, but in this instance it signifies that Demi-Sel is a deserter from the army.

"Necessary to know how to handle them, the *moukères*,"[1] Tête-Rouge pontificated. "You probably don't know what to do with them."

"Yes," Demi-Sel admitted. "I've always been told that I'm a little stupid with the kids. I don't like thumping them, so they take no notice of me; they lead me a merry dance."

The three friends shrugged their shoulders with commiseration; then, after a brief conference, Tête-Rouge went on: "We'll choose you a woman, for a man without a chick is good for nothing; he falls into the dirt. Gonesses are there to make cash. Try to make her walk straight. There are some who no longer have a male. It's necessary that women don't remain alone—it gives the others ideas. Remember this well—it's necessary that the chicks bring their galette back to their man; that's what they're made for, after all!"

Tête-Rouge reflected momentarily, and said to Boubouroche: "Go and see if you can see Françoise. Make her a sign to come."

Boubou obeyed, going out momentarily and making a particular appeal audible outside; then, when he had attracted the Bretonne's attention, he raised his arm in a gesture of summons.

She understood, and immediately started running toward the café, into which she penetrated fearfully, always in dread of having discontented her omnipotent master.

Her eyes went to him—she only saw him—and she was reassured, not reading any anger in the amethyst gaze that fascinated her.

"Say, kid, do you know Jeanne-la-Blonde . . . you know, Gros-Tas?"

"I think so; she's in a shop in the Rue de la Charbonnière. She's out of luck, the sister—her fellow, a strapping cove, received a bang on the head one evening when he was with the La

1 The term *moukère* is employed literally later in the text to mean a North African woman, but it was also used in Algeria to refer to a prostitute and in Paris to refer to a mistress.

54

Chapelle lads settling a score with those of the Sebasto. He was sent to Cayenne. Jeanne was floored, as you can imagine. Since then, she's recovered courage and is working herself to death!"

"Go to her pad," ordered Tête-Rouge. "If she's occupied, leave it for a moment . . . necessary never to spoil a deal, the times are too hard, but tell her as soon as her mark has gone that I'm waiting for her here . . . and right away . . ."

"I'll run, and I'll send her," she replied.

And she left, without even having noticed the newcomer.

He, by contrast, had stared at her throughout the time that she was there, her hands in the pockets of her apron, listening to Tête-Rouge, and his eyes were still following her, marveling, as she went out.

Boubouroche noticed that persistence and informed Demi-Sel, charitably: "That's Françoise, Tête-Rouge's kid. She's not bad, the sister, eh?"

"You can say that again," replied Demi-Sel, simply.

Tête-Rouge leaned backwards against the moleskin back of the bench, his hands joined behind his head, still gazing at Demi-Sel. After a few moments of examination, he let speech fall from his august lips, in an important manner, dominating him with all his superiority of a powerful and strong male, while the other seemed timid, hesitant, paltry and amorphous.

"You see," he said, "without any claptrap, it's necessary to be like me. I don't care about the police. I'm a somewhat cleaned-up mec. All the ruffians of the Quai des Orfèvres can rub, but I'm lily-white; nothing to be done against me. I lead my woman with an eye and a finger—a woman of my homeland. That's no joke. I'm tranquil with her; it's amour! She works a little . . . Bah! She does what she can. She's still young. She doesn't know all the tricks yet for getting as much money as possible from the clients. In time, she'll be a marvelous woman, who'll do what she likes, sweetly. Whether she finds chic types or layabouts, she always brings in for me . . ."

"You're lucky," said Demi-Sel, simply, with contained admiration.

Abruptly, a tall blonde woman came into the bar, whose opulent breasts rolled all the way to her waist, and whose waist was confounded with the respectable perimeter of her hips.

"What do you want with me, Tête-Rouge?" she asked. "It appears you have to talk to me. That's no story, at least?"

"No, shut up. Bring your lard, Gros-Tas and sit down."

"Go on, what is it?"

"It's already some time since your man, Sac-d'Os, took a tumble. You haven't yet replaced him, which proves that he has sentiment. But you know full well that women need to have a man behind them, someone to protect them, to reckon with fellows who want to cut up rough . . . and also to have some fun with. Here's a brother who's come back from Poissy . . . he no longer has a gonzesse, which works out nicely. You're going to come to an understanding . . ."

Jeanne-la-Blonde looked Demi-Sel up and down from head to toe, and made an imperceptible moue of disdain. That little fellow, thin and paltry, didn't appeal to her; she would have preferred a more solid mec, to clasp her forceful bosom in his arms. *A fellow like Tête-Rouge*, she thought, caressing him with her green eyes.

But the uncontested chief of the boulevard had decided and it was necessary to obey. Without daring to raise the slightest objection, she accepted, without enthusiasm, the project of an entirely morganatic union.

"Demi-Sel," Tête-Rouge then said, solemnly, "from now on, Jeanne-la-Blonde, otherwise known as Gros-Tas, is your chick; she'll give you money. If she gives you any trouble, give her a slap—but don't forget that you owe her aid and protection. Defend her against fellows who cut up rough, and especially against the cops. Now, order a liter of white wine, something nice! And you, Jeanne, pass your purse to your man . . . he'll pay for the round!"

When the white wine was poured, the friends raised their glass to the new couple, who, to seal their union, drank from the same glass while the others made lewd remarks with double meanings.

"Hurry up and go to bed!"

"Demi-Sel is hungry!"

"Don't stifle him. Gros-Tas!"

"Demi-Sel, you'd never be seen again!"

Soon after shaking hands with Tête-Rouge and his friends, Demi-Sel and his woman retired in order to consummate their hasty union with a brutal embrace.

Gros-Tas took Demi-Sel to her lodgings, as was her duty. She walked ahead to show him the way; he followed meekly. In front of a small shop with permanently closed shutters she lifted up her skirt and took a key from her stocking. A door grated; she lit an oil lamp and the room appeared, cold, sad and miserable. A large cretonne curtain separated it into two parts. The first, overlooking the street, was furnished with a threadbare red velvet armchair; the other hid an iron bed.

Demi-Sel contemplated Jeanne momentarily; Jeanne examined him in her turn. The door remained open, letting in, with a gust of wind, bursts of drunken laughter from the neighboring shops.

Gros-Tas approached her new master and, with a disdainful moue, threw in his face, crushing him with her scorn: "Well, what do you want me to say to you? You disgust me!"

III
Demi-Sel

Decidedly, Demi-Sel had no luck. He was "not blessed," as he had the custom of saying.

Jeanne-la-Blonde had seen immediately who she was dealing with, and, instead of submitting and allowing herself to be led by the omnipotent master, she had rebelled. In truth, yes—a strange spectacle, never seen before—Jeanne, perhaps the only one of all the women of the boulevard, had made her decision, and without hesitation, she mistreated, insulted and sent packing the master whom Tête-Rouge had given her.

Demi-Sel supported all the abuse patiently, defending himself as best he could, but when it came to raising his hand to bring his woman back to just respect for his dignity with a violent slap, he carefully refrained.

Every day, Jeanne brought him a tune, and that sum, which only represented a part of the product of her activity, was sufficient to satisfy his modest tastes. If, by chance, Demi-Sel raised a furtive objection, she said: "What, you're not content? What are you going to do, then? You imagine that . . . a tune! Five bullets: that's enough for your portrait, ape."

Without saying a word, Demi-Sel pocketed the hundred sous and went away meekly, summoned by memorable games of manille in some bar in La Chapelle. Because of his incomprehensible weakness and his unqualifiable docility, he soon became the butt of all the mates' jokes; they had never before seen a brother so inadequate to the role. In addition, Demi-Sel passed for a dodger, fleeing the mates, preferring to sup his blue tranquilly, in order to avoid settling the bill—a glory for which everyone criticized him loudly. It is only fair to add, in his defense, that while all his friends had deep pockets filled with fine louis, only wretched silver coins—sometimes infimal *billons*—sounded in his pocket.

It is true that, being an economical man, Demi-Sel possessed secret funds that he did not touch—something like two hundred francs, amassed during his last sojourn in the Centrale of Poissy.

Oh, he never borrowed from those savings; he respected them, in anticipation of future needs. Prudently, for fear of mates in need or an unfortunate taxation, he had sewn the two blue bills into the lining of his jacket.

Little by little, his existence with Jeanne-la-Blonde became intolerable.

One day, when she had accepted a few glasses from a client, an extraordinary courage animated her, and, on returning to the house, as her man had just lost four rounds of cards and asked her for some money, she administered a magisterial slap, about which people were talking for a long time on the exterior boulevards.

Demi-Sel did not respond, but collapsed, devoid of will, like a rag. He threw himself on the bed and the next day, when he awoke, after having drawn the blue cretonne curtains, on looking at himself in the mirror of the wardrobe, he perceived that a formidable black bruise, an immense swelling, ornamented his right eye. That black eye was the object of numerous gibes when Demi-Sel arrived at the boulevard café where Boubouroche, Nez-de-Coq and Tête-Rouge were holding their assizes. It was greeted by a volley of bitter jokes. His face gave rise to noisy laughter and formidable thigh-slaps.

Misfortunes never come alone, according to Clément Marot.[1] Two days later, Demi-Sel was subjected to an even greater affront—which he welcomed with the same passivity.

When he returned to his house in the evening, he found Gueule-d'Amour, a mate, installed in his stead and his place, sprawled on the bed alongside Jeanne-la-Blonde.

The greatest patience has its limit. Demi-Sel went pale and made the remonstrances usual in such circumstances. But Gueule-d'Amour, soon on his feet in a pink chemise and velvet trousers, said to him while Jeanne writhed with laughter under the sheets. "Yes. I'm taking her, the chick. Dry up! If you're not content, we can settle it. Take out your blade or your pistol . . ."

As he pronounced those words, Gueule-d'Amour had picked up his revolver, placed on the mantelpiece.

---

1 The Protestant poet Clément Marot (1496-1544) was as famous for his misfortunes as for his work.

Demi-Sel differed in this respect from the seigneurs of olden times: he had no intention of sacrificing himself for his beauty. Prudently, he avoided the combat and beat a shameful retreat, slamming the door, while Gueule-d'Amour and Jeanne-la-Blonde, after having shouted at him: "Go, then, coward! Demi-Sel—rat-meat!" fastened their lips again.

Crestfallen, Demi-Sel set forth for the Bar des Amis, counting on finding Tête-Rouge there in order to tell him about his misfortune and take him as an arbiter.

Another disillusionment—the least—awaited him there. He only found Boubou and Nez-du-Coq at table with two other mates, La Levite, a fellow from Belleville, and Panaris, a brother from Ménilmuche.

"Tête-Rouge isn't here?" he asked, anguished and still under the blow of the affront.

"Tête-Rouge?" said Boubouroche. "As you can see..." Then, after having examined him: "No, but what's the matter? Your face is upside-down."

"Perhaps your woman has talked back?" added Nez-de-Coq.

"No," said Boubou, laughing, "perhaps she's beaten him up?"

"If you don't have the courage to respond," remarked La Lévite, "you're not a man."

"It's not that," said Demi-Sel. "It's more serious."

"What, then? You don't need to make money with the girls. What has she done to you now, your moukère?"

Slack and inconsistent, Demi-Sel tried to elude the interrogation, but they became increasingly pressing and increasingly ironic. Finally, he was forced to admit, with a resigned gesture: "Well, this is it: my woman has dumped me."

"Your woman has dumped you?"

"His woman has dumped him!" howled the others, writhing with laughter. Then, when a relative calm was restored, someone said: "She's dumped you? With whom has she taken up?"

"With Gueule d'Amour," he replied, heart-broken.

"Gueule d'Amour!" said Nez-de-Coq, self-importantly. "In that case, old chap, you're finished—you're a widower. Gueule-d'Amoutr is a marvelous fellow, and no woman—apart from ours—has ever been able to resist him. You can look elsewhere."

Demi-Sel lowered his head, confused, while the four friends let out the same burst of laughter.

"Since that's the way it is," said Nez-de-Coq, in his whistling, incisive voice, "you can settle up. Pay the bill."

Demi-Sel went green. He did not have a sou in his pocket, having spent his last tune the day before and Jeanne having cut his rations abruptly, having banished him from her bed

"I don't have the cash," he admitted, piteously.

The four friends shrugged their shoulders, with commiseration.

"What! You don't even have a dozen darts? No, then, you're truly in the lurch, old chap. Necessary to get it from your woman's nose-bag."

"Get away, you're only a Demi-Sel!"

Boubouroche who, always charitable, sustained mates in difficulties, winked and said: "Peace! It's not his fault if he's on his uppers. I'll pay for the round, and I'll even offer another. Waiter, bring another . . . and what about you, Demi-Sel; what'll you have?"

"A barley-water!" hissed Nez-de-Coq, biliously.

"No," responded Demi-Sel, cheered up by a benevolent glance at Boubou. "A large purée!"

"So," asked Boubou, after having downed his tomato juice in a single draught, "what are you going to do?"

"In truth," replied Demi-Sel, tracing designs with the tip of his index finger in the liquid spilled on the table, "I don't know whether I'm going to be forced to take up my old trade. Perhaps I can find a place as an apprentice hairdresser."

"No, you're joking! Work, become a barber, a pomader! You can't think so."

"You want to go back to shaving beards! That will never do! Do you want to spoil the métier?"

"You can mock! I have to earn a crust until I find another woman . . ."

Eventually, after reflecting maturely, and having examined the pros and cons, Demi-Sel, who felt a serious embarrassment, abandoned his first idea of resuming his old trade, and opted for a more dangerous liberal profession. He set about picking pockets.

Every day, he, wandered idly through the crowds on the great boulevards, researching the groups; then, taking advantage of the slightest jostle or the most minor encumbrance, he dipped into bags and withdrew purses with an incomparable dexterity. However, he only had recourse to that means as a last resort, for he still lived in fear of the fatal conviction that would send him overseas, out there to the tropics. Such a voyage, along with its consequences, did not tempt him at all.

As he never had any luck, it often happened that he filched a purse that was poorly furnished. One day, as he was passing a stall, he could not resist the temptation, on the one hand, and to keep his hand in, on the other, to take possession of a bottle of old Medoc. After having tucked it under his jacket he drew away, proud of his acquisition by sleight of hand and even more so at the thought of the pride he would experience in sharing it with the mates.

And, in fact, when he exhibited the liter in the back room of a shop in the Rue de la Charbonnière, he uncorked it and, with infinite precaution, poured the contents into the glasses. Triumphantly, he raised his own to the health of his comrades, and each of them drank in a single draught.

But a frightful grimace was painted on all the faces.

"Damnation! What are you giving us? I swear that you're trying to poison us. In that case, it's necessary to see!"

Poor Demi-Sel understood then what had happened.

"Filthy grocers!" he cried. "It isn't wine that they put in their displays, its water colored with I don't know what! I've stolen a liter of the fake stuff!"

"You'll never be anything but a Demi-Sel" Nez-de-Coq let fall, spitting out the adulterated liquid fearfully and launching a terrible glare at him, shrugging his shoulders disdainfully.

A few days after that little incident, Demi-Sel, having appropriated a relatively well-furnished purse in the vicinity of a large store in the Chaussée-d'Antin, espied a pretty street-walker who was going past, provocative and made-up, with promising eyes. His veins were ferrying the effluvia of spring that were emanating from all of nature in fête. Like a bourgeois whipped by desire, excited by the occasion, the tender grass and all the rest. Demi-Sel accompanied the creature of pleasure into a hotel in the Rue de la Victoire.

After having drunk with full lips from the enchanting cup of sensuality, he fell asleep for a few moments. When he woke up he was alone, for the pretty girl had made off, taking with her the purse of her temporary client, so true is it that there is never any profit in ill-acquired wealth.

Utterly ashamed, he was still prey to his chagrin when he arrived at the Place de la Trinité. He had to stop on a refuge in order to let a long file of carriages, omnibuses, coupés and automobiles go by.

He was about to continue his route, going back to La Chapelle, when, through the window of a sumptuous "electric," shiny and varnished, he thought he recognized a comrade with a young woman, bejeweled and richly dressed, with a vast hat whose long plumes were swaying to the jolts of the vehicle.

"Tête-Rouge!" he exclaimed, in a low voice.

He was not dreaming; it really was Tête-Rouge, elegantly dressed, looking very prosperous, who, abandoned to the imperceptible lurches of the automobile, was holding tightly in his large fist a little hand delicately-gloved in suede.

"Damn!" exclaimed Demi-Sel. "He's doing well, the fellow! He needs women of high society! Monsieur doesn't refuse himself anything! It goes without saying that he must be earning good money!"

But the circulation, momentarily interrupted, was reestablished, and while the auto continued on its way with explosions of the engine, along the Rue Saint-Lazare, toward the classy quarters, Demi-Sel, bewildered, plunged into immense reflections. It was the face of Françoise-la-Bretonne that appeared to him in his reverie.

"She's pretty, though, his kid!" he exclaimed. "And that's not sufficient for him . . ."

Only then did he explain to himself why Tête-Rouge was seen so infrequently in La Chapelle. He had better things to do than to come and sit down at table in a music bar, sipping drinks of inferior quality. Did not pretty powdered arms, blood-red lips and passionate embraces await him?

That unexpected encounter dissipated the sad memory of his ridiculous adventure slightly. Swinging his hips and leering at the women under his nose, he went up the Rue Blanche. At the square, feeling fatigued, renouncing the pleasure of shaking the hands of all the friends who were working on the boulevard, he took the Metro and went down to La Chapelle.

Almost immediately, he ran into Nez-de-Coq, Boubou and Georges-l'Algerien in the process of playing zanzi on the zinc of a bar in the Rue de la Goutte-d'or.

"Do you know," he said, "who I saw just now? Tête-Rouge, in an auto, with a woman, all that there is of high-class."

"If you imagine that it's news that you're giving us," replied Georges-l'Algérien, "it's no secret for anyone that Tête-Rouge has found a good thing . . . a real vein. Liline Aubray is stuck on him. She met him at a wrestling match at the Casino de Paris, and since then, Tête-Rouge is making her very happy . . . and she gives him as much money as he wants!"

"I didn't know!" said Demi-Sel, humbly, resigned to that new disappointment, "but it was a shock for me for me when I saw that!"

"Not surprising: Tête-Rouge is a top man, not a demi-sel like you," added Nez-de-Coq, bitterly.

Crestfallen, Demi-Sel had fallen silent, although a question was burning his lips: What about Françoise-la-Bretonne? What had become of her in all this? He dared not formulate his question, fearing the gibes that would inevitably assail him.

But Georges-l'Algérien who was enthused by a well-served purée, explained: "Tête-Rouge is making as much money as he wants, but he doesn't lose his bearings for that. He comes to re-join his chick every evening so that she can render her accounts to him. As men with a good head go, he's one! Necessary that she gives him his four tunes every day, or there are slaps in the air, and on Françoise's face."

The next day, a fine sunlit Sunday in April, Demi-Sel went for a walk all the way to the Île Saint-Ouen—a trek of which he was fond, and the goal of which was La Peniche, a small wine-shop where fries and mussels were sold, which Demi-Sel washed down with acidic wine. Then he took a turn along the edge of the green and ammoniac water, dirty and stinking water the color of bad absinthe. The trees were beginning to turn green, and at every bend in the towpath, as if to mock his celibacy, he discovered amorous couples tenderly enlaced, hand in hand, their eyes shining, and their lips meeting at intervals.

As dusk fell, when the mist descended over the river, striped by the wakes of tugs and pinnaces, he returned to Paris via the Rue de La Chapelle and the Poterne des Poissoniers. The streets were crowded with people in their Sunday clothes, families coming back from the country, talking loudly, with joyful faces.

The Boulevard de La Chapelle had an appearance quite different from the usual. Only two or three prostitutes were soliciting the gaze of passers by; the others had flown away to the country in mad parties with their little men.

In the shadow of a pillar on the Metro, Demi-Sel perceived a woman whose silhouette he recognized immediately. His heart began to beat more rapidly and his forehead moistened. As he approached he recognized her and, trembling with troubling emotion, he murmured in a breath: "Françoise-la-Bretonne."

Yes, it was her, still at work in order to satisfy the demands of Tête-Rouge, the master abhorred and beloved at the same time.

While she accomplished her métier automatically, she felt within herself a vague, imprecise, ill-defined sentiment: a sort of obscure hatred against the man who had thrown her on to the sidewalk. But he only had to reappear; it was sufficient for his eyes to seek hers for an instant, for them to gleam momentarily with the same glare, for her to become a little helpless thing, limply submissive to his every whim, to his slightest caprices. She forgot everything, her being abolished, her thoughts concentrated on one unique objective: her man.

Fascinated, hypnotized and dominated, she went forth, having no other sentiment but his will.

Days of rest—Sundays, of which her peers took advantage to go and seek enjoyment on the bank of the Marne or at Billancourt—were unknown to her.

Incessantly, relentlessly, it was necessary for her to toil while Tête-Rouge amused himself, leading a joyful existence in the arms of pretty women, bejeweled and elegantly clad. He only made brief appearances in La Chapelle; he arrived like a gust of wind, always in a hurry, treated Françoise roughly, accorded her a kiss, and after having claimed the day's receipts, having made her swoon in his arms, he disappeared.

Demi-Sel was timid and awkward in the company of women in general, but as soon as he approached Françoise an undeniable sentiment invaded him; his pale and glabrous face went crimson, and a strange tremor shook him.

"What, Françoise," he said to her, striving to steady his voice, "you're still at work?"

"Who are you?" she demanded. "I don't know you. What do you want?"

"Have no fear, I'm a friend. They call me Demi-Sel; I'm a mate of Tête-Rouge, your man. You don't remember me?"

"Yes," she said, "I seem to have heard that name before, but I don't recall the face. Anyway, what do you want?"

"Nothing, but let me tell you . . ." he pronounced, hesitantly, leaning against a Metro pillar and turning into the darkness while Françoise remained under the light of an electric bulb, the glow of which gave her features a mysterious charm. "I remember very well, Françoise . . . the first time I saw you was good . . . I was smitten with you immediately . . . not like the other times, for the gonzesses of the quarter, no! I felt that I had you in my skin. Since then, I've never forgotten you . . ."

Motionless, frozen, her lips taut, Françoise was troubled by that language, which her ears had forgotten.

Encouraged by her mutism, Demi-Sel went on: "You see, it's not to feed you claptrap, but I adore you! It's true. Tête-Rouge has too much luck to have a woman like you and not to care about her. Oh, if you wanted . . . I'm a good fellow. I'd never beat you . . . If you wanted, Françoise . . . but I'm afraid of displeasing you . . . For a long time, since the day when I first saw you, that's tormented me . . . only . . ."

She looked at him, suspicious and intrigued. Never before had anyone spoken to her like that.

They walked side by side for a moment under the vault of the Metro, without saying a word. Above their heads the trains succeeded one another with a thunderous racket.

Demi-Sel, embarrassed, was searching for his words.

"They call you Françoise-la-Bretonne," he said, after a pause. "It's Tête-Rouge who brought you from his homeland. I'm from out there too."

That revelation had the immediate result of causing the ice to melt. Demi-Sel had found a solid terrain of connection.

Françoise departed from her coldness and asked, in Breton: "Where are you from?"

He opened astonished eyes and admitted, confusedly: "I don't understand . . . I don't speak Breton."

"What! You don't speak as we do? But in that case, you're not from the land . . ."

"Yes, Françoise, I'm from Nantes, from the city; I've never lived in the country. I quit the homeland when I was very young to come to Paris. And then, where I lived, people haven't talked Breton for more than a hundred years . . . since the Chouans . . ."

She looked him up and down rapidly. "A Breton who doesn't speak Breton," she thought aloud, "isn't a Breton. He's a Gallo . . ."

Nonplussed, Demi-Sel remained silent for a moment longer. He no longer knew himself, since he had been walking on the boulevard next to Françoise, toward whom all his desires converged. It was neither a sensual amour nor an interested amour, but a true, pure sentiment that he was experiencing, perhaps infantile but sincere. He would have liked to take her far away from Paris, to some provincial town, to hide his passion there.

There, shielded from the mates and the cops, they could spend happy days, thanks to the produce of his prison savings, which he had always conserved preciously, perhaps in anticipation of this romance, which he summoned with all his prayers.

Awkwardly, he made his "pitch" to Françoise.

"With me, you'd have nothing to fear, you wouldn't have to work any longer. I'm a former apprentice hairdresser. I was a very tranquil fellow until a mate put it into my head to raid the patron's cash-box. We got caught. I got two years . . . I did them . . . since then I've collected others, and if I get another conviction I'll be good for Guyana.

"In Monparno, as in Sebasto, the mates called me Demi-Sel because I didn't know how to handle women. You see . . ." He had stopped addressing her as *tu*, as much by virtue of respect as intimidation by the gravity of the conversation, "I've never been much of a mec. Can you imagine that, instead of getting money from gonzesses, it was me who gave it to them ... not much, but in the end, I paid! Then, they didn't give a damn about me ..."

He would have liked her to say something, for her to lament, for her to make him confidences, but Françoise refrained carefully from laying bare the secrets of her soul and her heart, contenting herself with listening to him with a complaisant ear. A bizarre thing! Although she did not experience, in reality, any attraction for the pseudo-Breton, who did not even know the language of her petty fatherland, she was interested by what he was saying. What he was causing to shine in her eyes was an entirely new existence, an honest existence, such as she had desired when, in the evening, on the health, before the sea, with Mathurin, she had dreamed, her eyes lost in space ...

The wretched life was still repugnant to her; custom and adaptation had taken a long time to set in within that rustic girl with an excessively docile brain, in which all influences were engraved.

While he was speaking, her dilated pupils stared straight ahead of her, lost in an indefinite dream, and her breast heaved in anguish. It was as if Demi-Sel's words had rendered her insensible, put her to sleep; momentarily, they had caused her to forget the bruising of the powerful chain that riveted her to Tête-Rouge.

In the following days, during her promenades on the asphalt in quest of clients, she encountered Demi-Sel again, once in Babés, another time in the Rue Guy-Patin when she had just run away from the moral police. They chatted then for a moment. Demi-Sel, the timid Demi-Sel, was deeply amorous and never ceased to surround Françoise with fond and polite phrases, compliments on her youth and her freshness, and, above all, to talk to her about future projects.

From day to day, although he was no psychologist, he sensed her will flexing, and mistook for amour what was, in fact, merely the result of the weakness of that indolent, malleable soul. But the next day, when he approached her again, he found her firm again, impenetrable and grim, still impregnated with the kisses of Tête-Rouge and her last embrace—a fugitive embrace that bewitched her.

A moral combat was delivered within her, while Demi-Sel strove to make her share his amour. She passed through terrible alternatives. Ready to yield, she collected herself abruptly and rejected energetically the propositions of her suitor, whose passion was becoming increasingly violent, exasperated by the very resistance that it encountered.

One evening in May, Françoise told Demi-Sel, whom more than a month of waiting had not discouraged, and who, still amorous, roamed from the Boulevard Barbès to the Rue du Faubourg-Saint-Denis in search of her, that: "Tomorrow, I'll no longer see you."

Demi-Sel became livid.

"Don't look at me like that . . . I'm moving . . . I'm leaving La Chapelle. I'm no longer making enough here; all the clients know me, and the cops have it in for me. Tête-Rouge is taking me to the Île de Beauté, in the Marne, a place where there are lots of marks. It's the fine season; it appears that there's a lot to do out there . . ."

"What! Then I won't see you any more?" said Demi-Sel, his voice strangled.

"Bah! We'll see one another again in winter. Between now and then . . . but look out, there's a fellow eying me . . . I'm lighting him up . . . I haven't finished work today . . ."

And Françoise set off toward the passer-by, took him by the arm and murmured a few propositions in his ear, while Demi-Sel, devastated, his heart bruised and his head empty, disappeared into the night, insensible to everything but his passion.

IV
The Flight of Françoise

The Red Sorcerer Pen-Ru, who raped and abducted the daughters of the heath in order to make them flesh of pleasure, which he threw into the gaping and insatiable mouth of Parisian lust—the terrible Tête-Rouge, whose gray eyes with violet glints disengaged powerful magnetic effluvia; the handsome male whom men respected and women adored and feared—increasingly abandoned La Chapelle in order to move in another society, not better but more elegant, more polite, more refined and more distinguished.

His success with Liline Aubray—the "delightful divette" as the newspapers qualified her, who showed off more than fifty thousand francs' worth of jewelry every evening and sang some inept ditty with far more enthusiasm than talent, whose dresses were described minutely in the fashion magazines; a woman who recruited her lovers in all strata of society, for whom three or four unfortunates had committed suicide—was Tête-Rouge's most beautiful conquest, and he was exceedingly proud of it. So he had begun to consider his old friends with a certain haughty scorn, a nuance of new superiority.

He was seen everywhere now beside his mistress, on Sunday in the paddock at Autueil or Longchamp and during the week at all the chic establishments, where women pampered him and fêted him, attracted by that secret charm, ready to throw themselves recklessly into his arms. He only had to make a sign or cast a glance, and they were his, rubbing their bloody lips against his moustache, infatuated with his muscular body and his strange eyes.

With his pockets well-garnished, his fingers ornamented by expensive rings, his waistcoat cut by a heavy gold chain, he had the fine self-assurance that fortune confers. But triumph had not intoxicated him to the point of forgetting Françoise-

71

la-Bretonne; he conserved her in anticipation of future days. With an astonishing psychology he had deciphered the soul of that girl; he knew that his gaze set her in motion as a motor activated a machine—that if the motor were to break down the machine would immediately become inert. He also knew that his presence was necessary to the maintenance of his power.

If Françoise had not seen him for several days, her personality might have regained the upper hand. Perhaps, too, she might have attempted to escape the existence that he had created for her. But he forgot nothing, and every day, with an implacable regularity, he returned to La Chapelle to remind her, to recapture the woman, who tried in vain to liberate herself.

And, as June had chased a good number of Parisians from the capital, and business became worse day by day, he had decided one evening that Françoise-la-Bretonne would depart for Nogent, on the Marne.

The next day, after having dressed her anew, he went to install her in a delightful corner of the Île de Beauté, making her the usual recommendations:

"Be alluring, eh! Don't tell anyone who you are. If anyone asks, only respond that you're a seamstress taking a few days' holiday. Pretend to be respectable—that pleases the old men out here. There's money to be earned, a place like this is a gold mine. Think, then, that on Sunday, chic folk come to go boating. It's up to you to cheer them up. In the evening, they're all drunk; they go to conclude the day with a blow-out with the locals. That's a windfall for you. Keep your eyes open; I need a louis a day . . . otherwise, look out!" he threatened, adopting his powerful gaze.

Tranquil, sure of his prey, he quit Françoise in order to return to Liline Aubray, whose caprice he doubtless still believed to be violent and who, vibrant with desire, thirsty for amour, was waiting for him in her brightly-decorated boudoir.

However, he found her different, preoccupied, worried, nervous and anxious. The pretty woman who had offered herself to him, who had gladly admitted him to her bed—the celebrated bed in which princes, statesmen and men of the world had wallowed—suddenly showed herself less passionate, less tender, and even rebellious to the forceful embrace of her lover.

He perceived that change of attitude immediately, and asked her the cause of it.

"But I assure you that absolutely nothing is wrong."

"Come on, then!"

Already, his arm was around her waist and he was looking at her tenderly, but she defended herself, evading his caress.

"Oh no, not today . . . I'm not in the mood . . ." And after a pause: "You know, my dear, today, I can't give you a brass farthing. The vicomte is hard up; Lapaire, my friend the banker of the Rue de Provence, is up against it, expecting catastrophe at any moment. For my part, I have settlements that are late; I owe my servants eight months' wages and nine thousand francs to my dressmaker, almost as much as my milliner . . . so you see . . ."

In spite of those assertions, Tête-Rouge remained skeptical. *Well*, he said to himself, *her infatuation for me has passed. She has someone else in her sights!*

He remembered that the previous evening, at the Folies Olympiennes—exactly where he had met her two months before, she had been excessively ecstatic abut the admirable physique of a wrestling champion, a certain Rodolphe-le-Boucher, whose deplorable morals were known to All-Paris, to its amusement. "To sleep with me," he said, brazenly, with a conceited expression, while an entire circle of bewigged ladies darted shining eyes at the protuberance of his muscles, "it's five louis and two bottles of chartreuse—and I have no lack of choice."

That high tariff did not prevent emplumed beauties in quest of new sensations from disputing his costly favors. Why should it be astonishing, then, that Liline was smitten with that wrestler?

An inextinguishable lustful thirst for sensual pleasures moved the ardent Liline; no one could keep count of the infatuations and more-or-less eccentric whims of the beautiful creature with the gilded eyes and fleshy lips, who emanated from head to toe an intoxicating perfume of troubling perversity. And it was in the depths of Parisian society that she sought her favorites—favorites of a night or several days, who enabled her to know more delightful minutes than the men of the world who covered her with gold every day to pay for her favors.

Tête-Rouge's vogue had been of long duration; everyone was astonished by it in the milieux in which Liline multiplied her charms. Only the women had understood that attachment when, by chance, Tête-Rouge's eyes had taken possession of them in passing. That reign, however, seemed to be on the point of termination.

But Tête-Rouge, with his marvelous instinct of divination, had the prescience of it, and it was not with a glad heart that he made that observation. He glimpsed the end of generous subsidies, and also the end of the joyful existence that he had been leading for two months. It would be necessary for him to limit himself to the louis that Françoise-la-Bretonne brought him with difficulty. And he would recommence confining himself to ridiculous activities in the cafés of La Chapelle and Rochechouart.

Before that catastrophe occurred, he wanted to try to reconquer the lost favor, throwing all his chips into the pot and using his hypnotic power.

However, in order to bring that off, it was necessary for him to remain with Liline for several days, in order to isolate her and cut her off from any foreign influencer.

Yes, but there's the other one, out there on the Marne, he thought. *If I don't wind her up, she's capable of getting away from me . . .*

He reflected then, at length. She feared him too much. She knew that he would find her again, wherever she went.

Less anxious, he put his plan into execution.

Three days passed thus, three days of caresses and amorous pleasures; he regained hope. On the fourth, however, Liline, satisfied, her senses sated by Tête-Rouge, escaped, eluding his narrow surveillance, slipping through his hands like an eel, and went to throw herself into the arms of Rodolphe-le-Boucher.

Vexed by having let go thus, Tête-Rouge initially meditated a terrible revenge. He rolled frightful projects around in his head—but he resigned himself to a less violent course of action, and also much wiser.

One lost, ten discovered! After all, I'm crazy. The mother of whores isn't dead. I'll make a tour of La Chapelle to say bonjour to the mates before heading for Nogent to rejoin my kid. Oh, I'm quite sure that that one will never dump me! I'll still have her, whatever happens.

As he went past a café near the entrance to the Metro on the Boulevard de La Chapelle, a particular whistle followed by a "Hey!" made him turn his head toward the establishment. It was Nez-de-Coq who was calling to him from the terrace.

"Well," he said, when they were sitting face to face, "what's become of you? We no longer see you!"

Tête-Rouge maintained a mysterious silence as to the reason for his absence, although it was no secret for anyone. In order to change the subject, he said: "You've changed bistro, then?"

"Yes, the other was full of police vermin. One couldn't talk there any longer, to the point that Panaris has been shopped and picked up. Oh, a bagatelle—an old score that was settled belatedly. He'll get himself out of it with a few bribes. But what about you?" Nez-de-Coq continued, with his habitual bitterness. "It appears that you're always tucked in with upper-class gonzesses now . . . the like of Liline d'Aubray, posh women . . ."

"That's still none of your business," Tête-Rouge replied, with a particularly sharp tone of voice "Do I occupy myself with your Mort-aux-Gosses and her abortions? No, but when one thinks . . . you have no reason to brag!"

That reflection calmed Nez-de-Coq down instantly, although his eyes were still gleaming with rage.

When they had talked about the news of the boulevard, the daily gossip, Tête-Rouge emptied his glass and said: "Now, old chap, I'm going to Nogent to rejoin my shepherdess . . ."

Nez-de-Coq's eyes sparkled with contained malice; he was about to obtain his revenge.

"You're shepherdess? Well, the shepherdess . . . no, let me laugh . . . your woman . . . she's almost never on the Marne; she spends all her time making perfect love with . . ."

"What's that you're saying?" roared Tête-Rouge, angrily. "Don't joke about that—it would end badly!"

"Don't get carried away. I'm simply telling you to render you a service. It appears that she's head over heels . . ."

"No! You're joking!"

"I swear."

"Oh, the vermin, the slut! I'll . . . I'll . . ."

"Come on, calm down . . . and reflect. You're in the wrong. You're living in grandeur, lost in Liline d'Aubrays . . . so Françoise has taken advantage of it to give you the slip. She even steals from you . . . she only gives you half of what she brings in. As for the rest . . . I'd rather keep quiet. What is certain is that if my name were Tête-Rouge, I'd take care of it. All that might be nothing, but the worst of it is that she's stuck on a mate . . ."

"Stuck on a mate? Who?" howled Tete-Rouge, grinding his teeth. "Tell me who, so I can take him apart!"

"Who? Are you blind, then? You haven't seen anything . . . no, the posh dolls have turned your head. With Demi-Sel!"

"With Demi-Sel!" he pronounced, unable to hide his anger. "Oh, the choleras!"

He got up precipitately, leaving Nez-de-Coq with the care of paying for the drinks.

"Au revoir; I'm taking the Metro right away as far as Vincennes. There I'll jump into the Nogentais. I want to have a clear heart about all these stories and to know the truth. If it's like that, there'll be news this evening!"

As he descended to the tramway he fell upon a band of unusual strollers, with joyous faces beneath their caps, and a nonchalant and debauched appearance: former or future jail-birds. He knew two or three of them, including La Levite and Le Laquais, two burglars.

When he perceived him, La Levite came to Tête-Rouge with his hand extended.

"Why, here you are . . . we no longer see you nowadays, what have you been doing, then? Is it true that you're the lover of . . . of the love-machine . . . what do they call her? Liline Aubray, an actress at the Folies Olympiennes? Good for you, mate, you must be in clover, always in the money, with a gonzesse like that!"

Tête-Rouge shrugged his shoulders and changed the subject. "I'm looking for my woman . . . you won't have seen her for a while with the others."

"Your woman? Françoise-la-Bretonne? But she's with thingy . . . with Demi-Sel . . ."

Tête-Rouge went white. He was beginning to be seriously annoyed to see that everyone was informed of his misfortune.

Wounded in his self-esteem, he no longer had any but one haste: to find her and recover her, no matter what the cost.

But in that regard, he was to suffer many affronts that day. As he went down toward the passenger platform he encountered friends at every step who had been on the spree, and who greeted him with mocking smiles as they recognized him; some of the boldest even joked: "There he is, Tête-Rouge! His chick is in the process of having a good time!"

"For sure she's making a fool of the man who flattered himself that his woman would only ever be fond of him!"

"Not good! That's because he wanted to swim in the heights. One can't run after two hares at the same time!"

"They're having fun at my expense," Tête-Rouge murmured. "They're making digs . . . what, then?"

Before climbing on to the ferry to cross the Marne he was stopped again by Frise-à-Plat, a mate who whispered to him in a mysterious tone:

"Are you in the clear?"

"Well, yes . . . I have nothing to fear from the cops. Why? I've paid . . ."

Frise-à-Plat looked suspiciously to the right and the left in order to make sure that no one was listening, and whispered: "There's something nice to do!"

"What?"

"Old houses are being demolished out there, and there's a good thing on the side. You, know, I know something marvelous, personally!"

"Ah!" said Tête-Rouge, rather indifferently, more preoccupied with finding his woman, in order to inflict the correction merited by her aberration, and the fact that she had cast ridicule upon him, thus diminishing his prestige in the eyes of the mates.

"A good haul . . . only has to be taken; it's easy!"

"Oh, I know all about that," declared Tête-Rouge, disdainfully.

The other laughed, sarcastically. "I understand—you're thinking about your woman, Françoise. She's shacked up with Demi-Sel . . ."

And Frise-à-Plat drew away, shrugging his shoulders and whistling. But he had not gone ten paces when Tête-Rouge murmured between his teeth, in a menacing tone: "There's an idea, and a nice one! It's the two of us now, Demi-Sel."

The morning after the day on which Tête-Rouge had installed Françoise-la-Bretonne in Nogent, as she was coming downstairs from her room, she had found herself face to face with Demi-Sel.

"What are you doing here?" she asked, anxiously.

"You see, Françoise, I was too bored without you. I asked the mates where you were . . . and here I am!" he explained, with suppliant eyes.

"Make sure that Tête-Rouge doesn't see you here. If he even suspects that you're making up to me, he'll smash you."

"Do you think so? He can't do any harm to you now; he's always in the skirts of a renowned whore, Liline Aubray, who gives him as much money as he wants."

"That makes no difference. You run after me with your smooth talk, your claptrap . . ."

"Oh, Françoise, we could be so happy, though, the two of us! I have a few sous that I earned at Poissy, in the Centrale. With that we could rent a little villa somewhere near here. We'd be as tranquil as Baptiste. You'd have nothing to do but let yourself live, drink, eat and sleep!"

"Shut up! Don't say stupid things. What would Tête-Rouge sing to me when he comes back, if I had no galette to give him? And then, he's my man . . . I only ought to listen to him."

The day was fairly clement to Françoise; the weather was splendid, strollers numerous. In the evening, she waited in vain for her man in order to give him the two louis that she had harvested. She waited for him until midnight; he did not come.

It was the first time that he had forgotten her thus. It appeared to her that it was a little liberty and independence that she was recovering; she breathed more easily. The night was warm, bright and mild; loud laughter departed from the woods. It seemed to her that a little happiness invaded her heart.

The next day, when Demi-Sel came to play his role of be-sotted lover with her, proposing that she take a little walk with him, her hesitation was of short duration, and she accepted.

The two of them wandered along the water's edge. Françoise threw stones into it. She did not resist the pleasure of crossing the arm of the Marne when Demi-Sel proposed: "Come on, let's go take something at Père La Tasse's place. It's very popular ... nothing but fat barons ..."

The afternoon passed thus, idling in the vicinity.

At nightfall she perceived that she had not earned a sou, and a sudden terror invaded her. What if Tête-Rouge arrived!

She prepared her defense ... she still had two louis ... she would say that she had earned twenty francs yesterday and as many today ...

But that terror dissipated and gave way to a happy quietude. For her man did not come that evening any more than the previous one.

"You see, he's dumped you for his Liline Aubray ..."

And Demi-Sel, although not very persuasive, ended up reckoning with Françoise-la-Bretonne's scruples. He took her to a little villa of very modest appearance, which he rented for a month and in which he installed her, spending without counting his meager savings, which his rent alone would scarcely have eroded.

He finally attained happiness—him, Demi-Sel, whom luck had never favored; his desires were finally granted. He had the woman he coveted.

How fleeting that semblance of happiness was!

Françoise and he were not made to understand one another; there were continual contradictions, quarrels and disputes. She was nervous and irritable, haunted by the memory of Tête-Rouge, whom she still feared, and dreaded seeing surge forth, terrible and menacing, with yellow gleams shining in his eyes. Her conscience was not tranquil; she had a kind of remorse;

the night did not bring her any more tranquility; nightmares frightened her, and in spite of the novelty, Demi-Sel did not make her forget Tête-Rouge.

Into what folly had she just launched herself? She was no sooner engaged in it than she already considered Demi-Sel with the scorn of a criminal for his accomplice.

Oh, decidedly she had him in her skin—her man—in spite of all the dread that he inspired and the yoke of slavery that he caused to weigh upon her shoulders. How superior he seemed to the little Demi-Sel, a thin, weak, frail being devoid of consistency, who did not even know how to speak Breton: a Nantais, a dirty Gallo!"

She almost regretted the fist that abused her, striking her pitilessly.

And yet, she did not want Tête-Roge to come to take her back; her soul was divided between various sentiments; she had gone astray; her audacity had unhinged her; she only knew how to obey, she did not know how to direct herself; she was a passive creature, whose will had been atrophied by authoritarian masculinity. A victim of events, she let herself drift, drawn by the current, with the same automatism as a piece of cork thrown into a stream, following the watercourse and meekly going toward its destiny: the river.

She did not do anything to escape; her dearest desire was to return to Bretagne, but she did not have the moral strength necessary to attempt such a flight.

She had been with Demi-Sel for three days, but it seemed to her that it had lasted for months.

And he, who had dreamed of a happiness beside that woman very different from the previous relationships he had had: what a disillusionment!

He had already exhausted his petty reserves of money; they were obliged to ask for credit at the grocer's, the wine-merchant's and the butcher's, which was only granted with a grimace.

Demi-Sel took care of everything, carefully dissimulating that situation from Françoise-la-Bretonne, and their differences were complicated by money troubles. But as he did not have much more initiative than his mistress, he abandoned himself to destiny, to fatality. What would be would be . . .

And destiny did not take long to make its appearance in the little furnished villa, because of the proximity of the river.

One evening, as they were dining together on an assortment of charcuterie and two bottles of white wine, a man was silhouetted in the door-frame.

"Tête-Rouge!" breathed Françoise, dropping her fork.

"Tête-Rouge!" stammered Demi-Sel, frightfully pale and trembling all over.

He got up painfully and tried to dissimulate his disturbance; he went to meet the newcomer.

Françoise got up so abruptly that the chair fell back on the red tiles without her having the time to pick it up, and she drew away, backwards, into the depths of the room, distressed, expecting to endure the wrath of her master.

The latter did not seem bellicose; he came into the dining room very calmly, his face even smiling; he sat astride the chair that Demi-Sel had advanced toward him, mechanically. And in a disengaged manner, without his gaze settling on either of them, he said: "Well, my old Demi-Sel, you're living in luxury. You refuse yourself nothing, then! I've encountered mates who've said to me: 'Go and see Demi-Sel, then; he's settled, he's rented a house.' I come and I find you with my woman! You're not putting one over on me, by any chance?"

"Me? You're crazy," yapped Demi-Sel, his throat tightened by a very legitimate emotion.

"Then it's all above board? That's good—but if ever you wanted to pass on to love-making, that wouldn't be the same thing. I'd break your neck right away . . ."

His voice had no hint of anger.

Demi-Sel, emboldened by the fortunate turn that the adventure was taking, without suspecting the deceptiveness of that attitude, responded firmly enough: "There are things that aren't done between mates."

Less tranquilized, Françoise had approached the table, picked up the chair, and sat down.

She did not say a word, and her eyes remained attached to Tête-Rouge. He had not yet looked at her.

"It's nothing like that," Demi-Sel pronounced. "Have you dined?"

"No."

"You can have a crust with us. We were just beginning."

"That's not to be refused. I had a few aperitifs on the way . . . with mates that I hadn't seen for a while. I need to back them up.

Françoise brought a plate, cutlery and a glass.

While they ate, the banal conservation continued. They ate with a good appetite and drank thirstily. The provision of wine was soon exhausted, and Françoise had to fetch another two liters.

"At the same time, bring a packet of tobacco, cigarettes and two three-sou cigars," ordered Demi-Sel, playing the generous host.

The meal finished in gaiety; the two men drank and smoked abundantly.

There was so much smoke in the dining room, transformed into a smoking room, that Françoise was seized by a fit of coughing and went out into the little garden that surrounded the maisonette. At the same time, she felt the need to be alone in order to reflect, because she was not so unintelligent as not to have found Tête-Rouge's conduct strange. Why was he, usually so violent and so jealous, acting with that mildness? His friends must have told him on what terms she was with Demi-Sel. What vengeance was hidden beneath it?

She divined that he was inflexible, ferocious. He had seemed to read her with his eyes, attractive poles that bewitched her.

And she prolonged her absence, while Demi-Sel, abandoned to the relaxation that drunkenness provokes, became communicative, forgetting that he was facing a terrible rival.

Tête-Rouge, his face reddened by drink, but his head perfectly steady, gently steered the conversation in the direction he intended to give it.

He made him say, in the most natural fashion in the world, that he was not a client but a genuine lover, and that the fact that he had been "stuck" with Françoise had been, for him, instantaneous. To which the other replied, with false bonhomie: "Women are like that; they pass from hand to hand. Yesterday, it was me; today, it's you; tomorrow it will be another. She'll see many others yet!"

Drunkenness obstructed Demi-Sel's brain; he was no longer seeing clearly, and delivered himself stupidly to his enemy. Sliding down the slope of confidence, he arrived at confessing, with tears in his eyes: "Between us, mate, I'm very stupid. I've obtained credit and I have no more galettte—not a sou, not a dart! It's all gone."

Tête-Rouge shrugged his shoulders. "You have no more money? Well, there's no need to fret about that. It's easy to find . . ."

"How?"

"But there are affairs all the time in these parts. They're full of money."

"You think so?"

"I'm certain of it. Look, if you weren't a demi-sel . . ." He stopped dead, hesitating to continue.

The other perceived it, and took the bait. "What would I do?"

"No, I can't tell you that. You've departed with my former woman. You'd imagine that I was doing it deliberately."

"What? Tell me anyway. You're a mate, old chap. I trust you. I know that you wouldn't do me a bad turn."

"In that regard, you're right, Demi-Sel. It's nothing, it's stupid."

"Go on; keep talking."

"Since you insist, here it is! If you want to make a big score ... there are ten sacs."

"Ten sacs! For sure, that's good to take," replied Demi-Sel, not at all decided to accept the proposition. "But think, I'm on my third strike; if I get pinched again, I'll go to wash my feet. Guyana, no thanks! Bad idea!"

"No, old man! There's no danger, it's a good affair; it's pure gold, nothing to fear."

"Ugh! One never knows."

"Come on, Demi-Sel. Think—ten sacs, ten thousand bullets! That's worth the risk. Enough to amuse yourself for a while with the gonzesse. You don't have a sou, and you're refusing that!"

The other was still shaking his head, indecisive and fearful.

"You'll never get out of trouble, then, old chap! What I'm proposing here is a nice coup. You'll be all square again, old man. It's good. It's there to be taken, as much as you want: silverware and pricey bronzes. A coup to make a fortune, what!"

Tête-Rouge's intonation was so persuasive that Demi-Sel's fears gradually evaporated.

"You're stupid. It's all there is to be done to get you out of the mire. It's tranquility; you can go straight; it will go like clockwork. Think, ten thousand bullets! And perhaps there's more than people think."

"Where is it?"

"At the other end of the island, where the demolitions are, you know? There's a villa inhabited by an old artist. It's there."

"Yes, I know the place; the house is surrounded by little railings, and they go all the way to the Marne."

"That's it; you've got it. The fellow has gone overseas; there's no one there. It's a dream, what! Once again, there for the taking."

Demi-Sel procrastinated, hesitantly, expressing fears that Tête-Rouge dissipated eloquently, making the "ten sacs" shine in his eyes, plus the rest that no one knew about.

"Well, that's all right," Demi-Sel ended up saying, making his decision. Then he added, now decided: "I'll get going right away, then."

"No, it's necessary to go in two hours, otherwise, it's no good. And disguise yourself, old chap, make up your face. You might be recognized."

The conversation was interrupted by the return of Françoise-la-Bretonne.

"What? What's the matter with you, kid?" said Demi-Sel, catching her around the waist. "You don't look so good."

He drew her toward him and his mouth, reeking because of the libation, sought the young woman's fresh lips.; she uttered a cry and pulled away from that drunken caress, fixing her blue eyes, widened by fear, on Tête-Rouge. Her face was distressed, livid. She perceived, in the shadow that was invading the corners of the room, Tête-Rouge's mouth, which was sniggering frightfully.

"What, kid, you don't want to let yourself go? That's because Tête-Rouge, your former man, is here. You're afraid that he'll slap you? Don't make a fuss; he knows full well how it is. Isn't that true?"

"For sure," affirmed the other, in a sinister tone.

"And then, do you know something, kid? I'm going to bring you money soon. We'll be happy, the two of us. Come on, let me kiss you."

He advanced toward her again, his lips extended; but she made him stumble with a punch, moved by a will other than her own: a will so imperious that it could have led her to crime.

Demi-Sel resigned himself meekly.

"We'll catch up this evening, won't we?" And, turning to Tête-Rouge, an impassive spectator of the scene: "It's agreed, eh? You've told me everything?"

"Yes, we're in complete accord, old chap, you can prepare yourself tranquilly. It's as if you had the ten sacs in your pocket."

Demi-Sel rubbed his hands joyfully. "Good! I'll go prepare myself. Stay with the kid, eh? I'll be back."

The door banged, and Françoise, backed up against the wall, found herself alone with Tête-Rouge.

He crossed the room in two strides and arrived before her without a word, in a menacing mutism.

Sensing the approaching storm, she buckled, her legs weakening and her shoulders slumping.

Outside, the monotonous song of the flowing river could be heard, and the splash of oars. The dining room was in a half-light darkened by clouds of smoke.

Tête-Rouge raised his arm in a surge of anger, and his hand fell upon Françoise's face with a resounding slap.

She collapsed, vanquished, annihilated, while her man launched, in a stinging voice that whipped her:

"Slut!"

V

The Master's Revenge

At ten o'clock, a man was going along the bank of the Marne, talking to himself in a rather loud voice.

Every ten paces he made a zigzag, then started again in a straight line, to recommence ten paces further on.

The night was quite dark and he scarcely stood out against the obscurity. At one moment, as he thought he had lost his way, he climbed up to the quay. He appeared then in the raw light of a gas-lamp.

It was Demi-Sel, disguised, unrecognizable, and completely drunk.

At his feet the water was splashing, making the moored boats dance.

He slid into one of those boats.

A fresh breeze was blowing, which dissipated his intoxication somewhat. He began to row in the direction of the island.

Ten sacs . . . ten thousand bullets, at least, he was about to bring back from his perilous enterprise!

That was what he was thinking. With that, he and his kid could let good days go by. They could do this, and that . . . they would be as happy as cocks in clover . . .

"I've had enough misery until now . . . it's my turn to have some good times."

And he constructed in thought a thousand future projects, with which he naturally associated Françoise-la-Bretonne, whom he considered as his henceforth.

"I could see by Tête-Rouge's face that he'd had enough of her. He's quite content that I rid him of her. He's stuck with a chic woman . . . Françoise would have been an embarrassment. So she'll really be mine . . . but for all those plans to work, I need the ten thousand bullets. Forward ho, Demi-Sel!"

He had never felt so much courage in undertaking an operation of this sort.

After having crossed the river, he went along the shore of the island cautiously. He had no difficulty recognizing the property that his mission was to burgle.

Before landing, he took off his boots and put on espadrilles, as Tête-Rouge had recommended him to do.

Thanks to a little pontoon, the disembarkation was utterly facile. With precaution, Demi-Sel attached the boat and went up the narrow stairway that led to the villa's grounds.

Placed behind a tree-trunk, he examined the surroundings; a great calm reigned.

You can go on, old man, he said to himself.

And he slipped through the trees.

He found a spade easily, and thanks to the implement it was easy to reckon with the lock. Like a conqueror, he set foot in the house.

The place being entirely new to him, he took a few minutes to get his bearings, with a small lantern, and then commenced a minute search.

On the ground floor he opened a door at random, and perceived blue enamel cooking-pots lined up on the wall along with the household items indispensable in a kitchen. He did not take the trouble to examine it and went into the next room.

A very ordinary little dresser, a sideboard, a table and a few chairs furnished the dining room. Conscientiously, Demi-Sel searched the drawers—all of them—breaking the locks. He found cracked plates, chipped glasses and pewter cutlery, but not the slightest piece of silverware.

"Doubtless it's all stored in a cupboard."

The third door that he opened led to a drawing room—a poor little drawing room in red velvet, the thread of which could be seen in more than one place.

"For rich people, they're not very lavish!"

He was still searching for the treasure, which he would doubtless discover in a corner. Again, there was nothing in the room. A glazed display cabinet contained trinkets; hoping to find some object of value there, he forced the lock. Imitation Saxe, plaster statuettes, porcelain figures, a candy-box in simulated old silver were offered to his sight. He left them where they were with a just disdain, in view of their scant value.

The mantelpiece was ornamented with a clock and candelabra. Demi-Sel pulled a face again. "There's nothing here! Twenty-nine francs' worth at the most; it really isn't worth the trouble."

He went up the narrow staircase and found himself confronted by four doors. Three bedrooms were furnished uniformly with a bed, a cupboard and a pitch-pine table; the fourth served as a library.

He overturned the beds, and emptied the cupboards from top to bottom. He found nothing but poor underclothes and papers devoid of interest.

"Where can they have lodged the ten sacs and the silverware—especially the ten sacs?"

The dressing-cabinet, the wardrobe and the water closets were subjected to a minute inspection in their turn . . . and nothing, still nothing. Not the slightest little thing to scratch. Decidedly, the affair was not as good as Tête-Rouge claimed.

In spite of those fruitless searches, however, Demi-Sel was not discouraged, sustained mentally by a residue of drunkenness that made him consider everything from a favorable angle. He had a smiling optimism this evening, and he would not have operated with more tranquility if he were in his own home. He had made his first tour without haste, with a sang-froid to which he was unaccustomed; usually, he was always in a funk at the moment of action.

"There's only one thing to do and that's start again," he said. "After having searched the house from bottom to top, I'll search it from top to bottom. And I'll be damned if I don't find the ten sacs this time. The old painter must be a maniac; he'll have hidden all that in an impossible place."

The smallest corners did not escape him. He looked behind the paintings—vulgar "croutons" surrounded by gilded frames—in the vases, and turned over the mattresses to make sure that there was nothing hidden in the springs. He ravaged all the room of the upper floor in that fashion, leaving an indescribable mess behind, in which the most various objects were mingled and tangled in piles of linen, sheets and blankets, the furniture overturned, disemboweled and gaping.

The rooms on the ground floor were subjected to the same outrage. He lifted up the carpets, unfastened the wall-hangings, sounded the armchairs and searched inside the piano.

Nothing. Absolutely nothing.

A suspicion dawned in his mind.

"They're not making a fool of me again! No, no! It's not possible . . . it can't be!"

One hope still remained. Had maniacs not been known to hide their silver in the kitchen utensils?

One by one, he unhooked the cooking-pots, took the lids off the spice-jars, emptied the beech-wood dresser and cupboard and looked inside the stove. Nothing . . . still nothing.

The doubt became firmer in his brain.

"Is Tête-Rouge messing with me?"

But he reassured himself again. His face cleared and he slapped his forehead. A luminous idea had just occurred to him.

"I forgot to look in the ashes of the dining room hearth. I have a presentiment that it must be there."

He ran there, knelt down on the floor, and sifted the ashes with his hands.

The floorboards behind him creaked, and before he even had time to turn round, a hand fell upon his shoulder.

He stood up with a start, and, suddenly sobered up, was amazed to see surging forth before him, emerging from the shadow, two police agents.

"Thunder!" he cried, without trying to defend himself. "Caught on the job! I'm done for!"

And while the two men took hold of him solidly, each by one arm, Demi-Sel went pale, devastated. Before him, the prison camp and forced labor were painted; this time he was good for "washing his feet."

And yet, he had not found a sou in that accursed villa; the wretched old painter who lived there had rented it furnished and there was nothing there but appearances.

Then he thought about his kid, Françoise-la-Bretonne, and especially of Tête-Rouge, whom he suspected. Was it not to avenge himself on him for having stolen his woman that he had meditated the coup?

"I was drunk ... I didn't perceive his ploy ... but now, it's all coming back to me ..."

It was, alas, a trifle late.

"I'm Monsieur le Bon, what!"

And, abandoning himself to the fatality that dogged him relentlessly, he allowed himself to be led away, docile and resigned.

"There's nothing to be done. They'll expedite me to Les Traves! Just my luck!"

And while poor Demi-Sel went to the police station with his escort, in the shadow of the muddy, sticky and grassy Marne, in the bottom of a wretched little boat, under the eye of the moon, which made an appearance from time to time between the clouds, a couple embraced, tightly united in the same sensuality.

The man suddenly straightened up, grimly, while the woman stretched herself, languid and swooning.

"You'll always belong to me," he breathed, in a hoarse voice. "You can't escape me. You're my thing."

"Yes, Tête-Rouge, I'm yours ... entirely yours ... no one but you ... forever!"

"And if you ever take it into your head to recommence, remember what happened to Demi-Sel!"

She dared not ask questions.

He brought her up to date, telling her about his encounter with a mate who had indicated a good coup to make, and how that had suggested to him the idea of launching Demi-Sel on a false trail. It was thus that he, Tête-Rouge, avenged himself!

Demi-Sel had no sooner set forth on his expedition than he had sent a mate to carry a little word to the commissaire: "A burglar is going to introduce himself into the villa of the painter Christian Mérof this evening, at about half past ten. Suggest to

Monsieur le Commissaire that he do his duty and take care to intervene."

"You'll understand that with that, the citizen couldn't escape. Now he's good for New Caledonia; he'll go to bathe his feet. That's nice, eh?"

She looked at him with eyes in which admiration was alloyed with dread, struck once again by his superiority and his power.

At that moment, the moon emerged completely from the clouds; it resembled, in the violet sky, an enormous, improbable electric globe, and its white and blue light sprinkled the undulating water with flecks of silver.

In the boat, which was oscillating at the mooring, Tête-Rouge abruptly enlaced Françoise's waist and took hold of her entirely with his gaze, rendered even stranger by the lunar light. He murmured to her in his harsh masculine voice, which the girl found melodious:

"You're mine, eh, kid! You're my thing, I have you entirely. Look into my peepers."

Hypnotized, fascinated, she obeyed him. And the fluid disengaged by his eyes was so powerful and so sweet that she half-closed her eyelids, and whispered in a breath: "I love you!"

VI
The Partnership

He had reconquered her body and soul. She was perhaps more his than ever after that flight.

It was not a mystery for anyone among the mates of the Boulevard de La Chapelle that poor Demi-Sel, the failed brother, had been the victim of the just vengeance of Tête-Rouge; a man of his importance could not, in fact, allow himself to be mocked in his renown and his amours without reprisals. And they jeered the black luck of the one, while admiring without reserve the felony of the other. His prestige had grown in consequence, and after having mocked him for allowing his woman to be taken, all were unanimous in declaring:

"Tête-Rouge is a first-class skewer! There's no way of putting him to sleep. Others in his place would have used a knife or a gun, but there's no danger of him compromising himself! He does everything quietly, and effectively. As for Demi-Sel, oh, the brother! He deserves to have his feet washed. Guyana for him! It appears that he wrote to Gros-Tas from the Île de Ré asking her to send him some cash. You can talk! He's a colonist now—he needs money to establish himself!"

While sarcasms rained down on the subject of the unfortunate Demi-Sel, Tête-Rouge continued to dominate his entourage with the nuance of superiority that his conduct had conferred upon him initially and then the recent favor of a woman like Liline Aubray. There was even a hint of disdain in the way he treated his friends of earlier days, as well as the sleazy bistros and the furnished rooms on the ground floor; all of that now inspired repulsion in him. All his desires summoned a more comfortable life in a better, more distinguished environment; but in order to realize those adventurous future projects—with which, of course, he associated Françoise—he needed money . . . a great deal of money.

Courageously, the Bretonne had returned to work with ardor, but what she brought back—a louis or two, depending on the day, the disposition and the generosity of the clients, was only enough to support their habitual expenses. Those subsidies were insufficient to launch his woman suitably.

While he sought the means of procuring the sum necessary to the satisfaction of his ambition, Tête-Rouge lived with Françoise in the Marne. The season was fine, with the result that strollers, and hence clients, were relatively numerous. On Sunday, especially, the affluence was considerable. That permitted Tête-Rouge to indulge in the consumption of varied aperitifs, or even to make long excursions by boat toward Joinville, Bry or Lagny.

With his powerful torso tightly-wrapped in a white leotard, his muscular arms manipulating the oars of the pinnace vigorously were, in those circumstances, the object of many feminine gazes, a discreet homage to which his male vanity was not insensible. Several times a week he absented himself, after having made his habitual recommendations to Françoise; he took the train to Paris, doubtless running to temporary amours, furtive and passionate infatuations.

One Sunday afternoon, when Tête-Rouge had flown away to some alcove, Françoise experienced a great emotion.

She was at table under the trees of a waterside guinguette with a bank employee or shop worker whose acquaintance she had made five minutes before. Already, he had his arms round her waist, amorously, and his hands were straying over the opulent rotundities of her bosom, his eyes shining with covetousness at the approach of the felicities that she would soon lavish, in exchange for an honest retribution.

Around them, other couples were drinking, and straying into the bushes. Men were playing bowls with their sleeves rolled up and their arms bare, or making savant reestablishments and great loops on the trapeze. The cheap wine was having its effect. Further away, children spilling out their silvery laughter were balancing on a swing, pushing and jostling one another, shrieking in insouciant joy, intoxicated by the open air, sunlight and liberty.

Françoise accorded that living tableau of dominical idleness a smiling gaze, indifferently, finally resigned to her destiny. Incessant comings and goings, spicy exclamations, coarse laughter and the cries of frightened women animated the spectacles. Her gallant of an hour, with the caustic wit of the Parisian street-urchin, caricatured the new arrivals and those departing with a word or a phrase, which provoked the bright laughter of his beauty from time to time.

He straightened up then, proud of his repartee and of his conquest; drunk on success and claret wine, he tugged the stray hairs of his nascent moustache.

"Look at those two pompiers with their moukères. Look how they're strutting. They're putting on airs because they feel well-dressed, more chic than the other soldiers."

"Pompiers?" stammered Françoise, in an anguished voice. "Pompiers . . . where?"

And her eyes searched among the couples, between the trees.

The other, who had not noticed that sudden emotion, replied: "Can't you see them, over there, to the left of the orchestra, beside the big chestnut-tree. Their backs are turned to us."

At the same time, he pointed with his finger at the two military men.

An unspeakable terror was painted on Françoise's face; her bulging eyes stared ay the blue uniforms.

"Mathurin!" she breathed, oppressed.

"What's that you're saying?"

She did not even hear the question. Very gently, with an instinctive gesture, she removed herself from the embrace of her temporary lover and stood up—but the young man took hold of her waist again and made her sit down.

"Hang on, child! At least finish your glass and your brioche."

"Yes, wait; I'll come back."

Only then did he perceive how pale she was. "What's the matter? You're not ill, all of a sudden?"

"It's nothing—it will pass. It happens to me sometimes. Wait for me a moment; I'll be back directly." Painfully, she drew away, traversing the garden, and went into the trees in order to head for the gate opening on to the road,

She would have liked to run in order to escape more rapidly, but her tottering legs refused; she only advanced with small steps, staggering like a drunken woman.

"She's drunk . . . not possible," her client murmured, following her with his eyes.

It seemed to Françoise that she was in one of those exhausting dreams in which, in spite of painful efforts, one cannot succeed in putting one foot in front of the other, or even standing upright, while one is pursued by terrible imaginary enemies.

The more she examined one of the two pompiers, the more she found him similar to Mathurin. He had the same slightly massive build, the same bearing, the same chestnit-brown hair. And she experienced an anguish at the thought that he might turn round, see her and recognize her.

A vision passed before her eyes; it was no longer the slow and calm river that was flowing there through the vegetation, but the big blue, the sea, the wild sea of her homeland. Mathurin was there, courting her, his "sweet"—and an old refrain came to her mind:

> *Until the return of the beauty,*
> *Soon we'll meet again,*
> *Soon we'll meet again . . .*
> *In the imminent season*
> *We'll sing in the round:*
> *Taderi dera lon la.*
> *Lire lire,*
> *Traderi dera lon la*
> *Lire la!*

Then the dream dissipated. All her scruples were reborn, more solid than ever; regrets assailed her in confrontation with Mathurin—which is to say, her past, her old life, which loomed up before her like a judiciary phantom.

She forgot that she only had one master, Tête-Rouge, and one will, that of Tête-Rouge . . . and that nothing else ought to exist for her.

A mystery of the feminine soul and its unfathomable meanders: that girl, whom a powerful ascendancy dominated, whom an energetic intelligence subjugated, that slack and amorphous being was still able to rebel at the memory of her first and chaste amour, the troubling memory of her petty fatherland.

And before having been able to reach the gate that closed the garden, she had a supreme emotion and uttered a cry, ready to faint. The man, the pompier, had turned round abruptly, and was looking at her.

For another second, she was the victim of her obsession.

Then she perceived her mistake; it was not Mathurin. She had been duped by a vague resemblance.

The soldier, unable to explain the emotion provoked by the sight of him, started smiling, while she continued walking toward the exit, unconsciously, confused, her head buzzing and her thoughts in disarray.

She took a good five minutes to recover her senses, with her hand on her breast to suppress the tumultuous beating of her heart, backed up against a living hedge. The people who passed by looked down their noses at her, curiously and ironically, also mistaking her for a drunken woman.

When calm was gradually restored, she reassembled her scattered ideas and, recalling the client who was waiting for her, experienced an insurmountable disgust and an immense lassitude.

It was, therefore, going to be necessary to smile, to be tender, to lend herself to the impulses and the caresses of that stranger, to submit to the embrace of that boy, who was indifferent to her, whom she had not known half an hour ago, whom she would quit in an hour, forget immediately and never see again.

And it came to her mind to flee straight ahead, at random, no matter where.

Yes, but what about Tête-Rouge?

The violet gleam of his eyes whipped her courage; mechanically, she returned to her duty.

"Well, what have you been doing? I thought you weren't going to come back; I was beginning to think the worst. Are you better now?" he asked, ironically.

"It was nothing," she said, forcing herself to smile.

But he, excited by the wait, enervated by contained desire, put his arm around her waist gently, with a significant wink.

She understood, swallowed her brioche in two mouthfuls and emptied her glass. Then, while he settled the bill, she got up, bracing her figure in a gesture that was customary to her, and they both moved away, along the river bank, going up as far as a hotel in Nogent.

Hastily recoiffed and dressed again, she found herself an hour later back on the bank, crowded with strollers, but instead of soliciting men again, she started fleeing, her flesh inert and her heart crazed. She wandered thus until sunset, somber, sad and disorientated.

When it was time to return to her master, there were only two miserable hundred-sou coins in her pocket. She only went up tremulously to the hotel room that had sheltered them since she had quit the humble villa where Demi-Sel had loved her.

She was certain in advance of suffering a terrible outburst of wrath. Now that she was a little calmer, she heaped herself with reproaches, and she already approved of Tête-Rouge without qualification, if he beat her.

"He's my man ... I ought only to think about him ... I ought not to care about anything else ... but I'm so stupid!"

Tête-Rouge had not yet come back, and she waited for him meekly until past midnight.

She recognized his footsteps on the stairway and went to open up to him before he reached the door, doubly anxious, for if he was drunk, his anger would be terrible.

She saw right away, by his face, that he was only cheerful, and made haste, seductively.

"Bonsoir, kid," he said, planting a kiss on her mouth that made her shiver all over. And instead of the inevitable and primordial question: "What have you done today?" she had the astonishment of hearing him say: "There's news . . . something good."

She dared not interrogate him.

"I'm sick of it here . . . there's nothing to do here for a woman like you . . . but in order to decamp, I need this . . ." He rubbed his thumb against his index finger with the particular movement by which one translates valuable coins. ""I need cash . . . a lot of cash . . . and it isn't as easy to find as people think, damn it. But now I've got a good seam . . ."

With a tenderness that was not habitual to him, he took her on his knees and caressed her with his stage eyes, with an expression that resembled love.

Happy and delighted, she erased the sadness of her afternoon from her memory, put her arms around his neck and forgot everything else in order to drink his changing gaze, his violet or gray gaze, which flowed into her with a indefinable sensation. And she smiled at him as she only smiled at him, her lips extended, ready to give herself to the desire of the master, and her entire body—her beautiful supple and curvaceous body—was run through by a delectable frisson to which he alone gave birth in her.

But she was extracted from that sweet softness by the shocking reality.

"Give me your galette," said Tête-Rouge.

She gave him the ten francs.

"Only ten francs!" he observed, without getting carried away. "It's time we left . . . there's nothing to do here . . . a kid like you ought to have a hundred . . . two hundred francs a day. Only, for that, it's necessary to arrange you. You need fashionable hats and dresses . . . harness, what! Within a month, you'll have all that, and then you'll be able to make big money, if you follow your man's advice . . ."

"I'll do whatever you want; I'm you're kid, eh?"

"Good—it gives me pleasure when you talk like that. You need plumage; we'll soon be with fancy folk. You understand, the likes of us aren't made to live in La Chapelle . . . we need something better than that. And the old lady is there for a coup . . . necessary to see that she coughs up!"

And Françoise, naturally incurious, confident in her man, did not ask any more.

Every day of the following week, Tête-Rouge was absent for a good part of the day, simply saying as he left: "I'm going to see the old woman," and when he came back: "It's going well . . . going well . . ."

She did not know exactly whet he was contriving in the shadows, and who the old woman was to whom he alluded incessantly. It did not matter, anyway; she had only to let things proceed and to obey.

And Tête-Rouge was increasingly radiant. He had, as he put it, "discovered a good seam": an old lady striving to mask her sixty years under a thick layer of make-up, which could not dissimulate her wrinkles.

She had been seduced by the vigor, the charm and the savant caresses of the Breton; she was madly smitten with him—and he, scenting a fine affair, had condescended to become her lover.

She had beautiful jewels, superb diamond ear-rings, rings on her fingers, golden crosses, clothes of a rich elegance, and he had immediately said to himself, on seeing her: *That one has the sac! Let's open our eyes!*

And even though she was repulsively ugly in spite of all her fine clothes, he had started to circle her, using his strange charm, for he had divined the unhealthy passions of that woman, who, in spite of her physical degradation, did not want to renounce amour.

With her shiny little eyes, ringed by a thick layer of kohl, her plastered complexion, her blood-red mouth deformed by the rictus of insanitary wounds, her entire person respired vice and perversion.

And he had captivated her so well that she took him home with her at their first meeting to the Rue Caulaincourt.

In the carriage, he coaxed and cajoled her, permitting himself certain liberties against which she had not protested, and when she took him to her apartment she was congested, intoxicated by desire. She drew him into her bedroom like a madwoman.

He contemplated, with an interior irony, the decrepitude of that female body . . .

He played his role of lover so well, deployed all his talents with such mastery to flatter her sensuality, that she was soon ready to make the worst extravagances, the greatest sacrifices, on the sole condition that he came every day to hold her in his powerful arms.

As soon as that first meeting, and to encourage him to return, she slid a hundred-franc bill discreetly into his hand, which he pocketed with a visible satisfaction.

In the meantime, he had been able to cast an eye over the apartment: superb furniture, a rosewood bed covered with satin and lace, artistic bronzes, sumptuous carpets, master paintings and silverware.

No doubt about it, she has galette, the sister!

And as she had maintained anonymity, he concluded: *She's an old comtesse who has retired from society and is blowing her income giving herself satisfactions.*

His first concern, on quitting her, was to obtain information.

He learned that her name was Irma Delmair and that she owned one of those bizarre boutiques in the Rue Province in which demi-mondaines in embarrassment can exchange jewels and clothes for ready money.

That's good, that—very good, even. Just wait, my old lady, I'm going to make you pay a little. Oh, you old shin of beef with a face like a herring, if you believe that anyone is going to embrace the fat with their eye . . . no, you haven't looked at yourself!

He was rigorously exact at his rendezvous, surrounding her with cares. He bewitched her, putting a spell on her with his marvelous power, and when he sensed that she was completely hooked, that he had her well in hand, he began to exploit her.

In spite of the generous subsidies she accorded him incessantly, he did not take long to borrow from her.

She could not refuse anything to a lover who gave her so much joy; she advanced him five hundred francs, then a thousand...

"Don't worry about it ... give it back to me when you can ..."

He put her to sleep, intoxicated her with words and promises, and she lost her head, crazed ... and gave him whatever he wanted.

"I've never known a man like you, my child," she repeated, incessantly

Tête-Rouge experienced nothing but repulsion for old Irma, but that did not prevent him from lavishing his caresses on her, doubtless in expectation of some grand coup in her regard. Benevolently, she believed it to be a real passion, not imagining that it was only deception.

The money that she had already poured out generously had permitted him to quit Nogent with Françoise in order to install himself in Paris, in a house in the Rue Douai, in the heart of the Fontaine quarter.

To begin with, he had bought his wife a new outfit and a rather simple hat, and simultaneously fixed a new itinerary for her. The Passage Jouffroy, the Passage Verdeau and the Galerie Véro-Dodat became her places of exploitation.

That was a debut, while awaiting the realization of more grandiose dreams.

Françoise had got a taste for the work; she brought back to her man between fifty and a hundred francs a day.

In the meantime, he continued to entertain the best relations with old Irma, for the moment was approaching when he would attempt a supreme and definitive step. He was only waiting for the opportunity.

One evening at the end of August, in one of those stormy heat-waves when the ambient air is saturated with electricity, he judged the moment particularly favorable.

"If you want, this evening, we can go to dine somewhere in the environs of Paris," he proposed. "I offer you a pleasant mouthful in a private cabinet. You'll see ... you can tell me what you think ..."

A rascally play of his physiognomy enabled her to glimpse, after the enjoyment of a succulent meal, pleasures even more refined and intoxicating.

She accepted very gladly; they stopped an auto-taxi and departed for Saint-Cloud.

Tête-Rouge said many things, and the champagne flowed abundantly, especially into his companion's cup; she did not take long to get drunk. That was what he wanted.

Before dessert, she came to nestle against him, requesting his caresses, and he took advantage of a moment when she was particularly weak to make the request that he had been holding in reserve for a long time.

"By the way, my love," he stammered, after a few kisses on her ear and a few amorous phrases, "I have a martingale at the racecourse, but I need money ..."

"All that you wish, my love ... I don't care about that. You before everything ..."

"Yes, but it's a matter of a large sum."

"How much?"

"I daren't tell you ..."

"No! Are you embarrassed with me, by chance?"

Skillfully, Tête-Rouge's caresses became more urgent, his gaze more troubling. Irma Delvair was fainting with pleasure.

"Go on, ask," she pronounced, her voice faint. "How much?"

"Five thousand francs ..."

"You'll have them . . . you'll have them . . . Oh, I love you . . ."

"How sweet you are. I'll return them, you know, within the week. Only, as I need them tomorrow morning and perhaps I won't see you, I'll ask you to sign a check for me right away, since you have a deposit at the Crédit Lyonnais . . ."

Subjugated, she signed, and the next day, Tête-Rouge was in possession of five lovely thousand-franc bills, which rendered him mad with joy. Naturally, there was no question of a martingale; that sum had an entirely different destination.

He began by transporting his possessions from the Rue Douai to the Rue Pigalle, where he rented a small apartment overlooking the street and another, more modest overlooking the courtyard. He furnished them sumptuously, especially the former, spending lavishly.

At the same time, Françoise became unrecognizable; she no longer bore any resemblance to the wretched whore of the Boulevard de La Chapelle. She was a beautiful young blonde woman, her waist delicately encased in a corset from a good manufacturer; she had vaporous and lacy underskirts, costumes in the latest fashion, and plumed hats. Her blonde eyelashes were darkened and lengthened with mascara, her complexion rendered even fresher by the skillful employment of creams and powders; her hair was introduced to curling tongs and she had abandoned her chignon for a complication of shells and torsades.

As always, she had inclined before the will of the master, neither satisfied nor discontented with that change of situation. It was thus, and that was all.

Tête-Rouge rubbed his hands. Finally, his dream was realized. They were on the way to making a fortune, or at least living large. Here, there were no more hundred-sou amours, but at least twenty bullets.

With an admirable carelessness he had spaced out his visits to the home of Irma Delvair since the famous evening when he had extracted her signature and her check. She complained about that bitterly, as well as his sudden amorous indifference.

"I no longer recognize you. You were once so punctual . . . so affectionate . . . so delirious. How you've changed, suddenly! You're no longer the same!"

And he had to suffer reiterated crises of tears and supplications, to which he remained deaf.

"You no longer love me, I can feel it; I displease you. Alas, I'm no longer young, but admit that I've been good to you . . . everything that you've wanted, I've given to you."

He changed the subject as cleverly as possible. The scene having been worse than usual, one day he no longer came to the rendezvous at all.

Then the poor old woman lost her head, maddened, wrote him pneumatique after pneumatique, letter after letter. He recognized her handwriting and tore them up without reading them, exclaiming: "Old crampon; haven't you finished pestering me? What a raquin!"[1]

At first, believing it to be a temporary infidelity, imagining that he would come back to her, she only talked about amour, but gradually she despaired and her missives took on a different tone.

She commenced by demanding the money that he owed her, the five thousand francs that she had lent him without the slightest suspicion, so much had his maddening caresses ensorcelled her.

Soon, she threatened to attract the eye of the police to him . . . there were no threats that she did not formulate.

---

1 Liteeraly, a *raquin* is a ramekin, but it is possible that Tête-Rouge has Emile Zola's lustful heroine Thérèse Raquin in mind. Zola claimed, in response to criticism of the alleged immorality of his 1868 novel, that it was a study of "temperament" rather than character—a remark that became one of the foundation-stones of the philosophy of his version of Naturalism. Delphi Fabrice certainly considered himself as a Naturalist in that tradition, and might well have offered a similar defense of *Le Sorcier rouge*.

Tête-Rouge remained impassive and without dread.

"You can put on mourning, old mole, for your five thousand bullets. You'll never see a sou. You don't have a tranquil conscience either. I know your history, and I hold you. At the slightest imprudence, I'll talk."

Never receiving a response, her patience exhausted, Irma Delvair came to the Rue Pigalle one morning, at ten o'clock.

Tête-Rouge opened the door in a dressing-gown. "Oh, it's you!"

"Exactly, it's me. I've come to get my five thousand francs. I need them immediately, or else watch out! I think you've mocked me enough, you that I loved so much, you who promised me . . ."

He looked at her hypocritically and sniggered. "Do you imagine that I'm afraid of you, you old trout?"

"You're a thief, a crook, a poltroon, a coward. You came to my house for as long as you didn't have the money you needed, and that day, you said 'Bonsoir, old woman, I have enough of your cash!' I can see your game clearly now, but too late, you scoundrel!"

"Enough, no! Don't pronounce another word! I've learned things on your account, old slut! You didn't hold me in such contempt when you made me come to your home. Mére Maca! Procuress!"

Those last two insults made Irma Delvair pale, and she remained nonplussed for a moment.

"Ah, that hits home, that. You imagined that you plied your dirty trade in hiding, without anyone knowing anything about it. I've been fixed on your account for a long time. Oh, fine things happen in the back room of your boutique! And if I wanted to talk, you'd go to make the acquaintance of the coffee-grinder . . . the correctional, what!"

"But that isn't true . . . it isn't true, all that," Irma tried to protest, with an evident disturbance throughout her person.

"What! It isn't true? You've got a nerve. Do I have to dot the *i*s? You don't receive early fruit every day?"

"Shut up . . . shut up, I beg you!" howled the procuress, prey to an invincible terror. Shut up!"

"Oh, so it's the truth!?"

Frightened, the aged coquette no longer knew what countenance to affect; she would have liked to be a hundred leagues away.

"You have two choices," posed Tête-Rouge, triumphantly. "Either you leave me in peace with your five thousand francs, and you arrange matters so that I no longer hear mention of you, or I give you to the cops and go to tell the commissaire de police of what the commerce consists that you dissimulate under the decorum of a clothes-merchant. Ogress! Seller of children!"

"Hush, shut up! Not another word. Promise me that you won't say anything . . . ever."

"Then you swear to leave me in peace with your five thousand bullets?" sniggered Tête-Rouge.

"Yes, yes . . . whatever you wish . . . but above all, don't talk. You promise me . . . you swear to me . . ."

"On my honor!" declaimed Têtte-Rouge, ironically, raising his hand. "But as I like things to be regular, you can start by signing me a little receipt for the settlement of the whole account."

In haste, he scribbled on a piece of paper and then passed her the pen, saying: "There; sign here . . ."

He took a receipt-stamp out of his pocket, which he stuck over the invoice.

"And there, on the vignette and the paper, write: 'paid in full,' the date and your signature."

Tête-Rouge folded the receipt into four and the old woman left, ashamed and trembling, chased by his imperious gaze and one more insult:

"Get out, you old slut!"

VII
The Hortensias Bleus

They were, therefore, installed in the heart of the Fontaine quarter.

Every evening, at about five o'clock, Françoise stretched herself in her bed and got up, for the time had come to resume work.

The prospect of the evening that was about to commence, similar to the previous ones, no longer caused her to experience lassitude, but not because she was any happier with her fate be-cause she was well-dressed—was it not fundamentally the same thing?—or that, instead of dealing with workers on the spree, as in La Chapelle, the men here were more chic, foreigners having a good time. The latter, after all, were no better than the former. The tranquility of mind that she now experienced she owed to the increasingly preponderant influence of Tête-Rouge. It only happened very rarely that she evoked the memory of her native land, her parents and her childhood . . . and Mathurin.

She was carried away in the whirlwind of Parisian life and she forgot everything in that milieu of luxury, noise and perversion, even though her nature was so scantly adapted to it.

In any case, in spite of the clothes and the extravagant hats she had preserved a certain cachet of naïve grace, which the other prostitutes, her rivals, mocked; she did not yet have their aplomb, their carelessness; she conserved an indelible imprint of savagery in her big blue almond-framed eyes, and through-out her person.

Tête-Rouge had tried in vain to combat that innate reserve, and he had ended up resigning himself to it, all the more so as it did not displease a number of amateurs, who preferred Françoise precisely because of it.

She commenced her evening with an aperitif, which she took in a café in the Place Pigalle. Already, she knew everyone there, the habitués of both sexes and the manager.

Regularly, before dinner, she found a monsieur who almost always kept her for the meal. Afterwards, she went into the houses where people sup, and obtained what she wanted there, moneywise.

In the morning, toward four or five o'clock, she went home, her hair undone and her face no longer fresh, her mouth thickened by numerous glasses of champagne; and in spite of an immense lassitude, it was still with intoxication that she delivered her body to her man.

She made the acquaintance thus of all the places in Montmartre where people amuse themselves: music halls, café-concerts, nightspots and shady bars.

Tête-Rouge was proud of his pupil, proud of what he had made of that humble little peasant girl; he had initiated her into the secrets of Parisian vice.

So, when he chanced to encounter a few former mates, Boubouroche, Nez-de-Coq or others, he cited himself as an example, with pride and vanity. He pointed out his woman in the distance, laughing in bursts with some party animal, parted his waistcoat in order to show off his torso, embellished with a thick gold chain, and said: "There! That's my work! Do as much, friends!" And he darted a glance of disdain at a petty streetwalker who was soliciting at the corner of the Rue Forest and the Boulevard de Clichy.

As for him, he continued to seduce; the men feared that he might steal their woman from them, but he did not have any such fear. Françoise only had eyes for him when her task was accomplished.

For his part, he evidently did not observe the same fidelity. He ran around the nocturnal establishments, where he did not disdain to fork out.

Such was their existence. They only met up again in the morning, wearied by orgiastic nights, and if Françoise sometimes had a slight rancor, it disappeared on the semi-conjugal couch. It was there that she armed herself with the courage and indifference necessary to return to her extenuating life the following day.

And she lived thus, from day to day, confiding to her man the hundred or two hundred francs that she harvested in the course of her evening.

She did not think about the day after tomorrow, the future; that was unknown, it never crossed her mind. She had never wondered what might happen to her and what would become of her when she grew old—when she had lost her charms—and then, afterwards, death . . .

No, she did not think about all that; it was as if her brain were anesthetized under the subjection of Tête-Rouge. She no longer had time to think about the past, why would she think about the future? It would have been pointless, anyway. Tête-Rouge, her *deus ex machina*, was there to foresee everything. In their association there were two bodies but only one head, which governed and directed everything. And in that head there was a great deal of ambition . . .

What Françoise had done so far was good, but he wanted to climb even higher; he dreamed of making her a petty Liline d'Aubray.

By frequenting the nocturnal establishments he had acquired numerous relationships in that heterogeneous society; he knew the managers, directors or owners of the places where people amuse themselves. There was a continual demand for women to sing or dance. He wanted to take advantage of that and launch Françoise-la-Bretonne in that manner, but she was not cut from the cloth of an actress, and she was met with pitiful checks everywhere. Her beauty was favorably welcomed, but the awkwardness of her gestures was mocked. Tête-Rouge conceived a sharp anger in consequence, and for the first time in several months she experienced slaps and harsh treatment.

"There's nothing to be done with you, dummy! You're not good for anything."

"But I assure you, Tête-Rouge, that I'm doing all that I can ... only I can't succeed ... I'd like to satisfy you, though ... I'd like nothing better. Tell me what it's necessary for me to do."

"You're too clumsy with your arms and legs. They're like two potato-sticks."

She endured yet another scene, resignedly.

A few days later, Tête-Rouge recognized his error in wanting to make her a Parisian dancer, and he said to her: "I've just had a wonderful, miraculous idea. Did you dance the *dérobée* in your homeland?"[1]

Bewildered, she took a second to respond. "Well, yes ..."

The homeland and the *dérobée* were so distant in her memory.

"Right, that's what I thought. I'm going to send for a Bretonne costume for you ... or rather, no, I'll have one made here ... it will have an even greater cachet ..."

"And I'll dress as a Bretonne?" she interrogated, with amazement. "As in the days at Carnac?"

"Yes. That pleases you, eh? I'll find you a fellow who can play the biniou, and another as a partner ... one of those fellow in Montmartre who can do anything and who can dress as a Breton. Only, watch out, eh?" he added, widening his eyes in order better to dominate her. I'll keep my eye open you know. Remember Demi-Sel!"

"Oh, you have nothing to fear. But I haven't yet understood what I'm to do, costumed like that?"

---

1 The Breton dance known as the *dérobée* [literally, "surreptitiously"] is associated with various festivals, most famously the Saint-Loup festival in Guingamp, which has now become a kind of annual exhibition of Breton folk-dancing.

"Well, you'll dance the dérobée; I'll have you rehearse it, for the gestures and the play of physiognomy. I believe that you'll be delightful in that ...

Thanks to the tenacity of Tête-Rouge, Françoise made her debut a fortnight later at the Hortensias Bleus in the Rue Fontaine. It was a memorable night when she appeared on the little stage hung with crimson velvet and ornamented with banderoles of furze. A murmur rose up among the diners—a flattering murmur, provoked by her charm, further heightened by her picturesque costume. Her dress of fine black cashmere, garnished with oblique strips of velvet, molded her bosom tightly, uncovering in the deeply-cut cleavage the beautiful line of the base of the neck, where a golden chain and a cross sparkled. Her skirt, rising in broad creases, made her waist slightly heavy, broadening her hips, in the manner of the daughters of the heath, and uncovered the ankle and the foot, shod in delicate yellow clogs. Only a small apron of green silk broke the monotony of that uniform black, while over her blonde hair, gathered at the nape and twisted at the neck, a head-dress flapped in the air like the wings of a seagull

Before the spectacle commenced, someone in the hall gargled Mayol's[1] latest success:

You're very dainty
My little Bretonne ...

Soon, the biniou made its shrill music heard and the conversations stopped momentarily.

The dérobée was new for all those blasé individuals; they suspended their noisy pleasantries in order to listen, and above all to see.

---

1 Félix Mayol (1872-1941) was a camp cabaret singer best known for performing the extremely popular "Viens poupoule ..."

It was, therefore, in the most profound silence that Françoise executed her first steps, and in spite of the extreme emotion that gripped her heart, she was so gracious, so ingenuous and simultaneously so troubling, thanks to a savant play that Tête-Rouge had taught her, that the entire hall was conquered from the outset.

It was a veritable triumph. There was an encore, and then another . . . and when Françoise passed between the tables for the collection, silver coins and louis fell on to the tray she held out, accompanied by the most flattering compliments. The receipts were magnificent. One of the spectators had thrown her a two-sou coin wrapped in a hundred-franc bill.

All-Paris filed to the Hortensias Bleus to see Françoise dance the dérobée, and all were unanimous in declaring her exquisite. She interpreted the dance with a mixture of Bretonne naivety and Parisian perversity which made it something new, never seen before. She offered herself and withdrew, by turns, with an infinite grace; and the few gestures and knowing winks that Tête-Rouge had taught her illuminated desires in men already excited by an abundant menu and varied drinks.

She experienced a vogue.

She was disputed. The body that she had once sold for forty sous, she only abandoned henceforth in exchange for a large sum. She had dresses from the great couturiers; she was sparkling with jewels and coiffed with sheaves of plumes.

And success did not go to her head. She continued to live her life with indifference. She was only an automaton; the brain that activated her was in another body—Tête-Rouge—and it was him who enjoyed her success, him who was intoxicated by her triumph.

"Where shall we go?" interrogated one of three men, indecisively.

They stopped on the edge of the sidewalk, under an electric bulb.

They had just emerged from the Moulin Rouge, in the flood of spectators who were scattering in all directions. They had watched an end-of-the-year revue, very much in the flesh, which, after a good dinner, had contributed greatly to exciting their desire to conclude the evening—or rather the night—joyfully.

"What if we were to have supper at the Hortensias Bleus in the Rue Fontaine?"

"An excellent idea . . . one of my friends mentioned it to me only the other day. It's very good, it appears."

"Isn't it there that someone dances the dérobée, the Breton dance that has had so much success?"

"Exactly—you're right, it's there. One no longer sees anything but that in the theatrical columns of the newspapers and the front pages of magazines."

"There are also postcards . . ."

"It's the great success of the year, in a word. They're dancing it in all the music halls; but it's at the Hortensias Bleus that it was created, by a delightful little woman, so far as one can judge by the photographic reproductions."

"Let's go, then!"

They set forth at a brisk and joyful pace, content with their inspiration.

A few minutes later they penetrated into the hall of the Hortenias Bleus, inundated with light.

"Let's choose a table near the stage," said the oldest, who seemed to be directing the other two.

There was one free, and very well placed with regard to the view; it was there that the trio sat down.

"Have you been here before, Fargeau?"

"No, Dordive; it's the first time."

"It's chic," said the third, with a circular glance.

For a second, all three were absorbed in the contemplation of the rectangular hall streaming with electric light.

The walls were almost entirely covered with mirrors, in which the lamps were reflected and multiplied to infinity; two panels that remained bare, as well as the ceiling, were ornamented with paintings by a Montmartrean maser; a fresco from the same brush ran all around: a realistic farandole of Parisian society fêting Amour and Bacchus in a disheveled whirl.

There were flowers everywhere, natural, artificial and electric: large bunches of blue hortensias, which filtered gently the resplendent glare of the bulbs.

The supper had scarcely commenced, so all of that was still in good order, but gradually, a hubbub was rising; black suits, dinner-jackets and low-necked or ultra-tight dresses arrived, numerously. It did not take long for all the tables to be occupied. Never had such an affluence been seen in that establishment, favored by noctambulists prior to the launch of the dérobée.

The joyful trio had abandoned their contemplation in order to occupy themselves with the confection of a delicate and well-chosen menu, with heady wines. When that was concluded, the great preoccupation was studying the women.

"Not bad, that tall blonde in the mauve dress over there near the door; what do you think, Morin?"

"Ugh! I prefer that little brunette who's chatting with a waiter," Dordive replied, caressing his salt-and-pepper beard.

"We need to decide to drop the handkerchief," said Clodomir Fargeau, his eyes sparkling; "we're spoiled for choice."

Morin and Dordive were approaching fifty, with their upper bodies thickening out, their foreheads balding and their hair graying; Clodomir Fargeau, with his white hair and his carefully-trimmed moustache, his skin still fresh but wrinkled around the eyes, appeared to be over sixty. He was still very upright, his eyes keen and his speech clear—very green, people said of him sometimes, jokingly.

None of the three friends had yet made the traditional signal to the questing beauties who were circling the table when the dérobée was announced.

Françoise-la-Bretonne appeared to them in her picturesque costume, and all three of them were dazzled by that seductive beauty. Charmed and conquered, they did not take their eyes off her for as long as the dance lasted.

"She's wonderful," said Morin, when it had finished.

"Extraordinary!" Dordive overbid.

Clodomir Fargeau remained silent.

"What are you thinking, you who know Bretagne? You're even a Breton, I believe?"

"Yes, I'm from Auray . . . and I'm very much mistaken if that girl isn't also a Bretonne. A Parisienne could never wear the costume and interpret that dance in such a personal fashion . . ."

"Ask her, then, when she passes by for the collection."

From that moment on they were no longer occupied with the other women; all their attention went to Françoise-la-Bretonne, on whom their desires converged.

And they joked among themselves:

"Who's going to march?"

"You, Dordive."

"Ha ha! It wouldn't astonish me if that damned Fargeau trumped us, in spite of his white hair."

"Don't joke, you're no longer twenty, the pair of you."

"Yes, yes, we know that we're always here to amuse you."

"What do you expect, we're no longer children," retorted Dordive, bursting into laughter.

"Then let's take advantage of it. But think of us—it's said that it brings happiness."

Drunkenness was gradually invading their brains; their voices rose, they felt bolder in the enterprise of their amorous conquest.

They waited with an undisguised impatience for Françoise to make her collection.

"There she is, she's starting," said Morin, suddenly.

They followed her with their gazes, moving between the tables, a smile on her lips, holding out the tray on to which generous obols were raining down, at the same time as slightly daring compliments were buzzing in her ears—the risqué propositions of customers cheered up by libations.

"It's astonishing," said Dordive. "That woman doesn't have anything of the appearance of other Parisiennes. I don't know whether it's the costume that does that."

Clodomir Fargeau had also noticed that divergence; and that timidity and gaucherie of sorts, which only augmented the dancer's charm in his eyes, had seduced him.

Finally, she approached their table, giving each of them the same smile—a smile of command that seemed fixed on her lips.

Simultaneously, they each deposited a gold louis d'or on the tray while devouring her with their eyes. She thanked them with a smile of her white teeth, ready to draw away and continue her task, indifferent to their banal flatteries, but a question formulated in a rude language that was particularly dear to her woke her dormant attention.

"You're a Bretonne?"

It was Clodomir Fargeau who had said that. She looked at him with astonishment, and before she had time to respond he asked her the same question, again in Breton but in a different dialect.

Her astonishment reached a crescendo while she was caressed in the most profound depths of her being by those few words in her native language. That simple phrase, pronounced unexpectedly, reawoke in her all her dormant memories, and she said, with a smile that she had not had for anyone else:

"Yes, I'm a Bretonne. I'm from Carnac. You too, doubtless, since you speak Breton?"

He did not reply to her question; he had not even heard it, he was drinking her smile. "Sit down," he proposed, "and have a drink with us."

"Thanks you, but it's necessary that I finish my collection first . . ."

"Well, do that . . . but promise to return afterwards?"

"Agreed—until then."

The Bretonne drew away with a movement of the head that made the white wings of her head-dress dance.

Morin and Dordive turned to Clodomir Fargeau, who was radiant. They assailed him with benevolent repartee in a slightly bitter tone.

"You're marvelous!"

"You conquered her right away!"

"Don Juan that you are, give us your recipe . . . you fell them all!"

"Could one believe, given your modest air, that an adolescent heart is seething under your frock-coat?"

"Mistrust dormant water!"

"Monsieur Clodomir Fargeaiu, debauchee . . ."

The sallies overlapped, while the old man, proud of his success, rolled eyes that were shining with impatience.

Less than half an hour later, a young woman, odorous and dressed up, came to sit at their table beside Clodomir Fargeau. It was Françoise-la-Bretonne, now clad in a Parisienne fashion.

Without worrying about his friends, the old man started talking to her in Breton, as if he suspected that it would complete his facile conquest.

"Me too; I'm from Morbihan . . ."

And, sensing that she was ready to accept what he proposed to her, he put his arm around her waist tenderly and whispered in her ear: "Then I'll accompany you . . . ?"

She acquiesced immediately.

Transfigured, illuminated, he put on his overcoat and winked at his friends, who watched him draw away, enviously.

"Where are you taking me?" he asked in the street, seizing her round arm in his clenched hand.

"To my home, nearby, in the Rue Pigalle."

"Hurry up, my beauty; tonight I feel twenty years old!"

VIII
Capital Execution

That same evening, as Tête-Rouge, satisfied, smoking his cigar blissfully, came to escort Françoise to the Blue Hortensias, he encountered Nez-de-Coq on the Place Pigalle.

"Say, old chap?" interrogated Nez-de-Coq.

"What?" said Tête-Rouge.

"You're still a mate?"

"You can ask me that?"

"Good. This is what it's about. There are suspicions about Boubouroche; it's thought that he's a failed mec, a cream-puff. For a fortnight he's been watched; it appears that he's becoming peevish. And then, rude remarks all the time about Gueule-d'Amour, nonsense!"

"So?"

"So, as we want to know what to think, we're taking him gently to Vincennes . . . to the zone . . . we're counting on you."

"Well, all right!"

"Let's jump on the Metro, then."

Half an hour later, five individuals of bizarre appearance could be seen sitting in a circle on the far side of an embankment, in grave discussion.

"I don't understand. Tell me what happened. You couldn't have warned me, Gros-Tas, if there was anything to steal? You ought to have known, though!" said a man's voice, that of Nez-de-Coq. "One is better informed than that! Only it's Boubouroche, that failed friend, who didn't do what he was supposed to do . . . so I wasn't able to warn the mates . . . otherwise, I'd have made a sign . . ."

"One isn't blessed, for once," pronounced a soft voice, that of Gros-Tas. "For sure, it was bad luck. A mark who always had his wallet full of bills and gold stuffed in his pocket . . . but this evening he had nothing . . . not a dart . . . empty, mown . . . oh, it's enough to disgust you with the métier . . ."

"And who's fault is all that? Boubouroche's," said Nez-de-Coq.

"How it is my fault?"

"Of course, regarding everything, soft-head. You spoiled everything," Gros-Tas put in.

"Me! Shut it, insect!"

"Be careful, Boubou," observed Nez-de-Coq. "Gueule-d'Amour isn't a demi-sel like the other and if you say too much, he'll soon fetch you a good distribution."

"For sure, that's all you're looking for, slut!" protested Boubouroche. "You're not content when no one's being thumped . . . but deep down, you're hopping because . . ."

"Because what?" protested Gros-Tas.

"Because I didn't want to follow your plan. And yet you sought me out, sweet-talked me, made me nice propositions in secret from your man. I didn't want to get involved with a slut like you . . . you're too fat, you turn my stomach. That's why you want to avenge yourself by stabbing me in the back. You said to yourself, *Boubou is Monsieur le Bon; he'll cop for the others; that'll teach him not to want to romp with me!*"

"Kid," Gueule-d'Amour put in, "you know that I don't joke about that question . . . if one weren't in society, I'd give you a beating you'd remember. Wait till we get home, and you'll see! As for you, Boubou, you've said enough. Nail it, or I'll get my shooter out . . ."

Another voice intervened, imperious, sententious and doctoral: that of Tête-Rouge. "Your count is full, Boubou," the chief said, his voice full of rancor, "without responding to the accusation. We know what it's about . . . you're no longer a brother . . ."

"You're playing the bourgeois," opined Nez-de-Coq, in his incisive tone. "Your woman earns money, you put it aside. She works hard, so you think you're someone . . . you put on airs with us . . . but that won't do!"

"Yes," agreed Gueule-d'Amour, passing his silver-ringed hands with black fingernails through his curly hair. "We've had our eye on you for some time. You're wavering . . ."

"Oh, you're all starting to annoy me," said Boubouroche, abandoning his habitual bonhomie and placidity.

"And you're annoying us," replied Tête-Rouge. "Nez-de-Coq is right; you want to play the artiste with us, braggart, but it won't do."

"You don't even work," said Nez-de-Coq, supportively. "What's with that fashion of continually leaving pockets turned out when one searches them, as you did with Gros-Tas' last client? That's not work, that; one always leaves the pockets in place. You ought go know that, at your age."

It was on Boubouroche that all the disappointments experienced by his accomplices were rebounding.

He protested, and defended himself energetically, but the others, spurred on by the amorous rancor of Gros-Tas, darted dirty, hateful looks at him. His entire person was a pretext for reproaches.

"And then, one doesn't have the idea of having a belly like yours . . . look, mates, what a paunch!" said Gueule-d'Amour with an ironic laugh, which the other three reinforced.

And Nez-de-Coq whistled: "One doesn't have a belly like that . . ."

"For sure, you'd like one like it, you're as thin as a hundred nails."

"I've always been as solid as you, at any rate."

Boubouroche jibbed. "Oh yes, let's talk about that!"

"You daren't go out when the wind's blowing; you're afraid of being knocked over," sniggered Gueule-d'Amour.

"You're becoming insolent now," Tête-Rouge put in.

"Why are you getting mixed up in it? I'm talking to Nez-de-Coq, it's none of your business," said Boubouroche, aggressively. "I know what's what on your account . . . you're a fine swindler. It's only because you need money that you've come back to your old mates. Deep down, you don't give a damn. I know your story, and if I wanted to talk, if I wanted to reveal all the bad turns that you've done . . . you've got enough on your conscience . . ."

Tête-Rouge went white with anger. It was the first time that anyone had dared to attack him personally, and he was greatly affected by it. However, he made no response, contenting himself with staring at Boubou, who continued, carried away by excitement: "You're here, all three of you, showing off, but I'm not afraid of you. I'm an honest man, me, whereas you . . .! You, Nez-de-Coq, who's maintained by a dirty child-killer of the Rue de la Goutte-d'Or—yes, an abortionist. She practices the trade in her boutique. She's already caused the death of two women, not counting the babies that she uses to light her furnace.

"And you, Gueurgueule, frogs' mirror, you're a wonderful card-player! You go into jewelers' shops dressed as a minister, you negligently place a card coated with wax on a brilliant and slip it into your pocket as naturally as anything.

"And you, Tête-Rouge, you imagine that everyone is afraid of you, that no one dares to tell you the truth to your face. But it's all the same to me. I don't fear you any more than anyone else. And if you continue to annoy me, I'll give you all to the cops. Beware of dancing at the Tour Pointue! Above all because I know who's good for going to the far side of the big blue!"

"What are you saying?" exclaimed all three, in chorus.

"Be careful—you talk too much! You have a loose tongue," pronounced Tête-Rouge.

It was Gros-Tas who unleashed the latent storm by insinuating: "You heard: he says he's going to turn us in. Believe me, if he says that, it's because he's already done it."

Flashes passed through the eyes of the three men, who shivered. Gueule-d'Amour slid a set of American knuckledusters out of his pocket; treacherously, he slipped behind Boubouroche and struck him a terrible blow on the back of the head,

Boubou uttered a cry, tottered and in spite of the pain, stood up in order to respond, but he did not have the time; Nez-de-Coq and Tête-Rouge came to Gueule-d'Amolur's rescue and fell upon him, arms raised, with such effect that in a few seconds, succumbing under the weight of numbers and blows, Boubouroche slid to the ground, stunned, tied up and gagged, unable to flee or defend himself.

Under the pale light of the silver star, the five individuals now took on a fantastic, Hoffmannesque appearance. Their shadows extended immeasurably over the thick short grass of the slope.

They spoke in low voices. Nothing could be seen but their gestures, exaggerated by the dubious clarity of the summer night.

"There's no mistake, he's no longer a brother . . . he's threatened to give us to the cops," said Gueule-d'Amour.

"And then, that manner of playing holier-than-thou," muttered Nez-de-Coq. "He makes a heap of chichis with his apartment. He makes a glory of paying his landlord well . . ."

"The imbecile! He must be a nark!" exclaimed Gros-Tas.

"Does one pay one's landlord? That isn't done! It's good for bourgeois . . ."

"And then, his woman, he hides her; one might think he's afraid that someone would steal her," said Tête-Rouge. "We have better looking ones than her, haven't we?"

"Julia-la-Cerise! A dirty gonzesse! Vermin! Such prey! She's as thin as a plank . . . it's as if one could see her bones. And eyes like a lotto ball . . . and hair as black as ink. Oh, she's fresh, his chick!" said Gros-Tas, exhaling all her rancor at having been disdained.

Tête-Rouge smiled at that very feminine exaggeration, and Nez-de-Coq said: "There are a heap of stories with all that, which have never been seen. He puts money in the savings bank. One day, when I was with him in the café, he took out a notebook in which he inscribes all his moukère's takings . . . his accounts!"

"He doesn't do anything like others, that artiste . . ."

"But all that wouldn't matter, if he weren't dangerous; there's only one thing to do: kill him," proposed Tête-Rouge.

"That's true; it has to be done," opined the others. "Take away his appetite for bread."

"What if we threw him into the ditch of the fortifs?"

"He'd get away with a broken limb; it's not sufficient—necessary that he croak."

"A good blade in the belly, then?"

"A gunshot in the noggin?"

"No, all that might backfire. It's necessary to find something better," said Tête-Rouge.

"I have an idea," said Nez-de-Coq, nasally, with a glint in his eye. "It's original, never been done."

"What's that?"

"Necessary to hook him behind the Nogentais."

"You're crazy!"

"You've lost . . ."

"It's solid gold, mates, at this hour," he replied, cruelly, looking at his watch. "It's one-fifteen . . . the sweep passes at half past. We have just enough time . . ."

"You're crazy—we'll get caught."

"No danger. Half the people going home at this hour are shaken . . . they don't perceive anything. If you listen to me, we'll be fine. For sure he won't spoil, Brother Boubouroche . . . he'll be done before having gone a hundred meters . . ."

Tête-Rouge, Gueule-d-Amour and Gros-Tas reflected, perplexed.

"You think it'll work?"

"Of course it'll work—it's wonderful. No danger that he'll escape . . . we've gagged him, and we'll attach him by the neck to the wire that draws the trolley. The conductor will sound his horn without perceiving anything. And off we go! The tram sets off like a mad thing, and our Boubouroche begins to make perilous leaps, at ten kilometers an hour. He's wheezy; after ten minutes he'll catch . . ."

"That's good," said Tête-Rouge, after reflecting for a few more seconds. "There's one who won't talk any more. Let's go, lads!"

With his habitual sang-froid, he took the direction of the affair.

"You, Gueule-d'Amour, and you, Nez-de-Coq, each grab Boubouroche under one arm. Drag him as best you can. Gros-Tas, go on ahead, to make a sign in case of alert. I'll bring up the rear."

"Understood," they approved.

And they set to work immediately.

Nez-de-Coq, the author of that plan of capital execution, untied Boubou's legs, only leaving the arms secured along the body. The latter was still unconscious, half-stifled by the gag applied over his nose and mouth.

They did not experience any difficulty, but they had to renounce each taking him under one arm; as he could no longer stand up, he was very heavy because of his corpulence.

Silently, the cortege set forth and penetrated into the Bois de Vincennes, all observing the greatest prudence, ready to flee at the slightest alert.

"There it is; we're here," breathed Gros-Tas, when she perceived the platform of the Nogent tramway.

Tête-Rouge leaned to the right and the left, and, perceiving nothing unusual behind him, hastened to catch up with Nez-de-Coq and Gueule-d'Amour; and they conferred in low voices.

"Put him on the ground," ordered Tête-Rouge. "The tram doubtless won't come right away. Listen to what I tell you. You, Gros-Tas, go to stand at the edge of the sidewalk. When you perceive the lights of the tram give us a sign. You two, catch hold of Boubouriche and hook him on to the trolley-wire. You understand the trick, Nez-de-Coq, since it was your idea. In the meantime, Gros-Tas and I will chat to the conductor. When it's done, whistle through your fingers, Gueule-d'Amour, and we'll let the bone-shaker set off again.

The prostitute went to her observation-post. They waited for more than ten minutes, somewhat anxiously.

"It might have gone past?" suggested Gueule-d'Amour

"No, no chance—it's late," explained Nez-de-Coq.

Finally, Gros-Tas summoned them. Briskly, Tête-Rouge joined her on the opposite sidewalk, while the other two stayed hidden behind the tree-trunks.

The tram arrived at top speed. Gros-Tas made energetic signals to the driver.

"Stop! Stop!"

The vehicle stopped.

"Is this the tram to Nogent?" interrogated Tête-Rouge, climbing on to the footplate.

"Yes, of course. Hurry up, let's go," replied the employee, rendered surly by his haste to go home.

"Do you stop at the Porte-Jaune?" asked Gros-Tas. "That's as far as we want to go."

"Yes, we go through it, Madame . . . but hurry, I beg you; we're already late."

"How much is it, in first-class?" asked Tête-Rouge.

The employee stamped his feet and briefly ran through the tariffs, adding, impatiently: "Hurry up, Monsieur et Madame—are you getting on or not? If all the clients were like you, we'd never get home. We ought to be in the depot already!"

A strident whistle-blast departed from behind the vehicle. Tête-Rouge descended from the footplate, saying: "On reflection, we'll walk as far as the Porte . . . we'll find a cab there."

"You could have made up your mind sooner!" grumbled the conductor, ill-humouredly. And he sounded his horn.

The driver, also in a hurry to go home, launched the vehicle along the long ribbon of the track at top speed.

"That's it," pronounced Nez-de-Coq and Gueule-d'Amour joyfully, rejoining Tête-Rouge and Gros-Tas, as the tram pulled away

"It's on . . . he didn't give you any trouble?"

"No, he was sill half-stunned," replied Nez-de-Coq. "I caught the trolley-wire, I made two turns around the tow-hooks with a slip-knot at the end, which I passed around Brother Boubou's neck . . ."

"Necessary not to be asleep to do all that in such a short time," said Gueule-d'Amour, proudly.

"Instead of talking, you'd do better to look," pronounced Gros-Tas, with gaiety in her voice. "Can't you see him trying to run with the tram . . . he's picking up speed . . ."

At that moment, the vehicle reached maximum velocity, going along the long avenue like a bolide.

Poor Boubouroche tried to follow it, conscious of the danger . . . but his belly prevented him from running, his gag cut off his respiration, and his hands, tied behind him, impeded his course. If he stopped for a moment he would be strangled by the slip knot tightened by the weight of his body.

Abruptly awakened from his daze, he took account of the full extent of his comrades' cruelty.

For a second, he hoped to escape their frightful vengeance by holding on to some part of the rear of the tram, but his bound arms rendered him impotent. He had not taken ten steps when he lost his equilibrium; his bruised feet bumped into a rail . . . he stumbled, made an effort to regain his aplomb, tottered again, tried again to straighten up, in a supreme leap, but collapsed definitively.

At the same time as the wire strangled him, the jolts of the electric vehicle that continued its vertiginous course made his body leap this way and that on the track, colliding with trees and lamp-posts. He was soon nothing but an inanimate quivering rag, a formless mass that the vehicle was dragging behind it, tracing a long trail of blood . . .

And in the distance, lost in the shadow of the wood, his executioners, after having followed him with their eyes for as long as the night permitted, laughed wholeheartedly, exchanging the most joyful repartee regarding that sad end.

"It will have helped the brother to lose weight, rolling his lard like that," said Gueule-d'Amour.

"We haven't earned much money," replied Nez-de-Coq, "but we've had a laugh . . ."

"Oh, if I live for a hundred years, I'll remember it," gurgled Gros-Tas.

"Necessary to have some fun occasionally, in life!"

"Now we can go drink a glass to the health of Boubouroche . . . would you like to, mates?"

"Yes, if we can find a bistro in the vicinity . . . and we'll clink glasses gladly."

"We're rid of a failed brother."

"No," said Gros-Tas, "I can't help writhing with laughter when I see him again, trying to run . . . with his big belly . . . ha ha!"

"All snitches ought to finish like that," said Nez-de-Coq, by way of a funeral oration.

"For sure . . . he's taken something for his cold . . . he'll arrive at the home of the Mec of Mecs in pieces," concluded Tête-Rouge, with a cynical gleam in his violet eyes.

And he quit his friends, rubbing his hands, in order to go and rejoin Françoise, the beautiful Françoise, who had just lifted a good haul . . .

IX
A Very Proper Old Man

"He's delightful, that little old man," Françoise said to herself when Monsieur Fargeau had quit her, at five o'clock in the morning, their meeting having been prolonged far beyond the usual interval.

It never happened to her to linger over the thought of her clients. As soon as they had handed over the price of her favors and had crossed the threshold of her room, they no longer existed for the Bretonne, to the extent that she had failed to recognize men who had come home with her twice. They had been obliged to remind her. But that little old man had been so polite and respectful in her regard, and had treated her with so much delicacy, that she had retained a very different impression of him. She, who never delved deeply into anything, had understood by his gaze and his speech that he was not the banal passer-by who only asks of a young woman the satisfaction of a momentary desire. In addition, he had announced, as he left, that he would probably return the following Thursday.

Empty words, she had thought, at first. When the intoxication of the night had dissipated, he would no longer think about her.

No, she had an intuition that it would not happen like that; there was a bond between the two of them, a bond that she did not know yet how to analyze—doubtless the petty fatherland, Bretagne, the joy for Françoise of hearing the language of her homeland spoken, that of the region of Vannes.

And, in fact, the following Thursday, as he had promised, Clodomir Fargeau presented himself at the Bretonne's apartment with a pretty bouquet bought at a nearby kiosk before going up.

That delicate attention delighted Françoise, who had never been the object of such forethought. She departed from her habitual indifference and became amiable, smiling and obliging the slightest amorous caprices of the old man.

She was particularly able to flatter the taste that men in the decline of their potency have for relative satisfactions, and she conquered him even more than at their first meeting.

That was the origin of a veritable liaison between the old man and the young woman.

Twice a week, at a fixed hour and day, Clodomir Fargeau came to the Rue Pigalle, and, strangely enough, it was always with pleasure that Françoise anticipated their rendezvous. In addition to the pecuniary necessity that obliged her to lavish her caresses, he pleased her greatly. His manners were so mild, so tender in her regard; he acted with so much tact!

At each of his visits, he left her a hundred-franc bill, but he arranged matters to do so discreetly, as if he feared offending her, slipping it into a bouquet or a bag of bonbons, or into a case with an item of jewelry.

Like all women, she was sensitive to those small attentions and she gradually became attached to that sexagenarian lover who treated her so gently. She always made arrangement to be free, to be exact at their rendezvous, rejecting if necessary the offers that were made to her, so as to be his as soon as he arrived, without him suffering the affront of perceiving anyone who had taken his place.

That was not to the taste of Tête-Rouge, and when he perceived it, there was an inevitable scene.

"Say, Françoise, who's this old man who's always rummaging in your skirts?" he began by interrogating her, looking her up and down.

"He's a friend," she replied, nonplussed, foreseeing a storm. "A friend like any other."

"Isn't it rather an infatuation? I've perceived that you've given him a passport . . ."

"Oh, Tête-Rouge, I assure you . . . Think, an old man . . ."

He eyed her suspiciously.

"That makes several times that you've neglected others for that one. Necessary not to cuckold me, you know . . . that would be bad . . ."

"I assure you that he's only a temporary friend. He gives me a hundred francs regularly, every time he visits. At that price, you know very well that one doesn't find many, and it's not a matter of letting them get away when one has them . . ."

"Of course, but you have no need to occupy yourself with that. I've told you more than once already—I'd prefer that your friends gave you less and you had more of them."

"Yes, but that one's a regular. I can't send him packing . . . I repeat that he's not like the others."

"What? What does that mean—he's not a friend like the others? What more is he? He's a prince, then?" He rolled his terrible eyes, and approached her face very closely. "Pay attention, you know; I'm keeping my eyes open and if I ever perceive anything . . ." He concluded his sentence with a threat. "Do you have information about that fellow?" he questioned, suspiciously, after a pause of several seconds. "What does he do? What is he?"

"I don't know anything, Tête-Rouge . . ."

"Is that true?"

"I swear to you . . ."

"What day does he come?"

"Saturday, between three and four . . ."

That afternoon, he watched out for Clodomir Fargeau's visit, which was easy, because their other apartment was on the same floor as the one where Françoise received. When the old man left, he made a sign to a mate, whom he had been careful to bring, and to whom he had given instructions.

"Say, pal, you're a good fellow; you'd like nothing better than to render me a service?"

"You don't have to hold back with me. Tête-Rouge."

"This is it: you'll follow the old man who'll come out of my woman's place. You'll tell me where he lives. You'll try to find out what he does."

"Understood."

And Clodmir Fargeau had not reached the bottom of the staircase when the obliging friend, transformed into an amateur policeman, was on his heels.

In the evening, he was able to make a complete report to Tête-Rouge on the old man who had inspired anxieties.

"His name is Clodomir Fargeau."

"Clodomir! A name to put on the door of a lodging-house, Clodomir Fargeau. Where does he nest, that bird?"

"32A Rue de Turenne in the Marais; he's a wholesale jewelry manufacturer."

Tête-Rouge whistled, and said: "Nice. He must have money, then, the fellow?"

"Yes, his business is doing well; he's on top."

"Married?"

"No. Old bachelor, rather miserly, tranquil and comfortable."

"That's good, that's good," said Tête-Rouge, mysteriously. And to thank the mate they went to have a drink together at a boulevard café.

He did not communicate to his woman the information that he had collected regarding her principal lover, and Françoise would doubtless have been unaware of his identity for a long time if hazard had not revealed it to her.

One afternoon, as the old man was about to quit her, she perceived a wallet on the ground. She picked it up, and the first thing she saw when she opened it was an engraved visiting card:

M. CLODOMIR FARGEAU
WHOLESALE JEWELRY
32A Rue de Turenne

With a very feminine curiosity, she searched all the compartments without disturbing anything, glad deep down to penetrate the private life of the man who had become part of her life, and of whom she only knew the forename Clodomir—Cloco, as she addressed him in intimacy.

She found, in addition, in a morocco leather pocket, a few business letters, two hundred-franc bills and one of fifty francs. She replaced them all in the same order, made a small parcel and sent it to the indicated address, in secret from Tête-Rouge.

How he would have mocked her honest scruples if he had known that! He would certainly have conceived a frightful wrath in consequence.

Fortunately he did not know anything about it, and she felt very happy about her action, her conscience tranquil. For nothing in the world would she have wanted to commit a dishonesty, less with regard to Clodomir than anyone else. She had a very special consideration for him, in spite of the scene that Tête-Rouge had made on his subject, and if it was not love, it was at least a very sincere sympathy.

As for him, he was passionately smitten with that young and beautiful mistress ready to satisfy his whims without disdain for his senility. The incident of the wallet only consolidated the confidence that he had in her. He had judged right away that she did not resemble the other prostitutes of the boulevard with regard to morals; he was not under any illusion, divining perfectly a man in the shadows who was exploiting her charms; he knew that she only danced at the Hortensias Bleus to facilitate the traffic of her flesh, but he excused that privately.

It's doubtless circumstances that have led her to that. Perhaps she has been seduced, then abandoned—the habitual story of all those women. I've no need to think about all that. She's a good girl, who has a great depth of honesty and even of restraint—a rare thing.

He sensed that Françoise responded to his amour differently than with the ordinary indifference of women for whose caresses one pays, and he was infinitely flattered by that.

In fact, she became increasingly attached to him; he became part of her life; he had a very small place in her heart, alongside Tête-Rouge.

And she experienced a real chagrin one afternoon, when she waited for him in vain at the hour when he was accustomed to come. He did not come . . . and the next day, and the day after, there was no news.

She dared not let her anxiety show. Tête-Rouge mocked her. "Well, he's dumped you, your old man. You see, it was well the trouble of making lovey-dovey with that old man, for him to dump you like that!"

Françoise could not believe it; it seemed to her that a great void had suddenly opened up in her existence.

So she uttered a sigh of relief and a flash of joy illuminated her face when, after a week, she received a letter addressed her, thus conceived:

> *My dear little friend.*
>
> *It has been impossible for me to write sooner, for I was suffering greatly. I thought that I would never see you again.*
>
> *Finally, I'm out of danger now, and my greatest joy would be if you came to see me at home, 32A Rue de Turenne, today, if possible. It seems to me that that pleasure alone could put me back on my feet.*
>
> *In the meantime, my dear little friend. I embrace you very tenderly, as I love you.*
>
> *Clodomir*

Will he let me go there? Françoise asked herself, when she had finished reading. *My God, how sad I would be if he refused me that!*

She communicated the letter to her man, and, contrary to expectation, it provoked an explosion of joy in Tête-Rouge.

"So much the better, so much the better! It couldn't be going better . . ."

"You want me to go, then?"

"I should think so. Since you have the old man's confidence, all is for the best. We can take advantage of it . . ."

She did not give any further thought to that last enigmatic remark, so glad was she to be seeing her old friend again.

"Admit that you're fond of him, that old mec?"

She blushed, embarrassed. "Which is to say that . . ."

"Enough, enough. Go!"

At two o'clock she took the Metro to go to the Rue de Turenne, where she was awaited impatiently.

Clodomir Fargeau was still in bed, his face distressed by several days of illness; but a surge of blood came to tint his cheeks when he saw her.

"You! My dear, if you knew how impatiently I've been awaiting you," he said, his voice trembling with emotion, extending his arms.

He seized her little gloved hands and covered them with kisses; then he lifted the sleeve of her mantle, and his lips encountered her skin . . .

"My dear child! My little Françoise . . . I dreaded so much that I might not see you again . . . you who have already given me so much happiness since I've known you."

His eyes became moist and tears rolled between his wrinkles.

Françoise, gained by emotion, felt her throat tightening, and she had difficulty asking him:

"Poor old friend! What has been the matter with you? I was very anxious, you know."

"Is that true, my little friend? You, so young and loving, have been able to regret a poor old fellow like me? Let me take your gloves off, so that I can hold your little hands in mine . . . your dear little hands . . . I want to cover them with kisses. I've had a touch of fever for a few days and I thought about them . . . I would have like to feel them placed on my forehead . . . it seemed to me that that would have cured me, that simple contact. You'll permit me, won't you?"

"Of course, Cloclo . . ."

"Cloclo . . . oh, when I hear your voice, as sweet as music, call me by that diminutive, my entire being shudders! Don't pay any attention, child—one is stupid when one gets old, one attaches importance to a heap of petty details . . . one is sensitive to everything . . ."

He unbuttoned her gloves slowly, extracted the fingers one by one, then seized the bare hands one after the other, caressed them between his own, applied them to his cheeks and finally covered them with burning kisses.

"But I beg your pardon, my beauty, I'm pestering you instead of inviting you to relax. Take off your mantle and hat . . . I'll tell the nurse to prepare you something. What would you like—tea?"

He was only occupied with her, urgently.

"Here, put your jacket at the foot of my bed, with your hat, where I can see them. It's yours . . . it's a little of you . . ."

And as she arranged her hair in front of the mirror, he gazed at her very amorously.

"You're pretty, my little friend . . . come and sit down here, beside my bed, very close . . . as close as possible . . . I've been very deprived of you these last few days."

She smiled at him tenderly and proposed, mischievously: "Well, in order to be even closer, I'll sit here, on the edge of your bed . . . would you like that?"

"It's just . . . that you're going to tempt me thus, my darling . . . and it's necessary for me to be good . . . otherwise, beware of complications . . ."

"Since it's like that, I'll take a chair, then . . ."

"No, no; I don't want that. Come; I'll make you a little room . . ."

She hoisted herself on to the edge of the bed.

"Now, Monsieur, pay attention," she said, menacing him with her finger. "Be good, won't you?"

"You're delightful . . . and I'd have the right, I suppose, simply to put an arm round your pretty waist . . ."

"Yes, I'll permit that, but no more. You'll tell me what was wrong with you?"

"What I had, my little friend, was a chill. You'll recall how foggy it was when I quit you, the last time. It was warm in your room . . . outside, I was gripped by that damp air, and as I've been overdoing it a little recently—how can one do otherwise when one has a little friend like you—that complicated things. I had a fever, and all that goes with it. Anyway, let's not talk about it any more, it was nothing. Two or three days' rest and it won't recur."

While speaking he caressed her round waist and hips, went up to her shoulders and her round bosom, and closed on her corsage . . .

"Look out! That isn't permitted to invalids . . ."

"Oh, my dear . . . I can never keep my resolutions . . . only in seeing you, only in sensing your presence, next to me, my poor old head is spinning madly . . . your odor intoxicates me like a heady wine. Give me your lips; I haven't tasted anything today."

She dared not refuse him, and leaned over, almost horizontally, in order to reach his mouth. He plunged his hand, clenched with passion, into her blonde undulations, and their lips met, in a reciprocal crush.

"That's not reasonable," said Françoise leaping on to the carpet. "Haven't you been recommended to the greatest caution, my friend?"

At that moment the nurse irrupted into the room, cutting the scene short and returning the sexagenarian to calm.

That afternoon was the beginning of a new phase in their liaison.

Clodomir Fargeau slowly got better, surrounded by the affection and caresses of the Bretonne, who came twice a week to spend the evening with him.

He was grateful for her solicitude and became more and more attached to her, testifying an unlimited confidence where he had once been so suspicious. He contracted thus pleasant habits that he did not want to give up when he had recovered completely; Françoise therefore continued her twice-weekly visits.

It was the first time that the bachelor had introduced a woman into his interior; in fact, he had never been smitten to that extent. The Bretonnne held him by the senses and the heart.

"You're the little blue flower of my old age," he repeated to her often, holding her close to him, on his knees.

He was no longer able to do without her, and if she happened to be late she found him pale and anguished.

Well before her arrival, everything was ready: the pink floral peignoir that she put on, and the pink satin slippers; in order that their intimacy would be greater, he prepared the tea himself, on a table in the bedroom, with little cakes and a bottle of liqueur.

He was a maniac, and Françoise was able to conform to his manias and flatter them.

He opened the door to her without her needing to ring, hugged her momentarily in the antechamber, his heart hammering, and then drew her gently into the bedroom and invariably asked her:

"Will you permit me to undress you?"

Then he sought out the hatpins in the midst of her feathers, withdrew them one by one, placed them in a vase, and, with a religious care, placed the hat on an armchair; then he unfastened her cloak, her bodice and her skirt, his hands impatient and his nostrils palpitating, taking an infinite pleasure in seeing the beautiful curves of her bosom, her waist and her hips appear.

After having arranged all that, in a place that never changed, he put on her peignoir.

"Now, she's my own little Françoise . . . I believe that it's in that peignoir that you're prettiest. That pink does such justice to your fresh complexion . . ."

Then it was the turn of the ankle-boots. When he had laid her feet bare he remained kneeling momentarily on the carpet, retaining her feet in his hands, kissing them frantically.

They lingered thereafter in the platonic caresses that delighted his exhausted senses.

In the meantime, they drank their tea, while chatting. Clodomir Fargeau talked to her about his past, about his family. He had left Auray and Bretagne when very young, to come to seek his fortune in Paris. First there had been difficult years; a petty worker, he earned his living miserably in the establishment of a jeweler, in the Rue Charlot; then he had found a new method of stamping, and his employer had associated him with his commerce. On the latter's death he had continued to run the business on his own, which had prospered in his hands, and was now one of the most highly esteemed in Paris. Fargeau fashion jewelry was well-known in all the clothing stores. He also brought her up to date with his manufacture and his commerce, taking her to visit the workshop when all the workers had departed. For her he opened his cupboards and coffers, initiating her into the slightest secrets of his organization.

"In this cupboard, you see, there is the gold leaf that we employ for stamping . . . Here are the ingots of silver . . . It doesn't look like much, but there's a small fortune here . . . something like thirty thousand francs . . .

His apartment, which was adjacent to the workshop, no longer had any mystery for Françoise; she knew where the silverware was kept; he had even pushed confidence so far as to reveal the secret of his personal strong-box, where he accumulated, carefully and meticulously, the produce of an entire life of work and saving: two or three hundred thousand francs in bonds and banknotes.

"No one knows the secret of my strong-box, but I have nothing to hide for you. Look, it's simple; it's sufficient to write the word *vici* while turning the knobs like this. You don't know Latin, child; *vici* means *I have conquered*."

Françoise-la-Bretonne only attached a secondary importance to these revelations. They simply proved the extent to which Clodomir Fargeau was attached to her, but the idea never occurred to her to commit an indiscretion in that regard, in the direction of Tête-Rouge.

The latter, in any case, made no allusion to the aged regular who had initially inspire a certain anxiety in him. He was generous; that was sufficient to have everything forgiven; he was no longer astonished that his woman neglected other clients in order to go on set days to the Rue de Turenne.

She was, therefore, relatively happy for a few months; next to the attentive and passionate old man she forgot Tête-Rouge's fits of ill-temper and the turpitude and baseness of her métier as a merchant of amour. He was a ray of sunlight that gilded her murky existence as a slave.

Her heart was constricted, her breast oppressed and her throat anguished when she envisaged the possibility that all of that might suddenly cease. It was a kind of somber presentiment that assailed her from time to time.

She strove to chase those clouds away while she was in her pink peignoir, nestled against the sexagenarian's breast, and all her serenity of soul returned on hearing him talk, softly and tenderly, in the Breton language.

And the evenings went by, almost similar, without either of them finding monotony in their tête-à-têtes.

141

They were in the process of drinking their tea, in little sips, at about nine o'clock one evening, when the ring of the doorbell made them jump.

Clodomir Fargeau had the custom of giving his housekeeper leave in order not to be embarrassed by importunate and indiscreet comings and goings; he was thus obliged to go to open the door himself.

It was the first time that anyone had come to trouble their intimacy, and Françoise wondered with a little anxiety who it might be.

"Oh, it's you, Christian?" said Monsieur Fargeau's voice, with a hint of embarrassment.

"Yes, uncle. It's been some time since I've had news of you. I was beginning to get anxious. How are you?"

"Very well, thank you. Come in then, pray."

He switched on the electricity in the drawing room and for a minute or two the uncle and the nephew chatted about their health and their affairs. The jeweler was embarrassed, even though his nephew was no longer a young man, to exhibit a mistress before him, but he had too much esteem for Françoise to insult her by hiding her.

"Permit me," he interrupted. "My young friend is in the next room; I'll summon her."

"Please do, uncle."

"Come in, Françoise," said the old man, advancing to the bedroom door.

She arrived timidly and hesitantly, and saluted the officer of pompiers who had risen to his feet and bowed respectfully."

"Damn! She's pretty, your little friend!"

The sexagenarian seized the compliment and straightened up with a gaze full of amorous gratitude toward his young mistress, at whom the captain darted admiring glances, surreptitiously but unambiguously.

Fargeau approached her, and with his habitual tenderness, said: "My dear, would you bring us the bottle of chartreuse and the little glasses? You know where it is, don't you?"

"Yes, my love."

She went out with a rustle of skirts. Then the officer turned to his uncle with a knowing smile.

"My compliments. You're not suffering from ennui, are you? You have good reason! There's nothing but good in that . . . amour, women . . ."

"Yes, I know that you're a terrible skirt-chaser. And yet, you have a charming wife . . . a pretty baby . . . You're not like me, all alone in the evening between my four walls. Fortunately, I've found in that young woman a delightful little friend . . . and you'll pardon your old uncle for wanting to ameliorate his old age."

Christian Bataille protested. "But it's entirely natural, uncle. You don't have to justify yourself to me."

At that moment Françoise returned to the drawing room, bringing the crystal glasses and the bottle on a tray.

She filled them with a gracious ease, silently, observing her gestures.

Clodomir Fargeau and Christian Bataille, a handsome fellow in his black dolman and blue trousers with a broad red stripe, talked about one thing and another while moistening their lips in the little glasses, where the liqueur was shining, as luminous as topaz.

"How is your business going, uncle?"

"I can't complain. What about you? When are you going to be promoted to commandant?"

"You're in a hurry. It not so long ago that I became a captain first-class."

They chatted thus for a few more minutes, and as half past nine sounded on the clock, the captain got up to take his leave.

"You have plenty of time," said the uncle, benevolently.

"No, I mustn't importune you any longer. Anyway, I only came to say bonjour as I was passing through the quarter; my automobile is waiting for me downstairs, at the door."

"Is it still the staff car . . . in fact, are you still attached to the barracks of the Cité?"

"Yes, uncle, still the other side of the water."

And the old man said, curiously: "Do you still have the same driver?"

"No, I've changed . . . advantageously. In fact, he's one of your compatriots who guides my machine now."

"A Breton?"

"Yes."

"A compatriot of my little friend too, in that case, for she's a Bretonne."

"Ah! Mademoiselle Bretonne?"

"Yes, from Morbihan . . . !

"Eh, my chauffeur too! Oh, a worthy, honest, conscientious fellow. I'm very satisfied with him. Anyway, you'll have the opportunity to meet him when I send you a commission."

A Breton pompier from Morbihan! Françoise felt a disturbance, but she chased away the fugitive impression; it could only be a coincidence.

After having bowed graciously, the captain headed for the door of the drawing room.

"It's getting late," he said to his uncle, who accompanied him, "and the worthy Mathurin must be getting impatient in the car."

"If you'll permit, I'll see the captain out," said Clodomir Fargeau.

Françoise tried to smile, but she had gone frightfully pale.

"Mathurin," she stammered, letting herself fall into an armchair. "Always him!"

It was the past that loomed up before her once again, irrupting into her life, to trouble the serenity of her passive soul.

IX
The Eye that Hypnotizes

All fashions pass in Paris.

The clientele of the Hortenias Bleus, wearied of the Breton dance that Françoise had renewed; the dérobée fell into forgetfulness, going to join the cake-walk and the mattchiche.[1]

Tête-Rouge was heart-broken, for his woman's receipts felt the effects, even though Clodomir Fargeau's had increased the figure of his allocations considerably in order to possess his countrywoman more exclusively. It happened quite frequently now that she went to dinner in the Rue de Turenne, and sometimes even spent the night there.

The dread that she had of encountering Mathurin there had gradually vanished; in any case, there was no proof that the Mathurin to whom the captain had alluded was really her former fiancé, that forename being quite common in Bretagne.

However, she had not recovered the tranquility of mind in which she had lived for a while. Since she was no longer at the Hortensias Bleus, Tête-Rouge was irritable and violent; continually, for the most futile reasons, he made terrible scenes, always finding that she did not bring back sufficient money.

He had, in fact, created great needs; money flowed between his fingers as if by enchantment without her ever daring to ask what he might be doing with it.

One day, when he had gone out, she chanced to fall upon a wad of papers that he had doubtless forgotten by mistake. She had the curiosity to cast her eyes over them and learned with amazement that Tête-Rouge was deep in debt. They were all demands and threats from discontented creditors, multicolored claims and notifications from bailiffs.

---

1 The briefly fashionable mattchiche, or Maxixe, was also known as the Brazilian tango.

She was dismayed by that discovery, having imagined that their affairs were perfectly in order. She divined easily that that financial embarrassment was the cause of the ill-humor that rebounded on her, but she did not permit herself to judge her man in that matter; he was the master, the tiller of their boat was in his hands; too bad if it was adrift.

However, Tête-Rouge was too skillful a pilot to arrive at that extremity. He had a good instrument in his hands, Françoise-la-Bretonne, that being whom a single glance subjected to his powerful will. He had always been able to make use of her, thus far; she was still there to get him out of difficulty.

One morning, as she came in after having spent the night with Clodomir Fargeau, she found him somber and frowning, his gaze harsh and his mouth peevish. She only approached him tremulously.

"Oh, there you are! It isn't too soon. I thought you were going to stay there, with your old man."

"But ... but ... Tête-Rouge, I'm not late. Look at the clock; it's eight o'clock ..."

"I don't care that it's eight o'clock! What do you want to do with that fellow? I've had enough of your old man. You're always tucked up with him ... you spend nights there ... and for what?"

She opened her mouth to respond, but he did not leave her the time and advanced toward her, menacing.

"In the end, I believe that it's me who's being played for a fool. You're cuckolding me with that old fellow ..."

"Oh! Tête-Rouge ..."

"Shut up. Don't try to defend yourself, or I'll smash your head, camel, slut, poison ... there's no mistake, I'm cuckolded! If it brought me anything, fine ... but hardly anything ... dribs and drabs ... nothing. Not necessary to support me ... I'm Monsieur le Bon! You have yourself pampered by that old ape ... you're at home in his house ... you have your peignoir, your slippers . . . you might as well be washing the dishes. You're settling in! And me, while you're laughing at me, I'm scraping . . ."

Leaning against the wall, she lowered her head, not attempting any reply.

Tête-Rouge, whose anger increased while he was speaking, drew closer, his gaze irritated and brutal.

"Lift your blinds and look me in the face, wretch . . ."

She obeyed, fearfully.

"Don't put on your imbecile expression, you disgust me when you're like that . . ."

She clung to the wall, even more fearful, and a mighty slap descended upon her face, turning her cheek crimson.

"That's to civilize you, insect!"

He took her by the arm and took her into the middle of the room.

"When I think of what I've done for you," he growled, through clenched teeth. "You were good for nothing . . . I took you from the cowshed, in a skirt and clogs . . . and what have you become, thanks to me? Almost a woman of the world! They wouldn't recognize you, the dirt-grubbers of Carnac, if they saw you decked out as you are now. You're dressed up like a princess: hundred-bullet hats on your head, marvelous dresses, lingerie like a doll . . . and all that thanks to who? Thanks to Bibi! What? What's the matter? Now you're blubbering! Oh, no! It's not the day for big waterworks. I'll dry up your spring . . ."

He let go of her painful wrist; she recoiled, terrified, trying to repress the sobs that oppressed her breast, while large tears rolled from her eyelids.

Tête-Rouge's hand described a circle to arrive at her right cheek with such force that she uttered a groan and vacillated on her legs. Humiliated, shrunken, she strove nervertheless to remain impassive, in order not to exacerbate the situation further.

He contemplated her with a sardonic laugh and continued, his voice hoarse: "I don't want to be a bed-warmer, me! I've been enduring your old man too long . . . your crush, for you can't say the contrary, it's a crush. Go on, respond, stupid!"

"No, Tête-Rouge, you know full well that he gives me, every week . . ."

"Three hundred bullets! What's that? I tell you that it's a crush, for that old Kroumir. You've been too impressed, running to his house . . . and then, all these tricks to receive you in his home . . . it's not natural, all that. And if you weren't so smitten you'd be able to take advantage of it to bring the galette back to your man. I'm on the scent, me. You remember what happened at Nogent with your Demi-Sel, your failed mec. I soon got rid of him. Well, it won't be long before I do the same with your old man . . ."

"Oh! Tête-Rouge!"

"What? What's the matter? You're taking his defense now . . . you're jibbing . . . oh, carrion!"

He fell upon her, his eyes crazed, and knocked her to the floor with a blow of his fist.

"Vermin! Filth! Slut! If I weren't restraining myself, I'd tear you to pieces. Make sacrifices for women, and this is how they repay you!"

He grabbed her hair and pulled, pitilessly. Pain extracted dull plaints from Françoise . . .

"Don't squeal, rat-meat, or I won't leave you any hair on your head . . . get up!"

As she stood up she resembled a poor beaten dog; she had the same fearful and fugitive manner . . .

His hands behind his back, Tête-Rouge seemed a little calmer after that brutal frenzy.

"When are you due back to your old man's house?"

"Tuesday," she replied, imperceptibly.

"Well, it's necessary to make him pay up."

She shuddered, and cringed, her eyes haggard.

"You hear . . . necessary for him to pay up, the old swine. I'm broke . . . I need money . . . lots of money. There are two terms to pay to the landlord ... contributions ... and a heap of late demands. The gobsek[1] has already come to bring me summonses ... I'm a respectable man, me!" he howled, striking his breast. "I've never had dealings with the bailiffs and I don't want to start, damn it! You hear? I need the cash in forty-eight hours."

"How much?" breathed Françoise, increasingly terrified.

"Ten thousand bullets!" he said, looking her full in the face.

She went pale, in utter disarray ... and her lips stammered, desperately: "Ten thousand francs ... ! Ten thousand francs ... !"

"What's up now? That doesn't suit you? Perhaps you find that it's too much? I need it ... I need it!" he growled, terribly. "If not ..."

A sinister gleam traversed his feline eyes. Françoise closed her eyelids, terrified.

"I can count on you, eh, kid?"

She found the strength to make a negative movement of the head.

"What? Come on, respond ... respond, camel!"

"I could never ... !" she pronounced, feebly, her shoulders drooping.

The roar of a wild beast escaped Tête-Rouge's breast; he bounded from one extremity of the room to the other. Over the beautiful body of the Bretonne there was a hail of kicks and punches, which rained down so thickly that she thought for a moment that she was going to die.

And when he had slaked his ferocity, she lay on the ground, extended, bruised and in pain, no longer having the strength to weep, to moan or to budge.

He grabbed her by her beautiful hair in order to put her on her feet again, and, satisfied, sniggered cynically.

"There's nothing like a nice dance like that to change your ideas. Have you reflected?"

---

1 "Gobseck" or "Gobsek" is one of several titles attached by Honoré de Balzac to one of his early novelettes, first published in 1830 subsequently rewritten for inclusion in the *Comédie humaine*. The eponymous character is a money-lender, and his name was appropriated by later writers as a generic term.

She was haggard, dazed, her brain and her limbs numb. She found no response.

"You've suddenly lost your voice?"

"Pity!" she implored, her hands joined.

"Eh? What's that you say? Damn! Go to bed, so that I don't have to look at you, and I'll make you a broth."

Leaning on the wall, she went out, accompanied by a formidable kick in the lower back, which left her insensible.

"Weakling! Imbecile!" he launched at her, scornfully.

She fell on the bed like a dead weight, not even thinking about taking off her disordered garments or putting up her hair; she was so weary, so very weary, that she fell asleep, in spite of the frightful alternatives that weighed upon her.

It was another shove that extracted her from that prostration. Tête-Rouge was before her.

"Well, kid, are you going to sleep like that all day? What about work?"

She took a moment to come to herself; the morning's scene was the first thing that she thought about, with a contraction of the heart.

Her man was looking at her, planted in the middle of the room, his hands on his hips.

"I'll be ready soon," she said, fearfully, seeing on the clock that it was past four o'clock.

"Before you go, we need to talk," pronounced Tête-Rouge. "We didn't settle the question this morning . . ." He paused briefly, and continued slowly, emphasizing the words and the syllables. "I've reflected since this morning. It troubles you to make your old man pay up. Perhaps you're not wrong, fundamentally. We'll make other arrangements . . ."

Françoise's face cleared; she uttered a sigh of relief, while a strange gleam was ignited in the depths of Tête-Rouge's eyes.

"Ten thousand bullets, that's not enough. I need more than that. So this is what I've decided . . ."

Attentive and relieved, she listened.

"We're going to skin the old man!" said Tête-Rouge, emphatically, staring at her.

She recoiled, huddled up, thinking that she had misheard. "You're saying..."

"I said that we're going to skin your old man. Are you deaf?"

A cry died in her anguished throat. Alarm, fear and terror reached their paroxysm on her livid and contracted face.

"You know where everything is kept, in the joint?" Tête-Rouge went on. "There's no time to lose..."

A horrible and bloody vision presented itself to Françoise-la-Bretonne... Her teeth chattered.

A rapid labor was accomplished in the convolutions of her brain. What could she do against the implacable will of Tête-Rouge? Rebel, refuse energetically to be the accomplice of his horrible plan? Alas, it would be the contest of the iron pot and the clay pot, and she would soon be broken, vanquished by his brutality and violence.

However, the prospect of the abominable crime terrified her; all her honesty of a daughter of the fields rose up in an indescribable turbulence of the soul; that revolt was further reinforced by the sympathy inspired in her by the man that Tête-Rouge had chosen to service as a holocaust to his cupidity. No, never... never! She could not accomplish such an ignominy.

What could she do? What could she do to escape that Tête-Rouge, who, after having made her wallow in the mire, wanted to roll her in blood?

One unique solution presented itself to her brain in slow conceptions: warn Clodomir Fargeau and flee, flee... But where? How could she escape the perspicacity of the master who dominated her?

She had only one refuge: death. Yes, death... To run recklessly to the Seine and hurl herself into its green-tinted and translucent waves, which would bear her away into annihilation, into death and beneficent bliss.

She raised her frightened eyes toward Tête-Rouge, internally decided to put her plan into execution.

The latter, with the gift of sorcery that comprised his redoubtable strength, had divined what was passing through her frustrated soul, and promised himself to triumph over her scruples, as he had always triumphed thus far when he had something in mind.

"That doesn't suit you, I can see. It troubles you, to kill that old fool . . . you have a little something for him. But you'll do it; it's me who tells you that. Not worth the trouble of trying to play me . . . I know you, kid. Get it into your head that if you try to run away I'll catch up with you. You won't take two steps in the street before I'm at your heels. You know full well that when there's something here"—he slapped himself on the forehead—"it's there, and there's no thunder of God that will get it out . . ."

"I . . . I . . ." stammered Françoise, distressed.

"Don't mumble! And don't oblige me to recommence fetching you a slap . . . I'll leave you on the floor, but you'll march . . . you'll march, you hear. I want it!" he added, emphasizing the syllables.

As he said that, Tête-Rouge's gaze drilled into the Bretonne's and an indefinable sensation flowed within her without her being able to defend herself against it.

Her good resolutions abandoned her, her scruples evaporated; and the more she stared at those fascinating eyes, the more her conscience was anesthetized; her instincts of revolt were tempered and extinguished entirely.

Under the empire of the hypnotic charm radiated by Tête-Rouge's violet eyes, she yielded, dominated and subjugated . . .

And her soul soon communicated with the soul of her man, and became his, at the same time as their mouths united in a burning kiss that stirred her from head to toe.

"You'll march?" he interrogated, his voice caressant.

She smiled at him, conquered and intoxicated, and, swooning. She replied: "Yes."

"Oh, my dear . . . what a happy surprise! How nice it is on your part to have brought forward the hour of our rendezvous."

Radiant, Claude Fargeau put his arm around Françoise's waist and kissed her hands; his eyes sought hers.

"You seem very thoughtful, very sad. Nothing has happened to you, at least?"

"No, my friend, I assure you I've only come sooner in order not to rob you of a part of the time that I devote to you . . ."

"How's that?"

"This is it: it's necessary that I be at home between eight-thirty and nine o'clock, so I need to quit you at eight o'clock."

"But you'll come back, I hope?"

"If you wish . . . but after ten o'clock."

"Understood," said the jewelry-manufacturer, without committing the indiscretion of asking her why she was absenting herself. "I feared that you might deprive me of your presence all night. It's the best of my life, and I'm even happier than before that you want to grant me that favor from time to time. In fact, you ought to dine with me as well. How are we going to arrange that?"

"My God, the easiest thing would be quite simply to eat late. If you wish, my friend, we can have a snack at about five o'clock and at ten o'clock, when I come back, we can dine . . ."

"My dear little friend! You always seek to give me pleasure . . . it's truly a treasure that I've found in you. When you're not here and I think of all the joy that you've already given me . . . if you knew how grateful I am . . . Here, let me kiss your neck . . . in the place that I love . . . my little corner . . . your skin is so soft, it smells so good . . . !"

He kissed her passionately, sensuously, and, eventually satisfied, smiled at her.

She strove to respond to him, but her smile was slightly artificial.

"It's odd," said the old man, with an anxious crease in his forehead. "I find you quite different today. You're not ill?"

"Ill, me? There's absolutely nothing wrong with me. Don't worry."

"Smile at me, then, I beg you; be as sweet and affectionate as you usually are . . . otherwise, I'll get a heap of things into my head and I'll be very unhappy . . ."

He installed her in the bedroom, amiably and hastily, and then excused himself.

"Permit me, my dear, to absent myself for five minutes. I have some orders to give in the workshop, for commissions and deliveries, and a glance to cast here and there. Afterwards, I'll be entirely yours . . ."

"I beg you, Cloclo, not to put yourself out for me."

She remained alone in the bedroom, and immediately, she took her head in her hands, and her face, which was striving to smile, contracted frightfully.

"Wretch that I am! Oh, if he could know . . . it's abominable!"

She held back the tears that were ready to slide from her eyes; nervous and agitated, she went back and forth, her eyes following the designs of the moquette that covered the floor. From time to time she stopped, staring into the void.

"What if I were to warn him? That would be better . . . he's always been so good to me . . ."

And she set off again, entirely contracted.

"Yes, that's it . . . I'll tell him when he comes back . . ."

But immediately, she started, took a step backwards, her eyelids enlarged; she seemed to be contemplating an invisible gaze . . .

"No, it's necessary that I obey him. He wants it . . . and I'm his thing . . . yes, I'm his, entirely his, nothing but his . . . Oh, his eyes!"

She fell into an armchair, playing mechanically with her cross.

Clodomir Fargeau came in; she got up and went toward him, radiant.

"I was beginning to find the time too long without you, Cloclo..."

"Is that true, my little friend?"

He took her by the chin and tapped her cheek.

"There we go! There's your beautiful smile, back again! I'm no longer anxious..."

"You're alarmed for very little, my friend!" she said, bursting into laughter that rang false.

"Good," exclaimed Fargeau, without perceiving the nuance.

And their tête-à-tête took its habitual turn, apart from a few clouds that obscured the Bretonne's face from time to time.

A little before eight o'clock she prepared to depart, but when she was ready, she could not decide to leave, continuing to talk, hesitating, heading for the door and then coming back. The sexagenarian attributed that to the annoyance she experienced in quitting him, and was proud of it.

Finally, at quarter past eight, she fled.

"See you soon, little friend. I'll prepare a nice little dinner... for ten o'clock, without fail, no?" Clodomir repeated, escorting her to the door.

"Understood, ten o'clock," she replied, as she went downstairs.

Monsieur Fargeau went to the window, in order to follow her with his eyes as far as the corner of the street. She turned round, as she always did and he blew her a kiss; then he closed the window and went back inside to give his orders to the housekeeper, who was to prepare the dinner.

He occupied himself with setting the table, enlivened the tablecloth with garlands of flowers, laid out the silverware, the porcelain vessels and the crystal glasses; all that scintillated under the illuminated dining-room chandelier.

Then he went to make a tour of the kitchen, where delicate odors were mingled.

"Everything's in progress?" he interrogated.

"Yes, Monsieur."

"Good. Take care of everything, won't you, and tell me when it's ready."

He returned to the dining room, set two bottles of fine champagne on the dresser and various bottles of liqueurs.

Clodomir Fargeau did things well when he received his little friend to dinner in his home. Although he was economical, even miserly, at ordinary times, he became prodigal in that circumstance.

At quarter to ten the housekeeper came to inform him, in accordance with his desire, that everything was ready.

"I've covered the dishes, which are keeping warm on the stove. Monsieur has only to fetch them."

"Thank you. You can go now. And tomorrow morning, be here early."

"Monsieur knows very well that I'm always punctual."

Left alone, Clodomir Fargeau took a small object out of a box and slipped it under his napkin.

"A souvenir! I hope my little Françoise will like it . . ."

At the same moment, he was surprised to hear the doorbell ring. He looked at the clock.

"Ten o'clock! It's her . . . I was so occupied that I didn't hear her come up."

He went to open the door, and Françoise penetrated joyfully into the apartment, resplendent with electric light. He led her by the hand into the dining room.

"Oh, the beautiful table!" she said.

"Isn't it? Nothing is too good for you, my dear," he replied, seeking her lips.

But she suddenly assumed a grave expression and fell silent.

"What's the matter? Have you lost something?"

"I no longer have my purse."

"Your golden purse?"

"Yes, you can see that I no longer have it . . ."

"Perhaps you left it at home?"

"No, I still had it in the Metro. Where can I have lost it? Oh, I have it," she said, after a moment of reflection. "I stopped at the bottom of the staircase to recapture my stocking in my garter. I must have put it down beside me, and I can no longer recall . . ."

"Go down quickly and see. In the meantime I'll prepare the dishes on the table, we'll hurry dinner . . . and then to bye-byes!"

In the dark stairway, Françoise whispered, imperceptibly: "Tête-Rouge!"

A shadow surged forth from the darkness.

"I'm yours . . ."

On tiptoe, the Bretonne went back into the apartment, holding her accomplice by the hand; she took care to switch off the electricity before traversing the antechamber.

From the dining room, situated to the right, the clink of cutlery and crockery reached her ears, as well as Clodomir Fargeau's voice, which was singing; she pushed the bedroom door, to the left, on the side of the drawing room.

"It's there," she whispered in her man's ear.

"Good. Go away—and pay attention, eh!" the latter replied, closing the door with precaution.

She went back into the dining room, slightly pale, dominating an interior tremor.

"I found my purse; I'm very glad," she said, with an entirely artificial joy.

"Ah! You'd forgotten it downstairs, then, little scatterbrain!"

"Yes. I was very scared . . . I love that purse; it's you who gave it to me, Cloclo . . ."

"Little dear! Come on, sit down, darling—you see, I've served the soup."

She got ready to unfold her napkin, and found in the fold the jewel that Monsieur Fargeau had hidden earlier, with her intention.

She was momentarily nonplused—delighted, he thought—contemplating that new generosity on her aged friend's part.

Her throat contracted, as if caught in a vice; she remained mute—mute with joy, the jeweler told himself.

Finally, she addressed a smile to him, put the ring on her finger, and said:

"It's splendid."

She made the large ruby scintillate under the powerful glare of the electric chandelier.

"It pleases you?"

"Very much, my good friend . . . but you're being foolish . . . it's too pretty . . ."

"Too pretty," he pronounced, very tenderly, leaning toward her over the table. "Is anything ever too pretty? You, perhaps, because you render me more and more amorous."

"Dear Cloclo," she pronounced, striving to match his tenderness and his joy.

"You don't seem content with my little souvenir?"

"But yes . . . very content . . . one can't be more content . . . since I even tell you that it's too pretty . . ."

She extended her lips toward him and he kissed them, closing his eyes as if to appreciate their exquisite softness more fully . . .

"You know that we're celebrating a demi-anniversary this evening . . ."

"A demi-anniversary?"

"Yes, it's exactly six months ago, to the day, my beauty, that I made your acquaintance at the Hortensias Bleu . . ."

"Six months!"

"You don't remember? It was the sixteenth of December—a great day for me—and it's now the sixteenth of June. I perceived that yesterday ... and I didn't want to let that memorable date pass without commemorating it, first by a souvenir, then a little meal in tête-à-tête ... and finally, a beautiful night of amour ..."

Françoise repressed a shudder.

"You like that, my pretty? We'll love one another," he implored.

"Yes, Cloclo, we'll love one another well," she repeated, her mind absent.

Again, he contemplated her, his expression serious.

"What's the matter, darling? You're not as cheerful as usual."

"Yes, yes, my friend, and I too want us to celebrate the demi-anniversary of our liaison joyfully. Here, pour me another glass of champagne. Let's drink, laugh, sing ..."

With an exuberance that he did not recognize, she fell from one extreme to the other, gesticulating and crying out, seized by mad laughter when the champagne cork flew out with the habitual explosion.

She scarcely touched the dishes, but, by contrast, she drank full glasses of champagne at a single draught, trying to get drunk. And she talked randomly, leaping from one subject to another, with the sole objective of stunning herself, preventing herself from thinking.

At dessert, her face was congested; she was agitated and nervous.

It's the champagne, thought the sexagenarian. And he was amused, teasing her and tickling her.

Suddenly, the Bretonne's face became pensive, her eyes fixed on the ruby ring that was shining on her finger, frightened—ecstatic, Monsieur Fargeau thought.

"One might think ... one might think ..." she stammered. "That it was a large drop of blood."

"Oh, how I wish that it was my own blood that had tinted that stone, in order always to have something of me on you, my adored!" he declared.

She bit her lip in order to overcome her sudden weakness, and held out her glass. "Give me another glass of chartreuse, then," she said.

"There, my sweet. Drink . . . and then we'll go into the bedroom, if you wish?"

Those words, pronounced in Breton, caressed her delectably, and tears rose to her eyes.

"What's the matter—are you weeping?"

"Not at all. It's the chartreuse; it's a little strong; I've never been able to get used to it, you know; it's stinging me."

She continued to drink even so, slowly, in little sips, as if to delay the fatal and imminent moment when it would be necessary to go into the bedroom.

In order to increase his strength at the approach of the felicities that awaited him, Clodomir Fargeau had secretly put a pinch of powder into his glass, and he was beginning to get impatient.

"Hurry up, darling!"

"Just a second, my love, I've just finished . . ."

She had suddenly been gripped by a terrible panic, and she had ended up emptying her glass.

The sexagenarian tried to draw her away; she resisted.

"What! You're not in a hurry, today. Normally, you're always the first . . ."

"It's just . . . I'm . . ."

He put his arm round her waist, gave her a kiss on the neck, and they penetrated thus into the bedroom, where the big bed with an old blue baldaquin, raised its imposing mass in the middle.

She had need of all her energy and all her courage now not to weaken.

Very amorous, excited by the champagne, the liqueurs and the aphrodisiac that he had just absorbed, Clodomir Fargeau did not let go of the Bretonne's waist, pronouncing amorous and sensual words in her ear

"I'd like to undress you myself... all the way... would you like that?"

"Yes, my love, whatever you please..."

He proceeded slowly, meticulously.

When the arms appeared, round and white, as well as the birth of the breasts emerging from the low-cut lace corset, his hands commenced to become hasty and feverish. Her underskirts fell with a rustle of crumpled silk; the face of the libidinous old man went white, contracted by a violent desire.

His fingers trembling, breathing in delightedly the exquisite odor of woman given off by her bare shoulders, he unlaced and unfastened the corset; his eyes were wild, his eyelids growing heavy, and while he quavered tender words, he contemplated the beautiful body, indiscreetly unveiled beneath the transparency of the lawn.

"My darling... my love... my treasure... my little blue flower... you're beautiful... too beautiful... you intoxicate me ... you're intoxicating me, darling... my little darling..."

There were sobs of happiness and lust in his throat. His eyelids filled with sweet tears.

The Bretonne, a smile fixed on her lips, contemplated with an interior effort the disturbance to which she was giving birth in that man, and was striving to appear tender, as usual, when a frisson of horror ran over her epidermis, and her eyes were terrified every time an invisible fluid drew them toward the head of the bed, where two eyes appeared from time to time behind the curtains: two eyes that subjugated her.

Tête-Rouge was there, dissimulated by the old blue baldaquin, and he was observing that scene of erotic folly with a pitiless cynicism.

Clodomir Fargeau, whose senses were exasperated more and more in confrontation with that young and fresh woman, whose senile arms could only grip her imperfectly any longer, detached the epaulettes of the ribbon that retained her chemise.

The last veil fell. The Bretonne surged forth, ideally beautiful, ideally tempting.

He could not see her face, the smile of which became a rictus and the eyes of which were bulging; he only saw her beautiful body, more beautiful than that of a statue, which was like a mockery of her youth to his white hair and his exhausted being.

His veins were seething, his arteries in fusion, his blood beating his temples with great dull blows, in a supreme rebellion of his entire being against old age and impotence.

His jaws clicked, his lower lip was drooping lamentably, his hands extended, tremulously toward that flesh of amour and intoxication . . .

And he finally found a little appeasement in parading his avid fingers over that epidermis quivering with fear—quivering with amour, he thought. They lingered over the firm and well-proportioned breasts, and then ran over the shoulders and arms, gripping the supple waist and the full hips . . . the uniform and smooth abdomen that no maternity had come to render ugly.

But on contact with her femininity, all his disturbance was reborn; he drew her toward him violently, almost lifting her from the floor, and carried her to the bed. And while he kissed her recklessly, Françoise saw Tête-Rouge's two eyes emerge from behind the tapestry.

That gaze sufficed to reinforce her courage, which was weakening, at the same time as it reminded her of her man's instructions.

Clodomir joined her; then, appealing to all her energy, she whispered into his ear.

"Oh, yes, my darling!" he stammered, "I love you!"

The Bretonne positioned herself in such a fashion that the sexagenarian could not see what was happening at the head of the bed, whereas she, by contrast, was directly facing it.

While she lavished maddening caresses, Tête-Rouge watched her from behind the baldaquin. She could only see his eyes, which were riveted to hers, and the mysterious fluid of that fascinating gaze had never been so powerful. She sensed a will that was not her own implant itself in her soul. She was ready to obey the signal.

Clodomir Fargeau, entirely given to the intoxication that the unfortunate woman was pouring into him, had closed his eyes.

Tête-Rouge's hand emerged from the drapes then; he extended his index finger, the middle-finger, and then the thumb, while articulating, fully, with his mouth:

"One . . . two . . . three . . ."

At the same time, a slender green cord, passed through the ring of the baldaquin, descended upon the drunken old man.

With a rapid gesture, commanded by the fascinating gaze, Françoise, while continuing her work of amour, commenced her work of death.

She passed the broad noose around Monsieur Fargeau's neck. Before the latter had had time to perceive it, Tête-Rouge pulled the other extremity of the cord.

His senses exasperated, his breast heaving, the man did not realize immediately what was happening. A second sufficed, however. He felt his throat powerfully gripped, raised from his couch at the end of the green cord, which the weight of his body tightened further with every passing second.

The man uttered a gasp of lust and agony; his eyes, revulsed by drunkenness and horror, opened one last time, and in an ultimate glance, they embraced the whole room. They did not see the Bretonne leaning over the bed, shaken by spasms of pleasure and death, nor Tête-Rouge, impassive and cynical, who emerged partly from the baldaquin, still sustaining her with his eyes, which hypnotized her.

The door had opened abruptly; a man had irrupted into the room.

In a supreme glimmer of intelligence, Clodomjir Fargeau recognized him; he tried to pronounce a word, but his eyelids covered his revulsed pupils again and his body was agitated by a profound shudder. His mouth open, his tongue protruding, he expired without having had the time to comprehend the crime of which he was the victim.

One single image had struck his retina in that moment of agony and death: that man who had unexpectedly entered the bedroom and stood there, terrified, mute with fear in confrontation with the spectacle that was offered to his sight. His haggard eyes went from the victim to the two accomplices, and he uttered a loud cry on recognizing the woman:

"Françoise!" he howled. "Oh, Françoise!"

At the noise that he had made when opening the door, the terrified Bretonne had quit Tête-Rouge's eyes, and, immediately released from their hypnotic radiation, felt weak, devastated and repentant, assailed by terrible remorse, in confrontation with the cadaver of Clodomir Fargeau. And that sentiment attained its paroxysm when she saw, and when she recognized, the face of the newcomer.

She went pale, trembling; she felt her strength suddenly abandon her.

Her conscience reproached her for the crime that she had just committed under suggestion. Everything in the room spun around her and she fell over the inert body of her victim, while her blanched kips stammered, dolorously: "Mathurin! Oh, Mathurin!"

PART TWO

I
The Maddening Vision

"Her . . . ! Her . . . !" Mathurin never ceased to murmur, dazed and haggard.

One hand on the steering-wheel of the automobile, he guided it through the streets at random without knowing where he was going, so chaotic were the ideas in his topsy-turvy and disordered brain.

He did not see or hear anything, indifferent to everything that was not the horrible vision that he had before his eyes and which haunted him terribly.

He had launched his vehicle at a crazy speed, operating the alarm horn with a mechanical gesture, and although the passers-by were beginning to become less numerous at that hour, more than once at the corner of a street or traversing a crossroads he had nearly run over pedestrians, who had cursed him violently

"Brute! Can't you pay attention!"

"Animal! Crusher! He thinks everything is permissible because he's driving an automobile!"

"Damned idiot! Does one go at such a speed through the streets of Paris?"

It was a miracle that he did not hit a tram, or an omnibus, or that he did not crash, in a fashion as unexpected as it was inevitable, into some café.

He traveled thus along the Rue des Francs-Bourgeois and the Boulevard Beaumarchais, traversed the Place de la Bastille like a gust of wind, and reached the quays, straying into the side-streets, which his machine filled with a terrible racket and crazy appeals of the horn.

He fled, fled recklessly, wondering whether he was really awake, if he were not dreaming, if it was not a frightful night-mare that he has just had.

Alas, it was certainly reality, brutal reality, a reality that terri-fied and froze all his faculties, crystallizing his ideas in his head.

Oh, he had had no suspicion of the horrible spectacle and the terrible surprise that awaited him in the home of Clodomir Fargeau when he had descended joyously outside the old build-ing inhabited by the jewelry manufacturer.

He knew the worthy Monsieur Fargeau well, to whom his captain often sent him to carry letters, to carry out a commis-sion—the good Monsieur Fargeau, who welcomed him every time in Breton, who poured him a drink and went so far as to slip him a silver coin.

Furnished that evening with an urgent letter by Captain Christian Bataille, Mathurin had gone upstairs whistling gaily. And what stupefaction on opening the bedroom door to see the old man half-strangled, his eyes bulging, imprinted with an expression of terror and amour, his own eyes fixed, desperately, trying to conserve one last and durable vision of that ultimate minute.

When that first second of alarm had passed, Mathurin's gaze had fallen upon the two accomplices; and he had sensed a breath of madness traverse his brain on recognizing Françoise-la-Bretonne . . . his countrywoman, his sweetheart, the woman he had loved and still loved, silently, allying her memory with that of his chaste amours and his attachment to his natal soil.

And the man who had appeared at the head of the bed, was that not the Red Sorcerer, that No'zour with the sinister face, whom the people of Carnac had made into a spell-caster?

Twenty times already he had evoked that scene, and always it returned with the same intensity.

He saw himself again, quitting the bedroom, lost, maddened. He had slammed the door and tumbled down the stairs four at a time; he had leapt into his automobile, which he had launched in third gear.

And that blind course continued; he was now at the Pont d'Austerlitz, without taking account of the direction he had taken.

The rumble of the Seine, which was rolling its somber waves, dotted with red fires in the vicinity of the bridges—that dull noise enlivened by the splashing of the river along the banks, reminded Mathurin of the notion of the situation in which he found himself.

He stopped momentarily in order to get his bearings.

"Good God! The Pont d'Austerlitz!"

He put his hand to his forehead, as if to reassemble his scattered ideas, to clarify slightly the pell-mell of his brain.

And he suddenly recalled . . .

"Mon Capitaine! Mon Capitaine, who's waiting for me! I have to go there, right away. But what have I done with the letter that he gave me to give to Monsieur Clodomir Fargeau?"

He must have dropped it . . . back there.

That "back there" reminded him of the obsessive vision . . . and his eyes became haggard again; an intense trouble disturbed his soul.

Oh, to no longer see that . . . to forget . . . no longer to think . . .

But that was impossible; the horrible memory haunted him incessantly; the terrifying scene returned before his eyes.

His temples throbbing, his head on fire, his hands agitated by fever, he felt his reason abandoning him. Everything fled before him, his vehicle went on into the unknown. His throat dry, his eyes staring ahead, his hands glued to the steering-wheel, he went implacably toward his destiny.

Fever clawed at his slack body; only his senses still guided him.

A morbid thirst extracted him from his hallucinatory dream. A bar offered itself to him on the corner of a busy street. He stopped and went into the establishment, where he drank, in a single draught, one after another, several glasses of wine before the bewildered eyes of the owner.

Somewhat dazed by the drink, he climbed back into his vehicle, remembering his captain, who was waiting for him at the Porte Maillot. He departed at top speed, zigzagging through the back streets to reach the Rue Rivoli, as far away as possible from the Rue de Turenne, which he fled instinctively.

The wine he had absorbed only stunned him slightly; the vision still returned, painfully.

He stopped again at a wine-merchant's at the entrance to the Rue du Temple and asked mechanically for a rum, then two, which he absorbed with his eyes absent . . . and set off again like a madman.

"What will my captain say when he finds out? But I won't tell him . . . In fact, what could I tell him? How could I explain to him that I'm not bringing back a response to his letter? However, I can't say anything to him, because of her . . . her! her!"

His madness recommenced, and while the auto, launched like a whirlwind, went down the Rue de Rivoli, an entire past was gradually evoked before his eyes.

Slightly reassured, he took pleasure in reviving the years that he had passed in the homeland.

At first, there was his childhood in the cottage of his parents, the Dagornes, mariners, father and son, for generations. He had been no more than ten years old when the angry sea had buried his father in its moving tomb. Mère Dagorne had thus been left a widow with three children, two girls and a boy, Mathurin. She had always had a hint of preference for the latter, and she had imposed the hardest sacrifices on herself in order to send him to the communal school until he obtained his certificate of studies. She went right and left all day to the surrounding farms, mending nets and following twenty petty métiers, difficult and poorly-paid, in order to bring together the few sous necessary to enable her small family to live.

She experienced a terrible rancor against the sea, which had stolen her husband from her affection, and so many other members of her family, so she had decided that her Mathurin, breaking with tradition, would not be a mariner. It was to the land that she intended to consecrate him.

When he was of age, therefore, she placed him with local agriculturalists; he proved himself to be active, industrious and, at harvest time, occupied himself very intelligently threshing grains, testifying a keen liking for mechanics, and rapidly specializing in the operation of the agrarian instruments that progress has placed at the disposal of the modern cultivator. On Sunday, closely shaven and clad in a costume in the Parisian fashion bought in a shop in Lorient, he went to the ball at which all the lads and lasses of Carnac came to dance . . .

And it was there that, one spring evening, he had felt his heart beating faster for the first time, on perceiving Françoise, the daughter of the Le Goffs, small farmers of the neighborhood. The lads who courted that youth, as beautiful and fresh as a flower opened in the morning, were numerous, so Mathurin had not had much hope. However, be had invited her to dance, gauche and intimidated; and the girl, blushing and lowering her eyes, had accepted. Neither of them daring to proffer a word, they had turned in a waltz to the sound of the biniou. Two days later they had encountered one another while returning from the fields. Françoise was carrying a basket of herbs on her head, for the rabbits. With a slightly heavy gallantry, Mathurin had offered to take charge of it. She had refused at first, but he had insisted . . . and they had made the journey together, chatting about indifferent things, about Yves and Marie-Anne, Martin or Catherine . . .

And they had loved one another for a long time, without daring to admit it.

But one morning in May, when the air was carrying the perfumed scent of wild flowers and the marine breeze, when the sun put nature in fête and the heart in joy, Mathurin had been emboldened.

At the foot of a gigantic cromlech—a vestige of one of the most remarkable alignments of stones that the Celts had planted in order to render homage to their gods—in the shadow projected over the heath by the centuries-old block, he took her hand gently and tenderly, and bore it to his mouth amorously. Françoise smiled at him, embarrassed. He drew her toward him, chastely, and, not daring to take her lips, kissed her on her cheeks, crimsoned by emotion.

People were beginning to talk in the village; the nascent tenderness of the two young people had been perceived. Mère Dagorne had said to her son: "It appears that you're circling the Le Goff girl, Françoise. She pleases you, then?"

"Yes," the young man had replied, embarrassed.

"Well, my lad, it's necessary to ask her parents for her. She's a nice girl, a hard worker, and she pleases me very much. I'd like her as a daughter-in-law, only it's necessary that she wait; you haven't done your military service yet."

Mathurin had been accepted by the Le Goffs and their betrothal had been celebrated. The presents that each family would make to the young couple had been agreed, and the marriage had been fixed for Mahthurin's return.

Françoise was a good girl; he had nothing to fear. She would wait faithfully; and he would therefore pay her a patient and chaste court, distancing the thought that he would one day possess that beautiful virgin body in order not to trouble the placidity of his senses. Oh, there had been a terrible release of passion within him, the day after Christmas, when Françoise had disappeared, at the same time as Pen-ru, the rapist and mysterious sorcerer, had disappeared.

What had become of her? Superstitious peasants claimed that, on stormy nights, when the roaring wind unleashed the waves against the rocks of the coast, Françoise appeared, frightful and sinister, playing hide-and-seek among the cromlechs of the heath, with the No'zour with the tawny hair.

Mathurin shrugged his shoulders, skeptical of all that nonsense; but he had become taciturn, somber and silent. He enclosed himself in his dolor, his heart broken.

He quit the fatherland and his old mother almost joyfully, all the more so as his service summoned him to Paris—to the regiment of sapeurs-pompiers. There, more than elsewhere, it would be easy to forget his chagrin.

In the barracks, he did not find himself too homesick, and he gave evidence of good will. After a month of that new existence he was, so to speak, liberated from the memory of his fiancée.

It was then that a countryman, encountered in the quarter of the École Militaire, had spoken to him about a girl named Françoise, a Bretonne like them, whose obliging mores rendered her accessible to all. That had awakened a terrible suspicion in him . . . he had wanted to see her . . . but, by a strange coincidence, the woman had suddenly disappeared.

He had been more amply informed by his comrade, and there was no longer any possible doubt he had recognized Françoise, his fiancée, by means of her description. That, therefore, was what the so-called sorcerer, the vulgar white slave trader, had done with her; he had transformed that chaste and modest girl into a creature of pleasure and prostitution!

He swore to find her again and searched the quarter. He learned that she had departed. He attempted to renounce her again, and the wound in his heart slowly closed.

In order to cauterize it entirely, he ran to temporary and rapid embraces, but they only calmed his senses; in the depths of his heart his first amour and the ever-cherished image of his sweet fiancée lay dormant.

So, what an emotion for the poor boy to find himself confronted by her again, at the moment when he least expected it—and in such tragic circumstances, most of all!

Her wondered whether his reason was not about to founder. It had received such a blow!

Françoise, that Françoise he had known as innocent as an angel of purity, that Françoise whom he still adored, even though she had rolled in and been dirtied by the filthy Parisian mud, was it possible that her heart had gone astray to the point that she had become . . . what had she become? He scarcely dared to formulate the terrible word that came to his mind . . . it scared him . . .

Françoise, a criminal! Unfortunately, he could not doubt it. He had seen her, leaning over, in an amorous attitude, that old man who was dying, his neck strangled by the green cord, his tongue hanging out, his eyes bulging and revulsed.

How her sentiments had changed in a few months!

But he forgave her; he excused her; he divined that she was animated by an invincible force, an alien will—the will of those two violet eyes that were shining at the head of the bed.

They were the true guilty parties. It was them that had done everything.

He was seized again by his chagrin, his anguish, the painful evocation.

I want to chase all that away, he said to himself. *I'm going to drink, to get drunk—it's necessary that I'm no longer thinking . . .*

From that moment on he stopped every time he encountered a wine-shop that had not yet closed its doors. His brain became obscured as the intoxication provoked by alcohol increased; his tongue thickened and his legs became unsteady. The memory blurred in the mist of drunkenness, but it was still there, as obsessive as a remorse.

And he continued his vertiginous course, forgetting his goal, no longer knowing where he was going, no longer recalling that his captain was waiting for him at the Porte Maillot.

His vehicle zigzagged, progressing at hazard; he piloted it mechanically, his sight as clouded as his brain.

He was astonished to find himself, at one moment, in a wine-shop in Billancourt. He had wandered around Paris, passing the Porte d'Auteuil without taking account of anything, stage after stage, ingurgitating alcoholic drinks in order to inebriate himself.

When he wanted to settle the price of his drinks he perceived that he no longer had anything in his pocket but a single twenty-five centime coin. He was thrown out without any other action being taken, in view of his uniform.

He collapsed in the vehicle, his head lost in drunkenness. It was a full five minutes before he was able to set it going again, but in the end, it pulled away.

In a flash of lucidity, he remembered that he had to go to the Porte Maillot and return to Paris.

As he went through the Porte d'Auteuil without caring about the formalities to be fulfilled, the employees of the customs post called to him.

"Hey, soldier, one doesn't pass through like that. What about the gasoline? I recognize you—you went through before like a madman. It might be late, but excessive speeds aren't permitted."

Extracted from his torpor, Mathurin applied the brake, and, bewildered, asked the customs officer who hoisted himself up on to the footplate: "What? What do you want?"

"How many liters of fuel do you have?"

"Liters of fuel?" he stammered, his eyes fluttering with drunkenness, seemingly not understanding.

"Of course! You don't know, then, that it's necessary to declare them?"

"Declare them . . . I didn't know."

"You're lucky you're a pompier, otherwise . . . come on, how many liters of fuel do you have?"

"You're annoying me. I don't know, I tell you. Leave me in peace."

He declutched suddenly, released the brake, liberated the engine and departed without warning.

The employee only just had time to descend from the vehicle, and swore violently

"Animal! What's the matter with him? He's drunk, damn it! Just wait, my lad, I'm taking your number."

Mathurin swerved abruptly and engaged in the Boulevard Suchet, which he went along at top speed. He had soon passed the Porte de la Muette, and sped along the dark and deserted Boulevard Lannes.

He perceived the glimmer of a small wine-shop, and wanted to stop there again, in order to complete his drunkenness. His head was spinning and his legs were giving way. He fell on to a chair, his elbows on a table.

"What would you like?" asked the owner, looking askance at the soldier, whose uniform was in disorder and who seemed very drunk.

"Give me a glass of brandy," he said.

The owner served the glass, which Mahurin drank in a single draught.

Then he put his hand in his pocket, opened his purse and perceived that it was empty. He rummaged in all his pockets in vain; he no longer had a sou.

The shopkeeper, who had not taken his eyes off him, sensed anger rising within him, but, in view of the inebriated state of the customer, found it preferable to take him by the arm and throw him out.

And, tottering, Mathurin drew away, without occupying himself with his automobile, and without perceiving that it had disappeared.

He marched straight ahead, staying on his feet by virtue of a miracle of equilibrium, stumbling over stones and bumping into trees.

After the Porte Dauphine he climbed the slope of the fortifications and continued his route, his reckless flight.

Anesthetized by drunkenness he went as if in a dream, murmuring phrases in Breton, swearing, his voice thick:

"Gaste de gaste! Ma doué! Ma doué!"

His vacillating shadow was profiled against the violet sky studded with silver. His feet trod on the short, thick grass.

Suddenly, however, he tripped over a clod of earth; he lurched and fell, like a mass, face down, so awkwardly that he could not get up again in spite of the efforts he made to do so.

His thoughts accelerated; for a second, he saw again all that night of horror and madness. He became torpid, with the maddening vision that always came to offer itself to his eyes, troubled by drunkenness . . .

II
Mathurin Hoisted by His Own Petard

"Colleague, I believe that it will be fine today. Look at that mist."

"Yes, it's a sign of good weather. It'll be warm this afternoon."

The two policemen were walking the beat at their regular pace, inspecting the surroundings indifferently. Suddenly, one of them shivered and stopped, a hand over his eyes.

"One might think that there's someone lying there on the glacis . . ."

"Indeed . . . a man, no doubt."

"Let's go see."

They climbed the slope without accelerating their pace.

"A soldier," said one of them, perceiving the blue and red uniform.

"A pompier," the other completed.

They drew closer and leaned over

"Well, what are you doing here?" exclaimed the first, shaking him furiously.

"He's fallen asleep on his feet . . ."

"I believe you . . . poor devil, he's going to cop it, having missed roll call and not having returned to barracks!"

"Wake up, damn it . . . you can't sleep like that . . ."

By virtue of being shaken, Mathurin ended up opening his eyes. He remained bewildered on perceiving the two policemen leaning over him and making efforts to lift him up.

"What? What do you want with me? What's the matter?"

"Come on, get up, necessary to return to barracks, my lad. You're going to get yourself punished. Get up, damn it!!"

They succeeded in getting him to his feet.

"We know how it is . . . we're men too . . . you've been amusing yourself . . . you've drunk too much, and you didn't have the strength to get back. We'll put you in a carriage . . ."

"What barracks are you from?"

Bewildered, Mathurin looked at them, one after the other, without responding to their question, not seeming to have understood.

"What barracks are you from?" repeated the policeman,

"General staff, barracks of the Cité," he said, mechanically.

"The Cité . . . good. We'll treat you as a mate . . . we'll put you in a carriage," said the worthy guardians, while going down the slope, still supporting him under the arms.

Mathurin came to slowly; his head was heavy, his face swollen . . .

His first thought disturbed him to such an extent that he stopped abruptly and stammered: "Ah! The murderer! The murderer! It's him who killed him!"

The agents shivered and looked at one another

"What's that you're saying?"

"The murderer! The murderer!"

"You know a murderer?"

"No…"

"Then what are you saying?"

"Me? Nothing… nothing…"

The two policemen exchanged a particular glance. They reached an understanding and, instead of going in quest of a carriage, they headed toward the police post.

The man had mentioned murder. One never knew … duty before all!

Mathurin allowed himself to be drawn, without resistance, without even asking where they were taking him. His brain was even more clouded than before his slumber, his nightmares mingling the terrible reality with frightful memories in a dense and inextricable confusion.

He emerged slightly from that prostration when he found himself in the commissaire's office, facing the secretary, who, after having made him state his name, forenames and qualities, interrogated him regarding the word "murderer" that he had recently pronounced.

"To what murderer were you alluding?"

"Me … a murderer … no … no murderer!" he stammered

"Take this pompier away," he ordered. "He's drunk. When you've made him absorb a little ammoniac and he's sobered up a little, I'll start again."

He was put in a special room under the surveillance of an agent.

Collapsed on the bench, he still had his bewildered countenance, in spite of the sal ammonic that he had been given to drink.

"The murderer ... the murderer ..."

That word returned incessantly to his lips, which stammered it confusedly.

And he remained indifferent to what was happening around him when a man was brought in who was laid down, awkwardly, on a camp bed.

He had just been found in the Bois, at the Porte Maillot, and the guards had summoned two agents, who had carried him to a pharmacist's shop. After having bandaged a few wounds that were not serious, the latter had made him absorb a cordial.

He had come round, although he was very weak, and the policemen had brought him to the post in order to establish his identity, but scarcely had he entered the commissariat than he had fainted again.

While he was given the necessary care, the secretary had observed that he was not just anyone, since the red ribbon of the Légion d'honneur ornamented the buttonhole of his frock-coat. He examined the bruises that had damaged his face searched his pockets—quite empty—and concluded immediately that the man had been the victim of a nocturnal attack.

In spite of energetic cares, the man remained unconscious,

"It'll be necessary to take him to the hospital, since he hasn't decided to come round," said the secretary.

At that moment, Mathurin, disturbed in his somber reverie by the comings and goings, turned toward the unknown man. "Ah!" he said, stupefied, widening his eyes.

"What? What's the matter with you?"

"My captain ..."

"Your captain? This man is your captain?" said the secretary, examining him suspiciously from the corner of his eye. And between his teeth he muttered: "Just now he mentioned a murderer. He didn't want to explain himself, and this wounded man is his captain. Well, well, what has this fellow done? It could be ... could be ... It's necessary that I clarify this matter."

The cares began to produce their effect, The captain came round, slowly. When he opened his eyelids, his eyes made a tour of the room. Perceiving his driver, he stammered: "Mathurin, here?"

The Breton could not succeed in dissipating his confusion, because a frightful alternative had loomed up before him at the same time as he had recognized his captain

What am I going to respond when he asks me what his uncle, Clodomir Fargeau, said?

He remained on the bench, seemingly anxious and frightened—to the great joy of the secretary, whose eyes were sparkling, because he saw in that embarrassed attitude a commencement of proof in favor of his presumptions.

"Well, Mathurin," said the captain, sitting up, "what are you doing here?"

"Me, *mon capitaine* . . . ? Nothing."

"What, nothing? On the contrary, I find it very odd. And where is the automobile?"

"The automobile!" he said. "The automobile!" He had not yet thought about that. He had not noticed that it was missing. "The automobile, *mon capitaine* . . . the automobile . . . but . . . but . . . I don't know . . . I don't recall where it is . . ."

"What? What are you saying? Is it really you, Mathurin, who are saying that? I don't recognize you. What has happened to you? Have you been attacked too by nocturnal prowlers?"

"I believe I understand," interjected the commissaire's secretary. "I believe I understand that Mathurin Dagorne, sapeur-pompier, serves as a chauffeur to drive your automobile?"

"That's correct, Monsieur le Secretaure."

"Well, captain, I would like to ask you to give me some information, as soon as your strength permits."

"At your disposal, Monsieur. I'm still in some pain, but it won't prevent me from speaking."

The officer followed the secretary into his office. The latter closed the door behind him, advanced a chair and then sat down and began asking questions.

"Permit me first, captain, for form's sake, to ask you for your name and forenames."

"Of course. I'm Captain Christian Bataille of the sapeur-pompiers of Paris, barracks of the Cité."

"Thank you. I shall now push indiscretion further and ask you to be kind enough to give me details of the aggression of which you have been the victim—for there was an aggression, in all probability?"

"Indeed, Monsieur le Secretaire. I'll tell you what happened without omitting the slightest detail. I made the acquaintance a few days ago, in the vicinity of the Gare du Nord, of a young woman of easy virtue. Her slightly plump beauty pleased me and I was the first to propose a meeting, in a restaurant near the Porte Maillot and the Bois. She accepted my proposition with pleasure, and yesterday, was very punctual at my rendezvous. I ordered a nice meal, and we dined together. She was charming.

"The evening passed very rapidly. The moment came to settle up. I summoned the waiter, who brought me the bill. I reached for my wallet, opened it, and perceived that it only contained papers—which never happens, because I always go out with several hundred francs in my pocket. All I had was two five-franc coins in my fob pocket.

"I informed my companion of my disappointment and thought immediately of sending my driver, Mathurin, to fetch a hundred francs from my domicile. But in acting thus I would be exposing myself to a terrible scene at home; I had told my wife that I was dining at the Military Club with comrades from the regiment, She had seemed slightly skeptical in accepting that excuse; she would be entirely so if I committed the imprudence of sending my chauffeur to my home a such a late hour.

"Only one solution presented itself in the circumstance: to address myself to my wife's uncle, Monsieur Clodomir Fargeau, to whom I had had recourse many times in almost similar circumstances. In haste, I drafted a letter, which I gave to Mathurin, my driver, who was waiting for me with his automobile, asking him to take it as quickly as possible to the Rue de Turenne, where my uncle lives. The hour was late, but Monsieur Fargeau is not in the habit of going to bed early, so everything was for the best.

"Scarcely had my chauffeur quit the café when the manager, brought up to date by the waiter who had served us, advanced toward me.

"'I beg you not to worry, Monsieur. These things happen. You can pay another time. We have confidence in you; you're a good client.'

"I thanked him and explained that the harm would soon be repaired, that my chauffeur would return soon.

"I waited for more than an hour and a half. Seeing that he was not coming back, I accepted the manager's proposition. My companion and I went out. 'Let's take a walk in the Bois,' she proposed. 'It's so pleasant this evening.'[1]

"I acceded to her desire. After having taken a few steps, we sat down.

"I was beginning to get impatient, Mathurin still not having returned; it was more than two hours since he had left."

"Aha!" the secretary put in, with a particular smile at the corners of his lips.

"My friend offered me a cigarette; I allowed myself to fall into the trap—for it was a trap, without a doubt—and as I no longer had any matches, she invited me to ask a stroller going in our direction for a light.

---

1 This makes no sense, as the captain has already explained to the prostitute that he has no money on him, but it is by no means the last lamentable failure in the logic of the narrative.

"Benevolently, without reflection, I obeyed. The man started to shout: 'Stop, thief!' and then I received a head-butt in the chest. I fell to the ground, and felt myself assailed with blows."

"Did you recognize your attackers?"

"My word, no . . ."

"Aha!" said the secretary, In a sententious tone. And you didn't have any suspicion? You don't know anyone, in your entourage, who might be the author of that aggression?"

"My word, no."

"What is certain, though—for you as for me, I imagine—is that the woman is an accomplice . . . perhaps the instigator."

"Evidently; but she would only have been the bait . . ."

"Well, I have suspicions," said the secretary. "They certainly need to be confirmed, but in the end . . ."

"Who?" interrogated the officer, curiously.

"Your driver, this Mathurin Dagorne."

"Never!" he replied, with a start of indignation. "He's an honest fellow, with whom I'm very satisfied."

"Permit me, captain, to tell you that there are many things that militate against him. First of all, he was found on the glacis of the fortifications in the vicinity of the Porte Maillot. He was lying on the ground, dead drunk. The agents lifted him up and asked for explanations. All that he was able to say was: 'Oh, the murderer! The murderer!'"

"You astonish me, Monsieur le Secretaire. I've had him in my service for a year, and I've never seen him drunk. As for the word murderer . . . evidently, it's strange, but he was doubtless not fully awake when he pronounced it . . ."

"He repeated it thereafter several times, as if he were pursued by remorse . . . and you weren't able to see his face a little while ago, when he recognized you in the post. He seemed inhibited, embarrassed . . ."

"Evidently, it must have appeared strange to him to encounter me in a commissariat, wounded, half-unconscious, when he had quit me a few hours before, cheerful and well . . ."

"And how do you explain that he had . . . lost your automobile?"

"That's impossible for me . . . for I repeat to you that Mathurin's conduct has always been very good . . . he must also have been the victim of an attack. Apaches are afraid of nothing . . ."

"One can't easily attack a moving automobile . . . he must have left it somewhere. Afterwards, frightened by the coup he had just committed, he no longer thought about it . . . and came to collapse on the glacis, where he was discovered this morning . . ."

"Monsieur, that boy isn't capable of having committed the crime of which you're accusing him. In any case, he knew that I had no money on me . . . so . . . ?"

"Evidently, but as you had sent him to obtain some money from your uncle, he doubtless wanted to take possession of it . . . and it was with that goal that he . . ."

"Excuse me for interrupting you, Monsieur le Secretaire, but that hypothesis isn't admissible . . ."

"Why is that?"

"Mathurin, as I've already said, has been in my service for more than a year. I let him go into my home, into my bedroom, into my study. I've never locked a drawer because of him, and never . . . never, you hear . . . has a single centime gone missing. And yet, he could have taken possession of sums much more considerable than my uncle can have given him, admitting your hypothesis."

"That doesn't prove anything. He doubtless had need of it at that moment, when he might have found himself suddenly embarrassed, afflicted by a pressing need . . . a woman, gambling, or something else. All means were good to him."

"I'll contradict you once again, for I'm absolutely sure of that boy, who is neither a womanizer nor a gambler. He has only been in Paris since he was summoned here by his military service. He had never left Bretagne before. No, Monsieur le Secretaire, I repeat, I'll never admit that accusation, unless you support your suspicions with undeniable facts."

"Evidently, they're only presumptions as yet . . . they need to be sagely investigated. With your permission, captain, I'll summon your driver, and in your presence I'll ask him a few questions in order to clarify the matter . . ."

"As you wish, Monsieur le Secretaire."

He left for a moment in order to give the order to bring Mathurin.

The latter, conducted by an agent, soon came into the study, his expression bewildered, his head bowed and his eyes fugitive.

Christian Bataille could not help finding that strange, but attributed the attitude to drunkenness and emotion.

The secretary looked at the pompier momentarily, and then questioned him: "Mathurin Dagorne, can you explain why you were heard to say, several times: 'Oh, the murderer! The murderer!' Who is that murderer."

"The murderer! The murderer! I don't know . . . I don't know anything . . ."

"You persist in replying in that evasive fashion, so be it! Well, tell me what you did with your time after the moment when your captain charged you with going to the home of his uncle, Clodomir Fargeau?"

The Breton shivered, and stammered, uncertainly: "Clodomir Fargeau . . ."

"Come on, reply clearly. Did you go there? Captain Bataille had given you a letter to deliver to your uncle; what have you done with it?"

"I . . . I don't know."

"What? You don't know what you've done with his letter? Then you didn't go to Clodomir Fargeau's home in the Rue de Turenne?"

"Rue de Turenne . . . Rue de Turenne . . ." said Mathurin, excitedly, emerging from his torpor. "Oh, no, I haven't been to the Rue de Turenne, I swear it!"

"You have no need to swear it. What did you do, then, instead of carrying out your superior's commission?"

"I don't know . . . I . . . I walked . . ."

"Aha! And where did you walk? You doubtless had a rendez-vous with friends?"

"Yes . . . yes . . . friends . . . from the homeland . . . Bretons."

"You'd been drinking to give you courage?"

"Yes."

"Afterwards, you returned to the Bois to put your plan into execution?"

"I returned because my captain was waiting for me at the Porte Maillot."

"You're not being logical; since you hadn't carried out his commission, you had no need to return."

Mathurin became embarrassed, and ended up replying: "Yes, I would have explained to him; my captain would have understood."

"And what had you done with your automobile?"

"I remember now. I had gone into a café, I no longer remember exactly where; when I came out, I no longer thought about it. I walked . . . walked. Then I stumbled and fell . . . I could no longer get up."

"How is it that you got so drunk, since you don't have the habit of it? You must have a reason."

"A reason . . . a reason . . ." he stammered, troubled.

Seized again by his obsession, he put his hand over his eyes, where the terrible vision had just been evoked again. Unconsciously, he pronounced words again: "The murderer! Oh, the murderer!"

The secretary exchanged a glance with the captain, which signified: *You see, you see . . . there's something shady behind this* . . . And he rang for one of the agents, whom he commanded: "Take this man away."

They found themselves in a tête-à-tête again.

"Do you persist in believing that he had nothing to do with your attack?" he interrogated.

"Yes, I'll answer for that man . . . I'll take responsibility for him."

"Then you don't want a report to be made in his regard?"

"On the contrary; I'd be very obliged to you if you can keep this matter as quiet as possible. It might attract inconvenience for me, first with my wife and also with my superiors."

"In that case, captain, I'll accede to your desire. We'll set you at liberty."

While saying that, the secretary unfolded a morning news-paper mechanically, turning the pages and casting a glance over the headlines.

"Another crime," he said, when he arrived at the heading *Latest News*. He read: "Mysterious murder in the Rue de Turenne."

"Rue de Turenne?" said Christian Bataille.

"Yes. An old man strangled in his bed. The crime seems to have been motivated by theft."

"Will you permit me to look at that, Monsieur le Secretaire?"

"Of course," said the latter, passing him the paper.

The officer immediately searched for the article related to the mysterious crime, and had scarcely read the first lines when he uttered a sharp exclamation.

"What is it?" asked the policemen.

"32A Rue de Turenne . . . a jewelry manufacturer . . . but that's my uncle!"

"What are you saying, captain?"

"I'm saying that it's my uncle, Clodomir Fargeau, who has been the victim of that murder . . ."

The relative to whom you sent your chauffeur to carry a letter?"

"Exactly."

"But then . . . then? This affair is getting murkier and murkier. This Mathurin Dagorne, in whose innocence you're obstinate in believing, claims not to have carried out the commission that you had given him—which is to say that he didn't go to your relative's home. On the other hand, he doesn't know what he did with the letter, and we learn from this article that Clodomir Fargeau has been murdered. That's a strange combination of circumstances."

The secretary was interrupted by his superior, whom, after having saluted Christan Bataille, asked his subordinate: "Is there anything new?"

The latter brought him rapidly up to date, in a low voice, with what had happened: the captain found in the Bois, inanimate, the victim of an attack; his chauffeur found a short distance away on the fortifications; the incoherent words pronounced by the latter; his ambiguous responses; and finally, the coincidence of the uncle murdered that same night.

"It seems to me that there's no error," he said. "The guilty party, in both cases, is this Breton who serves as chauffeur to Captain Christian Bataille, here present. And in those circumstances it seems to me to be difficult to release him, in spite of the captain's desire to suppress the rumor of the attack of which he has been the victim."

"Indeed, captain, we regret it, but your chauffeur must remain in custody until more ample information . . ."

Christian Bataille was still under the blow of the emotion that he had just felt. He was no longer thinking of defending Mathurin.

"I beg you to excuse me, Monsieur le Commissaire, but I'm so distressed by the news that I've just learned that I honestly no longer know . . . if it's all right with you, I'll take my leave of you immediately and have myself taken to the Rue de Turenne right away . . ."

He saluted the two policemen precipitately and quit the post, slightly unsteady on his feet.

After his departure, the commissaire expedited the current business swiftly, added a few signatures to documents, and then summoned Mathurin.

The latter had fallen back into his prostration, and came into the study with an appearance ill-made to plead in his favor. He had lost all energy, and was utterly confused.

"You claim, then, that you didn't go to the home of Clodomir Fargeau in the Rue de Turenne, as your captain had instructed?"

"Rue de Turenne . . . me . . . no . . . no . . ."

"Then you don't know that Clodomir Fargeau has been murdered?"

Mathurin was unable to suppress a violent start and murmured, feebly: "No . . . no . . ." But he could not sustain the commissaire's stare, and lowered his eyes.

Everything around him was spinning. His brain was seething. He defended himself maladroitly, although it would have been so easy to justify himself, and he did that for *her* . . . for his beloved.

The commissaire could only extract monosyllables from him, and like his secretary, arrived at the conclusion that the fellow must be implicated in it.

"There's only one thing to do," he said to his secretary. "Take a carriage and conduct him to the Depot immediately. There they'll take the necessary steps with regard to the military authorities.

Meekly, Mathurin climbed into the carriage, without asking where he was being taken, without suspecting what was happening around him. It mattered little to him, in any case. He no longer existed . . . he only belonged to his somber memories . . .

And as the vehicle rolled for more than a quarter of an hour, the secretary, who accompanied him, heard him murmur again, fearfully.

"Oh, the murderer . . . !"

He threw himself backwards in the carriage, his eyes widened, and stammered, terrified:

"Oh, those eyes! Those eyes!"

III
A Mother's Heart

"Where are you coming from like that, Mère Dagorne?"

"Me? Such as you see me, I'm coming back from Trinité-sur-Mer, I've been doing laundry at the Le Thiecs. What do you expect? One earns one's living as one can?" said Mathurin's mother, bringing back the strings of her white bonnet, which the wind had displaced.

Her interlocutor, an aged peasant from Carnac, had just met the old woman a hundred meters from the town, and they were walking together, chatting.

"It's just that you're no longer young, Mère Dagorne. If I recall rightly, we're almost the same age, the two of us, with your man Urbain? I can still remember the day when you were married as if it were today."

"All that was a long time ago, Père Le Coail, and I'm no longer young, for sure; I'm nearly seventy years old. My man would have been seventy-five."

"And that doesn't prevent you from still being very valiant. There's no one more courageous than you in the region."

"What do you expect, Père Le Coail. Necessary to work to earn a few sous—without that, where would I be? It's not my daughters who can nourish me, since they have a heap of children, nor is it my lad. You know that he's in the regiment . . ."

"You have nothing to lament; Mathurn is a worthy fellow."

"Oh, I don't complain . . . but it's a pity, all the same, when I think that I could have him close by . . . and then not at all . . ."

"Don't worry, old woman; he'll soon have done his time, and he'll come back to you nicer than ever. Do you have news of him?"

"He usually writes to me every week, but this time I don't know what's up . . . I haven't yet received the letter. I'm in a hurry to get home precisely because one might be waiting for me. It's my neighbor who reads them to me. My God, as long as there is one! I'm so anxious, Père Le Coail, knowing that he's all alone in that Paris . . . so many things are said about Paris that scare you . . . and when I think that it's the fault of Françoise Le Goff that he left . . ."

"What do you expect? Young men, when they have a girl in the head . . . but he'll have time to forget her, out there. When he comes back, he'll no longer be thinking about that . . ."

"Does one ever know, with those girls? Who can tell? If one could ever have believed that one capable of going away like that! With . . . with . . ."

She dared not finish; the sinister face of the Red Sorcerer rose before her eyes. She fell silent, trembling, frightened; and, her face somber, she took her leave of her traveling companion . . .

She went through several side-streets and finally found herself outside her dwelling, a modest hut with a little courtyard closed by a fence.

Before going in she went to knock at the next house, and asked through the door: "Are you there, Marie-Anne? Hasn't the postman brought me a letter?"

From inside the house, a feminine voice replied: "No," in a shrill tone. A second after, a woman appeared at the top of two or three steps.

"The postman hasn't brought anything for you. Mère Dagorne, but the gendarmes have come and . . ."

"The gendarmes . . . ! The gendarmes? Do you know what they wanted with me?"

"No. It must be about your son. The brigadier said that you should go to the gendarmerie . . . he'll explain there. You're not weeping, Mère Dagorne?"

Yes, Mère Dagorne was weeping. Large tears were rolling down her wrinkled cheeks.

"Necessary not to be afraid. It often happens that the gendarmes summon you when you have a son in the military," said the charitable neighbor.

The old woman made no reply, shook her head, and drew away, wiping away the tears with the back of her hand.

She only went into her house to change her apron, and came out again; then, heavily, her shoulders hunched under an invisible weight, she traversed the locale.

Two or three people of her acquaintance, whose path she crossed en route, were astonished by her attitude; she did not respond to their greeting, and did not even see them.

When she perceived the gendarmerie she was seized by a tremor; her heart was gripped by a singular anguish; she had a presentiment that misfortune was about to fall upon her.

The brigadier was absent; she had to wait for more than a quarter of an hour, her breast oppressed.

Finally, he arrived, and had her called.

"Well, Mère Dagorne, I have some news to give you," he growled, in his harsh voice. "It's not good news, you know . . . it's even bad news. What can you do? It's necessary to expect everything in existence."

She listened, pale and devastated, her throat terribly contracted. And she pronounced, hoarsely: "It's not that he's . . . that he's dead. my lad?"

"Oh no . . . don't worry, it's not that . . ." The brigadier scratched his head, embarrassed, murmuring between his teeth: "Lousy commission!"

Finally, it was necessary for him to get to the point: "You know, Mère Dagorne, in the regiment, and especially in Paris, lads learn a heap of things that they didn't know in our villages . . . yours was doubtless led astray by his comrades . . . at any rate, he's accused of having committed an assault against his captain, and he's going to appear before a court martial."

"A court martial?" she repeated. "A court martial?"

"Yes, a court-martial . . . all the more so as he's been accused, on the other hand, of having murdered his captain's uncle . . ."

"Mathurin . . . Mathurin . . . a mur . . . a murderer! Oh no, that isn't possible, we're honest, in our family. Unless . . . unless it's that dirty Paris that has turned his head . . ."

"I can't inform you about that. I've told you what I was ordered to transmit to you. I don't know any more . . ."

"Me, I know full well . . . when he told me that he was going to Paris to do his military service, right away, something was squeezed in my heart. I told myself that it would bring him misfortune. First, it's the Noz'our who cast a spell on poor Mathurin the day he took Françoise Le Goff who knows where . . . and then this. What are they going to do to my boy?"

"Listen, Mère, I don't want to frighten you, but in the end, it's better that you know what's facing you. He could get ten or twenty years hard labor, unless . . ."

"He won't be condemned to death?"

"I can't tell you . . . no, I don't think so . . . but in the end, you know . . . it's so odd, all this."

"Yes, I can see that it's annoying you to tell me the truth. I might be nothing but an old peasant-woman, but I can see clearly. My lad Mathurin . . . I'll never see him again. *Ma doué* . . . how unfortunate I am!" the old mother groaned. putting her hands together piously.

And she quit the gendarmerie more stooped and even heavier than when she had arrived.

She shut herself in her house, grimly, not confiding to anyone the dolor of her mother's heart. She did not think of eating, nor of sleeping. She stayed up all night with her elbows on her table and her head in her hands, reflecting and weeping.

Paris . . . the Red Sorcerer . . . those two names were rolling in her head. She associated them, and made them the authors of her son's fault. That Red Sorcerer, above all, with his "evil eye"—for once, the reality gave reason to the superstition.

Oh, that Paris, which seemed to her to be distant and inaccessible, like a land of dream, that Paris of debauchery and perversion, that Paris of luxury and pleasure . . . oh, how she abominated it!

She summoned upon it the malediction of God, and also of all those personages that populate the superstitious imagination of the inhabitants of the ancient land of Amorica: korrigans, farfadets, sprites, monsters, demons and sorcerers; an entire fictitious and unreal world in which she believed with a religious dread.

First light found her in the same position, still pensive, anxious and indecisive.

Ideas had passed through her head since the previous evening; she had envisaged all hypotheses . . . but she had not yet found a solution.

However, an imperious desire was gradually born in her heart: to see her son again, one last time, for she still had the same love for him . . . the delectable maternal love that makes a mother always see in her son the little being that she had breast-fed.

She wanted to hug him in her arms, to hug him against her breast, murmuring to him soft words of forgiveness. But the prospect of his eventual death filled her with a dolorous disturbance and she still rejected that hypothesis, which seemed to her to be impossible, as it also seemed impossible for her to undertake a voyage to Paris, having never been to Auray, only once to Vannes, and a few times to Lorient and Quiberon, and all that in a carriage or on foot, for she had never wanted to hear mention of the railway. That scared her, those locomotives and wagons . . . she called it "the devil's machine."

She had sworn more than once, on her great gods, that she would never set foot on one.

But how could she go to Paris without taking the train? It was impossible. She was, therefore, frightened in advance.

Those who had made the journey talked about ten hours on the train . . . ten hours shut in a carriage that carried you at top speed along interminable rails!

It seemed to Mère Dagorne that she would never endure such an ordeal; she was terrified in advance.

And yet, it was the sole condition on which she might embrace her unfortunate Mathurin one last time.

Maternal love prevailed over all other sentiments; is a mother not always ready to make the greatest sacrifices for her son?

She counted the money in her purse. She had the sum necessary to undertake the journey; and her decision did not take long to be firmly made: she would go to Paris to see Mathurin.

Soon, there was no talk of anything in the little region of Carnac but that irrevocable decision, which astonished more than one person—just as they were astonished by the change that must have been produced in Mathurin for him to be able to do what he had been accused of doing—him, such a disciplined and gentle boy.

"The poor fellow," they said. "It's the disappearance of Françoise, his fiancée, that has turned his head . . ."

The day came that Mère Dagorne had fixed for her departure. She put on her best clothes and her most elegant bonnet.

As she got ready to mount the carriage that was to take her to Plouharnel, the nearest railway station, she found herself face to face with Madame Le Goff, Françoise's mother.

The two women looked at one another askance, for enmity had reigned between the two families since the strange flight of Mathurin's fiancée. They accused one another mutually of their woes, and that enmity had only grown in Mère Dagorne since she had known that her son was to pass before a court martial. So she could not help directing at Mère Le Goffm when she perceived her, between lips pursed in anger and resentment: "It's your fault . . . it's the fault of your daughter, everything that had happened. Without that, my son would never have turned out badly . . . he was too honest."

The other did not know what to respond, downcast by her own personal misfortune and the opprobrium that had been thrown upon her house.

Mathurin's mother darted a hateful glance at her and turned back to the carriage, into which she leapt briskly, in spite of her sixty-nine years.

At Plouharnel she took the "devil's machine," into which she only climbed with the fear mingled with hatred that simple folk have for all progress.

She saw the countryside filing past, league after league, through the narrow carriage window. She had to change trains several times, and when she arrived in Paris, she was literally dazed. It seemed to her that she had quit Carnac more than a week before. She had never felt as exhausted as she was; her arms and legs were bruised, her head was buzzing and her stomach upset. It was necessary for an employee to come and tell her that her journey was concluded, and that it was necessary to descend.

She was lost in the tumultuous station, where it was almost necessary to shout in order to be heard in the midst of various whistles, the rumble of carriages and the din of the hasty, bustling crowd.

She had a great deal of difficulty getting out, going astray and retracing her steps several times.

Finally, she found herself on the sidewalk, in contact with the Paris that she hated, without knowing it.

It was a magnificent summer's day, which the sun aureoled with gold. The city was beautiful.

The peasant-woman remained for a long moment, open-mouthed, facing the lively intersection of the Gare Montparnasse, where trams, omnibuses, automobiles and carriages were coming and going, crossing paths in all directions, and elegant men and pretty women were going by, threading a path through the tangle of vehicles launched at top speed, at the same time as a deafening racket assailed Mère Dagotrne's ears.

She was habituated to the calm and serenity of the small town of Carnac, where one knew everybody, to a simple and placid life devoid of agitation and fever; and she had fallen into this Parisian ocean, with its indifferent crowd, its frantic turbulence, its intense life ... And those houses ... those never-ending houses that rose toward the sky, gigantically!

Passers-by, in a hurry, jostled her without any regard for her great age. She was there, motionless, lost in a contemplation that terrified her. She seemed to be living a dream; she thought she had been transported into the domain of some unknown demon; she felt lost, drowned, submerged. Tears came to her eyes; she regretted not having listened to her daughters. What had she come to do in this inferno?

Her son! Would she ever succeed in finding him? She knew where he was; she had the address written on a piece of paper—a complaisance of the brigadier of the gendarmerie—which she had wedged into her corsage. But how could she make her way through these innumerable streets and this infernal, uninterrupted crowd?

However, she could not remain in this indecision. She decided to approach a passer-by.

She took a long time before she made her choice; the people who brushed past her seemed too elegant, too hurried; she dared not address herself to them.

Finally, she perceived a bare-headed woman of modest appearance. She accosted her, and showed her the piece of paper on which her destination was inscribed: the prison of the Cherche-Midi. The passer-by saw what she was dealing with, and guided her very amiably to the nearest guardian of the peace.

"The court martial," said the latter, a trifle peevishly. "Traverse the square, take the Rue de Rennes, the Rue de Regard, and you'll reach the Rue du Cherche-Midi. You'll see that it's at number twelve."

She only retained one thing from that rapid enumeration: "Traverse."

"Traverse . . . traverse . . . she stammered. "I could never . . . with all those carriages, I'd be crushed, *ma doué*!"

The agent looked at her and softened a little. "Come on, I'll accompany you as far as the sidewalk, Mère."

He took her by the arm. She only advanced tremulously, frightened by the vehicles going past incessantly. Finally, she arrived at the other side, more dead than alive, never ceasing to murmur: "Ma doué! Ma doué!"

"You see," repeated the agent, "you follow this street, straight ahead . . . as far as the Rue Regard . . . that's the second one after traversing the Rue de Vaugirard . . ."

She did not understand, did not think of thanking him, and set forth, her mind absent, stunned by the din and the movement.

She darted a haggard eye at the luxurious shops . . . she was jolted by the busy crowd. Increasingly, she thought she was in a fantastic city, so completely different was everything around her—people and things—from what her eyes had been accustomed to see during the sixty-nine years that she had been in the world.

And she marched thus, with her heavy tread of a peasant-woman fatigued by hard work. She only stopped when the time came to cross the Rue Vaugirard.

She would not have been afraid to climb into a boat and depart over a stormy sea, but she was absolutely paralyzed by the prospect of crossing that new intersection.

Finally, as best she could, aided by the indications of policemen and obliging passers-by, she found herself in the Rue du Cherche-Midi, facing the sad and black buildings of the military prison.

She examined them for a minute; a frisson ran through her whole body; her heart was constricted again, even more forcefully. She forgot all the terrors she had just experienced in the capital, no longer to think about anything but her son, imprisoned there behind those high walls.

She was seized by an impatient desire to see him, and bravely crossed the road, suddenly emboldened.

"I'd like to see my lad," she said to the sentry.

The soldier looked her up and down with a slightly ironic smile, because of the naivety of the question.

"Your lad? Where is he?"

She blushed, and replied, in a feeble voice: "In the prison."

"Well, ask the sergeant, there in the courtyard; he'll inform you, Mère."

The man opened the heavy door slightly, and awkwardly she went into the courtyard and asked the same question to the sub-officer: "I'd like to see my lad . . ."

As clearly as she could, she explained that she had arrived from Bretagne to see her son, Mathurin, accuses of having committed an aggression against his captain.

"Go up to see the captain-reporter of the third court martial," the guardian replied. "First floor, first door on the right . . ."

And having accompanied her outside, he indicated with his finger the corner of the wall where she would find the entrance to the staircase.

She followed the indications that were given to her without any error now, stiffening herself against the emotion that was invading her more and more.

She found a sentry when she reached the upper floor.

"I'd like to see my lad, Mathurin . . ."

The soldier had the benevolent face of a worthy fellow, and as her heart was overflowing, the old woman gushed, speaking without embarrassment, in a French emphasized by Breton words.

The other listened, responded "yes" or "no," nodded his head. She told him everything about her affairs and her woes, seeming now to want to delay the painful interview. The noise of a door that someone was unlocking beside her made her shudder, and she scarcely had time to turn round before a group of soldiers arrived.

She uttered a cry, and clung to the wall, stammering: "Mathurin . . . Mathurin!"

It was in fact, him, entering between four soldiers with bayoneted rifles.

The old woman recovered quickly from her initial surprise; she launched herself toward her son, her arms extended, articulating words of tenderness in her native language . . .

But she did not reach him; the soldiers pushed her away, repelling her, while she stammered, livid, distressed and trembling: "That's my lad . . . my lad . . ."

Mathurin shook off his torpor slightly; his eyes widening . . . but he had no energy, he seemed frozen, overwhelmed by the misfortune that was heaped upon him . . .

Surrounded by the four soldiers, he passed before his devastated mother and went into the office of the captain-reporter, Sylvain Corbigny.

"So," she said, addressing a sentry. "I won't see my son, then . . . I'd like to talk to him, though, to embrace him . . ."

"Wait, Mère," replied the soldier. "I'll go ask the captain whether he can grant you that permission . . ."

Five minutes later, she was in a bare room, with cold whitewashed walls, facing her son, the captain having consented to accord that interview to the aged mother . . .

They exchanged a long and silent hug, and when they looked at one another, they both had eyes full of tears.

"Mathurin!" and "Maman!" stammered the mother and son, simultaneously.

"It's true, then," she said, "that you've been condemned?"

"It appears so," he replied, simply.

"But you . . . you're not going to die?" she interrogated, trembling.

"I don't know."

"Oh, my son, don't tell me that . . . if that ever happened it would kill me on the spot! And all this is the fault of that slut Françoise . . .

He started, stared at his mother momentarily, and murmured: "Françoise . . . Françoise . . ."

"Yes, that whore Françoise . . . it's not that you still love her, that slut? It's her that's the cause of your being before the court martial now. If she hadn't left like that, abruptly, you'd never have come to Paris . . . you wouldn't have engaged in the pompiers . . . it's chagrin that made you do that . . . and it must really be true that you've changed, Mathurin, to have done what you've done . . . you who would never have hurt a fly when you were in Carnac, But tell me, finally, what could have been going through your head . . ."

"I swear to you, Maman, that it wasn't me who did that."

"What! It wasn't you?"

"No, it wasn't me who attached the captain . . . nor the other story."

"It wasn't you," the mother repeated. "Then how is it that it's you who have been accused? It's necessary to say that it wasn't you . . ."

"I have said it, but they don't want to believe me."

"Ah!" said the old woman. "You see what you get for coming to Paris. In our country, that wouldn't have happened to you. People would have believed what you said right away. But here . . ."

"What do you expect?" he said, with a strange resignation.

Mère Dagorne became grim in responding: "You see, Mathurin: in the time you laughed when we talked about the evil eye, you said that they were stories that didn't hold up. Well, you can be sure now that it's the Noz'our that is the cause of everything that has happened. It's him, the Red Sorcerer, who has cast an evil spell on you."

He shrugged his shoulders indifferently.

The poor woman considered him for a moment silently, and was deeply affected by his equivocal attitude, which gave him the appearance of a guilty man. She scarcely recognized her Mathurin in that pompier with a fleeting gaze and slumped shoulders, who bore so little resemblance to the boy, frank of face and bearing, that he had been before. And her tumultuous maternal heart cast terrible anathemas upon Françoise, and upon Paris, which she held responsible for that transformation.

As for the Red Sorcerer, she no longer dared evoke him, fearing to make even more terrible evils fall upon herself and those dear to her.

She talked to her son for a long time in a low voice, under the eyes of the soldiers who witnessed the conversation. She did not think of going away; she wanted that conversation to last forever. However, as it was prolonged excessively, the captain, who was waiting, had her called to order.

There was a touching moment of adieu, which tore the aged mother's soul terribly. She was about to quit her son, doubtless never to see him again. Her Mathurin was the dearest thing she had in the world; he was the hope of her old age and he was being snatched from her brutally. What a terrible blow for her sixty-nine years!

She suspended herself from his neck with her fleshless arms and hugged him forcefully, as if to give him what remained of life in her body worn away by toil . . . and she wept for a long time, without saying anything, silently, looking at him with infinitely sad eyes.

She had no reproach to make to him. She did not wonder whether he was guilty or innocent; she only accused fatality.

It was necessary for someone to take her by the arm to drag her away from her son, and her despair then attained its paroxysm.

"It's necessary, then, that I bid him adieu . . . I'll never see him again, my little lad! Oh, my little lad, if you knew how I loved you, you wouldn't take it from me thus . . . I'm old . . . I no longer have anything but you . . . and it's being taken from me. It's as if a knife were being plunged into my breast to cut short my days . . . oh, my little lad! Mathurin! Let me embrace him one more time, since it's the last . . . since I'll never see him again . . . they're going to condemn him, him, so sweet and gentle . . . It's not his fault, what has happened . . . it's surely not his fault . . ."

And as the captain became impatient, the sergeant intervened.

"Come on, Mère, it's necessary to go. You've already been here for more than half an hour . . . it's a favor that you've been given to grant you such a long moment. Let's go . . ."

"Listen, *Monsieur le sergent* . . . you have a mother too . . . perhaps she's old, like me . . . well, think what chagrin it would give her if she saw you in my son's place . . . think of that and be indulgent, *Monsieur le sergent*, for an old woman. When I think that I'll never see him again, my lad . . . oh, you see, when I think of that . . ."

Her voice was lost in sobs, which prevented her from continuing.

The sub-officer seemed touched by the sincerity of her chagrin; gently, he took her by the arm and conducted her to the door.

Her face hidden in her hands, she continued to sob, with hoarse hiccups that tore her breast.

When she lowered her hands, she was no longer in the bureau, she could no longer see her son; she found herself in the stairwell again, beside the petty soldier to whom she had recounted her woes.

And she continued to stammer: "They can't take him from me, my little lad . . . tell the captain that it isn't possible . . . I no longer have anything but him, his father died at sea, nothing will remain to me any longer . . . then. What am I going to do, alone in the world? I need my boy! Return him to me, he's an honest lad, I'll take him home . . . he'll work for his old mother . . . you won't hear any more mention of him, *Monsieur le sergent* . . . tell all that to the captain."

She let herself fall on to one of the steps of the staircase and wept . . . and wept . . . imploring heaven to annihilate her on the spot . . .

And while she was desolate thus, her son was taken away between two soldiers to face Captain Sylvain Corbigny, reporter to the third court martial, charged with the examination of the affair.

IV
The Examination

Captain Sylvain Corbigny was a man of valor and foresight, an officer of integrity and an impartial judge, but he had one terrible eccentricity: he detested Bretons.

Poor Mathurin was decidedly unlucky, and one could willingly have lent credence to the peasant superstition that attributed that to the evil spell cast by the Red Sorcerer. All skeptical minds know that reality sometimes accumulates the most overwhelming circumstances on the head of a single individual; the innocent suffer and the guilty triumph.

The enmity of the captain with regard to everything that emanated from Bretagne—people and things—had its source in a simple point of pride. Sylvain Corbigny had graduated seventh from Saint-Maixent; number six in his class was a Breton, whom he had promised himself to emulate, if not to surpass, in life. Now, the Breton had been decorated first; he was now the colonel of a colonial infantry regiment in West Africa, and was due to receive the stars at his next promotion by reason of the rapidity and skill by which he had put down the uprising of an indigenous tribe. That had brought his jealousy to a peak;

his envy had only increased with chagrin, and he had vowed an implacable hatred to the Bretons; everything that was Breton had no mercy in his eyes.

Although he was as scantly modern as possible, in his thinking and in his sentiments, he was gripped by the need that devours almost everything in the world nowadays: advertisement, fame, publicity . . .

Now, whereas journalists filled their pages with detailed accounts of the deeds of his former classmate, while the latter's portrait was reproduced everywhere, in the daily papers as well as the weekly and monthly magazines, Captain Sylvain Cordigny remained in the shadows; no one was occupied with him, and yet he was furiously ambitious for the intoxication of those fumes of glory, the consecration of the press.

The newspapers had made a great deal of noise about the affair with which he was charged: the aggression committed by the fireman Mathurin Dagorne against his superior officer and his eventual culpability in the crime of the Rue de Turenne, but discipline was rigorous at the Cherche-Midi; the journalists ran into an absolute silence imposed by the regulations, and, to the great despair of Sylvain Corbigny, they could not get as far as him, any more than he would have been able to grant them an interview.

Public opinion began to lose interest in the two affairs that attempts had been made to connect, all the more so because a political event arrived to deflect attention.

Captain Corbigny pursued his investigation with the particular state of mind that had made him say, on the first day; "He's a Breton. That doesn't astonish me—one can expect anything on the part of those individuals."

He had accepted the accusations as they had been formulated by the commissaire de police and his secretary, without trying to look any deeper, beyond the appearances. In brief, he did not act with his habitual conscience and impartiality because he was dealing with a Breton.

The affair was, however, sufficiently complicated and murky to impassion its examiner. On the other hand, Mathurin, by his attitude, laid himself open to all suppositions.

Today, after the touching interview that he had had with his mother, he was to submit to a definitive interrogation; and the deceptive torpor that he could not succeed in shaking off was not likely to dissipate the captain's animosity.

"Let's see, Sapeur Dagorne," the officer said to him, harshly, "you're going to try to respond clearly to my questions, so that we can clarify all this . . ."

Short and fat, with a drooping moustache, small eyes and a ruddy complexion, he was sitting at the modest little table of black wood that served as his desk, and his gaze tried to scrutinize the tall, thickset fellow with the bowed head and the almost disquieting manner enclosed in a persistent mutism that made him impatient.

"Let's take things *ab ovo*," he said. "Captain Christian Bataille had charged you with taking a letter to his uncle, Clodomir Fargeau, in the Rue de Turenne. You claim that you didn't go there?"

"No," said Mathurin, dully.

"No . . . then how do you explain your disobedience to an order given by your captain?"

Mathurin shrugged his shoulders and responded, mechanically: "I don't know."

"That's not an answer. Come on, at least try to defend yourself; you're aggravating your case by denying with such obstinacy. You're encouraging the supposition that you were equally involved in the crime . . ."

"The crime . . . the crime . . ." he stammered.

"Yes, the old man strangled, in a cowardly fashion, in his bed, and his house then burgled."

"I don't know anything, I swear . . . I didn't see anything!"

"However, when you came to bring the letter to Clodomir Fargeau . . ."

"I didn't give the letter to Clodomir Fargeau . . . I didn't see Clodomir Fargeau . . ."

The captain raised his eyes to the ceiling and muttered between his teeth: "These Bretons! What stubborn . . ." Then, in a loud voice, addressing Msthurin: "This is what happened: with your captain's automobile you came to the Rue de Turenne. You gave the letter to Monsieur Fargeau, who, after taking cognizance of it, gave you two or three hundred francs, perhaps more. On the way, you had encountered comrades . . . Bretons . . . you had been drinking in order to give you the courage to carry through your villainous task and finish what your accomplice had already begun . . ."

"My accomplice?" Mathurin repeated. "What accomplice?"

"The woman who was in intimate association with your captain and who must have served to lure him into the trap . . ."

"That woman . . . I don't know her," said the fireman.

At the same time, the story that he had heard while he was collapsed, in a profound somnolence, on the glacis of the fortifications, returned to him vaguely.[1]

On that sinister night, his brain had been so jolted, shaken in all directions, that his nightmares and the reality were mingled, and the conference that he had overheard without being aware of it was mingled with all that, without him being able to discern what role he had played in the affair.

And he confessed, naively: "That woman . . . I don't know her . . . I've never seen her . . . but it seems to me that I've heard mention of her . . . if I remember correctly, she was called Gros-Tas . . . yes, that's it, Gros-Tas . . . there were men with her, who had bizarre names . . ."

---

1 This evidently refers to an episode that is not in the text, which must have occurred in the interval between the end of chapter I of Part Two and the beginning of chapter II. It might have been omitted accidentally from the text prepared for printing, but it is more likely that the author, making up the story as he went along while it was being published on a daily basis, introduced it as a belated improvisation. It is not the only one, as can be seen in the remainder of the present chapter, which is replete with contradictions.

"How do you know that?"

"A nightmare...?"

"Not entirely ... what you're telling me happened ... oh, what does it mean? Were you also involved in that terrible crime? Until now, it had been attributed to apaches ... were you acquainted with those people?"

"No, not at all ..."

"Well then, what is the significance of all these stories you're telling? More strange coincidences ... there's nothing comprehensible in your entire story. What is certain, nevertheless, is that you've played a villainous role in this ..."

The hypothesis that had been envisaged at first, and which wanted to make Mathurin the murderer of Clodomir Fargeau, the captain had gradually set aside when he had learned from the housekeeper of the old bachelor that the latter had received a young woman on the evening of the crime, who had the habit of coming to his house once or twice a week, and with whom he sometimes spent the night.

Now, that young woman had disappeared abruptly, and no more mention had been heard of her. The concierge, who knew her, had given a description of her, but nothing else was known about her—her name or her address—with the consequence that she remained undiscoverable in spite of fruitful searches.

It was probable that she, with an accomplice, was the author of the crime.

The officer had asked several times whether Mathurin was that accomplice, and he succeeded in dispelling that suspicion almost entirely. However, he had not yet received the reports of the official physicians who had been charged with the autopsy of the cadaver, and they were about to shake his conviction.

A young doctor, wanting to attract attention to himself, had repeated with more success the experiments that an American scientist had carried out on animals, notably oxen. Those trials, still vague, had demonstrated that the last spectacle situated in the visual field of a dying being remained fixed indissolubly on the retina, and that a simple photograph of the eyes would cause the last objects that had impressed it to appear.[1] He therefore applied that discovery and photographed the eye of the victim, Clodomir Fargeau. He obtained a very blurred print, but in which the head of a man could be distinguished. He even found a certain resemblance to Mathurin.

"The pompier really is the murder," concluded the young scientist, in a detailed report that he had addressed to the captain reporter. "It's him that the victim saw, in a last glimmer of intelligence; his image was fixed on his retina, as if on a sensitive plate. The proof is there, material and overwhelming. Science is infallible."

That discovery made a great noise in all milieux, above all in that of medicine, where it provoked polemics. Old scientists, members of the Académie, contested its value, the invention of an American, as an infantile, utopian idea, an insane dream.

The young doctor's idea foundered under scorn and ridicule. The captain had had no need of the attestation of the princes of science to set aside the discovery of the young scientist ambitious for fame.

Sylvain Corbigny was not modern, and everything that emanated from science he held in perfect indifference, citing personal anecdotes in support.

"The proof that physicians are mistaken all the time is that I, myself, was nearly discharged because I had a cardiac affliction. Well, I've made campaigns, and that hasn't prevented me from still being solid . . . I was forbidden to smoke, but I smoke good cigars and it hasn't done me any harm. I was forbidden absinthe, but I drink it every day and I'm no worse for it . . ."

With that excessive disdain for science, he had not been embarrassed for long by the affirmations of the young doctor.

---

1 This ludicrous myth had a considerable pedigree in popular fiction; the author was undoubtedly aware of its spectacular deployment in Villiers de l'Isle Adam's "Claire Lenoir" (1867).

"A head in an eye!" he exclaimed, shrugging his shoulders. "A head in an eye! Is that possible?"

In that epoch, in addition, the letter that Mathurin had been charged with handing to Clodomir Fargeau was found by rag-pickers on the glacis of the fortification and handed in to the law. The unfortunate Breton must have lost it during his errant course. The discovery of that letter outside the domicile of the murdered man was the annihilation of the principal grievance that could be directed at the pompier in the matter of the jeweler's murder.

The captain reporter thus disinterested himself in the civil affair in order to occupy himself exclusively with the military affair: the aggression committed by the pompier on his superior officer. The crime of the Rue de Turenne was handed over to an examining magistrate, who pursued his investigation with no more success than the captain reporter.

Several times, Captain Christian Bataille was called to testify; he never wanted to accuse his chauffeur. On the contrary, he tried to defend him and to discharge him.

"That boy is innocent. He has my complete confidence; he has never abused it. Why would he have imagined this coup? He had no interest in carrying it out . . ."

"Does one ever know, with a fellow as sly and as secretive," Corbigny replied. "There was certainly an idea in his head . . . as for getting it out, it's necessary not to count on that . . ."

"The poor fellow is unrecognizable since his arrest . . . and that's understandable, given the blow he must have received. Before, he was very frank and open . . ."

"You're truly too good, captain, to want to disculpate him, when everything condemns him: his attitude, first of all, the lack of energy with which he defends himself and his contradictory allegations . . . his actions. What is the significance of the sort of madness that suddenly took possession of him on the night of the murder? A wine-merchant in Billancourt remembers having been obliged to throw him out; he had no more money and was very drunk. The employees at the customs post stopped him to ask about his gasoline; he did not seem to understand and departed without warning, like a madman. I've succeeded in gathering that information. Everywhere he passed, that strange madness was observed . . ."

"It was doubtless drunkenness that provoked it."

"Certainly he was drunk; but there was something other than drunkenness: remorse! In any case, he has not yet departed from that depressed attitude. And what about your automobile, which he abandoned without knowing what he had done with it? I presume that he got out, in the vicinity of the Porte Maillot, to which he returned, drawn by the obsession that attracts the guilty to the place where they carried out their crimes. Overwhelmed by drunkenness and remorse, he forgot it and set off no matter where, straight ahead, to end up on the glacis, where he was discovered by the agents."

"Circumstances seem to be conspiring against the poor fellow. I assure you, in my soul and my conscience, that he isn't guilty."

Unfortunately, Christian Bataille's conviction was unsupported by any evidence. It was a personal opinion, of which Sylvain Corbigny could scarcely take account; he only envisaged the facts, in their brutality.

Mathurin was imprisoned, in the claws of military justice; he only had to pronounce one word to liberate himself, but that word he never pronounced. He resigned himself voluntarily to his fate. He had made the sacrifice of his life to Françoise, his Françoise, whom he had always loved, whom he perhaps loved more than ever, in spite of her apparent ignominy. Without her, the future was unimportant to him; he was ready in advance to accept the verdict of fatality.

IV
The Obsession of Remorse

Tête-Rouge was decidedly a master. He had no peer for escaping the gleaming eye of the law when he had committed some crime. And it was thus that, on that tragic night, he had been able to conduct three criminal affairs without their resulting in any inconvenience for him. He had emerged with clean hands.

However, he had thought it prudent to regulate his landlord's invoices; he had sold his furniture, not wanting to embarrass himself with it, and had quit the Rue Pigalle for a more tranquil quarter, where it was certain that no one would come to look for him.

He had therefore taken up residence, with Françoise, in a furnished house in the Rue des Entrepreneurs. He had before him a tidy sum that permitted him to live well, all the more so because his woman continued to work; she had simply changed her field of operations.

Françoise no longer had anything in common with the coarse peasant girl that Tête-Rouge had abducted from her family. She was singularly slender and refined; she had a slim waist ad an elegant stride. In a word, she was one of those plumed, perfumed and well-dressed Parisiennes toward whom men turned with covetousness in their gaze. Nor was she any longer the outrageously made-up and provocative prostitute upon whose person every man fixed his intentions. On the contrary, she had an elegantly discreet, scrupulously engaging appearance. She could stroll nonchalantly before the counters of an elegant shop in the Chausée-d'Antin at the hour of affluence, playing the buyer . . . and never bought anything, her eyes ferreting, lying in ambush for masculine gazes.

From time to time she perceived a chic man in the crowd, with a suit and overcoat in the latest fashion and a tilted hat; that was Tête-Rouge, come to make sure that she was at her post and working conscientiously.

More than before she needed to feel his influence; as soon as she was alone, memories assailed her and she was clawed by the obsession of remorse.

It was always the crime that unfurled before her eyes, with its frightful peripeties . . . that unfortunate old man for whom she experienced more than sympathy, it had been necessary for her to kill, for the cupid pleasure of Tête-Rouge; and she had obeyed, fascinated by his violet eyes. She would never have had the strength if she had not felt them, very close to her, at the head of the bed.

And she had carried out her ignoble task without a tremor, without any hesitation.

But what an upheaval there had been when the door had opened abruptly and she had recognized Mathurin, her fiancé, the man she had been fleeing with so much care for such a long time. He had recognized her, he had stammered her name. Oh, why had destiny reserved such an encounter for her, at such a terrible moment, the most terrible of her entire existence?

Her calm had suddenly disappeared, giving way to an inde-scribable disarray, but the energetic hand of Tête-Rouge had fallen upon her, had lifted her up with a vigorous gesture, and it had been necessary for her to continue her abominable work to the end.

After having been a murderer, she had been a thief. It was her who had guided Tête-Rouge through the house where everything was familiar to her. It was her who had revealed the secret of the strong-box . . . and then, in haste, she had got dressed, no matter how . . . and they had fled, with a thousand precautions, while the old man, pale and decomposed, lying on the disordered bed, had accompanied them with his immutable and horrified gaze.

Oh, that gaze pursued her; that was what she saw when she closed her eyelids, whether she was going to sleep, or pensive, or in the arms of a temporary lover. It was only in the presence of Tête-Rouge that it left her in peace.

Her brain, which had known a relative quietude for a while, was more obsessed than ever. Mathurin had awakened the dear memories that were slumbering in her soul. Again she thought about her father and mother, her brothers and sisters, who remained out there is the homeland . . . and she thought about Carnac, about the heath, so beautiful when the gorse covered it with a living layer of gold; she thought about the vast field of great ancient stones where the two of them, she and Mathurin, loved so much to lose themselves in long reveries.

And she regretted her projects, the honest and placid existence of which she had dreamed, similar to that of her parents and grandparents . . .

Françoise was unhappy, therefore, very unhappy. However, she had not yet reached the climax of dolor; life still had rude ordeals in store for her. The poor girl, whose heart had remained pure and good in spite of the shameful compromises of her flesh, had always had a sincere amour for the man who had been her fiancé, the Mathurin who had been the companion of her existence, a solid sentiment having nothing in common with the strange bond that attached her to Tête-Rouge. So, what a chagrin came to hurt her pained heart, her bruised soul, two days after the fatal day.

It was always with new anxiety that she unfolded the newspaper every morning, and she could not retain a scream on perceiving the headline: ACCUSED POMPIER MATHURIN DAGORNE IN THE CHERCHE-MIDI.

He was accused simultaneously of the murder in the Rue de Turenne and the attack in the Bois de Bouolgne, when he was innocent of both!

And as Tête-Rouge was absent just then, she had been able to weep at her ease for that worthy fellow, who could have denounced her but preferred to say nothing, doubtless in order to protect her.

"He still loves me, in spite of the odious crime . . ."

She reproached herself for not doing anything to get him out of that trouble, although he had not hesitated to sacrifice himself. But she did not know how to do it; she was afraid of Tête-Rouge.

Several days passed, bringing her some relief—that of seeing Mathurin disengaged from the responsibility of the murder: *The law in searching in vain for the guilty parties*, the newspaper said; *they are undiscoverable . . .*

But the second affair continued to weigh upon the pompier's shoulders; no one seemed to want to disengage him from it.

She thought about writing to the captain reporter to reveal the true guilty parties to him, under the cover of anonymity, but she did not have the courage to undertake such a task; she was too cowardly for that . . . she feared the vengeance of Tête-Rouge.

To go there? That was scarcely possible either; the consequences would be felt.

She could not, however, allow him to be condemned; that would be unforgivable. What could she do?

Discreetly, she made enquiries of comrades, and learned that Mathurin might well be condemned to death.

A terrible struggle was engaged in her conscience. All her scruples vanished; she took advantage of an amorous caprice on the part of Tête-Rouge to escape from his authority on a day when he had a rendezvous with a famous singer.

She went to the Cherche-Midi, ready to reveal everything she knew in order to save Mathurin. She would denounce Gros-Tas, Gueule-d'Amour and Nez-de-Coq. She would dare to pronouce the name of Tête-Rouge. She would say where they had sold the captain's watch and gold pencil; she would indicate their lair, all the things that she had heard repeated several times before . . .

And the pompier would soon be cleared of the accusations unjustly brought against him.

She was so firmly determined that she did not have a moment's hesitation on the way. On the contrary, the closer she came to the military prison, the firmer her courage became. But a powerful emotion awaited her a few meters from the sad buildings.

She perceived, twenty paces away, an old woman dressed in a Breton costume who was coming out of the prison, and it seemed to her that she recognized her.

Her heart began to pound in her breast; she passed her hand over her eyes, looked again, and her legs gave way when she recognized the face, tanned by the sea breeze and wrinkled by old age.

She only went on unsteadily, her legs weak, and when she was before her compatriot she stopped, stammering incomprehensible words.

The latter looked her up and down, astonished to be examined thus by an elegant Parisienne, but as she stared at her, her eyes widened, and were soon impregnated with wrath.

"Françoise! God! Is it possible?" she cried, raising her arms to the heavens,

"Mère Dagorne . . . yes . . . it's me. You recognize me," the prostitute replied, feebly.

The old woman continued examining her, minutely, with amazement.

"Lord! *Ma doué!* How you've changed," she said, inspecting her from head to toe. "What are you doing in Paris?" she interrogated, still containing the anger growling within her.

Françoise blushed and lowered her head,

The old woman remained pensive for a moment, still studying her. She discovered the multicolored traces of make-up, scented a violent perfume, recoiled, opened her mouth, closed it again, and then murmured:

"Ah! That's what you've become in Paris . . . The life! Well, it's appropriate, my girl . . ."

Overwhelmed by all the disdain and criticism contained in that speech, Françoise could only lower her head. And the old woman, grimly, clenching her fists on her hips, lashed her with hateful phrases:

"Here you are, dragged, in the dirt, soiled, dust-rag! It's you who made the misfortune of my Mathurin. If he hadn't known you, good-for-nothing, he wouldn't be where he is. Everything that has happened to him is your fault. I've come to Paris, although I swore to the good God that I'd never set for in this infernal city . . . I've come even so, in order to embrace Mathurin one last time . . . but it's stronger than me. I can't go back right away . . . I want to be here until the day of his condemnation. Oh, yes, slut, everything that has happened is your fault . . . and I encounter you here. It's only you who could be still prowling around him, monstrous woman!"

"Oh, Mère Dagorne," she tried to interject. "If you knew . . ."

"I don't want to know anything about you. Go on your way. I curse you! Whore! Whore!"

Before Françoise had had time to make a gesture or say a word to retain her and explain herself, Mère Dangorne had shoved her aside and strode away, leaning on her blue cotton umbrella.

Françoise took more than five minutes to pull herself together, and, trembling she headed toward the sentry, her ears still buzzing with the insults hurled by the old peasant.

"Where is it necessary to go to speak to the captain reporter of the third court martial?"

The soldier replied, with a smile in the corner of his eyes: "Go across the courtyard, lovely girl, and take the first door opposite."

She thanked him, and drew away in the direction indicated.

"What is she going to do there?" muttered the soldier, following her with his eyes.

She had sensed that the soldier, like Mère Dagorne, was reproaching her for loose morals, and that constricted her heart. She took account of how disparate her costume and manner were, in this glacially bare military milieu, with the heavy chained doors armed with enormous padlocks and huge locks.

The soldier on guard at the captain's door scanned her slyly before going to announce to Sylvain Corbigny that she had expressed the desire to see him.

The officer was in a murderous mood that afternoon; his former classmate was still cluttering the newspapers; that was enough for him. So, when the sentry said to him: "Captain, there's a woman who wants to speak to you about the Dagorne affair," he cried:

"Good God! What does she want with me? What is her name?"

"She didn't give her name."

"What does she look like?"

"Oh . . . Captain, she looks like a very light woman . . ."

"A whore, here!" cried the officer, striking the table with his fist. "Have her thrown out . . . and right away. If one wanted to listen to women like that, one would never finish . . ."

With one bound he opened the door of his office and arrived facing Françoise.

"What do you want?"

"I'd like to talk to you about Mathurin Dagorne. I have proof that he's . . ."

"Leave me in peace! You're bothering me; I don't have time to listen to gossip of women of your sort . . ."

"But . . . but . . . Monsieur . . . Captain . . ." The poor girl stammered, utterly confused by that welcome.

"Throw that whore out, and right away. Go on! Move! Get out! There's no brothel here; there's no lantern or big number above the door."

And the soldier took her by the arm and dragged her toward the staircase. She tried to escape,

"Listen to me! It's a matter of a man's life! I have proof that he's innocent!"

Sylvain Corbigny paid no further attention to her; he went back into his office with a sigh of relief.

"No one's going go listen to me, then? However, it's the truth that I want to reveal. Mathurin is innocent. An innocent man is going to be condemned. Let me speak and I'll tell everything."

The soldier was not even listening to what she said, and dragged her away.

"If you think the captain has time to listen to your nonsense, girl . . . you've doubtless had a glass too many and it's loosened your tongue. Get out."

Heart-broken by her impotence to reveal the truth, Françoise started to sob painfully, and she quit the prison, overwhelmed, tottering like a drunken woman.

VI
The Relentlessness of Fatality

In the large, glacially bare hall, the court martial had assembled.

After having consulted his assessors, the president, a colonel, made a sign to the clerk.

"Bring in the sapeur-pompier Mathurin Dagorne," ordered the latter.

The Breton, in his service uniform but devoid of arms, made his appearance between four infantry soldiers bearing arms. He was bleak, as usual. When he penetrated into the room, however, and perceived the military tribunal that was about to judge him, he went slightly pale. He sank on to the bench of the accused. Two soldiers took their places to either side of him, and two others behind him.

"Stand up," commanded the clerk.

Mathurin obeyed, without daring to cast a glance around the room, his head bowed and his eyes bleak.

"Your name?" demanded the president.

"Mathurin Dagorne," replied a dull voice.

"Your age and place of birth?"

"Carnac, twenty-first of December 1884."

"You've been in service for a year with the sapeur-pompiers, at the Cité barracks, where you were Captain Christian Bataille's chauffeur?"

"Yes, *mon colonel*," the accused replied.

"You've been summoned before us today," the president continued, "for attempted murder with premeditation, acts of violence and setting a trap for the person of your superior. You fall under the scope of articles 295 and 296 of the Penal Code and article 14 of the Military Code, thus conceived: *Acts of violence toward a superior outside of the service or without there being any occasion of service: five to ten years of public labor.*"

Mathurin bowed his head, overwhelmed and impotent.

"Mathurin Dagorne," repeated the colonel, "we shall proceed to hear the witnesses; then we shall hear the official defender designated to you." And, addressing the lieutenant clerk: "Call the witnesses."

The military tribunal heard, successively, Captain Bataille and three or four pompiers; all were in accord regarding the honesty of Mathurin, who had been an exemplary soldier since his incorporation.

Then came the summoned witnesses: the employees of the customs post, and the innkeepers in whose establishments the pompier had stopped. Then the president gave the floor to his defender, a trainee advocate who strove to prove that he was innocent, with no great enthusiasm or conviction. He struck his breast awkwardly, juggling humanitarian ideas, the tearful old mother, and vituperated maladroitly against the inflexibility of military justice. The tribunal was not moved for a second by that speech, with produced instead an impression of coldness.

"Accused, have you anything to add in your defense?"

Mathurin, dazed, stood up from his bench and, not even having the courage or the audacity to disculpate himself, he said in a low, scarcely perceptible voice: "No, nothing."

"The floor is given to the commissaire of the government," pronounced the president

The latter—a commandant—stood up, and his and voice resonated in the bare room:

"Messieurs, the sapeur Mathurin Dagorne, in spite of his excellent antecedents, is undoubtedly the author of the aggression committed against Captain Christian Bataille. Although he has not confessed, his attitude alone would condemn him if there were not the evidence accumulated against him. Why does he persist in claiming that he did not carry out the commission entrusted to him by the captain, and without offering any excuses? And what does that hectic race through the streets of Paris signify? Was it not the result of panic, of remorse? I request, in consequence, the full and entire application of the law."

The commissaire of the government sat down again, and the president asked the accused again: "Mathurin Dagorne, have you anything to add in your defense?"

The Breton shook himself slightly, and replied, in a hoarse voice: "It wasn't me who did that . . . no . . . no!" And he fell back on his bench, his head in his hands, weeping hot tears, with sobs that tore his breast.

"The council will deliberate," announced the president, standing up, followed by the assessors. The military tribunal went into the chamber of deliberation.

There were few auditors in the hall, journalists and comrades of the regiment, and it was scarcely possible to make out, in the shadow of a pillar, a white Breton bonnet agitated by slight tremors. Almost all of them were indifferent to the fate that the tribunal reserved for Mathurin; she alone awaited the result of the discussion anxiously.

Her exceedingly wrinkled face had an earthen pallor, her eyes were reddened by tears; large sobs shook her, but in spite of that, she still found the strength to raise herself up on tiptoe from time to time in order to dart a glance at her son in the distance. And her chagrin was redoubled; dolor tore her breast; her head was on fire. Her teeth convulsed and started to chatter when the judges filed back in and resumed their respective places.

The president, with a piece of paper in hand, began to read the verdict.

"The court martial of Paris, united at the request of the colonel commandant of the regiment of sapeur-pompiers in order to judge Sapeur Mathurin Dagorne following an attempt of murder with premeditation, setting a trap and assault on the person of his superior, Captain Bataille, a crime foreseen and punished by the law, in the presence of the witnesses, the commissaire of the government in his conclusions and the defender of the accused, condemns the accused to ten years of public labor."

The poor mother opened haggard, crazed eyes; she hung on to a pillar, for she felt her legs giving way beneath her; her throat contacted atrociously and a strangled cry expired on her lips:

"Oh, my poor lad!"

The guttural exclamation resounded in the silent hall, and gazes turned toward the old Bretonne, who buckled and soon collapsed on the floor-tiles.

People hastened around her, but she seemed profoundly unconscious; a doctor who was there leaned over her in order to give her the necessary cares, but he stood up again, very grave, and said solemnly to the witness of the brief and painful scene: "The unfortunate woman is dead."

Dolor had struck Mère Dagorne down.

She had struggled courageously until the end, sustained by a supreme and last hope; the pious woman had prayed a great deal, convinced the God would hear her prayer and grant her wish . . . but fatality had continued to weigh relentlessly upon her son.

At the announcement of his condemnation—ten years of public labor—there had been an upheaval within her of which her heart and brain, worn away by old age and toil, had been unable to support the shock. Her ultimate thought had been for the Red Sorcerer and the influence of his evil eye, which she had not, alas, been able to ward off.

The old Bretonne, steeped in the traditions and customs of her homeland, who had always nourished for progress and for Paris—which summarized it in her eyes—a grim hatred, had just died in the city that she abhorred: a strange coincidence of destiny.

✳

The *Ville-de-Zéred*, the Bône mailboat,[1] was rolling strong—there was a heavy swell—and on board, almost all the passengers were sick.

Plaints, gasps and maledictions rose from the cabins, were the fortunate voyagers lost consciousness, exhausted by twenty hours crossing an inclement sea in the stifling atmosphere of the steamer.

On deck, alongside the engine, the other passengers where leaning, pale and silent, in front of the barrier to first class—distances were still maintained, whatever the milieu and in spite of the circumstances.

There were Italians there going to spend a season in Algeria, to work in tanneries or charcoal factories to bring back a few

---

1 The town of Bône in the French colony of Algeria, near the Tunisian border, which became an important industrial center under French rule, is nowadays known as Annaba.

sous; the inevitable Kabyle returning to his homeland after making his fortune—a relative fortune earned with difficulty selling Egyptian carpets bought in the Place de Clichy on the terraces of cafés, along with goatskins masquerading as sheepskins and wallets and purses braided with gold originating from the Rue du Sentier; and finally, coupled two by two like beasts of burden, soldiers, the refuse of metropolitan courts martial escorted by five gendarmes, sailing to Africa for public labor.

Pale and thin—the diet of military prisons is not fattening—they went like wild beasts, at the rear of the steamer, from the crew quarters to the bunkers, bleak and taciturn, tortured by seasickness.

Their garments—all that the chief could find in the stores of the most wretched at the moment of departure—hung loosely over their thin bodies, and, leaning over the side with curious eyes, they searched for the coast of Africa, the goal of their involuntary voyage.

Suddenly, they were seen to gather together like hungry dogs; a sailor brought a vast cooking-pot filled with a vague bean-soup. He placed it on the deck, distributed a piece of bread to each man and disappeared through a hatchway.

The sea had calmed down; they all rushed toward the cauldron, followed by the inquisitive and suspicious gaze of the gendarmes who were conveying them from Marseille to Bône, where they would hand the consignment of military convicts over to the penitentiary administration.

In a few seconds, those hungry jaws would have cleaned the plates.

Only one prisoner, still dressed in the somber uniform of the pompiers of Paris, had not approached; leaning on the rail, his gaze distant, he was following with a bleak eye the flight of a seagull, or perhaps the smoke of the engine, which was flowing toward France, carried by the breeze.

Since Marseille he had not taken any nourishment, enclosing himself in an obstinate mutism, not addressing a word to anyone. Ignoring his companions in misfortune, he was sunk in endless meditations; nothing could loosen his tongue.

"Well, you're not eating, Pompier?" said a sympathetic gendarme.

"The others have had my share," Mathurin said, in a low voice, without raising his head, without emerging from his reverie, contemplating the blue sea that reminded him a little of his dear Bretagne—the sea that had been the shroud and the tomb of his father.

But the worthy guard doubtless had his obsession; he returned to the charge, taking advantage of the fact that his brigadier was somnolent, exhausted by fatigue. He approached the convict.

"You don't seem to be a bad fellow. You have an honest face, you aren't like all these other rogues."

"I'm not hungry; I don't want anything; leave me alone."

"Leave you alone?" retorted the gendarme. "Are you mad? Come on, don't put on airs. What have you done to be transported?"

"Nothing."

"Nothing! You all say the same thing. If one listened to you, you're as innocent as a new-born lamb. Have you got a long time?"

"Ten years. It's nothing . . ."

"Don't be silly, old man; do as the others do, laugh instead of curling up miserably in a corner. Your companions—they're amusing themselves."

In fact, the other prisoners were going back and forth on deck; groups had formed at the whim of amities or countries of origin; watched by the gendarmes who, revolvers in their belts, were guarding the passage from port to starboard, they were singing a barrière refrain:

When a little kid
Wants to idle around
And not go to work
You have to kill her . . .

Insensible to that unreflective gaiety, the former pompier had plunged back into bleak dejection, his eyes lost over the sea, in the distance extending as far as the eye could see, blue, green and gray, translucent under the glare of the setting sun.

The benevolent gendarme was still examining him with an expression of commiseration; he had approached the rail on which he was still leaning and took him by his tunic

"What, then? You haven't eaten anything at all? You must be hungry?"

Mathurin shrugged his shoulders indifferently, which signified: *What's the point of eating, now? Why live?* Insensible to the pangs of his stomach, he was entirely given to the sorrows of destiny.

"Decidedly," said the gendarme, "you're not a fellow like the others, I've already taken loads to the labor, but I've never seen one like you. It's tedious, I know, but why torture yourself. One comes back, you know. So don't get upset!"

And as he still made no reply, the gendarme took a small bottle of wine, a hunk of bread and a few slices of sausage from his sack, which his far-sighted housekeeper had carefully wrapped in silk paper.

"Here, eat! That'll put a little heart in your belly!"

The soldier looked at him with astonishment, stupefied by such an impulse; he was not used to being so well treated.

"That's for me?" he interrogated, fearfully, like a beaten dog.

"Yes, of course," replied the gendarme. "Eat, old chap; you're hurting me. Eat, while the others can't see."

"Thank you," he stammered, gratefully, with tears in his eyes. "Truly, it's not worth the trouble . . ." Then, after a pause; "Worthy men exist, then?"

"Shut up and be quick."

But Mathurin, recaptured by his somber ideas, had already fallen back into his black reverie; his eyes were lost over the water, while he broke up his bread and swallowed it in large mouthfuls.

Moved, and content with his good deed, the gendarme drew away to call the other convicts to order, who were signing at the top of their voices, to the tune of the Marseillaise:

> *Ohé, you convicts,*
> *Raise your standards . . .*
> *Slash and break your guards*
> *To make black pudding*
> *For the dogs!*

The sea, in the vicinity of the coast, was becoming increasingly choppy; already, Fort Gênois and the Cap de Garde had been doubled; the cone of Mont Edough was making a delightful backcloth of verdure for the city, its wooded slopes, in the midst of vines and orchards, extended, white and elegant, all the way to the sea.

The brigadier and the gendarme took a few utensils from their pockets and, in a fragment of mirror posed on a packet of cables, made a summery toilette, saluted by the jeers of the prisoners.

"What—the polichinelles are going to make eyes at the natives . . . no, but we'll tell your wives . . ."

"Silence in the ranks," commanded the brigadier. "Shut your traps and get your things ready in your distribution sacks; we'll be arriving in a few minutes. Try to conduct yourselves like demoiselles at confession . . . otherwise, when we disembark, I'll make a report to the square, and watch out!"

The men fell silent under that threat, and packed their clothes; then, grouped to port, they examined the coast.

Villas elegantly posed along the shore, bathing establishment, the Rocher de Lion . . . The *Ville-de-Zéred* entered the outer harbor and came to dock as the sun disappeared behind the summits of the Djebel Edough.

There was then a rush of Arab commissionaires and merchants pressing around the passengers. When a relative calm had returned, the prisoners, still framed by their guards, their heads on fire, exhausted by a voyage effectuated in the worst conditions, were lined up on the quay.

A sergeant of the penitentiary was waiting for them. The brigadier of the gendarmerie exchanged a few words with him in a low voice, and then the soldier commanded: "By twos, forward march! And the little troop moved off via the Quai Warnier and winding back-streets—in order to avoid going through the town—toward the kasbah, guided by the sergeant, who examined the prey of the latest trip with a searching eye.

The ancient kasbah of Bône, which serves as the military penitentiary, has been entirely rebuilt since the capture of the town. Nothing remains of the old Turkish building but the entrance gate and a few cisterns. From the top of the hill of Sautons the view extends splendidly. It is an admirable panorama over the entire town, white under the blue sky, over the gulf with azure waves and the verdant plain.

As soon as the prisoners had crossed the threshold of the antique fortress they understood what had become of their liberty. An indefinable sentiment of sadness invaded the most insouciant, even those who had filled the air with their lewd refrains a little while ago.

Night had almost fallen. The sergeant summoned a tirailleur,[1] who came back after a few seconds accompanied by a sergeant-major.

"Oh, it's you, Crassni," said the latter, you've come from the port—you've been to fetch this rabble. There's a good measure this time, we'll be busy. There's exactly one person per cell." Then, to the brigadier: "Have you any complaint to make of these lascars? We could turn the screws on two or three, you know, to make our premises known to them. Necessary not to inconvenience you . . ."

"No, chief, everything went smoothly. These are the identity papers and documents that were given to me in Marseille at Fort Saint-Jean, as well as the list from the boat."

"Perfect."

The sergeant-major took cognizance of the papers, made the roll call and inspected each of the men, who had lined up in the courtyard, at an order from the sergeant, under the uncertain glow of a lantern.

When he arrived at Mathurin, he examined him and said: "Aha! A pompier . . . number 3474. That's good. What has this client done?" He looked through the papers and his face expanded when he saw the reason for the condemnation. "So Monsieur took against his captain," he insinuated, sarcastically. "Perfect! We'll take care of Monsieur . . . we'll make his existence so agreeable that he won't want to leave us."

That pleasantry terminated, he saluted the gendarmes, who, after having delivered their "merchandise" went into the town to await the departure of the next steamboat.

"Poor buggers!" said one of them. "You never know what can happen to you. They have no chance; I feel sorry for them."

When the heavy door had closed upon the worthy guardsmen, the "double" said to Crassni: "While places are found in

1 The *régiment de tirailleurs Algérien* [Algerian light infantry] was one of the principal native regiments recruited by the French colonial army. It still exists, but changed its name after Algeria became independent.

the lock-up for all these cocos, stick them in cells for me on a diet of bread and water . . . the crossing has fatigued their stomachs and it'll put them right. And you lot, pay attention: if we hear singing in the prisons, watch out! Tomorrow, reveille at four o'clock; you'll be given suitable garments and the depot barber will make billiard balls of your heads. By the left, march, and into the bin, you load of garbage!"

Mathurin spent a terrible night. He appealed in vain to sleep to put a little calm in his brain, put out of order by the succession of crushing events, pursed by disquieting hallucinations and painful memories: his poor mother, dead of chagrin at the announcement of his condemnation, and the face of his Françoise, lost to him forever. For the poor innocent did not even think of revolting against the injustice of fate; he accepted the dictates of his destiny benevolently, although the prospect of staying for ten years in this strange milieu frightened him a little, and he wished that death would abridge his torment.

Finally, at about three o'clock, he became drowsy, and had murky and fatiguing dreams, in the midst of which he was abruptly woken up.

"Well! What, species of idler," howled a thunderous voice, "not yet on your feet? Necessary to get up on time or things will go badly . . ."

It was Sergeant Crassni, who had just opened the cells and was bringing the convicts out.

Other disciplinary premises poured out their contents into the courtyard of the kasbah, under the eyes of a corporal of tirailleurs. A few prisoners had to harness themselves to the corvée of the quarter. They were put in single file and the chief, followed by a man carrying garments, passed before each of them. He examined their stature briefly and threw on the ground a pair of trousers, a gray vest, a kepi with a long visor, two undershirts and a pair of crude shoes.

"Let's go—put your uniforms on and put your other clothes into the store; you'll be given smocks and a blue belt. At the double, go!"

The men undressed, without modesty and put on the gray livery of *pégriots*.

The majority accepted their new situation philosophically, even cheerfully, and mocking reflections were exchanged.

"You can boast of having a fine appearance in that dolman."

"The general is nothing by comparison with us! Nice visor! One can catch plenty of sun with that!"

"And now for twenty-five years wearing this uniform!"

"Ten for me!"

"I only have five—that's quite enough."

"And all that for having sold his clothes . . ."

"I was an ordinary brigadier; I had an innkeeper give me a jug of wine."

"Oh, it's wrong to be condemned for trivia."

"So I got ten years for desertion," said a mocking voice. "I was barred from the battalion, had a sniff in Paris, and as it was the second time I was salted!"

"Don't upset yourself, old man. It'll go by without you noticing. What if you had twenty-five years, like me!"

"I've no desire to get upset either, old man . . . but in fact, you're a mate . . . you have the look of a good fellow. What do they call you?"

"I'm from Montparno and my name is Bengali, known as La Taupe."

"I'm from La Chapelle and the mates call me Nez-de-Coq."

"Well, we'll try not to fret, eh, Nez-de-Coq?"

Nez-de Coq! That soubriquet, pronounced twice, had made Mathurin shudder as he was putting on his new costume in a corner. He emerged from his invincible dejection to stare at the small thin man to whom that nickname belonged. His face was completely unknown to him.

"Well, why are you looking at me like that, sausage?" pronounced the other, approaching Mathurin.

The pompier turned away and Bengali, known as La Taupe, nudged Nez-de-Coq's elbow.

"Let him alone," he pronounced. "He's a bit mad, that fellow ... he never speaks to anyone. He should have been taken to Charenton."

"What did he do?" Nez-de-Coq interrogated.

"Appears that he drew his captain into an ambush in the Bois-de-Boulogne ... a dirty story ..."

"Ah!" said Nez-de-Coq.

"Yes, he got ten years for it. He's a Breton—called Mathurin, I believe ..."

"Ha ha!" sniggered the cynical Nez-de-Coq, and emitted a loud burst of laughter that astonished Bengali, alias La Taupe, who could not understand the cause of that hilarity.

"What? Why are you laughing like that?"

"No reason," the other responded. And his eyes returned to Mathurin. He saw large tears rolling down his cheeks and said, ironically, without any pity for the innocent man:

"Is he stupid to blubber like that!"

PART THREE

I
Le Banque du Travail et de l'Espargne

"Necessary to put on a new skin, Françoise," said Tête-Rouge one morning. "No more working in the Fontaine quarter and the cafés; we're going to launch ourselves in high society now, and it's your old fellow's money that will serve us."

And they went to take up residence in a pretty furnished villa in the Rue des Chatagniers, in Asnières.

That was the beginning of a new phase in the eventful existence of the couple.

"From now on," her man commanded, "you'll go to teas in chic grand hotels. They're full of foreigners with well-furnished pockets. You'll try to figure out how to profit from it, blockhead. Work hard, smarten up your ideas, Necessary that you're always working an angle. I only have a handful of your old fellow's twenty thousand bullets left—necessary that you earn, kid. In the meantime, I'll handle my own little affair . . . a marvelous affair . . ."

Françoise never knew anything about Tête-Rouge's occupations.

One day, she perceived him on the terrace of a café at the Gare Saint-Lazare, at table with strangers, making a speech accompanied by grand gestures. The next day she encountered him with Gueule-d'Amour. Finally, one morning, as she was returning to Paris after spending the night with a young Austrian, Tête-Rouge made her party to his secret.

"You know, Françoise, I'm setting up a bank."

"A bank!" she repeated, bewildered.

"Yes, a bank. When I said that I'd arrive at something, you see that I wasn't mistaken."

Françoise's astonishment did not last long. She expected anything on the part of her man.

"The future administrators will come tomorrow," he continued, "I've invited them to lunch. You'll take care of that. Necessary that we give them the impression of very chic people . . . whatever the cost. You understand, there'll be Monsieur Durand de la Bosselière, Comte Martinotte, Monsieur Miguel Ledesma y Caracas . . . wonderful fellows. It's a matter of being worldly people. You won't be at work this evening, so that everything will be ready. Here's some money, go to the market, and above all, no blunders!"

The reception was very successful, and the three guests marveled at the luxury of the table, the elegant installation of the villa, and the charm and grace of the mistress of the house.

More than ever, they put all their confidence in Tête-Rouge, certain that they were dealing with a man as honest as he was capable of conducting an establishment like the one they were planning to found.

A few days later the walls of Paris were covered with posters in which multicolored characters announced the founding of Le Banque du Travail et de l'Espargne, "an anonymous society with a capital of a million francs, entirely liquid, not counting the reserves."

And there was such a blizzard of publicity regarding the affair that clients flowed to the new establishment in the Rue Le Peletier from all the quarters of Paris, and even from the depths of the provinces.

The names of the administrators inspired such great confidence that the public was eager to obtain the company's shares; they sold "like hot cakes" at the exceptional price of two hundred and fifty francs, filling the coffers of the Banque du Travail et de l'Espargne.

The *deus ex machina*, the soul of the affair, Tête-Rouge, insisted, with admirable discretion, on remaining modestly in the shadows. He was content to supervise the cogs of the machine and to give it the impetus necessary to its good functioning.

Thus far, everything was working perfectly, of which the administrators were proud, although it was not due to their science. Their task had consisted of advancing the capital necessary to set the affair in motion. Tête-Rouge took charge of making it bear fruit.

He had done many things; the Banque du Travail et de l'Espargne was situated in one of the finest buildings in the Rue Le Peletier, in proximity to the boulevards. It occupied the entire entresol of the house, and its installation was very modern: brightly painted and papered offices, electricity in profusion, telephone, phérophone, etc., etc. The director's office was particularly sumptuous; nothing had been spared to impress visitors. The furniture was in a pure Louis XVI style, the tapestries in rich fabric It was there that "Monsieur le Directeur"—which is to say, Tête-Rouge—was enthroned, as elegant and chic as an English milord, his fingers ringed with diamonds and rubies, emitting the heady scent of *trèfle incarnat* perfume.

He was the one who received the clients when it was a matter of important orders.

One monsieur had made a placement of ten thousand francs. Tête-Rouge was able to give him good advice in order to multiply his capital tenfold in a short time.

"Buy shares in the Societé des Mines d'or de Seine-et-Oise … it's an excellent affair that we're presently in the process of launching. Take advantage of it. Since the introduction on the Bourse, they've been rising, … and rising…"

Another time, an old lady came naively to lament the meager interest on money nowadays, and Tête-Rouge, with a knowing wink, said to her: "All that depends on how one places one's money!"

The old lady, intrigued, asked for explanations, which Tête-Rouge hastened to give her. In the final count, Monsieur le Directeur learned that her portfolio contained bonds in Rente Française, Ville de Paris, Crédit Foncier, etc., etc.

"It's necessary to sell all that, dear Madame," Tête-Rouge advised, with apparent disinterest. "Those placements are not reliable . . . there might be a war . . . a change of government. So buy shares in the Mines d'or de Seine-et-Oise instead. That's a good, very safe investment . . . an investment for the father of a family, which will bring you, in spite of that, five or six per cent, if not more. It's worth considering. As for the added value, I won't mention that, although it will be considerable . . ."

The Director, on fire, launched into a dithyramb on the extraordinary fortune of certain gold mines, to which he assimilated the Societé des Mines d'or de Seine-et-Oise. He supported his affirmations with reports from engineers, plans, maps and mineral specimens . . .

The client, conquered, tempted by the lure of profit, did not hesitate for a moment, and traded her State and Ville de Paris funds for shares and obligations of the Societé des Mines d'or de Seine-et-Oise—which had never existed, of course, except in the imagination of Tête-Rouge.

Affairs marched as desired. The coffers were not emptied; the strong-boxes were garnished with varied and multicolored bonds . . .

Maids, valets de chambre, cooks, concierges, gardeners, country priests and provincial schoolteachers—all those who, by virtue of hard work and energy, had succeeded in putting a few blue bills aside—brought them or sent them to the Banque du Travail et de l'Espargne. Gold was shifted there by the handful; the administrators, although they had not yet received any indemnity, were delighted with the prosperity of their affair.

The shares, introduced in the Bourse, rose steeply, going up by several francs every session; the clients, increasingly content, since Monsieur le Directeur's predictions were being realized to the letter, put their bonds on deposit at the new establishment of credit . . .

Everything was going marvelously.

Tête-Rouge was admirably seconded by an elite personnel recruited no one knew where.

First, there was the cashier, a pretty monsieur, curled and pomaded, who handled the louis and the banknotes with an exemplary dexterity. One would certainly have had difficulty recognizing him as Gueule-d'Amour, Gros-Tas' pimp.

Gros-Tas put in appearances herself at the bank in the Rue Le Peletier. She was as elegant as her increasing embonpoint permitted. And as Gueule-d'Amour had interests in the house, in which he had invested, on Tête-Rouge's advice an inheritance of ten thousand francs from some American uncle—or, rather, a productive robbery—she believed that she had a right to make observations, at least on the female personnel.

It was thus that she gave a serious scolding to the steno-dactylographers whom she found, on several occasions, chatting to young employees who were making eyes at them. She even criticized their work, although it was not in her line. In sum, she was a shareholder in the bank, since Gueule-d'Amour possessed ten thousand francs' worth of shares himself, and she intended to enjoy her rights and privileges.

Gueule-d'Amour, behind his counter, presided majestically, manipulating the cash; and the mates of the boulevard would have been surprised to see a red ribbon flowering in his button-hole. Not that he was decorated . . . oh, not in the least . . . but when Tête-Rouge had founded the bank he had said to him: "It's necessary that a cashier should be decorated . . . it impresses the clients."

"That's unfortunate; I don't have any medal," the other had replied. "Perhaps, if I'd completed my time in the battalion at Gafsa, I'd have my colonial medal, but . . ."

"Don't be stupid . . . the colonial medal . . . the colonial medal! No you're mad . . . it's the cross you need, idiot!"

"The cross . . . but it's not as easy as that to get one; recommendations are necessary, and a heap of things I don't have . . ."

"It isn't a question of having it, old chap; it's sufficient to wear it. Stick a red ribbon in your buttonhole . . . and that's all."

"But what if I'm harassed for wearing a decoration illegally? You know that I don't like have dealing with the law."

"No, but you must be stupid. You're at home here. You can do as you like . . . wear any decorations that seem good to you . . . even the great sash."

Convinced, Gueule-d'Amour had capitulated, and had immediately ornamented his buttonhole with a very impressive multicolored rosette.

As for Françoise, she lived outside of all that. She never made the slightest appearance in the bank. She continued to "work" chic teas.

"One never knows what might happen," Tête-Rouge said. "I'm a prudent man. A woman always needs to have a métier and to know it. Necessary not to get habituated to idleness."

In the meantime, the Director profited from the good times. He took his meals in the chic restaurants on the boulevards; he dressed with a refined elegance. He treated himself to the most expensive women in Paris: La Belle Miguelo, Eliane de Buzy, Cloclo de Merolles, etc.

In order to meet his sumptuous expenses he drew with full hands from the coffers of the bank, and found that entirely natural.

The bank's motto was *The Maximum profit with the Minimum advance*: a fine slogan that Tête-Rouge interpreted from a point of view directly opposite to that of his clients.

All went well thus for several months, and the end of which complaints began to come in.

Some client, who had handed over several thousand francs for the purchase of obligations in railways or the Crédit Foncier waited in vain for his titles. The invariable response was: "They haven't yet arrived; the agent of exchange hasn't delivered them yet." In reality, the money had been pocketed and the order had not been transmitted, by design.

The people who had committed the imprudence of depositing their titles in the bank's vaults in order to put them in a safe place could never recover possession of them, for the good reason that they had been sold long ago.

As for shares in the Societé des Mines d'or de Seine-et-Oise, after having reached almost double the issuing price, they weakened, and when one of the initial purchasers wanted to negotiate them through the intermediary of a large credit establishment, he was told that they could not be sold.

So complaints rained down incessantly, impatient and menacing. Clients demanded to speak to "Monsieur le Directeur," but "Monsierur le Directeur" was not visible. He only made one brief appearance in the morning, and emptied the cash-box, to the despair of Gueule-d'Amour, who began to fear having made a bad placement of the ten thousand francs of his inheritance. He only dared communicate his fears to Gros-Tas; she treated him then as an imbecile, insulted him and glorified Tête-Rouge, the man of genius for whom she had always experienced a profound admiration, and even amour.

In order to compensate Gueule-d'Amour, Tête-Rouge had a delicate attention; he resigned his functions as director in favor of Gueule-d'Amour. Gros-Tas' man was very flattered by his new title. In spite of his resignation, Tête-Rouge continued to come every morning to take possession of the funds that were still in the cash-box.

One day, when he arrived, he was handed a summons from the commissaire of the judiciary delegations to appear in his office in the Palais de Justice, in order to give explanations regarding the conduct of the Banque du Travail et de l'Espargne; several complaints of abuse of confidence and criminality had reached Monsieur le procureur de la République.

"It's nothing," Tête-Rouge sad to Gueule-d'Amour, who was anxious. "I'll take care of it." And he quit the bank with his habitual tranquility.

Reassured, Gueule-d'Amour went to reinstall himself in the luxurious office that he had occupied since his appointment as director. Proud of his success, confident in the future and proud of the decorations, as strange as they were unknown, that ornamented his frock-coat.

II
Opium Dream

Françoise was now only living with foreigners; today it was a Swede, tomorrow a Serb, the day after a Russian or a Japanese. She had a great deal of success, especially with Americans and Englishmen, for she was slim and as blonde as anyone could wish.

One evening, she had made the acquaintance at the Fritz Hotel of a thirty-year-old Londoner, a tall thin man, dressed expertly and pretentiously, excessively perfumed, with his fingers laden with rings and a camellia in his buttonhole.

In his appearance and his slightest mannerisms one divined an eccentric, who did not know how to employ his fortune.

They dined together in intimacy, and Françoise had the leisure to examine his face, with strange eyes so bright that their irises faded into the veined white of the sclerotic. He scarcely spoke; his pale face and his blond moustache remained continually immobile and cold. At the beginning of their meeting he had made Françoise understand that he did not expect any amorous sacrifice on her part. She pleased him, and he had chosen her to finish the evening and pass the night. All that he asked of her was her garters.

Françoise had smiled. That maniac's particular caprice was easy to satisfy. Before quitting the private booth in which they had dined, he had detached the blue silk ribbon that circled the Breton's shapely leg himself. Then, with infinite precaution, he put the two garters into an inside pocket of his jacket,

"It's the five hundred and thirty-second pair in my collection," he said, simply. For that eccentric collected the garters of every woman he chance to encounter in his travels throughout the world.

Françoise was amused; it was the first time she had encountered such a maniac—and yet she had had so many lovers!

He hired an automobile-taxi, at which he launched an address. At half past eleven or thereabouts the vehicle stopped in the Rue de Helder, opposite a small white bar of the Mauclair or Zizi Voisin genre,[1] in which there were high stools with skating demoiselles perched on top next to party animals.

The Englishman gave a particular sign to the barman who advanced toward him, and the waiter conducted the couple to the back of the shop, where Françoise distinguished a staircase poorly dissimulated behind a Japanese screen.

In her incessant peregrinations through the shady nocturnal establishments that pullulate in the capital, Françoise had never had occasion to come into one like it, and she was slightly intrigued.

Behind the Britisher, who seemed to be familiar with the usages and customs of the house, she climbed the staircase,

---

1 The second name is sometimes referenced as that of one of the "professional beauties" who performed on the Parisian stage, presumably famous enough in her heyday to have a bar named after her.

which was short but rather steep and poorly decorated. They emerged into a kind of small drawing room, where the mistress of the place held her court between two frightfully ugly Tonkinese dogs, a Siamese cat with hieratical attitudes and a glass of choum-choum. She was a fat woman pushing fifty, and her abundant person was simultaneously reminiscent of the superior of a brothel and an aged concierge of the Madame Cardinal genre. She appeared to know Sir Walter, doubtless a habitué of the strange den—which astonished Françoise.

The Englishman traversed that first room with an automaton tread and lifted a saffroned door-curtain. An indefinable odor, both bitter and warm, suffocated the young woman—an odor that was unfamiliar to her, which she had never respired before.

All that she could see at first was heavy black smoke, which, according to Sir Walter's picturesque expression used to describe certain fogs, one could have cut with a knife: a sticky and dirty smoke, a Londonian smoke of November evenings on the banks of the Thames, reeking like the tanneries of the Bièvre. She breathed in lungfuls of something unnamable and vertiginous.

When Françoise's eyes got used to that murky atmosphere, she distinguished, in its details, a long, nightmarish room in which some frightful bad dream seemed to be materializing.

Here and there, men and women were lying down, with bamboo pipes in their lips or their hands, their faces illuminated by minuscule lamps that soiled the atmosphere even more with the reek of oil.

Françoise finally realized where her eccentric companion had brought her. She was in an opium den.

Her eyes widened by surprised, she contemplated with astonishment and stupefaction those people sprawled on bizarre attitudes, with their false collars or bodices unfastened, the buckles of trousers or corsets undone, their heads posed on a block of wood of sorts, which is the preferred pillow of the opium smoker, the legs covered by travel-blankets of goatskins.

She followed Sir Walter, who boldly stepped over the smokers, drowsy or stupidly unconscious—the final resolution of a night of drug-use—in the manner of an habitué of the place and the vice that was celebrated there.

Her soul, still naïve and superstitious, was strangely impressed by the sight of those living cadavers, unmoving in the ruddy light.

At the end of the improbable conduit, as narrow as a gallery in a mine, Walter stopped and sat down—or, rather, crouched down—on a mat of remarkable whiteness, inviting Françoise to imitate him.

She obeyed, although she was a little frightened, and took her place on the next mat.

With a flick of his thumb, the Englishman caused his false collar and cravat to spring away, and lay down. A waiter came to take his orders and soon brought pipes and a little cup of the drug. Sir Walter immediately began grinding a sticky black substance in the little recipient—not a liquid but rather a sort of jam, which he stretched and rendered syrupy by the adjunction, drop by drop, of warm water.

A slender and fantastically curved spatula served him in making that sabbat cuisine, and as he manipulated the drug, the Englishman's eyes sparkled with joy.

When the infernal sauce was terminated, there was a brown mud, a few drops of which he tried to retain at the end of a long, thin steel needle. And as he succeeded in that, satisfaction parted his lips in a smile of contentment.

He seized long and slender instruments of a bizarre form, reminiscent of flutes or oboes; they were opium pipes, bamboo shafts of various thickness, terminated by ivory tips.

Sir Walter initiated Françoise into the art of smoking the drug, proceeding for his part with method and an astonishing scrupulousness, rolling his little ball above the flame of the lamp and sticking it with circumspection to the flat bowl adorned by a minuscule hole and aspiring the bamboo. His atonal eyes became hilarious, and his face even paler, while he absorbed the opium smoke blissfully.

Françoise, with her habitual meekness, conforming with her companion's desire, imitated him awkwardly, since it was the only time that she had abandoned herself to opium.

An indefinable sensation of wellbeing invaded her at the commencement of the inhalation. Gilded dreams, agreeable visions and infinite enchantments populated her brain, which expelled the obsessive memories, the depressing thoughts and the maddening remorse. In order to render that magical and artificial happiness durable, she multiplied the pipes. She passed through the four psychological states of the smoking-room to fall, finally, into the redoubtable torpor, the terror of all smokers, the redoubtable sister of anguish and relative of the nightmare.

The smoking-room thickened with clouds, black-tinted vapors, and the floor took on the aspect of a battlefield after the action. Plaints and gasps rose up, and sometimes, the gigantic shadow of a clenched fist rose up the wall. Only incoherent words in all the languages of the world troubled the silence, very soft, almost whispered words, of an infinite candor or the most lubricious equivocation.

Françoise was no longer anything but an inert mass, invaded by a numbing torpor. She could no longer see or hear anything that was happening around her.

How long did that last?

When she woke up and came to her senses, she thought she was still prey to a hallucination. But no! The dream had dissipated. What was that rumbling, then? It seemed to her that she was being borne along by a jolting carriage.

She rubbed her eyes and looked around, to the right and the left. She perceived houses filing past on either side, through the windows of portieres.

"Where am I?" she murmured, putting her hand to her head, which was very heavy, and buzzing, as after a night of drunkenness.

Then she remembered the English eccentric she had met the previous day at the Fritz Hotel; she recalled the pair of garters that she had abandoned to him for his collection, and remembered their arrival in the den of opiumaniacs.

From that moment on her memories were blurred and she was astonished to find herself alone in a carriage that was carrying her who knows where!

She approached the portiere and lowered the glass; a fresh wind caressed her face and restored complete order to her ideas . . .

What time was it?

She perceived a few shops that were open here and there. It was early morning, but the night was still dark.

"Coachman, stop!" she shouted. She wanted to know where she was being taken.

The coachman obeyed, and tugged the reins of his horse.

"What is it, little lady?"

"Where are you taking me?"

"Me, nowhere; I'm waiting for you to tell me. There was a fellow who gave me a louis a little while ago and told me to drive until you had had enough.

She had herself taken to the Gare Saint-Lazare, where she intended to take the first train to Asnières.

Suddenly, though, she was struck by alarm. The Englishman had not given her anything as a retribution for the night she had spent in his company. What would Tête-Rouge say? She was scared, anticipating a terrible scene.

For several days he had seemed rather worried; the sources on which he drew seemed to have suddenly dried up, and he had become insatiably exigent again.

Instinctively, she opened her handbag, and took an inventory in the penumbra of the vehicle, which was rolling over more-or-less regular pavement of the streets of Paris.

A particular frisson extracted a cry of surprise from her; she had recognized a banknote.

Immediately, her apprehensions calmed down and she approached the parchment to the window in order to make it out more clearly when the fiacre passed a gas-lamp.

Her surprise was even greater when she perceived that it was a thousand-franc bill. She had never been the object of such generosity. So that sum—a small fortune for her—cast an extraordinary confusion into her soul. For some weeks she had been escaping slightly from the influence of Tête-Rouge, which had gradually relaxed, occupied as he doubtless was with the affairs of the bank and the excessive celebration in which he lived.

And the thought was born in her amorphous brain to get away from him . . . to rejoin Mathurin out there, on the far side of the Mediterranean, to procure a little relief for the innocent man, to live for the man that she had continued to love in spite of all the turpitudes and all the baseness of her unhappy existence.

There was scarcely a combat within her, as she evoked the terrible face of the man who bent her under his inflexible will and dominated her with all his power of domination.

She leaned out of the portiere and shouted to the coachman: "I've changed my mind; take me to the Gare de Lyon."

"She doesn't know what she wants, that one," grumbled the coachman, turning his horse in another direction.

A nervous excitement took possession of Françoise. She no longer had anything but a haste to be in the train that would carry her, at top speed, far from the Paris that she abhorred, since it was the source of all her evils.

Two or three times she stimulated the coachman, promising him a good tip.

And when she was finally installed in a third class compartment, she uttered a sigh of relief, only wanting one thing: for the train to pull away and depart.

She arrived in Marseille without incident, and booked into a hotel in order to repose while she awaited the departure of the boat. She was finally free of Tête-Rouge, and definitively. How would he be able to get her back? It was impossible.

It seemed to her that she was reborn to life.

III
The Good Apostle

The summons issued by the Commissaire aux Délégations Judiciares was a precious warning, of which Tête-Rouge took advantage with his customary skill.

"Don't worry," he had said to Gueule-d'Amour, "I'll take care of everything."

In reality, he had purely and simply stuffed the piece of paper into one of his pockets, after having conscientiously emptied his appointee's cash-box and the box of titles of any that might have any value.

In all haste, he had negotiated them; then, with a few thousand-franc bills in his pocket, he returned to the villa in Asnières. His intention was to depart again immediately with Françoise, because he did not want to stay any longer in the capital, where the sojourn threatened to be dangerous.; it was necessary to leave Paris as quickly as possible to avoid the investigations that would inevitably be undertaken.

He was surprised to learn that Françoise had not returned to the villa the day before, but his astonishment was not of long duration.

Immediately, with his profound knowledge of Françoise's weak soul, he had an intuition of what might have happened within her. For some time he had been seeing her less frequently, with the consequence that the fascinating influence of his eyes had become less intense. She had escaped the hypnotism of his strange gaze.

He went back and forth in the rooms of the villa, searching everywhere, in the hope of finding some clue.

Let's see, he said to himself, *she can't have run away with a lover. The adventure of Demi-Sel must have cured her. And then, I'd have noticed something. So? It can only have been a foolish impulse—but which?*

As he continued his research opening cupboards at random and examining their contents, he brought a stack of old newspapers out of the bottom of a drawer.

"What's this?" he said, intrigued.

He unfolded the papers. It was a collection of items reporting the Mathurin Dagorne affair.

"Idiot!" he exclaimed. "Triple idiot! What a blunder I've made, all the same! I didn't think of it! She's still thinking about her Mathurin. It's the memory of her pompier that has turned her head. No doubt about it. She'll have amassed a few banknotes and, repossessed by the thought of that imbecile, she'll have departed to rejoin him out there is Africa. Yes, but Africa is vast, and there are a lot of convicts in Algeria. She won't have fallen on the track right away . . . so . . . ?

"So, my old Tête-Rouge, there's only one thing to do: buckle your valise and go to Marseille; she'll have to pass through there!"

And he took the first express from the Gare de Lyon, not worrying at all about the fate of Gueule-d'Amour, the cashier and director of the Banque de Travail et d'Espargne.

At the hour when he left Paris, the Bretonne arrived in ancient Phocea.

Françoise spent the night there agitated by the impatience she felt to quit the soil of France. It seemed to her that only then would she be completely liberated.

In the morning, she leapt out of bed, dressed in haste and immediately headed for the offices of a nearby agency in order to book a passage for Algeria, for the first convenient port. It mattered little to her whether it was Algiers or some other port; the essential thing, for her, was to disembark in a corner of that land where her fiancé was expiating a crime of which he was not guilty. Once out there, she would find him; she was sure of it!

She obtained a passage on the *Indus*, and mechanically, a body devoid of a soul, she went down to the port in order to see the steamer that would bear her away.

The quays were filled with rumors and cries, people running and gesticulating. She went through the multicolored crowd indifferently, as if adrift, and yet hallucinated. For hours and hours she wandered thus, disarmed.

Suddenly, a hand fell brutally on her shoulder, and as she turned round slowly, fearfully, an exclamation of rage almost emerged from her lips . . . but she only pronounced a single name:

"Tête-Rouge!"

In a second, a profound change of direction occurred within her. She accused herself of having abandoned her master in a cowardly fashion. She felt recaptured, reconquered by his gaze, dominated by his powerful will. Her good resolutions melted instantaneously; nothing else existed any longer for her. She forgot Mathurin, the innocent man who was paying dearly for a crime he had not committed, the man who was suffering, doubtless maltreated by his chiefs. She no longer thought about any of that.

Nothing existed for her any longer but *him*, the fascinator.

He did not pronounce a word, but the glare of his eyes was eloquent. Françoise bowed her head, frightened, and started walking beside her man like a fearful and submissive beast.

He took her to a room in a hotel in the Rue de Belzunce, and only then, when they were quite alone, did he unseal his lips.

"I knew that I'd find you here. You had to pass this way. You thought, then, that you could escape me like that?" he grated, approaching her very closely. "You know, though, that I hold you . . . that you're mine, and will be for as long as you live . . ."

She lowered her head guiltily. He seized her wrist abruptly, and twisted it. She bit her lips in order not to scream.

"Where did you get the money to go away?" he interrogated, his voice terribly menacing.

She had to tell him all about her encounter with the English eccentric, the night they had spent together, and how she had found herself alone in the morning in a fiacre, with a thousand-franc bill in her handbag.

"Shut! Vermin!" he breathed, slapping her. "That money was mine! There isn't a sou's worth of gratitude in your filthy head, then? You ought, however, to remember that you were nothing, and that I made something of you . . . a Parisienne . . . a chic woman . . ."

Certainly, Françoise bore little resemblance now to the Bretonne that Tête-Rouge had knocked down on the heath, at the foot of a gigantic menhir. But that metamorphosis was only physical. Mentally, she was still the fearful and superstitious peasant girl who feared sorcerers, demons and korrigans. For her, Tête-Rouge was still a korrigan, a supernatural being. And he was proving it to her once again . . .

"Madame is dreaming of independence," he said, with a malicious irony. "She's bought a ticket for Marseille . . . she's imagined that she can go to rejoin her Mathurin . . . that species of brute . . . and that I'd let her do it . . ."

"How did you know?" asked the Bretonne her eyes immeasurably wide.

He sniggered, too prudent to recount his discovery of the stack of newspapers that had put him on the track.

"Don't I know everything? Don't I divine everything?"

She closed her eyes and slumped even further. Yes, he was still, for her, the Red Sorcerer!

"I'll show you indepenence!"

The blows and brutalities continued, which Françoise supported with patience and resignation.

"Ah, this is the way you idle your time away while I struggle to earn our living!" Tête-Rouge declaimed. "Necessary that you work—and hard!—because I've just lost my situation at the Banque d'Espargene et de Travail . . . a fine situation, in which I made gold . . . but what can you expect? That animal Gueule-d'Amour wasn't able to direct it . . . he made one stupid blunder after another. I'd told him, however, that in business it requires honesty to succeed. But he wanted to do it his way . . . he didn't want to listen to me and he's got himself into a nasty mess, although he had the good ball in hand. So much the worse for him; he's banged up. I read in the newspaper that he's under lock and key. That will teach him not to want to do things properly. It's quite natural that the law intervenes in cases like that . . . otherwise, it wouldn't be possible to live . . ."

With his habitual cynicism, Tête-Rouge passed over in silence the preponderant and shady role that he had played in the bank that was his work. The compromising of Gueule-d'Amour was the result of his own calculations. He had discharged on to the back of his cashier and friend all the faults that he had committed: thefts, abuses of confidence, frauds, etc.

Françoise never questioned his words. She listened to them religiously and did not permit herself any objection. None, in any case, was born in her amorphous brain.

His anger passed, Tête-Rouge drew the Bretonne to him in a rude embrace, after which she meekly handed him the eccentric and generous Englishman's thousand-franc bill. She had had hardly made a dent in it, only acting with economy, in order that it would last longer.

"Wait for me here," her man said to her, after pocketing the money. "I have to go get a shave. I have the time, since the boat doesn't leave until noon. Another two hours and both of us will be on the other side of the Mediterranean, in Algeria, to make the acquaintance of the Arabs. France, you understand, is beginning to be unhealthy for me with all these stories . . . there's nothing for me here . . . and after all, I don't want to cop it for the others . . ."

And he left the hotel, his face serene and his conscience tranquil, with his head held proudly high.

✳

Tête-Rouge and Françoise disembarked in Bône two days later. The Bretonne was utterly disorientated on that African soil, so different from every point of view from Bretagne, her native land, and also from Paris.

Pen-Ru, by contrast, had no difficulty. He had soon made a tour of the town and he was familiar with the usages of the land.

His lucky star also enabled him to encounter an old acquaintance there who might be useful to him. A few days after his arrival in Bône he was walking along the Cours Bertagna, between the port and the cathedral; at the end of the avenue the port raised its forest of masts and funnels. Strollers were numerous, the men in bright costumes, the women in white robes.

Tête-Rouge was perfectly elegant. His male beauty and athletic form were even more advantageous by virtue of the cut of a flannel suit; a panama hat coiffed his impeccably pomaded flamboyant hair. His entire person had a certain something that earned him eloquent glances on the part of the women who crossed his path.

He was conscious of that success, and proud of it.

As he prepared to cross the spacious avenue, accomplishing gracious twirls with his cane that made the expensive rings ornamenting his fingers stand out, he was obliged to stop: a speeder harnessed to two superb chestnuts arrived before him. He let the light vehicle pass, through the cloud of dust whipped up by the brisk pace of the horses, and perceived a friendly face.

"Georges!" he called.

The man who was driving, Georges l'Algérien, a former acquaintance of La Chapelle, the protector of the famous "earner," Mélie-la-Prune, who had an Arab domestic by his side, pulled on the reins and, leaning backwards, turned his head in the direction of the appeal.

"Ah, of course!" he cried, when he recognized Tête-Rouge.

Briskly, throwing the reins to his valet and leaping from the vehicle, he headed for Tête-Rouge, his arm extended.

"You, here!" he said, after a handshake.

"Yes, I've come to make a tour of your homeland. I wanted to take account of what it's like, Algeria."

"And what are you doing?"

"Me? As you can see, I'm taking a walk . . ."

"Lucky man!"

"And you?"

"I'm doing odd jobs. I can't complain . . . it's not going too badly."

"The chicks bring in money here?"

"The gonzesses? Oh, it's not that. I'm an honest man. I work."

"Come on, don't make a mystery of it . . . I'm a mate."

"Well, come and see me tomorrow, 35A Rue Mesmer . . . you'll see my place, and we'll have lunch together . . ."

"I accept. One's always glad to see mates again. All the more so as I can ask you for tips. I don't want to go on doing nothing . . . you know that it's not my habit . . ."

"That's true, you're no idler. In fact . . . what have you done with your woman?"

"Françoise? She's with me. It's always useful, old friend, to have a woman. One can make use of them in tight circumstances. And Mélie-la-Prune?"

"Mélie-la-Prune? You say that as if I'd left her in Paris. I wasn't going to get rid of her. Now, I only go with women of the world . . ."

"Wow! You're doing well, old friend. One can see that, anyway, by your fine horses . . . you have a chic speeder and are dressed like a prince . . ."

"It seems to me that you don't seem too badly off either . . ."

"Evidently, I have a little money . . . but it's not sufficient for me; I need more than that. I had a nice situation in Paris, but that animal Gueule-d'Amour . . . oh, you see, friends are like that. One tries to do them good, and it backfires on you . . ."

"Gueule-d'Amour, Gros-Tas' man? He didn't inspire confidence in me, that fellow."

"Oh, how right you were! Anyway, for the moment, be tranquil, he's in the shade . . . he got himself caught."

"I beg your pardon, old man," Georges interjected, "but I'm obliged to leave you . . . I'm in a hurry . . . I have a rendezvous with a woman . . . you understand. Tomorrow, without fail, we'll talk . . ."

"Don't delay, I beg you," said Tête-Rouge.

And the two friends separated after a vigorous handshake. Tête-Rouge continued his walk, very thoughtful, jealous of having encountered George-l'Algérien in such splendor.

He returned to Françoise with a surly expression, in a bad mood, already formulating a thousand schemes in his ingenious brain.

"Tomorrow, I need you," he said, simply, to the Bretonne. "You'll dress as elegantly as possible . . . without too much make-up . . . you'll put on a more respectable appearance." And in a low voice, he added: "One never knows . . . she might be useful."

They both went to the address indicated by Georges l'Algérien. On the way he brought the Bretonne up to date with what had happened, recommending her to hold her tongue—a superfluous recommendation, for Françoise never permitted herself any indiscretion.

A caleche deposited them in front of a house painted bright red, on which words stood out in golden letters:

I find anything.

The couple went in. An employee took them to Gerges l'Algérien. There were handshakes, salutations, welcomes—after which Georges took his friends to visit the offices and storerooms of his agency.

Then he took the two of them to lunch outside Bône, at Saint-Cloud-les-Plages, to La Cascade, a pretty Swiss chalet a few meters from the sea.

Then Tête-Rouge's curiosity was satisfied.

"You ask what I do," said Georges-l'Algérien, stroking his brown moustache, of which he was proud. "It's not very difficult to guess: I find things."

"That still requires a few explanations . . ."

"However, you must have seen on the walls of Bône posters representing a fat man with a thousand arms; the city is inundated with them, for there's nothing like publicity, you know, in commerce. When I returned to Algeria a few months ago, I happened upon a fellow who sold a little of everything. His commerce wasn't going well. I offered to improve it—on condition, of course, that he put up the money.

"He entered into the scheme, and was so happy with the results that he associated me with him. Nothing to fear with that brother; he has bags of cash. Our agency embraces the most diverse objects, so we sell wheat, sardines, tea, oil, wool, sheep . . . in a word, we sell anything, we find anything. I find anything!" the Algérien concluded joyfully, bursting into laughter.

While they were drinking champagne, a fat apoplectic monsieur decorated with a multicolored rosette irrupted into the private booth in which the two friends and Françoise were finishing lunch.

Georges made the introductions. "My partner, Monsieur Pedrazzi . . ."

After the salutations and handshakes customary in such circumstances, they sat down around a tablecloth cluttered with glasses, cups of various dimensions, carafes and bottles. Françoise, who was facing Tête-Rouge, felt a foot placed on hers. The ex-banker took advantage of a moment when Georges and his associate were conversing privately to favor the Bretonne with a wink.

She did not understand the significance immediately; her man approached her more closely over the table and whispered in her ear: "Pay attention! Entice the old man! Keep your eyes open!"

The conversation between the four guests resumed, only interrupted by the explosion of successively-uncorked champagne bottles. They swilled full glasses of the sparkling golden wine, so their heads did not take long to be warmed and their faces crimsoned by the alcohol.

Georges-l'Algérien's partner, whose fifty years rendered him even fonder of feminine graces, darted his shining eyes in the direction of Françoise, who smiled at him in a very engaging fashion.

Tête-Rouge perceived that conduct, which served his calculations, with pleasure. He already had an entire plan in mind, and that evening, when Françoise found herself alone with him, he explained at length what he expected of her.

"Pedrazzi has money. It's necessary for you to be his mistress, and that you entangle him to the extent that he'll do anything for you. To begin with, that will bring us a large sum, and then, gradually, I'll empty Georges in order to put myself in his place. Everyone has his turn down here to earn money."

The entirely Parisienne elegance of the Bretonne seduced the Algérien's partner, as Tête-Rouge had foreseen, and she soon became his mistress. The fat man was generous, all the more so because, following her lover's instructions, Françoise played in his regard the honest woman whose jealous husband does not suspect her treason; she had to tell lies incessantly in order to explain her frequent absences.

Pedrazzi blossomed, proud of possessing a young and pretty mistress; and it seemed quite natural to him gradually to ease out Georges-l'Algérien in order to put Tête-Rouge in his place. It was, he thought, the least he could do to compensate him thus for taking his wife! That was all that the latter desired. Once again, his wishes were granted.

L'Algérien conceived a terrible anger in consequence; he even threatened to employ trenchant arguments against him, but Tête-Rouge dissuaded him with his habitual finesse.

"I'll tell Monsieur Pedrazzi who you are and what you did in Paris," Georges threatened, "and Françoise, whom he imagines to be an honest woman . . ."

"Shut up, Georges, don't say anything. Pedrazzi wouldn't believe you, for he no longer sees anything but Françoise; everything she says is well said, everything she does is well done, so what's the point in burying us in stories? You know very well what I could say about you. I know all your dirty tricks, and I could denounce them. Anyway, don't get angry, you know that I'm a good fellow . . . I'll compensate you. I have something in view that will sort you out very well. I can't tell you any more today, but come and see me tomorrow and we'll talk . . ."

Georges-l'Algérien submitted to Tête-Rouge's will, who took the direction of the "I find anything" agency from then on, the traffic of which he extended further.

He was rich and highly considered in the country; he possessed a nice villa on the Route de la Pépinière, one of the most sumptuous habitations. Madame and Monsieur went riding in the mornings; in the afternoons they went out in a magnificent limousine that was the admiration of everyone in Bône.

As he got out of his auto outside his villa one afternoon, Tête-Rouge found himself face to face with a man he seemed to recognize.

Where have I seen that face before? he wondered.

The man had also winced on perceiving the grim Breton. Instinctively, as if seized by a sudden terror, he had lowered his eyes, seeming to want to sink into the earth.

Suddenly, a cry escaped Tête-Rouge's lips. "Demi-Sel!" he exclaimed.

The other man remained motionless.

"You again!" breathed the cynical Breton, approaching the man he had caused to fall into the famous trap in Nogent. "I always find you in my path. What are you doing here? Have you escaped from out there?"

The other looked at him piteously and replied, his eyes fixed on the ground: "Yes."

Then, in short phrases, trembling, he recounted his odyssey, his sojourn in the prison camp in Guyana and the various penitentiaries of Maroni. He had linked himself in close friendship out there with two of his fellow prisoners; he considered them as friends, brothers, even more. One day, in the hut that sheltered them, they imparted confidences. His two companions in chains had told him that on the Martigues coast they had murdered an old woman and hidden her savings in the neighboring forest. Then, all three of them had decided to escape together and one day, after the visit of the chief guard, armed with machetes that they used to clear the undergrowth, they had plunged fearlessly into the virgin forest.

Soon, however, one of Demi-Sel's friends had succumbed to marsh fever, and when they reached the bank of the river separating them from Dutch Guyana, the other hand drowned while trying to board an indigenous canoe. Animated by the energy of despair, Demi-Sel had reached the foreign territory, carrying with him the secret of his two brothers in misery. He had obtained passage, thanks to a few savings he had accumulated, on a ship that took him to Sydney; then he had embarked as a cook on a steamer that brought him to Bordeaux. In small stages he had attained Martigues, where he had found the treasure buried by his friends: neither more nor less than twenty thousand francs.

Gradually, he had changed his way of life. At first, for some time, he had been an apprentice to a hairdresser in the Rue de Phocée. Eventually, with his own money "honestly earned," Demi-Sel had bought a renowned public lavatory for himself. He had seduced his clients with his affable manners and in time he had become the most considered businessman in the street, to the extent that a group of his Phocean compatriots, afflicted by the ravages caused by societies of nervis,[1] had come to ask him to take the lead in an association destined to repress their exactions; and Demi-Sel had accepted temporarily. The society had been founded and the hairdresser had not disdained to speak at the meetings organized in the evening, vituperating against the wretches escaped from the prison camp, apaches who were terrorizing the bourgeois and the entire rabble of malefactors and law-breakers.

Unfortunately, it had been a bad idea for Demi-Sel to want to play the honest man. The nervis had avenged themselves cruelly by ransacking his shop and robbing him to his last centime one day when the hairdresser had taken a trip to the country. Mad with despair, not daring to lodge a complaint for fear of his identity being discovered, Demi-Sel had just abandoned Marseille in order to try his luck in Bône—the luck that was always so contrary to him!

And now, the first person he encountered was Tête-Rouge, the former terror of La Chapelle, his most bitter enemy!

"So," said the latter , with an evil laugh, when the other had finished his story, "you've never got out of trouble! But you still have funds—at least you sold up!"

"Yes, but at a loss, to my leading apprentice. I explained that I wasn't tranquil and wanted to liquidate as soon as possible. In two days it was settled and I crossed the water to come in search of tranquility here."

---

1 *Nervis* was the term used in and around Marseille for the local mafia.

"You'll have it! You'll have it!"

"Alas, I was so happy in Marseille; now here I am, without a situation, and, figuratively speaking, I no longer have a sou. My successor has signed notes to me, but I don't know how to negotiate them."

"Your notes are an embarrassment; pass them to me and I'll take charge of them. I can handle all that. Only, it's necessary that I no longer find you in my path; I've had enough of your face. Take that as said. Come on, imbecile, hand over your notes."

Meekly, Demi-Sel took the stamped papers from a wallet and gave them to Tête-Rouge.

The latter cast an eye over them and said: "All right, I can handle it. And as I'm a worthy fellow who can't see mates in difficulties, I'll find you a serious employment in which you'll be free of all worries. One of my friends is the proprietor of a coastal vineyard on the Tunisian frontier; I'll mention you to him and I believe that he'll be able to use you . . ."

"You'd really do that for me, Tête-Rouge?"

"Yes. Come on, you know that I'm not a bad fellow. What happened between us a while ago no longer matters; it's ancient history. I wish you well and I'll prove it to you. There aren't many friends like me. You know Georges-l'Algérien, a mate from La Chapelle—well, I encountered him here, he was in difficulties too, and I'm in the process of taking care of him. It's stronger than me; I can't leave people in trouble."

Demi-Sel looked at Tête-Rouge fearfully, wondering if it was really him who was talking like that—but his speech was so persuasive that he was convinced of his sincerity. Thus, when they separated, the ex-hairdresser shook the hand of his former rival effusively and thanked him warmly, in anticipation of all that he had promised to do for him.

Tête-Rouge played the character of the good apostle marvelously.

IV
The Beneficence of Tête-Rouge

Tête-Rouge had promised a compensation to Georges-l'Algérien, and he kept his promise. The same day, he enabled him to make the acquaintance of a woman he introduced under the pompous name of Madame Rose des Moulins.

She was a frightfully ugly old woman, heavily made-up and excessively fat, whose stout body was strapped into a corset that was more than tight, which gripped her like a vice.

What does he expect me to do with that old painting? Georges wondered. *She's a hundred years old!*

Tête-Rouge addressed sly winks to him, and l'Algérien, subjugated, made up to the voluminous Madame des Moulins, showing himself attentive and gallant. She was delighted, and played the coquette, still believing in the existence of her long-vanished charms and proud of her success with a handsome fellow like the friend Tête-Rouge had introduced to her.

The latter made arrangements to be alone for a moment with Georges in order to explain to him who the old woman was and the compensation that she represented.

"She's one of my friends; she isn't beautiful, I know—she's old—but what does that matter to you? You'll have no difficulty infatuating her with your physique and manners. The old woman represents fifty thousand francs for whoever is able to take her . . ."

"Fifty thousand francs! In that case, she's a delightful woman. Tell me quickly what it's necessary to do to get into her good graces . . ."

"Well, old man, it's not complicated. You have only to ask for her hand . . ."

"Eh? What are you saying? Marry her?"

"Yes, marry her."

"But that's easy to do. I can do it!"

"So, it's as if you had the fifty thousand francs in your pocket ... all the more so as I perceived immediately that she was smitten with you ..."

The return of Rose des Moulins interrupted that interesting conversation.

Georges redoubled his gallantry and attentions, praising the lady's hair, which was still blonde, thanks to the progress of chemistry and the skill of her hairdresser and wigmaker. Before they separated that day he had pushed boldness as far as kissing the lady's gelatinous neck; she had laughed, agreeably tickled.

Delighted with the fortunate turn that his marriage was taking, Georges l'Algérien thanked Tête-Rouge warmly, certain that he had found a fine windfall. He forgot the bad turn that his friend had done him by evicting him from the "I find anything" agency.

Things went well. On either side they were occupied with the imminent union. L'Algérien had already promised to "lift his foot" the day after the marriage—which is to say, the same day that he obtained the fifty thousand francs. He had the key to the enigma; that sum would be handed over by a lover of the lady in question as soon as he was absolutely certain of being rid forever of an old and ugly mistress who importuned him.

"That explains," Tête-Rouge affirmed, "why he'll only pay the indemnity the day after the marriage—which is to say, when he's absolutely certain that it's something irremediable."

Georges rubbed his hands, delighted with that magnificent opportunity to enrich himself; so he paid court assiduously to his fiancée for fear that she might escape him.

Eventually, the great day so much awaited arrived. The marriage was celebrated solemnly. In spite of her age and her more-than-problematic candor, the bride had thought it appropriate to put on a white satin dress; she had only neglected the orange blossom, which was doubtless superfluous. The husband was clad in a suit and impeccably gloved, as were the witnesses, of whom Tête-Rouge was naturally one.

The following morning, l'Algérien was on tenterhooks, impatiently awaiting the generous donor. That day was much more important for him than the previous one.

Alas, he waited in vain. The rich unknown did not appear; the next day and the one after it was the same.

The honeymoon was spoiled.

Heartbroken, Georges went to find Tête-Rouge, in order to inform him of his disappointment and to ask him to intervene, since he alone knew the man in question.

Tête-Rouge appeared quite astonished by that contretemps.

"I can't understand it. He had promised me personally . . . he had even sworn on his honor that he would give you the fifty thousand bullets. Don't worry, old man; I'll take care of it. I'll go and see him."

A little later, after a turn around the town, Tête-Rouge told his friend, with a heart-broken expression, that the monsieur had suddenly disappeared.

"It's bad luck for you . . . for there's no error, the affair was pure gold. But it's necessary to steel yourself. Yes, I know, you're pulling a face. You don't have the cash. Anyway, console yourself; if the money is gone, the woman still remains . . ."

"Oh, don't go on! I don't have the heart for joking . . ."

"What, then? You can't have trouble in the household already . . . don't get angry; it will pass . . ."

"All that's nothing! It's the woman who isn't funny. You can talk—a hundred kilos of lard to stir! That's not nothing! It's the quid pro quo that decided me . . ."

In reality, the generous lover had only ever existed in the inventive brain of Tête-Rouge, who had employed that clever means to get rid of Pou-Blanc, alias Rose-des-Moulins, whose acquaintance he had made since his installation in Bône and who was threatening to be inconvenient for him.

Georges-l'Algérien remained with that old woman on his arm, therefore, with no money and no situation. In addition, Rose des Moulins—or, rather, Pou-Blanc, as she was universally known in the shady establishments of Bône—was a limpet, in the full meaning of the term. She was infatuated with her husband and did not intend that he would deceive her or leave her. She followed him everywhere, not admitting that he go anywhere without her.

※

In the meantime, Tête-Rouge enjoyed in all tranquility the ease that he had conquered, more or less honestly; and as he was devoid of any scruple, he had no remorse—his conscience had died a long time ago.

He was happy, earning plenty of money and living well. Françoise was no stranger to all that, for she had acquired a great influence over Pedrazzi, who was madly in love with her. Always cunning, Tête-Rouge had judged the situation well, and preferred that the Bretonne had no other lover than his partner. In any case, she brought him enough for him to be content.

Françoise would, therefore, have been relatively happy without the remorse that haunted her continually, and the thought that Mathurin was engaged in public works and doubtless the butt of brutality and ill-treatment. How dearly he, the innocent, was paying for her crime and the crime of her accomplice!

During the several months that they had already been installed in Bône, how many times the desire had been born in her heart to go up to the kasbah, to the penitentiary, in order to see the former pompier! But she recalled the menacing expression with which Tête-Rouge had said to her: "And above all, make sure that I never perceive you trying to see him, or else look out—things will turn ugly."

Every day, when she went out for a walk on the Cours Bertagna or the Corniche, he interrogated her when she returned; it was necessary to give him a minute account of her movements . . . and she could not lie when Tête-Rouge's violet eyes, strangely troubling, stared at her, seeming to delve into her utmost depths.

As for him, he "played the caïd," as people say out there. Proud of the success that he had on the beach during the hour of bathing—for the pretty women loved his commanding appearance—he no longer counted his conquests. In spite of that, an innate need summoned him to low dives; he spent nights in the shady establishments of the Rue Gambetta near the Colonne Randon. A mixed population swarmed there: hideous women, outrageously-painted old Mooresses, and men of all countries and races: Italians, Jews, Arabs, Frenchmen, Maltese, etc. It was there, truly, that he amused himself and lived; it was his milieu. He reigned there as master, as he did everywhere he went, curbing everyone to his will for the success of his incessant calculations.

One night, as he came out of a Moorish café, he perceived a man collapsed in the gutter; he was moving away when a drunken voice pronounced his name. He retraced his steps and recognized Demi-Sel, who was making desperate efforts to stand up.

"What!" he said, angrily. "It's you again?"

"Yes, it's me again. I'm in a rude fix, old friend."

"You're as full as a barrel!"

"What do you expect—one has to forget one's chagrins," he said, finally succeeding in standing up.

Tête-Rouge burst out laughing on seeing him, dirty and ragged, his face wan.

"Well, you know, one can no longer recognize the honest man you were a few months ago. Where is the President of the Protective League against the Nervis?"

"It's my fault, I had a fright . . . and now I don't have a sou, after having possessed a magnificent situation. After having been on the point of making a fortune . . . in fact, have you cashed my notes yet?"

"Your notes? But they were worthless, old chap. I passed them to my banker . . . he didn't even want them, and in the final count, they were just enough to cover the expenses they cost me. I only made eleven sous profit, you see, but as good accounts make good friends, I don't want you to lose them. Here they are!"

So saying, Tête-Rouge took out of his pocket a silver coin and a copper coin, which he put in Demi-Sel's hand.

The latter, bewildered, contemplated them, vacillating on his legs.

"Eleven sous! Eleven sous . . . ah, decidedly I'm not blessed." A tear ran down Demi-Sel's cheek, and he went on: "You know, Tête-Rouge, that I'm still counting on you to find me a situation. You promised to occupy yourself with me some time ago, when I met you . . ."

"You're right; there's nothing like honesty . . . and as you're a good mate I'll give you the address of one of my friends; you can go to see him on my behalf . . . I've mentioned you to him. You can be sure that he'll employ you."

Tête-Rouge scribbled an address on a card and handed it to Demi-Sel, whose eyes, blurred by drunkenness, succeeded in deciphering: *M. Manfredo, Chapeau-de-Gendarme, near Bône.*

When he had recovered from his drunkenness, Demi-Sel immediately set forth for Chapeau-de-Gendarme, where he had been so charitably recommended by his good friend Tête-Rouge. His funds had almost run out; he did not have a sou, and instead of taking the Bône-Guelma, he had to make the journey—thirty-six kilometers—on foot, roasted and burned by the terrible sun. As he left with his eleven sous, the relic of his liquidation of the lavatory in Merseille, he had bought a liter of wine, three sous'-worth of bread and two sous'-worth of sausage.

Full of courage and hope, in spite of the pitiless sunlight falling from above, he set out on the road, dead straight for three leagues, singing Parisian refrains to give himself heart.

Toward midday, the heat being too intense, he stopped in a field. When he had consumed his meager pittance, he found the shade of an olive-tree and rested there for a couple of hours, dreaming that Tête-Roge had procured him a splendid situation; already he was the director of a domain where he would go to work, and his past was forgotten forever.

The sun, continuing its course, woke him up, darting its burning rays upon his face. In an instant he was on his feet, and he resumed his route. He still had twelve kilometers to cover, but nothing is impossible for a valiant heart. Arabs and colonists informed him on the way, and at nightfall he arrived at Monsieur Manfredo's farm, situated two kilometers from Chapeau-de-Gendarme, a little village lost in the midst of vines on an admirably colorful landscape.

He went into the interior courtyard of the farm, and a mastiff launched itself upon him.

"Oh well, you're not going to eat me," he said.

A voice departed from the habitation: "Here, Sultan!"

And immediately, a fat man, very red-faced, with a sunburned complexion, in his shirt-sleeves, emerged from the habitation.

"What can I do for you, Monsieur?" But, seeing the wretched appearance of Demi-Sel, her added immediately: "What do you want . . . a hunk of bread?"

Demi-Sel took Tête-Rouge's recommendation out of his pocket and asked: "Monsieur Manfredo?"

"That's me. What do you want with me?"

When he had taken cognizance of Tête-Rouge's card he looked at Demi-Sel pityingly and said: "All right; you've been recommended to me by a friend in Bône, What do you want to do?"

"I don't know, Patron. What do you have to do?"

"There's no lack of work here. Look around . . . there are fifty hectares of vines to dig. You can't dig them all on your own."

"Certainly not, but I have a good will and I don't have fat arms . . ."

"In sum, you know, I don't pay dear. I have Kabyles who work for ten sous a day. You mustn't expect to earn thousands or hundreds with me."

"It's necessary to live, Monsieur; what do you want?"

"I can see that you're an accommodating fellow; the two of us can reach an understanding. You look tired; to begin with you'd better rest. Tomorrow morning I'll give you a hoe, and you can go with the comrades to take up the vine-stocks. There's plenty of work, you know; you have enough for the rest of your days here if the two of us can reach an agreement . . ."

Demi-Sel was happy; finally, he was going to be able to earn a few honest sous and rebuild his life.

He set to work with ardor. His situation was certainly not brilliant. Monsieur Manfredo had promised to nourish him until he was familiar with the work; later he would allow him a modest retribution.

At sunrise, with the hoe over his shoulder, Demi-Sel departed with the Kabyle laborers; and until dusk, without respite, he dug and dug. The labor was exhausting, all the more so because he was poorly nourished—but what did those petty miseries matter to Demi-Sel, who was content to earn his living by his own means, and honestly? And when, sometimes, the gendarmes from Morisse passed on patrol alongside the vineyard, he looked at them boldly. He no longer had anything to fear from them now that he was redeeming his sins.

But it was in vain that he waited for the payments for which Monsieur Manfredo had let him hope. So, one Saturday, disillusioned, he asked for an explanation on that subject.

Monsieur Manfredo, at table in the yard of his farm before a well-filled glass of absinthe with his fists in his pockets, said to him: "Payments, Sidi! You're crazy! I know who you are now. You ought to deem yourself happy to be nourished, in sum . . ."

"What! Patron, I work like the others!"

"You work, that's possible, but in sum, you ought to be grateful, for if I wanted . . ."

Demi-Sel went pale. "If you wanted . . . ?"

"Yes, if I wanted to denounce you . . ."

"Denounce me? For what?"

"Come on, don't play the innocent. You know, eh?"

"But Patron . . ."

"No one puts one over on me. You've been out there in the land of coconuts and you've picked them. I know what they'd do to you if they caught you."

"Who told you that?" stammered Demi-Sel, completely bewildered, wondering whether bad luck was not as dead against him as ever. How could Monsieur Manfredo know who he was, where he had been and by virtue of what sequence of adventures he had been able to escape the prison camp?

Always naïve and a good fellow, Demi-Sel, in his candor, did not suspect that it was another trick of his friend Tête-Rouge.

Two or three days before, the latter had met Monsieur Manfredo in the market in Bône, and he had told him enough to have Demi-Sel hanged. "Necessary to make him work as if he were in the prison camp," he had advised him, as they parted.

Poor Demi-Sel was a victim again. And yet, he was worth as much as Tête-Rouge, his singular protector, and Monsieur Manfredo, whom Tête-Rouge had once known during a sojourn at Poissy. Manfredo, then in conflict with Parisian law, was serving a term in the Centrale of Seine-et-Oise.

And the former hairdresser who thought he had found an honest situation, where he would be regenerated by manual labor, experienced another supreme disillusionment. He had only escaped from Guyana, where existence was relatively possible, to fall into a more terrible prison camp, from which it would be impossible to escape.

V
Mortal Embrace

It was a superb sunlit morning, which promised a torrid heat for the afternoon. So the terraces of the cafés were already full of customers taking advantage of a few hours of relative coolness in order to sip their aperitifs tranquilly.

Under the arcades of the Palais Calvin, in the Café d'Orient, Françoise was sitting between Pedrazzi and Tête-Rouge. The conversation was slowing down,

"Why," said the fat man suddenly, his eyes staring at the far end of the road, "what's that I can see out there?"

His interlocutors leaned over.

"One might think that it's a file of convicts," replied Tête-Rouge.

Pedrazzi looked more attentively, and said: "I believe you're right."

Soon, there was no more doubt; they were "public laborers" that were advancing slowly, under the guard of tirailleurs, in the middle of the superb promenade that was the ornament of the town.

Fançoise had suddenly gone pale, a nervous tremor agitating her internally. Tête-Rouge stared at her momentarily. She understood what that meant. However, she could not succeed in dissipating the disturbance that invaded her as the column approached, amid the sound of iron-studded shoes and imperative commands. Thirty pale-faced convicts clad in gray, with enormous sacks surmounted by various tools on their backs, were advancing, framed by tirailleus with shouldered arms fitted with bayonets, their eyes watchful.

A sergeant of the penitentiary was marching at the head.

"They're not going to amuse themselves," said Pedrazzi. "The fellow commanding them isn't soft—a Corsican named Crassni. He's a brute, it appears. He's never so content as when he can make them turn or lodge a bullet—sixteen grams, as he says when he's had a drink—in the skin of some poor devil who tries to run away. Last year, Crassni was working ten kilometers from here taking up vine-stocks. Well, of the thirty men in his detachment, only seven came back."

"And the others?" aked Tête-Rouge

"The others?" replied Pedrazzi. "They were killed by fevers or the tirailleurs and fed the jackals." And he concluded by saying: "Crassni doesn't mess about. It's necessary to march straight with him, or beware of the grams!"

During that conversation the prisoners had arrived level with the café: a wretched column of suffering and misery. Some marched with heads high, looking at the cafés enviously; others kept their eyes on the ground, with bleak expressions. In the former category, Tête-Rouge had time to recognize Nez-de-Coq. Françoise also recognized him, but it was not him for whom she was searching in the group; and when the file reached its end, she perceived Mathurin, thin and unrecognizable, marching with difficulty, his shoulders curbed under the weight of his sack.

"Move, then, dummy!"

She followed the column with her eyes until she could no longer make it out, and she imagined all the vexations of which Mathurin must be the butt.

But Tête-Rouge took possession of her gaze, and imperiously, albeit in silence, ordered her to chase away those thoughts . . .

Five minutes later he left her alone with Pedrazzi in order to favor the liaison of which he was still pretending to be unaware and from which he was able to profit.

The fat man was very attentive to Françoise; he lavished terms of endearment on her, which depicted his ardent passion. She strove to be in unison.

"Well, my little kitten," he said to her, very tenderly, "let's not linger in this café—we have better things to do. I know a place where we'll be entirely at our ease . . . privately . . ."

He paid for the drinks and, proud of possessing such a pretty mistress, he braced his figure and drew her along the road, gallantly offering her his arm.

They stopped in the Rue Heliopolis in a hotel where they had been accustomed to come since the first days of their liaison.

Past fifty, his corpulence and lack of charm did not prevent Pedrazzi from being a passionate lover. So, as soon as he was alone with Françoise, he took her on his knees in order to cover her with caresses. Then he aided her to undress, with a refined pleasure, and carried her away in his short, fat arms, which were trembling with impatience.

Desire caused an afflux of blood to his apoplectically-colored face, and as he feared that age might betray him, he always absorbed a strong dose of an aphrodisiac beforehand. This morning he operated as usual, glad to embrace the supple young body of his mistress and to know divine enchantment once more . . . but he had scarcely tasted the delights of amour than he uttered a dull plaint, accompanied by a violent start, and he fell like a mass upon Françoise.

She did not understand at first why the man was suddenly inert and crushing her, but his immobility finished up by alarming her; she called to him and shook him, but he did not respond. Then, as best she could, she disengaged herself from beneath his heavy mass. Pedrazzi had not yet come round. She was afraid; had he suddenly died?

She examined him more attentively and perceived that he was no longer anything but a cadaver.

She was alarmed, foreseeing complications. Perhaps she would be suspected, accused and arrested? What should she do? She had no idea.

She seemed to be reliving the somber hours of the crime of the Rue de Turenne. It was less horrible, however, for in the present circumstances she had nothing for which to reproach herself. It was hazard alone that she needed to accuse.

Finally, come what may, she summoned the hotel bellboy. She could not remain alone in the face of the dead man. She explained to the man that came what had happened. Pedrazzi's pockets were searched, and his address was found there.

Françoise slipped away while a caleche took the fat man to his domicile. She had got away with a terrible fright, which had caused an immense disgust for her existence to rise within her again. In all haste she returned to the villa, hoping to find tranquility if, fortunately, Tête-Rouge was absent.

She had a bad headache that was manifested by dull shocks in her temples; she needed to lie down and rest. Tête-Rouge was not in the villa, and doubtless would not be back that afternoon or evening, believing her to be in the company of Pedrazzi.

She did not even take the trouble to eat; she was neither hungry nor thirsty. She put on a peignoir in which she was comfortable and lay down in a rocking chair, in the shadow of a magnificent orange tree in the big garden—almost a park—that surrounded the habitation.

Once again she was in one of her black periods of discouragement. She felt so weary it seemed to her that she no longer had the strength to live.

She closed her eyelids, wanting a complete annihilation that would rid her of her multiple cares.

She could do no more; this life overwhelmed her. She was not cut out to follow that métier, to sell her kisses and her flesh. She did it because she was under the empire of Tête-Rouge; but when she had the time to think and look into hersef, to recall the past, she experienced nausea.

She belonged to that man; she was bound to him forever because of the inconstancy of her will, which allowed itself to be subjugated by the fascinating gaze of the strange eyes. For her, he was still, in a sense, the Sorcerer; she did not love him; she feared him. Her heart had only ever had one love: Mathurin . . . yes, poor Mathurin, whom she had perceived a little while ago and for whom she could, alas, do nothing.

The poor man! How downcast he seemed! How dearly he was expiating her sin, the crime of Tête-Rouge.

All day long she passed those ideas back and forth in her head. She also wondered, which happened sometimes, whether her parents were still alive. She thought about her dear Bretagne, which she would doubtless never see again.

Gradually, a dull revolt rumbled within her, increased and became envenomed. Was she finally about to find the strength to rebel, to detach herself from her accomplice?

If she had had some money, she would have renewed her attempt at flight. But where could she go now that she no longer wanted to quit Algeria, still hoping that she might succeed in getting close to Mathurin, in order to soften his suffering?

The afternoon passed thus, and then the night.

Tête-Rouge came back in the morning, rather drunk.

She told him what had happened at the hotel, the amorous rendezvous terminated in a tragic fashion.

"Perdrazzi is dead!" cried the cynical individual. "So much the better! He's capable of having included you in his testament! In any case, I'll be able to profit from the situation!"

That event rendered him very joyful. He did not go to bed, so as to be at the "I find anything" agency early in the morning.

Immediately, he began to make up the accounts—an operation having no aim, of course, but to fill his pockets as much as possible. That was all the easier for him because Pedrazzi and he were the only ones familiar with the rather shady deals made by the company. He appropriated ten thousand francs in that fashion without Pedrazzi's heirs having any suspicion of it.

Contrary to his hopes, the fat man had not made any provision for Françoise in his will, which had been made prior to the liaison. The agency was sold a few days later, and Tête-Rouge judged it preferable to withdraw discreetly.

As he was accustomed to do after each of his "failed turns" he abandoned his villa, changed his quarter and his way of life.

In spite of her desire to liberate herself from the despotism of Tête-Rouge, Françoise was subjected to it once again, asking herself fearfully what he was going to make her do now, and into what cunning schemes he was about to launch her.

She did not take long to find out.

"I've found you a nice little engagement at the Casino de Bône," he told her one day. "It's necessary that you sing the Gavroches, my child. Bretonnes won't please here!"

"I'll never be able to do it! I don't have the voice!"

"No voice . . . no voice . . . is it necessary to have a voice to be a café-concert singer?" he mocked. "As long as one has chic, a figure and a nice face . . . and above all that one isn't surly, no more is necessary than to spout lewd things to the public, who find everything delightful when it's a nice girl who delivers them. It's settled, all right?"

"As you wish . . ."

"I've unearthed a good woman who followed the métier for twenty years . . . she'll give you tips. Then you'll go and introduce yourself to the director. The deal is done but I want him to see for himself that I haven't deceived him, that your legs are as well-made as your breasts . . .

"Needless to say, I've cleaned you up since the day when I extracted you from the midst of the peasants where you were lurking . . . and what a life, running behind cows and feeding the chickens and pigs! Instead of that, you're a delightful woman . . . you'll have success as a singer.

"Only it's necessary not to be proud, eh. Necessary to be a good girl when you pass through the crowd for the collection. It's there that you'll find your clientele, because the salary isn't even worth the trouble of talking about. It's not on the thirty francs that Monsieur Avela, the director, will give you, you understand, that we can live . . .

"Fortunately, the hall is always full, so the clients are all yours! Every evening, in audition to the regulars, there are colonists from the surrounding area, officers of the infantry and the chasseurs, mariners and tourists. Choose the latter for preference; they're richer and hence more generous. At the end of the concert taken them to supper on the beach, at the Chalet Suisse, where I have an agreement with the patron and an interest in his business . . . and above all, watch out for cops, or I'll slap you. For galette it's not as good as Paris, I know, but too bad—war is war. Anyway, you might find someone rich; that would be a real coup."

A week later, following a most summary apprenticeship, Françoise made her first appearance on the boards of Le Cadran du Bône, costumed as a gavroche.

Half-drunk, fascinated by the gaze of Tête-Rouge, who was sitting at the first table and did not take his eyes off her for a second, she launched, with a certain boldness:

> *I like having fun*
> *With all the mates,*
> *But I don't like the cops,*
> *I'm the fun-loving kid!*

After the first couplet she was at home; the public no longer existed, nor Tête-Rouge, nor anyone else. She sang as if in a dream.

When the orchestra fell silent, she understood that it was finished.

She was applauded, as Tête-Rouge had predicted, but not because the words of her song were very witty or because her voice charmed the ear; she owed her success entirely to her beauty.

When she made the collection she heard the same flattering words that had resonated in her ears before, when she had danced at the Hortensias Bleus.

The collection was excellent, the homages numerous—so Tête-Rouge was charming that evening.

From that day onward she was recaptured by her former life of partying. Again she knew long orgiastic nights, the kisses of drunken men, and brutal caresses. She had to yield to all the caprices of every stranger, provided that he paid well. As she was a good prostitute, her conquests were numerous. Even the Arabs, although parsimonious, wanted to know the white woman about whom everyone in the town was talking, and they too brought their four douros to Françoise.

One night, when she was supping with two officers, she had the surprise and emotion to hear mention of a certain Breton, a sly and imbecile numbskull who gave his chiefs a good deal of trouble. Her heart beat as if to burst in her breast.

"And," added one of the two officers, "the fellow isn't at all interesting. He drew his captain into a trap and was even suspected of murdering the latter's uncle."

There was no doubt that they were talking before her about Mathurin, the innocent man who was in the brush almost at the gate of the town.

From that night on she plunged deeper into the orgy, in order to stifle the remorse of her conscience, which always returned painfully...

As for Tête-Rouge, he "played the caïd." He spent without counting; money cost him so little!

Several times he met up with Georges-l'Algérien, who had finally managed to get rid of his wife and had become a caterer. It was in the course of one of those encounters that he also learned that Mathurin, as well as his old friend Nez-de-Coq, was part of a detachment to which Georges supplied food.

That's precious information, thought Tête-Rouge. *Necessary to keep tabs on the pompier, for if Françoise ever suspected that her former fiancé was so close to her...*

He asked Georges to keep him up to date with the actions of the former chauffeur. L'Algérien promised to inform his mate.

And life continued for the couple. Françoise had every success. Some lovers kept her for an hour, others for a night or a whole day.

About a month after her debut at the concert-hall of Bône, one of them wanted to take her out in a caleche on a fine afternoon all the way to Morris. On the way they passed an unfinished road on which the convicts of the penitentiary were working.

Françoise's heart filled with emotion—an emotion made of both hope and dread suddenly shone before her eyes . . .

What if she were to find herself face to face with Mathurin? Great God!

Certainly, she would never have dared to attempt such an adventure, but since the opportunity had arisen, why should she not profit from it?

"Would you like to get down?" she asked her companion. "I'd like to see those men working . . . those *pégriots*, as they call them here . . . it would amuse me . . ."

And she strove to laugh.

Her friend acquiesced, and ordered the coachman to stop.

Slowly, the couple approached the "public works." The elegant man and the gaudy woman provoked a stir among the thirty men bent over the ground, spade or pick-ax in hand. Almost all of them lifted their heads for a second and wiped away the sweat that was running over their foreheads in large droplets.

"My God, how unhappy they must be!" murmured Françoise, searching for Mathurin.

Instead of the visage of her fiancé she only saw the sniggering and grimacing face of Nez-de-Coq. He fixed his ironic and hateful eyes upon her, and his lips pronounced words that did not reach as far as her.

"Why, there's that slut! That means that her mec, Tête-Rouge, isn't far away! There's one that has luck . . . he doesn't stop to do failed turns and never gets caught. Do you see that chick, the rest of you? If you had one like that under our tent in the evening, you wouldn't get bored. No, but when she's finished staring at us . . . oh, I know who she's looking for . . . it's her Mathurin. Hey there, pompier . . . there's a little lady asking or you . . . don't you recognize her—it's Françoise!"

Mathurin, who was a few paces away, in the process of breaking rocks, only heard the word "Françoise." He raised his head instinctively, and he saw a woman in a bright costume. He recognized her immediately. It was her.

For the first time since he had been doing convict labor, the poor fellow emerged from his torpor. He stared at her, stammering her name.

That unexpected apparition caused him such a commotion that he went red and white by turns. He almost reached out his arms, not perceiving that she was not alone.

"Well, Breton," howled a terrible voice. "Haven't you finished idling? Do you imagine that you're here to dream? To work, damn it, or beware the silo, idler!"

A sly snigger burst forth—that was Nez-de-Coq, who was writhing with laughter. Abruptly extracted from his contemplation, Mathurin bent over his work again, trembling with fear and emotion.

Françoise had to lean on the arm of her lover in order not to collapse. She overcame her weakness and fixed her blue gaze on the sub-officer who was abusing the unfortunate Breton, Sergeant Crassni. He was not unknown to her; she had seen him before, but she did not know where, perhaps in the concert hall while making a collection. She remembered that physiognomy imprinted with brutality.

"Come on, let's go," said her lover, tugging her arm lightly. "It's not as funny as that, looking at these poor devils."

She followed him, after one last glance at Mathurin, who had resumed work, bent over the ground. After a few paces, however, she turned round in order to examine Sergeant Crassni.

She strove to appear cheerful and to laugh as she was lifted back into the caleche. She feigned exuberance.

Her brain, incapable of initiative, was traversed by a glimmer: the more she reflected, the more it seemed to her that she had encountered Crassni at the concert hall in Bône; perhaps she had even been the target of his gallantries. Why, then, should she not use the power of her charms to Mathurin's advantage, to try to ameliorate his situation?

That idea remained in her mind in the state of a seed, but it was to develop gradually, even in spite of Tête-Rouge.

Naturally, she had carefully concealed the encounter accomplished at the hazard of an excursion; she imagined that he would never know anything about it. But twenty-four hours after that scene, he had been warned by l'Algérien, informed immediately of the encounter by the mocking comments of the men of the detachment and by Nez-de-Coq himself.

So, one evening, Tête-Rouge launched at her: "Is he still doing well, your Mathurin?"

"Mathurin!" she stammered. "Mathurn . . . I . . . I don't know?"

"Ha! You don't know? But you saw him the other day on the road to Morris . . ."

"I . . . I . . ."

"Don't try to tell me the contrary. I'm informed. You must really be stupid, my poor girl, to have imagined that that would pass unnoticed . . . you ought to remember that I always know everything. Nothing escapes the Red Sorcerer, as they called me out there in Bretagne. Yes, nothing escapes these eyes!"

"But I assure you that . . ."

"Don't say another word. You have better things to do . . . or else, look out! So, I've learned that you spent a long moment, on the arm of a client, looking at the pégriots . . . especially Mathurin. What I can't swallow is that you looked at the pompier, a prisoner, a convict, and that you didn't dare admit it to me.

No, truly, you have fine relations! Madame is doubtless smitten with a convict. Well, you won't think about it any more! Keep to your rank . . ." And he continued, furiously: "Fortunately, I have people of my own on the spot . . . Georges-l'Algérien and Nez-de-Coq; I can do what I want with them, and I assure you that he's going to pass bad quarter-hours, your Mathurin. That'll teach you to play the fool! I want him dead within three months, you hear . . . and you know that when I say something, it's serious . . ."

"Oh! Tête-Rouge, I beg you, don't harm him . . . he's already so unfortunate!"

"What? You're taking his defense now? You feel sorry for the fate of that riff-raff. You want me to pulverize you, insect!" He fell upon her with clenched fists, ready to beat her with his customary violence and brutality.

He restricted himself to a slap, Françoise having darted a glance at him imploring his clemency, the gaze of a beaten and contented dog, full of submission to the omnipotent master who kept her on the end of a leash without permitting her the slightest swerve.

VI
The Recommendation

I've had my fill of the men of the Bois
Of all those types with manners
And I dream of going to live for months
With my little man near Asnières

Françoise sang, emphasizing the words with automatic gestures, opening her excessively red lips in a smile and underlining the scabrous passages with a wink of her blackened eyelids and a flick of her mascara-covered eyelashes.

At the end of each couplet she made a movement, always the same, in order to introduce her hands, with a lewd gesture, into the pockets of her vast velvet trousers, lift up her red flannel belt and plant a soft felt hat with a mischievous expression on her golden chignon, the rebel strands of which emerged in the most unexpected fashion and made an aureole of blonde light around her heavily made-up face.

She had already acquired a great ease on stage, and her eyes scanned the audience, seeming to search for conquests in advance.

In that direction, the singer had no complaints, and, according to a phrase repeated by comrades less pretty or less favored by chance, she "lifted the lot." All the men followed her with their eyes when she made the collection, inviting her to take a chartreuse, a glass of champagne or something else. All of them would have liked to have her at their table, to chat to her and whisper sweet nothings, stick flowers into the cleavage of her false collar or pinch her figure, poorly contained by her masculine costume.

Françoise was a good girl with all of them, and without giving herself gratuitously, she knew how to manipulate covetousness, give birth to desires and revive defunct infatuations.

What she was seeking, above all, in the concert hall darkened by the smoke of the customers' cigarettes, was a brutal physiognomy with abrupt features, a face that was too pale and also as hard as steel, with a nose as straight as a saber-cut surmounting a black moustache—one of those jet-black moustaches that give such a characteristic aspect of harshness and malevolence to the physiognomies that bear them.

That evening, her ditty finished, Françoise quit the stage very troubled, amid her habitual harvest of bravos. In the wings, a comrade had to help her off and obligingly handed her the tray covered with a napkin destined to make the collection.

"What's the matter, Françoise," she said to her, "do you have a flirt in the hall?"

"Me? Oh, no!"

"That's true ... you don't go in for flirtations; you're a woman in a thousand ... there are times when I tell myself that you don't have the temperament ..."

Françoise did not reply, and shrugged her shoulders as she drew away.

She traversed the wings and went through the door giving access to the hall. Then she became quite different, and commenced her tour with less lassitude and less disgust than usual, underlining the fall of the silver coins with a smile and a "Merci, Monsieur!"

A comedian had followed her on stage. Instead of listening to him, the spectators admired the pretty girl who was advancing, offering to their eyes, without false modesty, the dazzling flesh of her cleavage. Hands brushed her round waist, and the coins rained down.

Françoise did not see or hear anything, not smiling at anyone in a particular fashion. She only paid attention to the distance that separated her from the man with the brutal physiognomy that she had perceived a moment ago, from the stage ... and when she reached him, her attitude changed. She listened to Sub-officer Crassni's banal words, and her caressant gaze lingered upon him.

The sergeant immediately swelled with pride at the attention that the singer paid to him, tugged his moustache, straightened his torso and blushed with pleasure, looking around to see whether other people perceived his success. He was well-dressed in his black tunic with a collar embroidered with two little crossed gold keys; his red satin trousers would have given him the well-to-do appearance of an officer if his kepi, also ornamented with two fateful keys and excessively tilted over the left ear, had not corrected that initial impression and caused his apparent distinction to disappear.

He had no doubt that the prestige of his red trousers and his braid had impressed Françoise, and that he could go on to dally with her as he did with the sordid moukères of the brush. Crassni could not feel more joy, and while Françoise drew away after a long gaze, he was already making an entire plan to enjoy himself as soon as possible . . . for he had no doubt that he had just made a superb conquest.

In the intermission he went to prowl in the vicinity of the wings. As he did not see Françoise, he enquired about her. He was told that she had just left.

Crassni conceived a sharp chagrin in that regard, and swore to employ all means to encounter her again as soon as possible. How dare she leave him standing—him, the handsome Crassni, who turned the heads of all the Maltese women and at whom the curvaceous Jewesses of the souks rolled their eyes!

From then on he came every evening to the concert hall of Bône. And the Bretonne always showed herself attentive to him—but she was deliberately coquettish, making him desire her. She used all the tricks of the métier that she had learned by degrees in the course of her eventful existence.

When she deemed that Crassni had been waiting long enough, she provoked him with a long conversation. One evening, after the performance, when all the spectators had retired, some alone and others in the joyous company of other employees of the establishment, Françoise allowed the rutilant sub-officer to offer her a beer in a private room.

Under the gas-light, she had time to examine him in detail, and to divine him. Then, seeing the conceited way in which he puffed out his chest and tugged his moustache, recounting inept stories, she began by flattering the soldier's pride.

"I noticed you a long time ago, sergeant. I thought that you had such a masculine appearance, so proud and energetic!"

"Truly, dear beauty, you allowed your beautiful eyes to fall upon me?"

"And I was only waiting for a favorable opportunity to approach you ..."

"You're utterly charming. For my part, your beauty also seduced me a long time ago ... I'll even confess to you that I only come to the concert hall for you ..."

"I'm very flattered. Truly, we couldn't do better than meet one another ..."

"Isn't it so? I hope, then, that you'll agree to spend the end of the night with me?" Crassni's eyes were ablaze with amorous flames, while his pale face suddenly turned crimson.

"I'd certainly like to accept, sergeant, but I have a lover who is atrociously jealous. Your offer makes me smile ... it's very tempting ... but in staying with you I'd fear exposing myself to the just wrath of my lover ..." And in a sigh, Françoise, a skillful actress, murmured: "He's so jealous!"

That little scene having produced the desired effect, she turned her lovely eyes toward Crassni, stimulating his passion; then, very close to him, feline, she sighed: "Finally!"

But the sub-officer had stiffened, in a chivalrous manner, and said, with a bold expression: "Have no fear, Mademoiselle; I'm not a soldier for nothing and I'll be able to defend you ..."

"You're brave, I divined that, and I regret, in spite of that, being obliged to refuse your offer ..."

"Truly, it's impossible for you?"

"I assure you ... at least for today. But as I desire that the two of us become excellent friends, I'll make arrangements ..."

"Oh, how good you are and how happy you render me. Speak, I'm listening ... I'll do anything that will please you. But permit me, you're so kind ..."

And Crassni's head, the head of an overly handsome fellow, advanced toward Françoise: "Come on, you want to, eh? One kiss, for the trouble ... only one."

"Go on," said Françoise. "Only one, greedy ... and be quick!"

The soldier appeased the fever of his lips on that flesh, the source of desires. And as he lingered, Françoise recalled him to down-to-earth reality.

"Then, for our . . . for our rendezvous?" Crassni stammered.

"Right! Can you come to meet me here tomorrow evening?"

"Tomorrow evening?" the sergeant repeated. Then, after a pause: "I won't be free, but too bad. For you, beauty, I'll do the impossible. I'll leave the guard of my detachment to my comrade. Agreed, for tomorrow evening . . ."

"Come, then . . . I'll make dispositions to render myself free and to have nothing to dread. Wait for me at the Swiss Chalet; I'll arrive at midnight, or half past . . . and I'll be all yours!"

"You fulfill me, darling . . . all mine!"

"Yes, all yours!" Françoise repeated, smoothing the soldier's heavy moustache with her perfumed hand; he reared up under the caress and stole a kiss in passing.

That postponement was only a ruse on Françoise's part. Very proud of her politics, she went back to her dressing-room, followed by the sergeant.

First light was already breaking over the sea in the direction of La Calle when, having taken off the velvet costume in which she sang, she emerged from the casino in an elegant dress of blue linen that suited her perfectly, molding her hips and her breasts in the most troubling fashion.

"Then, truly, there's no means today?" implored Crassni one last time, his appetite stimulated.

"You know that, big beast! By patient until tomorrow, and we'll go mad . . . you'll catch up . . . we'll catch up . . ."

Françoise hailed a caleche, which deposited her at her home a few minutes later.

Tête-Rouge was asleep. All was going well.

As for Crassni, half-drunk on the heady promises that had just been made to him, he wandered around the port, awaiting with impatience the opening of the cafés and a barber. Before returning to his detachment, stationed thirty-three kilometers away on the road to La Calle, he wanted to make himself beautiful for the evening.

He passed a terrible day. The pégriots knew that something was up. Privations of wine fell like hail and, at the moment when, spick and span in his uniform and white-gloved, Crassni climbed into the carriage of a colonist that was to take him into Bône, the riflemen were taking two men whom Crassni had punished that afternoon to the "tomb" in order to put them in irons.

Nez-de-Coq saw the scene from the threshold of his tent and pronounced, mockingly: "The *pied* is going to make hay with the moukères . . . two numbskulls are going into irons. Everyone takes his pleasure as he can!" And he uttered a burst of laughter that made the other prisoners shudder.

Françoise had given Crassni a rendezvous at the Swiss Chalet, on the Saint-Cloud beach, about three kilometers from the town. It was there, in fact, that amorous projects generally reached an agreeable conclusion.

Crassni followed the minutes anxiously on his watch, and uttered a veritable howl of triumphant joy when he saw Françoise arrive, fresh, captious and exciting, more seductive than ever. Two heavily sugared pernods had put him in verve and he wanted to be witty. Having saluted her as ceremoniously as possible, he said: "It's Venus in the house of Mars!" And he put his arm around the supple waist of the Bretonne, who drew him into a private booth that the manager, a small red-faced man and a good businessman, had just offered to their amorous conversation.

When a rather elegant supper was served—a supper that Crassni's modest salary must have found uncomfortable—the sub-officer, whose ardor had been ill-contained since the previous evening, wanted to obtain his recompense.

But Françoise refused, pensively. "In a little while," she said. "For dessert . . . let's eat and chat, and afterwards . . ."

"Afterwards?" questioned Crassni, palpitating with passion.

"Well, afterwards, you'll be in command. I'll be your . . . how do you put it? . . . your subordinate."

The supper was very cheerful. Françoise illuminated the darkness of the sub-officer's complex soul like a ray of sunlight. It was a veritable amorous feast.

At the end of the meal, Françoise, whom Crassni had succeeded in seating on his knees, drank champagne from his glass. That was delicious.

But time was passing; Françoise seemed to be in no hurry to leave. Deliberately, Crassni allowed the conversation to lapse. He had already uttered several times a sacramental: "Shall we go?" But those three syllables, emphasized by the soldier, had the effect of prompting a new torrent of speech from the young woman. She rambled on and on.

Crassni had put on his kepi, settled the bill, considerably salted, and buttoned his gloves with a thousand precautions, his large hairy paws adapting to such promiscuity with icy goatskin poorly.

"We'll go, then?" he said. "Let's go back to Bône. I know a hotel where it'll be as if we were in paradise."

Françoise could not suppress a start.

"A hotel? Oh, yes . . ."

"It's still agreed, eh? Oh, come, I beg you . . ."

"Let's go."

Françoise had her idea. As she climbed into the carriage she made up her mind. "You'll admit, my lad, that I've been good to you?"

"Yes," said Crassni, foreseeing in his naïve soul the inevitable request for money, which would have the effect of a cold shower.

In sum, the wine was tugging, he needed a drink, all the more so because a long sojourn in the brush had exasperated his senses. And just in case, before departing, he had borrowed eight douros from his comrade, Sergeant Valotte.

He was so drawn—him, the goblin mirror, the feller of virtues, the heartbreaker—that he would allow himself to pay. So, wanting to keep on her good side, he would, like a veritable gentleman, offer Françoise a louis as the price of her future complaisance.

But she had divined too. "Oh, can you imagine . . . but my word, you're mad! It isn't for money that you please me . . . it's because you're handsome and robust . . . because you have nice eyes and a fine moustache . . ."

She underlined her words with caresses, which delighted the sub-officer.

In the meantime, the caleche, pulled by two apocalyptic nags, entered the town. "Poor dog . . . get away! Do you think that I'd ask you for money? Oh!"

"Then you'll permit me to make you a gift . . . a jewel . . . an Arab ring . . ."

"No, nothing at all; one kiss, and I'll be content . . ."

"Then you don't want anything?"

Nothing . . . which is to say, my God . . . am I stupid, when I think that, thanks to you, I can render a service to someone . . . and what a service!"

"Speak!" said Crassni, holding her in his arms, delighted to give her pleasure.

"It's really you who commands the detachment of military convicts who are presently repairing the road to La Calle?"

"Yes . . . It isn't that you want to take service in my company?" said the sergeant, laughing. "I don't see any inconvenience in that, you know—on the contrary, you can imagine the pleasure I'd have in reengaging then! Oh, the parties under the tent! We'd make the siesta all the time!"

"Get away, baby," said Françoise. "It isn't for me . . ." Then, after a pause: "You must have one of my countrymen under your orders, a Breton?"

"A Breton?" said Crassni. "There's only one; number 3474, a dirty fellow. What's yours called?"

"Mathurin Dagorne," said Françpise, painfully.

"That's the same one. What do you want with that convict?"

"Oh, my word, nothing . . . or not much. Only, if you could make life a little easier for him, you'd give me pleasure."

"He interests you, then, the clown. Damn! They're lucky, the pégriots, to turn the heads of pretty women like you!"

"Oh, don't joke . . . If you knew!"

"If I knew what?"

Françoise, unable to hide her embarrassment and her disturbance, said, timidly: "He's my brother. He merits compassion . . ."

"If it's like that," said Crassni, "I'll take care of it. You know that I can't refuse you anything, my darling. You can have confidence in me; I'll do everything possible to be useful to him."

"Oh, thank you!" said Françoise, taking the sergeant's hands. "I'd be so grateful to you."

And the Bretonne, softly rocked by the jolts of the vehicle, abandoned herself to Crassni's caresses.

When it stopped, the carriage extracted her from her torpor.

They were in a street in the old quarter, outside a hotel. Françoise, glad of the sergeant's promise, was about to be able to testify her gratitude to him.

Suddenly, however, the silhouette of an officer appeared at the corner of the street.

Before the door of the hotel opened, the officer—a captain of tirailleurs—was upon them. Crassni saluted. The officer responded mechanically and, perceiving the woman, examined her covertly.

He might have been about to draw away but, suddenly turning round, the officer came straight toward Crassni—who, immediately returned to reality, struck a military attitude.

"What are you doing in town at this hour, sergeant?"

"*Mon capitaine* . . ."

"Enough! I don't understand why you aren't with your men. It's not astonishing that they're all idlers . . . there are never any officers in the camp, and in the meantime, the indigenous tirailleurs are the masters. Show me your permission slip."

"*Mon capitaine*, I don't have one . . . I thought . . ."

"What!" howled the captain, turning as red as his kepi. "You don't have permission and you're trailing your gaiters in town at undue hours! But what does this signify? There's no authority, then? *Monsieur le sergent* abandons his post in order to come and party with pretty women. I know what the métier is; I've carried the sack; I don't want you to make up a story. Rejoin your detachment immediately, and don't do it again, or I'll make a report and you'll be demoted!"

Crassni, pale, more dead than alive, shamed of being subjected to such a sermon in front of his conquest, murmured: "*Merci, mon capitaine.*" But as he made as if to remain, the captain went on:

"Come on, kiss your friend and go!"

Cassini put a kiss—only one, very regretfully, on Françoise's cheek. She had time to say to him: "Remember!"

That word charmed him and annoyed him at the same time. How ought he to interpret it? Was it their amour that Françoise was telling him to remember, or the recommendation regarding 3474?

That was an enigma that was not clarified that day.

Scarcely had he turned the corner of the street, followed by the officer's eyes, than the latter, after having saluted Françoise with a gracious gesture, continued his stroll, muttering:

"They're all mad . . . going into town without permission . . . doubtless he thinks he's the general in command of an army corps . . . fortunately, I'm a good fellow . . ."

A few minutes later Françoise was at home with Tête-Rouge. He was in bed; her return woke him up.

"Where have you been?" he demanded.

"The concert hall. I was retained by a client . . . nothing new today; I have to see him again tomorrow. I believe it will be interesting," she added, sliding her thumb over her index finger in a familiar gesture.

It was the first time she had lied with so much assurance.

"If that's true, you've worked well, kid. Come and join me."

And Tête-Rouge made room for her on the bed, where she came to nestle.

VII
At the Camp

The entire detachment was already at work when Crassni returned to the camp.

The prisoners, under the guard of the tirailleurs and Sergeant Valotte, were some distance away, on the road that they were rebuilding. From the camp they could be seen distinctly coming and going; even the commands and reprimands were audible.

His mouth thick, Crassni scarcely responded to the greeting of the sergeant of the tirailleurs of the reserve; he went to the tent that he shared with his comrade, and in a few seconds changed his dazzling costume for work clothes: faded red trousers tightened at the knees in big yellow boots, a shiny dolman and a greasy kepi. Then he went out, not without having equipped himself with his revolver, enclosed in a yellow leather holster.

The camp was tranquil; Crassni uttered an "ouf" of relief. From the threshold of his tent he considered the landscape. There were the four marabout-tents of the prisoners—fifteen men per tent, as per regulations, and that of the tirailleurs of the guard; further away, separate, a seventh contained the food supplies.

The camp was surrounded by a shallow double ditch indicating its extreme limits, which the men were not allowed to cross. In the middle stood a small low tent, the "tomb," under which a man, a pégriot, his wrists bound and his legs secured in the bar of justice, was awaiting the end of his torture at six o'clock in the evening, singing barrière refrains while the tirailleurs, insensible to his martyrdom, were busy with their habitual occupations, washing their linen and cooking the stew.

Crassni judged the morning too far advanced to rejoin his work crew and waited patiently next to a glass of absinthe for his comrade's return. Under the tent, seated before a camp table, he followed with an indifferent eye the operations that preceded the return of the men.

To begin with, two prisoners, under the guard of a tirailleur, came back from the labor; they were the two cooks who would prepare their companions' meal. He laughed as he saw the difficulty they had in lighting the fire necessary to the confection of the meal.

Soon, he perceived Valotte giving the signal to return; and immediately, a long chaplet of men extended along the road.

It was six o'clock. The sun was blazing terribly.

Soon, the long procession arrived in the camp. The prisoners let themselves fall like beasts, under the eyes of their guards, while Valotte, sweating blood and water, took off his jacket and threw it, with an extended arm, toward Crassni, whom he had just perceived in the half-light of the tent.

"What, back already?" he said. "It didn't go well, then?"

"Yes, it did. Sit down. Here's a glass—have a drink with me."

"Right. How did you come back? I didn't see a carriage."

"I took the five o'clock train from Bône, which dropped me at the Marais station at six . . . three kilometers on foot and here I am."

"Then the moukère in question didn't turn up?"

"Yes, old man, on the contrary, but that's a whole story. I'll tell you, but in the meantime, to your health!"

The two sergeants clinked glasses; and with a luxury of details, remarks and loud expressions, Crassni brought his friend up to date with the various peripeties of his evening and night, until the moment when he had been so annoyingly surprised by a noctambulistic captain.

When he had told him everything, without omitting or neglecting the slightest detail, tugging his moustache he asked: "Well, Valotte, what do you think of that? In spite of sojourns in the brush, one still has customs, and one is able to please young actresses!"

"Possibly," said Valotte. "You're able to please young actresses, as you say, but you've gone a long way around . . . you failed to tie it up and, in sum, you didn't have the shepherdess. Oh, your ideas are too grand; rather than riding to Bône after women, why not do as I do?"

"Yes, I know, Arab women, moukères. Thank you very much. I only take medicine when I have a cold."

"It's not worth the trouble of being disgusted; there are Arab women who aren't bad. Look, at the douar that you can see over there by the lakeside there are virgins, old man, about whom I'll only say this: try . . ."

"I could never . . . all the more so with my advantages . . ."

"Your advantages! Good! Don't get on your high horse yet. Listen, Crassni—we're good mates, aren't we?"

"Yes . . ."

"We've been together for six years. You're commanding the thirteenth company, me the fourteenth . . . we always have the same job, we understand one another . . . let me tell you something . . ."

"Speak."

"Promise me not to get annoyed."

"Agreed."

"Well, I believe that the donzelle is stringing you along."

Crassni's pale face became livid, but he collected himself quickly and, after taking a generous swig of absinthe, his eyes bulging, he said: "What are you saying, Valotte? You're not talking sense; the chick is smitten with me."

"Possibly . . . possibly . . . but you know me, I'm skeptical. I no longer believe in anything, since my girl-friend . . ."

"Yes, yes, enough! You no longer believe in anything, you're the enemy of all women since your acquaintance ran away with a Tunisian. It's annoying, I admit, but in the end, it doesn't prove anything. There are men that women don't dump . . ."

"You're doubtless speaking for yourself. You have reason to hold on to your illusions, but, you see, it's necessary never to get carried away. I'd rather be cuckolded by a chic Tunisian who has money in his pocket than a numbskull."

"By a numbskull . . . Speak, explain yourself . . . I don't understand."

"You don't understand? Well, it's that the gonzesse has bewitched you, to the point of making you lose your reason. Come on, Crassni, an old jackal like you, an African soldier, who's fought I don't know how many campaigns in the brush, is letting yourself be turned over like a greenhorn. Your acquaintance is the mistress of 3474—Dagorne, the Breton . . . and you've been taken in like a novice."

"No!"

"It's as I say."

"Then . . . then . . . what's this about the brother? Oh, the slut, the slut . . . to put one over on me like that! No, I'll lose my stripes if it goes like that. Well, I'll take care of him, the client, since there's nothing to be done against her, I'll take charge of leading him by the paths that will make him reenlist without pay . . ."

"So you're not upset, Crassni? Perhaps I was wrong to tell you?"

"No, I thank you . . ."

"Calm down, come and eat. Georges, in the canteen, has prepared us a nice menu . . ."

The meal was rapid, but it was succeeded by drinks, varied and numerous. If Valotte did them honor, Crassni used and abused them with an evident weakness. When it was concluded, Crassni, predisposed to drunkenness by the emotions of the night, was greatly stirred, so he responded carelessly to the multiple questions addressed to him by the caterer and had enormous difficulty following the conversation. His head was vacillating, his eyes were red, and an invincible torpor gradually invaded him.

Georges did not stop talking, taking Valotte and Crassni to one side.

"Oh, truly, I admire you, sergeant, for leading such an existence. What a life . . . always in the brush with the villainous cocos you have to lead. You must have some in the bunch who aren't convenient . . ."

"Oh, not convenient!" said Valotte. "That's a manner of speaking, for the bad heads become good with us; it's a waste of time to act up or try to be clever . . ."

"For sure," said Crassni, supportively. "We have bracelets for the brazen. As for those who don't like our society and would like to give up the skip at any price, we always find a means to lodge sixteen grams between their eyes. Isn't that so, Valoltte?"

"Oh, you know my ideas about that, Crassni. As for shouting at the pégriots, and withholding a portion of wine if necessary, it's fine by me, but as for irons, the silo and the tomb, there's nothing doing . . . even less for the sixteen grams. Everyone has his own ideas . . . you have yours and I have mine."

"Right!" said Crassni. "You're only a damp chicken; you've never been able to make yourself feared . . ."

"It's not a matter of being feared, it's a matter of being obeyed. On the work-site, as soon as they perceive you, the pégriots work at full tilt, but as soon as your back is turned, they don't give a damn, whereas, when it's a matter of that good fellow Valotte, they don't go faster at one time than another, but at least they don't stop . . . all that in order not to tell me stories . . ."

"Yes, keep talking, old man," sniggered Crassni. "One day, the convicts will write to the minister to ask for a medal for you . . ."

"You're joking, Sergeant," Georges interjected. "But perhaps you're right, in a way. You have terrible men here. Thus, one of my friends in Bône told me, a few days ago, that he had recognized a bandit of the worst sort in one of the two companies working here . . . a bad lot who, it seems, tried to murder his captain. You understand that with fellows like that, one can't take too many precautions."

"What's his name, this client?" asked Valotte,

"In truth," said Georges, pretending to search for a name he knew well, "I believe it was a Breton . . ."

"A Breton!" Crassni started.

"Yes, a Breton . . . a former pompier. Wait, the name's coming back to me . . . it's Mathurin Dagorne."

"3474, then!" said Crassni, glancing at Valotte.

"Good—it's your protégé . . ."

And Valotte, who was certainly more stupid than malevolent, burst into ironic laughter, which caused hateful gleams to shine in the yellow eyes of his comrade.

In the camp, however, a shrtill sound resounded. With a little thrust of the tongue into his instrument, the trumpeter preluded the notes of the reveille—for in Africa, during the most intense heat, the siesta is imposed between ten o'clock in the morning and two o'clock in the afternoon, when all the men must resume their service. The reveille vibrated, alert and rapid:

> *Soldier, get up,*
> *Soldier, get up,*
> *Soldier, get up,*
> *If you don't want to get up*
> *Say that you're ill.*
> *If you aren't recognized*
> *You'll have four days more!*

The two sergeants had regained the tents in a few strides; at the appeal of the clarion the prisoners had come to line up in two files, and patiently, poor whipped beasts, awaited the order to depart.

The tirailleurs of the guard were there; with a customary movement they had loaded their rifles and fitted bayonets to the barrels, while Crassni and Valotte, after having equipped themselves with their revolvers, took the head of the wretched column.

"There's wind in the sails," said a mocking voice. "The galley slaves are on fire!"

"Shut up, Nez-de-Coq, you'll get yourself buckled," remarked a comrade, obligingly. "For sure, the slave-drivers are full up, but shut up, or you'll catch it out there at the site . . ."

And while the detachment went to work, on the interminable white road that it was necessary to terminate, Nez-de-Coq, ever hateful, replied: "What I do is my affair; at least I say what I think, I'm not a sly fellow like that Breton who doesn't say two words all day. That client," he said, darting a terrible glance at Mathurin, who was marching behind him, "must be a snitch—a fellow to rat on the mates, no? Eh, Breton—you can see that it's you I'm talking about . . ."

But Mathurin remained insensible under that torrent of sarcasm. What did insults and disobliging words matter to him? Bleak and annihilated, as if in a dream, he went to his destiny, whatever it might be.

The different events that had followed his condemnation had passed over him like a light breeze. The degradation, his arrival in Bône and the site of the public works all faded into the increasingly opaque fog of his memory.

Only his sojourn in the kasbah still caused frissons to run through him when he thought of the long martyrdom he had endured between the sad gray walls of the severe and sullen edifice that overlooked the blue sea—an obstacle between France and Bretagne, his homeland, everything that reminded him of his grand amour, Françoise, for whom he was there, and the wretched rag clad in ignominious livery that he now was.

During the whole journey from the camp to the work-site, Nez-de-Coq did not stop harassing Mathurin with coarse jokes in a more-than-dubious taste, which made the pégriots burst out laughing. The indigenous tirailleurs, without understanding all the savor of Nez-de-Coq's wit, were also overtaken by the general hilarity.

Finally, they stopped at the site; a whistle-blast resounded. That was the order given by Valotte, the senior in rank, to be quiet and set to work without delay.

The work commenced, a terrible labor. Blows of sledgehammers broke the stones under the eyes of the tirailleurs and the two sergeants, who went back and forth between the men shoveling fragments into wheelbarrows and going, with exclamations of pain, cursing the sun and thirst, to tip their loads on the road, which others pressed down forcefully, sweating like wellsprings, their long-peaked beige kepis plunging over their napes and their coarse cotton shirts soaked by large patches transpiration sticking to their backs and chests.

Mathurin was one of the latter, while Nez-de-Coq was pushing a wheelbarrow with evident ill-will. Entirely given to his hatred, he had just emptied the contents of his barrow over Dagorne's feet, who had not uttered a single ill-tempered or angry word in his regard.

"Idiot!" Nez-de-Coq had muttered, while Mathurin, like a good beast of burden, continued his task imperturbably, uttering a terrible "Han! Han!" at every blow of the piledriver on the ground.

He was there when Crassni arrived, his gaze evil, red-faced, his moustache in battle order, his kepi tilted and his unbuttoned tunic showing a mauve shirt.

"What's this? One is frozen?" he said, in his thick voice. "Move, damn it, move!"

Mathurin, entirely devoted to his task, had not even looked up, so the sergeant went on:

"Well, 3474 . . . I'm talking to you, idler! You can't hear me? Your ears are blocked . . . you're stupid . . . you doubtless need a little sojourn in the tomb with jewels on your four limbs to unblock them, sly swine!"

And while abusing him, Crassni circled Dagorne, while the other prisoners put down their tools momentarily in order to follow the phases of that unequal contest, whose outcome was easy to foresee.

"Poor Breton," said a compassionate voice. "He's rowing like a stag, but the foot is on his antlers . . . he's going to cop it."

"Silence, damn it!" ordered Crassni. He was now face to face with his victim, who immediately, with his habitual passive obedience, had struck a regulation pose, his hands by his side and his gaze fixed immutably fifteen paces away.

Crassni stood before him victoriously, his legs apart and his chest swelling; then, twisting his moustache with a nervous hand, he spat: "Come on, look me in the face, numbskull. What, you don't have the courage . . . you're good for nothing but idling. Oh, I know that working on the roads in Africa is less agreeable than going on the spree in Paris and trying to murder your captain . . ."

Under that insult, Mathurin went pale.

"Come on, respond—say something, dirty swine! Defend yourself!"

Mathurin remained closed in his habitual mutism.

"Go on, Monsieur, put on airs . . . Monsieur doesn't deign to speak to his superior . . . Monsieur is doubtless a Spanish grandee?"

As Crassni spoke his anger grew before Dargorne's silence.

"There are no more workers, then . . . there are only damp chickens . . . No, look at this, he doesn't respond, he shuts up . . . Sly bastard!"

"Bur Sergeant . . ." Mathurin ventured, timidly.

"Shut up, damn it! Will you shut up! Oh, you permit yourself reflections! Just wait, my lascar, you were recommended to me in a very particular fashion ..."

Crassni made a sign to the corporal of tirailleurs. "Take a man with you and take this citizen to the camp; put him in number one irons, and buckle him well—I'll see this evening how you've done. And on the way, if he takes a step out of line, shoot him."

"Yes, sergeant! Forward, you!" the corporal said to Dagorne. With a brutal gesture, the corporal gave him the signal to march.

Before setting out, after having picked up his smock, thrown on the edge of a ditch, Mathurin had time to hear Crassni launch at him: "I'll teach you, swine, to have women recommend you. It'll do you a lot of good, your shepherdess's recommendation! Oh no—when one thinks that this pégriot will send women up and that his sergeant will be taken in! No, that will never be seen. Oh, you won't sleep alone tonight, but it won't be with your former mistress ... it will be with Mademoiselle Crapaudine!"

At the work-site the day finished; the adventure of the former pompier supplied the banal conversation of the prisoners on the return journey.

"Poor fellow," said one. "He's very vilely treated. Crassni has it in for him; he won't let up ..."

"Too bad for him." said a thick voice.

"Oh, you again, Nez-de-Coq. You always want the mates to get cuts and bruises ... but the *pied* doesn't spare you either!"

"Possibly. The *pied* is a swine, but that doesn't prevent the Breton from being a failed brother."

When a blast of the whistle announced the end of the shift the pégriots lined up four by four and, in the same order as the morning, returned to the camp.

The sky was studded with stars when the column arrived at the tents.

The men spared a glance of pity at Mathurin, extended with irons on his limbs, but he, still immutable and indifferent, scarcely turned his head to watch them file past—although his breast could not repress a profound sigh containing all of his rancor and sadness.

After the meal, as soon as Valotte was lying on his summary bed, Crassni quit the tent and went to prowl around the camp. Everything was silent.

A douar dog barked in the distance, and its howl, reverberated by the echo of the neighboring hills, took on a tragic accent. Then the silence was troubled by the voices of the men on guard, who sent from the four corners of the camp, every five minutes, the traditional "Sentinels beware!"

Crassni made a tour of the tents. In their canvas abode the tirailleurs waiting for their turn on guard were playing cards; their guttural exclamations reached the sergeant's ears:

"*Inhaldin bou!*"

"*Terba! Inshallah!*"

His steps brought him close to the prisoners. Here, the real or simulated snores announced that everyone was asleep or . . . what did he care? He caught scraps of conversation, stifled as soon as the interlocutors heard his footsteps. Hoarse voices lauded Pantruche, the women of the boulevard, the mates of La Chapelle and Sebasto . . . And all of them cursed the injustice of fate, which, instead of leaving them to their amours back there with their chicks, who worked on the sidewalk, had exiled them thousands of leagues from the capital to make them exert themselves against their will in a terrible a poorly-remunerated métier.

Crassni arrived at the tomb, the little low tent under which Mathurin had been lying for eight hours.

The sergeant approached stealthily and arrived very close to the man; a ray of moonlight illuminated the scene crudely, in which Crassni found an evil pleasure.

The Breton was extended, his ankles imprisoned and locked in the bar of justice, his wrists enchained and raised above his head, his feet and arms fixed to the ground by tent-pegs, which prevented any movement. Crassni drew closer, still advancing and gazing. What he saw made him shudder: two large blue eyes, the eyes of a docile beast, staring at him without hatred, resigned. The officer's anger increased further.

"Ah! The swine isn't asleep! It's the fault of that imbecile of an indigenous corporal; these Arabs are useless; they don't even know how to put a man in irons!"

As he spoke, he applied a turn of the screw to the handcuffs, which dug into the flesh of the patient. The wrists, already congested by immobility, turned violet, swollen as if to burst.

Crassni tried to apply a second turn, but, either because his strength was exhausted or because the vice was at its limit, he could not succeed in tightening the torture apparatus.

But he had an idea. He went to the tirailleurs' tent to look for a bayonet. With that weapon, which he introduced into the hole of the lock, he succeeded in rendering to the handcuffs the maximum pain that they could deliver.

Dagorne's wrists were blue-black. Droplets of blood were oozing from the violet-tinted thumbs: a terrible sweat that did not extract a single plaint from the Breton.

"There, brute!" said Crassni, sarcastically.

The eyes turned toward him then.

"Ah, you've finally understood. Are you calmer, then, swine, louse! With me, you know, it's necessary not to be bold, or I'll make arrangements to give you to the jackals to eat, along with the carcasses of the strong heads. When I think that you had yourself recommended by your mistress . . . no, you don't refuse yourself anything . . ."

Then, wanting to torture Mathurin mentally, since the physical torture had not extracted a plaint from him: "The Bretonne you know . . . your former . . . well, I've had her too. She can't hold it against me—I've taken care of you!"

Then, to terminate the conversation, Crassni launched a kick against the Breton's ribs and returned to his tent.

Two minutes later, with the lack of conscience that was his prerogative, he was snoring, fully dressed on his camp-bed, while Mathurin, helpless, lying on his back, his ankles paralyzed, his hands bloody and his soul in disarray, was contemplating the beautiful violet sky, with its myriad stars, which reminded him of summer evenings in his dear Bretagne.

VIII
Mathurin's Luck

While Valotte was returning from the work-site with his detachment, a joyful voice called to him just as he entered the camp.

"Well, sergeant, that's another half day terminated. While waiting for the resumption of the work, do me the amity of coming to lunch with me; I have guests, a friend and his wife, and we're putting little dishes in the large one!"

Before making that frank invitation, Georges-l'Algérien uttered a loud burst of laughter and went toward the sergeant, his hand extended. He caught up with him as he arrived at his tent.

"Your colleague's not here, then? That's a pity!"

"What do you expect, Monsieur Georges; it's the work that requires him. The fevers have scythed down a few men, so, as the job has to proceed rapidly, Crassni went to the depot this morning to take delivery of a new consignment of convicts."

"Too bad; your friend won't be with us, but at least I can count on you?"

"Without fail. Give me time to dress properly and I'll join you in the canteen."

Valotte made himself handsome; Crassni not being there, he had no scruple in putting on varnished shoes and donning his comrade's best black satin dolman.

Georges traversed the camp and went into the canteen, where his associate, a Mozabite[1] as yellow as a lemon and bearded like a goat was waiting, making grand gestures and crying in his comical language: "You come! You come quickly! A carrossa is coming!"

Georges recognized the English carriage that Tête-Rouge had possessed for several days.

"There they are—you're right, Resgui," he said. "They'll be here in a few minutes. It's time to prepare the *bleue*. Go fetch fresh water."

Resgui had scarcely placed the bucket on the table set up in front of the shack than Tête-Rouge leapt down from the English carriage and appeared, clad in white flannel, with an elegant panama shading his face.

He aided his companion to descend from the vehicle. Was it the long journey in the sun, the memory of Crassni or the proximity of Mathurin? At any rate, Françoise was completely transfigured.

Taking her in his robust arms, Tête-Rouge set her down on the road in a flight of crumpled silk undershirts.

"Oh, how content I am with my excursion . . ." she said.

But he cut off her speech and shook the hands of Georges-l'Algérien vigorously, who had run to meet them.

"How content I am to see you again here, old friend, established as proprietor! It's a long way from Paris, my old Georges! Do you remember the little bistro in La Chapelle where we played manille? We've both come a long way!"

"Yes, one can't complain too much . . . what about you?"

"Oh, me," said Tête-Rouge, flicking away a few scattered speck of dust from his jacket, "things aren't going badly in Bône; I occupy myself with commissions and exports, and give business advice . . . I have a lot of friends, to the point that they want to nominate me for something in the imminent elections . . ."

---

1 The Mozabites were a Berber tribe originating in the northern Sahara; their homeland was annexed by the French in 1882.

"Ah," said Georges, sententiously, "it was always said that you'd do well. But we're chatting and the sun is hot. Let's go to the canteen; the aperitifs are waiting for us."

The meal was animated. Valotte, as handsome as a star, rutilant, lustrous and polished, his breast ornamented with all his medals, had come to join the guests.

Everything surprised Françoise; nothing interested Tête-Rouge, who knew everything and had seen everything.

Valotte, who had not seen a European woman for several months, darted glances gleaming with covetousness at Françoise. After he had drunk several glasses of wine on top of his absinthe, whether it was illusion of reality, Valotte thought he perceived that the wife of Georges' guest was testifying a certain amity to him.

As soon as he was almost sure of the fact, the "bench-foot" felt his blood turn, and something contracted in his chest and his throat.

Name of God, he thought, *she's rudely well-dressed. There's no denying that she's worth a lot more than the Africans.*

Throughout the meal he expended himself in amiabilities and gallantries while Tête-Rouge conversed with his friend Georges in low voices, so that he could not hear them.

"Well, old man, you've fallen on your feet. Of what do you have to complain? You've found a fine scheme . . . you're making a fortune."

"Oh, you know, it's necessary not to strut when one's making a living; necessary to deem oneself lucky. It isn't with the pégriots that I make money . . . I'm forced to serve them, at a certain tariff established by the military administration, various articles destined to ameliorate their ordinary fare—sardines, white bread, Sardinian cheese, figs, wine and so on, and on Sunday to sell them paper to write to mates back in Pantruche. Add to that what I do with the temporaries, colonists or indigenes, who go to the markets in Blandan, Turf and La Calle—not forgetting, of course, the clientele of Messieurs les Sergents . . . and you'll admit that I'm not too unfortunate."

"Possibly, possibly . . . you're well installed, you don't lack anything, but . . ."

"But what? What are you trying to say?"

Raising his voice, Tête-Rouge continued: "A simple remark. Do you think it's funny for an honest businessman to spend every day in the midst of the most dangerous criminals?" Then, addressing Valotte, who was swooning with admiration before Françoise, he said: "You don't share my opinion, sergeant?"

"Oh, you know," replied the bewildered sub-officer, suddenly extracted from the savor of his dream, "there are many cocos in the heap who aren't easy, but it passes. In my company, I don't have any complaint . . . but Crassni, my colleague, who isn't here today, has a few strong heads to keep in respect . . . apaches, Parisians, vagabonds come from who knows where, the refuse of courts martial. Only to cite one example, he has under his orders a certain Breton, number 3474, who gives him diabolical trouble . . . it's not that he acts up, no, it's the force of inertia in his case . . ."

Françoise, listening to the conversation, opened her eyes wide, which she shut from time to time in order to flee the glances darted by Tête-Rouge's eyes.

Valotte, excited by the drink and wanting to show that he could turn phrases before the fair sex, went on:

"The client is named Dagorne . . . he doesn't care for the site where he works. Crassni doesn't know to what to attribute that state of things, but he's almost certain the Dagorne—the pompier, as his comrades call him because he comes from the sapeur-pompiers of Paris—has turned the heads of all the pégriots in his detachment. He doesn't say anything but I don't make mistakes, you know; I have an eye . . . he's dormant water. He's brewing something, so I pointed him out to my colleague, who's taken his measures . . ."

And Valotte kept talking, responding to the skilful questions posed by Tête-Ruge, while Françoise writhed anxiously, casting troubled glances in the direction of the tents situated fifty meters away, fearing and wishing at the same time to see a well-known silhouette emerge therefrom, which Tête-Rouge had only been able imperfectly to banish from her heart.

The resumption of work had just sounded. Valotte quit his guests and, dragging the miserable cohort of convicts behind him, set off toward the path.

The sun was blazing in a terrible fashion; it was as if the landscape was on fire, and yet, in spite of the vigor of the climate, a considerable labor had to be accomplished before nightfall. The inspector, accompanied by the engineer of roads and bridges, was due to come the next day in order to "receive" what had been done on the road.

Valotte, his face illuminated and very cheerful, was singing barracks refrains or addressing paternal admonitions to his subordinates when he perceived the detachment that Crassni was bringing coming along the road.

The two comrades exchanged congratulations.

"Well," said Crassni, "did you find what you needed?"

"Yes, as you see; I was given strong heads at the kasbah. It's up to us to look after them. What's new at the camp?"

"Oh, something delightful, old man!"

And while chatting the two sub-officers drew away, while Valotte told his comrade about all the day's events.

"It's not only you who creates infatuation, old man; if you had seen how the chick looked at me . . . and a delightful woman, you know . . ."

Valotte launched into a very detailed description of Françoise-la-Bretonne, whose beauty had impressed him singularly.

"But . . . but, that's the same woman who recommended 3474 to me . . . unless it's a matter of an extraordinary resemblance . . ."

While talking the two sergeants had reached the shadow of an olive tree, from which they could embrace the entire work-site with a glance.

As if by magic, murmurs rose up in the ranks of the workers. "The *pieds* have gone, necessary to rest for moment!"

And with a unanimous gesture, all the prisoners dropped their tools.

Only one continued to ply his pick-ax with ardor, untiringly, delivering great blows to the sticky ground and straightening up in order to continue relentlessly, without stopping.

"Look," launched the mocking voice of Nez-de-Coq. "It's that idiot Dagorne again, working like a stag. Hey over there, 3474, you're not a little crazy to row like that. You're putting the friends to shame—necessary to see!"

Insensible to the sarcasms, which he did not seem to hear, Mathurin continued, his forehead streaming with sweat, his shirt stuck to his back and breast.

"Well," said Nez-de-Coq, "are you deaf? You can't hear me? I'm talking to you, insect! Oh, I see; you want to get in well with the *pied*, but you're wasting your time. It's midday! He's got his eye on you, and you're good for the tomb again this evening."

And as Mathurin did not even turn his head, Nez-de-Coq approached him, seized his pick and, with the aid of a large stone, broke the shaft, saying: "Go on, work now, idiot!"

The Breton was bewildered, uncomprehending. Everything seemed to abandon him; only Crassni's hatred pursued him, as well as Nez-de-Coq's malevolence.

Crushed, he remained motionless, his arms folded and his gaze bleak.

Suddenly, a familiar voice resounded: "Well, 3474, do you think you can spend your time doing nothing?"

It was Crassni, followed by Valotte, who was returning to the work-site. He was soon next to his subordinate and seized his collar with a sinewy hand.

"No, but you've decided to give me stories! If all the other pégriots were like you, the work wouldn't advance and I'd be in trouble. But it won't happen like that, swine . . . go on, resume work, or beware of the tomb. And quicker than that!"

As soon as they had perceived Crassni, all the prisoners had bent their backs and resumed their tasks.

"So it's only you who isn't doing anything?" continued Crassni, in a voice strangled by anger.

"But sergeant," said Mathurin, deciding to reply. "The shaft of my pick is broken and . . ."

He was about to continue, but the fear of denouncing a comrade made him fall silent.

"Well, go on—respond, speak, say something . . . defend yourself, idiot! So you've broken the handle of your pick so as not to be able to work. You're rebelling, you're an anarchist, your account is settled. My colleague has just told me who you are. Just now, at lunch, a friend of the caterer, a Breton like you, who knew you in Paris, has given me information on your account . . .

"Oh, it's something nice, your carcass! You led quite a life in Paris. And here you want to set a bad example, to preach revolt in the workyards. Have no fear, it won't happen like that, we know you . . . with your touch-me-not airs you're a sly one of the worst sort . . . if we didn't have an eye on you, you'd slip away like a zebra. Fortunately, I'm occupying myself with you. Let's go—you're lucky, it's time to return to camp."

Mathurin's luck was a sinister joke, for that evening, like the others, he was put in irons as soon as the column returned to the camp.

The first hours of the night passed tranquilly, but when, in the great silence of the plain, he heard bursts of laughter coming from the canteen and a familiar voice resounding in his ears, his chagrin was immense. He understood that Françoise was there . . .

Turning slightly, in spite of his shackles, he succeeded in perceiving the caterer's hut. The table had been set up outside the door, and by the light of a smoky lamp he recognized the Red Sorcerer, his tawny mane gilded by the reflections of the light, who was clinking glasses with Georges-l'Álgérien and Valotte; and, slightly dissimulated in the shadows, he perceived Crassni, who was murmuring gallantries in Françoise's ear.

All the dolors buried in the simple and honest heart of the unfortunate burst forth then. In an instant, he took account of all the bitterness of his situation.

Over there, the guilty were laughing and drinking, profiting from life; here, he, the innocent, was in pain, paying with his suffering for their share of happiness.

He could not suppress a sob; tears invaded his eyes, flowing down his thin cheeks, and sadly, in the night, his laments rose up like a *miserere*.

"Listen," said someone in the neighboring tent. "It's the Breton again. Poor fellow, he's paying his price . . . he'll surely leave his bones in the brush."

"Too bad for him!" yapped the stinging voice of Nez-de-Coq. "Rather than show off, he'd do better to be like everyone else . . . to be a mate like the rest. I was looking for a friend; we could have had an understanding. He didn't want to—that's all right!" And he concluded, sententiously: "Necessary never to show disgust for the pégriots!"

Mathurin's sobs reached as far as the joyful companions.

"Why, one would think that someone were lamenting," said Tête-Rouge.

"Yes. I can hear sobbing. Better go and see, Crassni, whether there's anything new in the camp—one never knows with those cocos."

"You're right, Valotte. I'll go."

Crassni disappeared, after a long glance at Françoise.

The closer he came to the tomb, the more distinct the lamentations became; he stopped for a moment and started to listen.

"There's no error," he said. "It's 3474 who's wailing. Necessary to make him shut up; we have guests."

Crassni soon reached his tent. He emerged a few moments later holding a small piece of wood and headed toward Mathurin, who was writhing in despair, filling the air with his lamentation.

"So, swine, you've sworn to annoy us till the end . . . but wait, that won't wash."

Crassni knelt down, maintaining Mathurin's head between his knees. After rummaging, he took a handkerchief out of his trouser pocket.

Mathurin, his eyes crazed, had fallen silent and was waiting. Crassni gripped his nose, in such a way as to cut off the respiration. The patient opened his mouth and his torturer took advantage of it immediately to introduce the handkerchief, rolled into a plug; then, taking the mysterious little piece of wood, he wedged it between the unfortunate's teeth, in such a way as to prevent the expulsion of the handkerchief, and tied it behind the head with a piece of string.

Mathurin Dagorne was gagged. Impotent, mute, pinned to the ground, he saw the sergeant draw away and return to his friends.

"What was it?" asked Valotte.

"Oh, nothing," Crassni replied. "A pégriot acting up. I've taken care of it."

"Another glass of anisette, sergeant?" asked Georges.

"With pleasure."

And Crassni swallowed the syrupy liqueur insouciantly, without sparing a thought for his victim.

At midnight, Tête-Rouge and Françoise took their leave of Georges and the two sub-officers. Soon, nothing could be seen on the highway but the lanterns of their carriage, drawing away at a rapid trot of their little horse.

"Well, would you say that she's pretty, the good woman?" asked Crassni.

"Yes," Valotte replied, "and she definitely seems to be smitten with you."

They returned to their tent.

Mathurin, vanquished, had lost consciousness.

IX
Toward Liberty

"It isn't fun here, old man, but in the end, one takes the time as it comes. We try to amuse ourselves a little by playing tricks on the mates. Thus, 3474, Mathurin, the pompier . . . you know, Tête-Rouge's protégé . . . what an imbecile! Oh, we make him see all the colors. Can you imagine, the other day . . ."

And Nez-de-Coq, with his inexhaustible verve and malevolence, told his former comrade Georges-l'Algérien, who had just stopped him at the moment of departing for the work-site, about all the miseries that he had caused poor Mathurin to support. They laughed together, without any pity for those injustices . . . but the caterer darted a glance to the left and the right, to see whether anyone was following his conversation with the convict. When he had that assurance, Georges continued to chat tranquilly.

His employment as a caterer had not relieved him of his pretentions to elegance; he was well-dressed, as in the past. In reality, he was only a caterer in title, for he discharged all the work on to his associate, the Mozabite Resgui.

But if the caterer affected to be on good teems with Nez-de-Coq, it was because he feared the latter's venomous tongue. Fundamentally, he detested him.

In Paris they had already had numerous quarrels provoked by the cruel mentality of Nez-de-Coq, ever ready to deliver thrusts of the beak and claws. And it was dread alone that had pushed Georges-l'Algérien—or, rather, Georges the Parisian—to recommend Nez-de-Coq particularly to Resgui, and to slip him some treats in secret from the others.

"For nourishment, I can't complain," Nez-de-Coq admitted, "And thanks to you, eh, old chap? All the more so for giving three-quarter portions to that imbecile pompier. What an idiot, anyway; if there were many like him, they'd get on with the work nicely ... not to mention that the sergeant is a fool, just between us. Oh, he lets me alone; he's perceived that it wouldn't be good to rub me up the wrong way. In the end, all that would be nothing—but there's no means of having women here ... and in the nearly six months that I've been here, I'm beginning no longer to know what amour is ..."

"Women, old chap? But I can procure them for you; don't be chagrined ... wait while I think ..."

And after a pause, the caterer went ob: "Try to escape from the camp tomorrow evening. You can say, if necessary, that you're going to wash your linen in the stream. An indigenous tirailleur will follow you, but as you're not Pantruche for nothing, you can arrange to give him the slip. At midnight, be at that spring over there. I'll send you a moukère and you can give me news of her."

"Really?"

"As I say!"

"You're not bad ... you, at least, are a mate. Put it there!"

"It's understood, then? At midnight?" said Georges, shaking his hand.

"You know, I'm beginning to have an appetite, it's been so long. You can send the chick ... I'll make her see that I'm not lily-livered!"

But Sergeant Crassni appeared, his gaze severe and his gesture menacing. Nez-de-Coq quit Georges-l'Algerien with a wink, and with a spade on his shoulder he went back to work.

The following evening—for Crassni had not given him the requested permission—he slipped out of the camp, in spite of it being closely watched, and when the moon rose, he was at the exact spot that Georges-l'Algérien had fixed for the rendezvous.

He hid behind a clump of oleanders and waited. He pricked up his ears, thinking that he could already hear footsteps. He was nervous and impatient . . .

But he waited in vain; the minutes and the hours went by; nothing happened. Nez-de-Coq was enraged.

First light surprised him, still waiting.

He was now in great embarrassment for the return to camp. His absence had surely been noticed and he was going to be severely punished. However, it was necessary to decide to return.

Out there in the plain he could distinguish the tents where the friends were. The obscure soul of Nez-de-Coq was suddenly invaded by an immense sadness, at the same time as a terrible dread.

Brave with his companions in misery, who feared his ill-treatments and the sharp darts of his faubourgian wit, Nez-de-Coq was exemplary in his submission to the sergeants. Rarely punished, he had been well-noted, his conditional liberation and his transfer to the African battalion being only a matter of four or five months. Was all that about to be compromised by a stupid flight, an imbecile mischief?

Hiding behind the olive-trees, trying to evade gazes, Nez-de-Coq tried to get back to the camp.

The reveille, sounded gaily by the tirailleurs' trumpeter, made him shudder. He was caught now; his return could no longer pass unperceived. He succeeded in reaching the tents without being perceived, however, when just as he was about to go into the shelter that he shared with fourteen other convicts, he found himself face to face with Crassni . . .

The sergeant had spent a bad night; the memory of the Bretonne haunted him, her image had pursued him into his slumber. He had dreamed that she was there, in his bed, by his side, and that they had delivered themselves to the most reckless caresses. But, waking up suddenly, he had yielded to the evidence. It was, alas, only a dream. Only Valotte's snores filled the tent.

By virtue of that, Crassni was in a bulldog humor. Scarcely was he on his feet than he had gone to "kill the worm" in the canteen. There he had found the patron, Georges-l'Algérien, in quite a state.

"Oh, sergeant, can you imagine?—something terrible has happened to me. You can't have the slightest idea . . ."

"Pour us two cassis-cognacs then, and tell me about it."

When the glasses were filled, after swallowing the sun-colored liquid in a single draught, Georges explained to Crassni in a tearful voice: "This is it, sergeant; during the night, some bandit introduced himself into the canteen through the poorly-closed door without making the slightest noise. He took possession of a sum of money that I kept hidden in a small trunk; there was nearly six hundred francs in gold there. Oh, if I get my hands on him, the animal! When one thinks that it was my entire fortune . . . money honestly earned!"

"Don't worry—I'll warn my comrade Valotte and we'll investigate. Perhaps it's a trick of the pégriots."

Crassni had returned to the tents, while Georges-l'Algérein and his associate continued to lament, bewailing their vanished small fortune.

Scarcely had the sergeant arrived at the camp than he perceived Nez-de-Coq, his expression piteous, trying to reenter without being seen

"Hey, 333, come here! Where have you been?"

"Chief, I . . ."

"Come on, don't mumble. You've doubtless been out of bed; tell the truth!"

"Chief, I assure you . . ."

"Don't lie, scoundrel. I'll tell you what you've done, wretch. Oh, my word, you've distinguished yourself! You want to award yourself a little trip to Constantine at government expense—you do well."

Bewildered, Nez-de-Coq did not understand. However, he pulled himself together sufficiently to respond: "I'd rather tell you the truth, sergeant. I know that I'll get a fortnight in irons, but too bad . . . this is it. I wanted a woman, so, knowing that moukères go to the spring during the night to fill their gourds, I went to lie in wait for them . . ."

Crassni, in a spirit of mockery, let him continue, adding, sarcastically: "All went well, then?"

"Very badly, chief, for I waited in vain; no one came."

"That's all? You've told the whole truth?"

"Everything; punish me and get it over with."

Crassni leaned back on his short legs, folded his arms over his breast, the peak of his kepi in battle order, and uttered such a burst of laughter that Valotte, who was getting dressed, emerged from the tent in haste.

"No," said Crassni, "you have no idea of such cheek! Here's a lascar, number 333, who tells me that he was running after a whore last night, when he was simply robbing poor Monsieur Georges' canteen. Anyway, it's not astonishing; this coco, 333, was recruited in Paris. He's a former batallionaire who killed an apache in a quarrel on the fortifs. Well, my colonist, with such an offence—theft with effraction—you're sure not to see the city again very soon. If you have a gigolette waiting for you, I advise her to get another pimp, because it isn't tomorrow that you'll be able to take care of her!"

Valotte, the regulation man, as soon as he heard "theft with effraction," had Nez-de-Coq taken to a tent where a tirailleur was to keep watch on him until further notice.

"Crassni," he said, "we'll inform the gendarmerie at Morris and the army commandant in Bône this evening."

"Agreed," the latter replied, "but that's no reason not to go to work. Let's go, the rest of you," he shouted at the pégriots, who remained silent. "Form up in fours and off to the workplace!"

In the meantime, Georges continued to lament in his wooden shack, turning over all the merchandise, searching the smallest corners, thinking that he might rediscover his savings.

Alas, the unfortunate fellow was wasting his time; the thief had taken his precautions. There was not the slightest indication to permit the slightest presumption.

Informed by Resgui, he learned of the suspicions that were weighing upon Nez-de-Coq.

"Oh!" he cried, lyrically, "that's friends for you! Render them a service, and that's how they repay you! No, I would never have believed that such a thing was possible! Oh, the swine—all my money, my lovely cash! Tête-Rouge was right when he told me to mistrust all the apaches there are here! One might have had little histories, but all that was the sins of youth . . . it isn't of any consequence. One remakes one's life, as Tête-Rouge has remade his, as I was in the process of remaking mine, but all those former mecs of La Chapelle are impossible to reform; thieves they were, scoundrels they remain!"

While indulging in his superfluous lamentations, Georges went to the tent where Nez-de-Coq was being kept out of sight, with irons on his feet. The tirailleur, who knew the caterer, to whom he owed money, let him go in.

"Oh, there you are!" said Nez-de-Coq, perceiving his tall silhouette outlined in the gap in the doorway against a patch of blue sky. "I've had a fine adventure, old man. Have you heard?"

"Yes; I would never have believed it of you. To play such a trick on me, a mate who loved you like a brother . . . on me, who was rendering you a service—to the point that if the thing were known, I would have lost my situation . . ."

"Oh, but you're as crazy as Crassni! It wasn't me who made the coup . . . I was at the spring waiting for the chick in question . . . but no moukéres! I didn't see anything, I waited for nothing."

"Yes," said Georges, "you say that, but you stayed out there all night, you waited until everyone was asleep and you came back. You broke down my door, which was poorly locked, you got into the canteen and you took all my money. That's bad!"

"I swear to you. Georges, on the Mec of Mecs!"

"Get away—nonsense, all that."

"Look, I tell you that I never want to see Pantruche again if it was me who lifted your cash . . ."

"It's stories that you're telling me. Do one thing—tell me where you've hidden the money and I'll call it quits; I'll settle things with the sergeants and you'll get away with three days in irons. Come on, where have you hidden it?—you don't have it on you, you've doubtless hidden it in the brush. Talk!"

Georges was softening, but Nez-de-Coq replied. "I tell you that I'm innocent; it wasn't me. Oh, if I knew where your cash was, I'd tell you, if only to get out of here. I only had forty-eight days to go, and I'd have been reintegrated into the battalion at Souk-el-Arba. I wouldn't have compromised my liberation!"

"Yes, exactly, you needed money to go on the spree out here. Perhaps, once free, you'd even have returned to Paris . . ." And, returning to his obsession, the caterer implored: "Come on, confess."

"I tell you that it wasn't me!"

"In that case, get out of trouble if you can—you'll see that you're caught. The screws will go to Constantine tomorrow; there you'll go before the court martial. Crassni will charge you, and after an offence like yours, you're sure to cop it. You'll get ten years . . . it's your affair."

Georges returned to his establishment in order to continue his search, cursing friends, Parisians and all humankind.

Left alone in his tent, Nez-de-Coq started bewailing his situation, weeping tears of rage and sorrow. "As being stuffed goes, I'm well stuffed! No, but that's just my luck! Ten years! I'm sure to get ten years! If I could only get away, go on the run . . . oh, to run away!"

"You want to run away," said a voice, suddenly. "You want to save yourself . . . I can help you with that."

In the shadows, Nez-de-Coq perceived a form draped in a burnoose. It drew closer.

"Who are you?" he asked.

But before the mysterious individual had time to reply, a gust of wind lifted the tent-flap taking the place of a door, and the prisoner recognized Resgui, Georges-l'Algérien's associate.

"What do you want with me?"

"Listen," said the Mozabite, approaching very close to the man pinned to the ground. "Listen to me, Frenchman; I know that it wasn't you who stole . . . I know the thief, but I can't denounce him . . ."

"Then what do you want with me?"

"I want to offer you liberty. I'm associated with Sidi Georges' work; I want to return to my homeland, far to the south. You please me . . ."

Moving closer to Nez-de-Coq, his eyes started to shine in a fashion that left no doubt as to his intentions.

"I'm looking for a companion to travel with me. Come—in Gardala you can work with us, you'll make a fortune, and whenever you wish you can quit us, to return to your homeland. Come, and you'll see the desert, so grand and so immense that the sky touches the sand; the palm trees are always green, the oases have springs that sing like virgins' voices, and the coubas[1] gilded by the sun's rays . . . Come; I'll love you like a son, more than a son, even . . . if you want, you won't work, you'll stay in the cabin, lying on a mat, smoking fine cigarettes of blond tobacco and drinking coffee that the women will prepare for you. You'll have nice burnooses of white silk and varnished shoes; you'll be the master in my home, and I'll be the slave . . . Come!"

---

1 Couba is a phonetic rendering of Qubba [dome].

Stunned by that flood of promises, Nez-de-Coq, before the quantity of joys that awaited him, did not know what to respond.

The commerce that Resgui was proposing to him, was not repugnant to him, but the memory of Paris . . . but bah! After all, he could return to Paris some day. What did he have to lose?

"You'll take me with you, then?"

"Yes, since I'm offering!"

"But what can you do? You can see that I have irons on my feet . . . and then, with my pégriot costume, the gendarmes will soon have recognized me."

"You talk like an infant at the tit. Look—I've taken my precautions."

And Resgui took from his burnoose a file and an Arab costume. In a few minutes, the padlocks of the irons were sawn through. Resgui helped Nez-de-Coq to put on the burnoose and the turban . . .

"Be quick," he said. "The sun's already high; the laborers will be coming back. I'll leave the tent and go talk to the tirailleurs of the guard. If necessary, I'll play a game of cards with them to retain them. I sent my luggage to Bône in the morning, from which it will leave for Biskra; you can go to wait for me over there, on the edge of the forest. As soon as I'm with the soldiers I'll sing: '*Ram ouldi y a Guelbi'Rak azizi y a saabi!*' Then you'll take advantage of that to escape."

"Understood!"

Resgui drew away. Soon, the Arabic chant resounded, sung by a nasal voice.

"It's time!" said Nez-de-Coq.

The bad mood of the morning had been succeeded in Crassni by a mad gaiety; Nez-de-Coq was the innocent cause of that.

In fact, the theft that 333 had just rendered himself culpable invaded Crassni with a delirious joy, not because he had anything against Nez-de-Coq more particularly than the other pégriots, but simply because the affair would procure him a journey to Bône—a rather long journey because of the instruction of the affair, which he charged himself with complicating deliberately, in order to prolong his sojourn in the elegant Mediterranean town.

At Bône, he would put everything to work to rediscover the Bretonne, whose beauty haunted him. He knew the approximate address of her and her lover. He would be able to find her, and this time, he would certainly have the woman, whose charm had ensorcelled him.

It was, therefore, very cheerfully that he went past the canteen.

"Well, Monsieur Georges," he shouted, "if you have any commissions for your friend—you know, the one who came with his wife—you can charge me with them; I'm going to Bône this afternoon, on the subject of your theft."

"Ah! Bon voyage, sergeant! Amuse yourself well out there. And while you're there, go say bonjour to my comrade. He lives in the Faubourg Sainte-Anne. You can find his house easily; he's well known in the quarter, where he gives judicial consultations. But to change the subject, your pégriot doesn't want to say where he's hidden the money, you know. Tell him that if he returns it to me, I won't make a complaint."

"I'm going to see him now, but it's a waste of time; the military authority will take charge of the matter."

Before putting on his uniform, Crassni, who was accompanied by Valotte, passed before the tent where Nez-de-Coq had been imprisoned.

"Let's go see one last time whether the client has decided to confess," he said to his companion.

The two officers penetrated into the canvas shelter

"Oh! Where is he? No . . . he isn't barred . . . oh, the swine . . . but . . ."

Valotte had just perceived the sawn-through shackles, and the twill trousers, shirt and belt abandoned by the fugitive.

"Yes, old man," said Valotte, laconically, "the bird has flown, but here are his feathers!"

"Oh, the dirty swine!" howled Crassni. "He's escaped. And where's the tirailleur? He'll be given sixty days of bread and water, which he'll do in Bône . . . Mount a search for 333!"

"It's pointless; he must have escaped as soon as we set off for work, in disguise, since he's left his garments. He must be far away by now. As for us, old man, if we don't arrange a story for ourselves, we'll be charged with failure of surveillance."

"Too bad! I'm going to town anyway to make a detailed report of these events!"

Crassni had his obsession, and he would rather have seen half the world crumble, see the remaining fifty-nine men flee and even lose his stripes rather than renounce his journey to Bône and the conquest of Françoise.

X

In the Sands

Crouching at the back of the stage, the Arab musicians were striving to make as much noise as possible; some were banging tambourines and darboukas, others scraping violins and theorbs; others, finally, were inflating the skins of their sakras immeasurably.

The singers, clad in sparkling outfits, dazzling with embroidery and tinsel, sitting in lascivious poses, were clamoring in chorus one of those Arab songs of which amour is the ordinary theme, and which depict so well, in their naïve harmony, the indolence of Orientals, their hatred of effort, and their resignation to what is.

Unused to such a luxurious spectacle, the Arabs of Kheroun were pressed in tightly-packed rows. Having come to see and to hear, it was indifferent to them whether they were seated, lying down or standing up. Their eyes widened by curiosity or admiration, they did not miss a single word of the chant. A woman in cherry red garments striped with embroideries, with a necklace of gold coins round her neck, was singing:

Ya Leïli, Ya Aïni!
If I had known you were coming, my friend,
I would have laid beneath your feet as a carpet
The crimson of my heart and the blackness of my eyes!

Ya Leïli, Ya Aïni!
If I had known you were coming, my friend,
I would have extended for your couch
The softness of my cheeks and the firmness of my breasts!

Ya Leïli, Ya Aïni!
If I had known you were coming, my friend,
For music I would have made you hear
The sweetness of my voice in passionate sighs!

To excite the spectators, the almahs addressed winks to them, or even called out to them, asking them, with loud voices and sonorous laughter for cigarettes or liqueurs, that they would sell later to the café-owner in exchange for an honest recompense.

Among the spectators nearest to the stage, to whom the singers addressed themselves most particularly, there was a group of three persons, two Arabs and a European, whose elegant appearance indicated a certain ease. The women never ceased to heap them with teasing and pleasantries.

"Well, Resgui," called one of the bayaderes, whose eyes were shining beneath the kohl, "is your purse empty? What advance is yours? O my heart, my throat is dry and you aren't even offering me a refreshment! Waiter, a lemonade on Resgui's account."

Without responding to that appeal, Resgui, clad in a fine burnoose of pink silk, with the puerile pride that is the prerogative of demi-barbarians, took out a scarlet silk purse ostentatiously and, making the coins that it contained clink, got ready to pay for the ordered drink. But his gesture was anticipated by that of his companion, probably a colonist, elegantly dressed in a white flannel suit, his dazzling tawny hair covered by an alder-wood helmet.

More agile than the indigene, the European had thrown a five-franc piece on to the knees of the singer, saying: "O my eye, one asks for flour from the miller and barking from dogs!"

That proverb, which was an ironic reproach, excited noisy laughter from the audience.

"Bravo, Roumi!" cried the woman. "Bravo, my heart! May Allah allow me to kiss the sole of your sandal! You are my lord!"

And she threw him her silk handkerchief.

The third person in the group, an individual of short stature, with an emaciated face and a hooked nose, wearing an indigenous costume gauchely, exclaimed then, in the purest French, ornamented with a strong Parisian accent: "Good, my old Tête-Rouge, you're always the same . . . you need them all! Oh, you're truly wonderful!"

"What do you expect, Nez-de-Coq; it's in my temperament; I can't see a woman who's all there without wanting to taste the dish."

Since his escape, Nez-de-Coq had been leading a charming existence, reaching Southern Algeria in small stages, accompanied by his friend and benefactor Resgui who spent money without counting it for his young comrade.

They had quit Bône, where their presence might be signaled, and, while traveling to Biskra, had encountered Tête-Rouge in a café in Kheroun, where he had gone on business: loans to recover or the defense of an Arab to undertake with regard to the administrator.

"It's not all this," Nez-de-Coq soon said to Tête-Rouge; "one doesn't get bored with you, but we're going to make tracks; I'll only be truly tranquil when there are no more polichinelles on my route."

"What, you fear the gendarmes?"

"Well, you know how I'd prefer not to re-engage without wages; I believe that it's preferable if the cops and I don't find ourselves face to face."

"Ah," replied Tête-Rouge, "in sum, you had good reason to slip away thus, without bidding farewell to the sergeants; it's not good for a clever fellow like you to row like a stag with pégriots. You have the right stuff; try to get out of trouble."

"All the more so," added Resgui, who was taking part in the conversation, "because, thanks to me, my friend doesn't lack anything. As soon as we arrive in my homeland, I'll arrange things for him to have an agreeable existence. In fact, Nez-de-Coq, we ought to go to the nearest railways station on mule-back; go and see if our mounts are ready and whether the guardians have already saddled them . . ."

Glad of that diversion, as well as their imminent departure, Nez-de-Coq went out, leaving Resgui alone with Tête-Rouge.

Scarcely was the deserter outside than the Sorcerer, having examined his interlocutor carefully, began:

"I don't like to say it, my dear Resgui, but I believe that you've put your finger in your eye . . ."

"A finger in the eye? What do you mean?"

"I mean, friend, that you're making a mistake. Your friend Nez-de-Coq, in whom you appear to have great confidence, isn't worth much—a scoundrel who will do you bad turns."

"Are you sure?"

"Yes, I'm sure . . . I'd bet my head on it. The mud on the streets is nothing by comparison . . . if I remember rightly, that client was a pimp in Paris, when he wasn't a burglar."

Having given those few items of information about his friend's past existence, Tête-Rouge, becoming familiar, put his hand on the Mozabite's shoulder, saying: "Look, Resgui, I haven't known you for very long, but you seem sympathetic to me . . . well, I'd like to render you a serious service. Listen to me. You and your . . . friend are going to continue your route together. He knows that you have savings; as soon as you're in some desert region, he'll kill you in order to take your money, so that he can return to Paris, where his mistress is waiting. That's what I wanted to tell you; now, act as you wish!"

Resgui had become thoughtful, and would probably have solicited further information if Nez-de-Coq had not returned, joyfully, and exclaimed in his faubourgian voice, contrasting with his Oriental attire: "The mules are ready, Resgui—mount up and let's get going."

After warm handshakes, the two travelers took their leave of Tête-Rouge, who, taking Resgui aside one last time, whispered in his ear: "You've been warned . . . be careful!"

Then, as soon as the indigene was attending to the mules, thinking about that last advice, Tête-Rouge summoned Nez-de-Coq and, while the Mozabite's back was turned, whispered in his former comrade's ear: "Don't trust him, you know; to venture into a land one doesn't know with a Bedouin isn't wise. I'll give you some advice: try to get hold of a little money and return to Paris; you'll be out of trouble there."

Jolted, bumped and jostled for long hours in the railway carriage that took them to Biskra, Resgui and his companion waxed ecstatic about the beauty of the country they traversed.

They had passed through Constantine in haste, had not paused in Batna, and were now rolling toward Gardala, the capital of the Mzab, the most beautiful town in the south. They had already passed El Kantara; the stations succeeded one another; to the right and left, the wonderstruck eyes of Nez-de-Coq discovered quantities of palm trees raising their metallic foliage toward the sky, agglomerations of gourbis, tents and, from time to time, the sparkling white dome of a marabout or the bold steeple of a minaret.

After having rested for a while in Biskra, Resgui and his friend climbed into the old patache, the ancient diligence that was to take them to Touggouri, from which they reached Laghouat, their final stop before traversing a part of the sands separating that town from the capital of the Mzab.

Scarcely had they arrived when Resgui put himself in communication with several of his coreligionists who, having made their fortune in Algeria, were returning to their homeland with full purses. While awaiting the departure of the caravan, comprising twenty camels and as many mules, Nez-de-Coq asked his friend to visit the town.

There was, before anything else, a multitude of palm trees; then, in the midst of that odorous verdure, a beautiful square, narrow streets bordered by European houses; and then, further away, the indigenous quarter with its tortuous and partly-vaulted streets and its white uncovered maisonettes, with mysterious doors giving them a particular and picturesque physiognomy.

That day, as it was the end of Ramadan, a troupe of Ouled-Naïls was giving a most suggestive performance. In spite of the scant enthusiasm that Resgui testified for persons of the fair sex, his friend succeeded in persuading him to go to that spectacle, always new and interesting for European eyes.

In a marvelous décor of palm trees, a dozen bayaderes were agitating. Those strange women caused new desires to pass through the abnormal and atrophied mind of Nez-de-Coq.

Clad in brightly-colored floating tunics tightened at the waist by a silk scarf, they agitated their bellies in a disorderly fashion, and Nez-de-Coq did not miss anything of those exercises.

To the sound—or rather the deafening racket—of a tambour, a rebec and a darbouka, the almahs of the desert executed, rhythmically, voluptuously nuanced choreographic torsions and emphatic movements, the poses becoming lascivious.

Soon, they put such a great charm and expression into the gyratory movement of the torso and the hips and the undulations of the naked belly, scarcely contained by a light gauze, that the breathless Nez-de-Coq experienced an immense joy at that parade, forgetting Paris, the prison camp, Resgui and his demands, and everything else, so absorbed was he by that pantomime of amour.

One woman, particularly lovely in her mantle of light fabric draped over her shoulders, her dainty diadem of golden silk—a brown-skinned woman with eyes enlarged by kohl, lips colored with rouge and fingernails dyed with henna—had captured the Parisian's attention. The inversions of her hands, beating the air like wings, the flexions of her body, her sudden leap, movements of the head and sudden light bound of a great hieratical art had all revived in the exile the memory of the joys of which he had been deprived since his arrival on African soil.

Resgui had a great deal of difficulty making him quit that spectacle. The night was completely dark when they emerged; the caravan, taking advantage of the cool air, was to set forth at midnight.

Nez-de-Coq was now only going southwards regretfully. Every step took him further away from everything that remained dear to his heart and his senses: Paris, friends, women—oh yes, women!

How was he going to adapt to this new life in an unknown country, with that madman Resgui, who would bend him to all his whims?

Rocked by the cadence of his camel, he went on. By his side, his friend boasted about the sumptuousness of his petty fatherland, Gardala, the eight hundred houses and the colossal minaret of which they would soon perceive, in the vapors of the nascent day.

Finally, after a march of six hours, the caravan stopped at a spring surrounded by palm trees in order for the animals to drink and rest for a while.

After slaking their thirst, the beasts collapsed on the sand, Drivers and travelers rolled up in their burnooses and dozed.

Still obsessed, Nez-de-Coq had resisted the ambient heat and the inclemency of the fiery sunlight, which descended from the clouds like a flood of molten lead. He listened momentarily. Snores could be heard; an Arab, dreaming aloud, addressed a long discourse to houris whose caresses he was demanding.

Nez-de-Coq started to reflect.

Old man, it isn't worth the trouble of being the son of your dab to have maneuvered like this! In truth, you've worked like an apprentice. You've got yourself into a pretty mess. You'll never see Pantruche and all the cut and thrust again. Oh, the good mominettes swallowed at the counter while waiting for the chick working on the street, where are you? And you, the mates, always ready for a hand of zanzi, I'll never see you again!

No, Nez-de-Coq did not want to say a supreme adieu to all those joys. What did the gendarmes matter to him? He only had to be careful; all deserters were not recaptured! Once in Paris, he would be able to elude all the researches of the bloodhounds.

Yes, but what about the money necessary to reach the coast, to pay for his passage as far as Marseille first and then his train to Paris? He didn't have a centime.

There, beside him, sleeping like a brute, exhausted by the heat and fatigue, Resgui was snoring. The belt that he wore next to his skin was well-garnished. One day, he had admitted that in addition to his savings he had a rather round sum—three or four thousand francs, to which were added the six hundred francs that he had stolen from his associate.

Knowing that Resgui was the thief, Nez-de-Coq experienced a bitter joy, at the same time as an ill-disguised rancor.

What, that villainous Moor had appropriated the savings of a mate like Georges, almost a Parisian! It was necessary that he avenge his friend. The solution was close beside him, within his reach. Nez-de-Coq made up his mind; he would act to take possession of the money that would procure liberty, pleasure, women, etc. etc., and, thanks to a camel, would return to Laghouat, from which he was not yet too far distant.

Resgui's silence and slumber encouraged him. Softly, very softly, he drew closer to the sleeper, parted the flaps of his burnoose, lifted the gandoura and unbuttoned his waistcoat. The liberating belt was beneath his hand: a belt of the red leather of the region, which, in its lining and its secret pockets, contained more than four thousand francs, as much in banknotes as in gold.

Nez-de-Coq no longer hesitated; with infinite precaution, he began to unfasten the clasp.

Already, his task was well under way; the sleeper had not made a movement and Nez-de-Coq was nearly at the end, when a voice suddenly howled: *"Redbalehoum el seracq!"*—beware the thief!

Immediately awake, all the men on the caravan were on their feet, and ten hands seized the unfortunate. In a few words, Resgui was informed of what had happened.

At that news, an immense dolor appeared to invade the strange and complex soul of the Mozabite.

"Oh, merciful God!" he exclaimed. "See how one is recompensed! Benefit is a camel, but the recompense is a rope! O my brother, O my best friend, why are you repaying me with such ingratitude?"

Nez-de-Coq made no reply; he was resigned to everything, weary of struggling against destiny.

"Resgui," said the bachamar, the leader of the convoy, "the roumi has acted badly toward you; he merits being punished, all the more so as entry to our town is forbidden to him. You know that among us, everyone works honestly. The child delivers himself to the occupations of his age, the father cultivates the gardens, the mother and the daughters weave the wool and the men go to earn their living in the towns. No, this man has given a bad example, we cannot conserve such an element of vice."

"What is it necessary to do?" asked Resgui.

"Punish him," the other replied. "The Quran, in a sura in the seventh book, says that the head that sins must fall, that the hand that steals must be cut off; let us heed the holy book, which is wisdom itself. As good muslims, true believers, that we are, we cannot shed the blood of an enemy incapable of defending himself; let us do justice otherwise. Let me handle it."

The man went to the mounts, took a solid rope, and, making a sign to Nez-de-Coq, made him understand that he was to back up against a palm tree.

In a few moments he was tightly tied up, pale and livid with fear—the fear of the torture that he redoubted without knowing what it would be.

After having bound his prisoner, without Resgui doing anything to hinder him, the Arab spotted the camel-drivers, who had just butchered a goat for their nourishment. The skin of the animal was lying on the ground; he picked it up and, with the aid of the sharp blade of his Bou-Saada dagger, cut it into large pieces.

Uncomprehendingly, Nez-de-Coq followed that operation mutely, his eyes extinct and his throat dry, watched by all the indigenes of the caravan, to whom the scene that was in preparation was not unknown. All of them, including Resgui, experienced an immense pleasure in seeing a roumi tortured who had wanted to wrong one of their own.

The man took Nez-de-Coq's right hand, and with his trenchant pointed blade he made four deep incisions in the palm. Nez-de-Coq uttered howls of pain that ripped through the burning air without finding any other echo than the laughter of the indigenes, who were extraordinarily amused by that spectacle.

Blood inundated his hand, but that did not intimidate the Arab, who continued his task very conscientiously. Someone passed him a handful of salt, and he stuffed the open and bloody wounds with it.

Nez-de-Coq suffered atrociously and his suffering was exhaled in shrill and piercing screams.

"Shut up, son of a dog!" said the torturer. "If you continue to howl like that, I'll gag you."

With an exemplary sang-froid he closed the patient's hands, in such a fashion that the fingernails plunged into the living wounds. Then, with the strips of goatskin, he wrapped the wrist and sewed it up tightly—a last refinement of cruelty, for the skin as it dried, would shrink, exerting an abominable pressure that would cause the fingernails to penetrate the wounded flesh even more deeply.

Nez-de-Coq's dolor was such that he closed his eyes and went white. Meanwhile, his left hand was subjected to the same operation. When it was concluded, he was half-unconscious.

Perhaps, at that moment, he regretted his existence of crime and misdeeds. Perhaps he remembered the atrocious death of Boubouroche, tortured in accordance with his indications, whose agony must have been as long and as terrible as his own.

In fact, he no longer doubted now the fate that awaited him. No one would come to deliver him. And within himself, he wished for a quicker death to put an end to the atrocities he was enduring.

It was settled. He would never see Paris again, He would never see the Boulevard de La Chapelle and its welcoming prostitutes . . . or Montmartre, the Butte on which he had been born, the old Butte where his childhood had gone by, where he had grown up in the company of pretty girls, the same ones with whom he had learned to dance at the Moulin de la Galette

... The Moulin de la Galette ... Montmartre ... and his entire childhood!

And while the unfortunate writhed, prey to horrible suffering, the caravan slowly drew away, sowing its white burnooses in the gold of the sands and the azure of the sky. Pinned to his palm tree, tortured by the fresh skin that was tightening its implacable embrace, Nez-de-Coq, wounded, dying of hunger, thirst and fatigue, was in agony ...

The caravan had disappeared; the sun, a terrible Southern sun, was darting its rays upon the solitary, who was howling with rage and dolor. Then dusk fell, one of those perfumed Algerian evenings. A breath of wind passed at intervals, so delightful and so subtle that it was scarcely graspable, and only the penetrating scents with which it was laden, playing in the leaves of the palm trees, awoke the senses.

In the profound calm, only troubled by the faint song of the wind in the branches, nature, delivered from the burns of the fiery star, seemed to be reborn to a new life of ecstasy and contemplation ...

Nez-de-Coq groaned softly. Suddenly, vanquished by dolor, his head slumped on to his breast. The sun, lost in the sands, set the sky ablaze with its last rays; in the confines of the horizon, a mirage effect designed the silhouette of a palm tree, but a red, bloody palm tree illuminated with violent hues by the last caresses of the dying daylight ...

And Nez-de-Coq, in his ultimate delirium, began to babble: "Paris ... the mates ... my slut ... it's over ... The camp ... Crassni ... Resgui ... the Sorcerer ... Oh, the Red Sorcerer!"

And having revered a little strength he murmured: "Yes, it's the work of the Red Sorcerer, Tête-Rouge ... I sense it ... I divine it! He must have told Resgui everything ... oh, Tête-Rouge!"

Night had fallen completely, the sky was studded with silver ... silence had returned ... no more wind, nothing but the plaints of Nez-de-Coq, who was slowly—very slowly—dying ...

XI
Crassni's Vengeance

After having wandered like a lost soul in search of Françoise, Crassni, confronted by the lack of success of his research, once he had made his report to the army commandant, had regretfully decided to return to the brush.

On his return to the camp, Valotte saluted him with laughter and an indiscreet question: "Well, have you had her, your good woman?"

"What good woman?"

"Come on, don't play the innocent; you needed to go to the square, I recognize that, but it wasn't the service alone that pushed you; you had another idea in your head."

"I assure you . . ."

"Get away! Don't defend yourself, I know what it is . . . your Bretonne . . . the civilian's wife who came the other day . . . was eating you up; you could no longer do without her . . . you need her. Oh, heartbreaker! But tell me—did it go well?"

All those crude pleasantries reawoke Crassni's chagrin; he had been beating Bône in all directions for two long days without being able to discover the woman for whom he had come. He had visited the terraces of all the elegant cafés of the Cours Bertagna and the Rue du Quatre-Septembre, searched the Arab quarter and the Colonne Randon. All those investigatons had been fruitless, including the concert hall of Bône, where the Bretonne had been replaced.

That new disappointment had put into the multiple detours of his soul a muted anger that would soon burst forth.

He had contained himself to support Valotte's pleasantries and had only accepted them with difficulty. His rage increased further when he received the midday dispatches, which brought him—as well as the innocent Valotte—a severe criticism and gross threats for lack of surveillance and negligence in service.

Valotte, with his force of inertia and his fine serenity, awaited with his habitual calm the punishment against which he did not even protest.

"Bah!" he said, philosophically. "It's an accident that can happen to anyone. A pégriot who runs away is annoying for us, but it would have been much more so for him if the tirailleurs had seen him! In fact, I believe that someone—I don't know who—must have helped him to reach the country."

And he, an eternal blunderer, out of a need to chatter, continued: "I know that people say that Resgui, the caterer's associate, was no stranger to that affair, given that he disappeared too, the same day, but all that is mere supposition. What interest did the Mozabite have in aiding the escape of a penniless apache, incapable of remunerating him subsequently?"

Crassni was scarcely listening to all that verbiage; the double disappointment he had just experienced was pursuing him incessantly. Never, perhaps, in his military life or his career as a feller of virtues, had he endured two such palpable blows.

All the pégriots who had attempted to give him the slip had been laid in the dirt by a bullet, just as all the women who had looked desirously at his mat complexion, his dark eyes and his conquering moustache had accorded him the ultimate favors he had requested. But this time, what a flop! What a failure!

The commandant of the central section, an old captain who has spent fifteen years in the colonial infantry at Noumea, did not stand any nonsense. On horseback before the regiment, he punished rebellious prisoners and negligent sub-officers with equal severity. Such an affair might hold back Crassni's advancement and compromise forever the military medal for which he was ambitious, the green and yellow ribbon of which haunted him.

The animation that reigned in the camp in the meantime could not extract him from his reflections, Valotte's words pursued him. Yes, someone had favored 333's escape—but who? How could the guilty party be found in that horde of wretches who would deny everything at the first question, or retreat into complete mutism?

The hour of labor had arrived; a whistle-blast resounded. The men emerged from the tents and lined up, mechanically. No one was missing; the fifty-nine detainees were all present.

Crassni passed between the ranks, stopping before one or another, addressing a brutal reprimand or a coarse insult.

Mathurin was in the second rank, motionless, his eyes distant, fixed in the regulation posture, with his little finger on the seam of his trousers.

At the sight of him, all the ideas that were torturing Crassni's senses and his brain took on an even greater acuity.

That Breton, that pig-headed, impenetrable, mysterious and enclosed being, reminded him of a blonde head with fresh cheeks, blood-red lips and languid eyes admirably shaded, a head that he would have liked to crush upon his breast—that of Françoise, for whom he had searched in vain, and which this prey, this Mathurin Dagorne, inmate 3474, had doubtless covered with kisses in some corner of a barn in Bretagne, or in the immensity of the heath embalmed with the scent of wild flowers.

All that crossed his mind with an insensate rapidity; his ill-contained wrath burst forth like a thunderclap.

"Ah. Let's see, 3474, do you think the government furnishes you with garments to put them in that state? No, but look at yourself! The mud on your shoes is disgusting; your trousers were white on the day when Maréchal Niel signed the order of the second of November 1863 on the interior service of places; the shirt is torn—it's not a shirt you have there but holes sewn together..."

Mathurin, resigned, listened without flinching, his gaze immutably fixed fifteen paces away. But Crassni was holding his prey and did not want to let go; he continued: "Respond, in the name of God! Don't mess with my head into the bargain."

In the ranks the men sniggered, as much at the Breton's stupidity as the sergeant's anger.

One voice mocked: "Leave him alone, sergeant, or the insect will slip away like the Parisian!"

"Silence in the ranks!" howled Crassni, "or I'll buckle all of you!"

The flight of Nez-de-Coq suddenly returned to his mind. The two men, 3474 and 333, were both from the military government of Paris, and if what the other convicts said was true, they had doubtless known one another before, in La Chapelle, where they both lived with women until the moment when Dagorne had nearly lost his head over an affair of murder. The animosity that seemed to separate them was doubtless only apparent. They had remained friends.

The truth suddenly appeared to Crassni as clear as daylight: the accomplice of the deserter, the obliging friend who had sawn through the irons and prepared all the details of the flight, he had before his eyes, at his mercy; it was Mathurin Dagorne.

He approached his victim very closely then and, eye to eye, tugging his moustache with a nervous hand, he sniggered: "Not content with dressing like a pig, you occupy yourself with things that don't concern you. Yes, I know what's happened—it's you who favored the departure of 333. You were doubtless mates in Paris; the two of you have doubtless committed many misdeeds there together. But this time, I won't fail you; you'll be clapped in irons right away. Tirailleurs, bring me monsieur's bracelets— and the rest of you, form up in pairs and off to work! You'll be escorted. As for you, my colonist," he went on, addressing the former pompier, "your affair is clear, you won't avoid the sixty days of bread and water that you'll serve in the Kasbah!"

Mathurin, annihilated and brutalized, was still silent, a veritable statue made man. And that immobility, that indifference, irritated the sub-officer to the utmost degree.

At the peak of his anger, he had seized his victim by the collar and shouted at him loudly: "Respond then, defend yourself, speak, say something!" And the more animated he became, the tighter his grip became and the more he shook the Breton.

Everything comes to an end down here, even the patience of people as placid as Mathurin. Bruised by the sergeant's fist, he suddenly recoiled, and with an abrupt gesture disengaged himself from the sergeant's grip, lifting his arm above his head as if he wanted to strike him.

The gesture had been so rapid that the sub-officer, at the time, believed that it was an impulse of anger or mad rage, and prudently stepped back. But as soon as he saw Dagorne's arm fall back, a terrible idea, a Machiavellian idea, took possession of his mind. That Dagorne, whom he hated, had wanted to carry out an act of violence against his superior!

With a gesture he summoned the few indigenes who remained on guard in the camp.

"You observed," he said to then, "that 3474 has just committed an act of violence on my person."

The Arab tirailleurs, as much in a spirit of flattery as out of stupidity, all affirmed that they had seen the detainee's gesture, and that only the firmness of the sergeant had saved him from being the victim of the Breton's brutality.

In two strides, during which the Arabs took hold of Mathurin and made it impossible for him to defend himself, Crassni had gone to his tent and came back carrying his military handbook.

He stood before Mathurin and, after having paused, he said in an incisive voice:

"Alphabetical list of crimes and military misdemeanors, and the punishments attached to them: Acts of violence against a superior during service or in connection with the service: *Death*.

"Now, I believe that with an offence like that, you can be tranquil for the rest of your days that you'll have bread on the plank, if not on the stake. You'll see the other side of the water, the Isle of Pines, if I have anything to do with it. You've already had one turn, you'll have a second. You have the habit of it; it was for a similar reason, I believe, that you tried to kill your captain. We have treatments for you; this time, you're going to get it. Go on, you," he said to the tirailleurs, "buckle him for me, with irons on his four paws, in my tent, at the foot of my camp bed . . . set two men to watch him, as well as me; we'll see whether he can succeed in vanishing, like his friend . . ."

And while Mathurin was bolted and padlocked once again, Crassni, entirely given to his evil hatred, ruminated the phrases of the report that he would send and which would cause the greatest harm to the Breton.

He did not experience any anxiety; already convicted once for an act of violence, he would certainly get the maximum, capital punishment!

At that prospect, the sergeant experienced an unhealthy joy, a morbid pleasure, and it was with a sprightly step, thinking about the journeys that these new incidents would procure him, that he went to the canteen, where Georges was waiting for him before a large glass of absinthe.

In a few words, the sub-officer brought him up to date. Scarcely had he concluded than the caterer, making grand gestures, raising his arms to the heavens in a tragic-comic fashion, cursed the depravity of present-day morality and modern mores.

"What! Wanting to strike you, sergeant! You, who are the cream of men, the father of the detachment! Oh, it's not possible. No, there must be rascally men on earth, even so. That fellow will be given to the good God without confession, in spite of his sly air; he has committed acts of violence against you! It's incredible. It's today's society, you see!"

And Georges, getting carried away continued with deafening volubility:

"It's like me, see—my associate has abandoned me on the eve of market day . . ." For the hundredth time, perhaps, he related in detail the theft of which he had been the victim, the disappearance of Resgui and the escape of Nez-de-Coq . . .

Suddenly, however, he returned to Mathurin. "He's quite something that Breton! For a villainous bird, he's one. The friend who came to see me recently with his wife—you know, the one who spoke so well, has brought me up to date with a heap of things. In the time when he had a brilliant situation in the capital, my friend heard much talk of this wretch Dagorne, and he confided to me in the greatest secrecy that the Breton was a scantly recommendable person, who lived with a woman before entering the service. A whim had made him enlist, and he had no fear of dishonoring the corps of sapeurs-pompiers when, in the company of his mistress, a prostitute well known to the prefecture of police, he murdered an old man—a senator or a big businessman, I no longer remember which—whom she had drawn into a trap. You can see that I'm informed, and that your 3474 is a great villain, monsieur."

Crassni listened to those lies and infamies with a visible pleasure. His heart, insensible to pity, had consecrated Mathurin Dagorne to the worst sufferings and definitive degradation. He was only thinking of crushing him, unjustly and cruelly—and all that because of Françoise's kiss!

The instruction of Mathurin Dagorne's case was conducted swiftly by the young captain of tirailleurs changed with the investigation. The witnesses were numerous and conclusive: detainee number 3474, according to the information collected by the investigation, had committed acts of violence against the person of his sergeant, sub-officer Crassni.

A complaint was lodged with the court martial and as the procedure was expeditious for men at the sites of public works, the order to send the accused to Constantine in order to be placed before the court martial soon arrived at the division.

Mathurin had accepted all that with an extraordinary detachment, an indifference that caused doubt regarding his mental faculties—a slackness verging on idiocy.

To all the questions posed to him he replied "No," without seeking to defend or disculpate himself otherwise. Mental and physical suffering seemed to have gradually ruined his intelligence, and if he still had in his heart a profound amour for Françoise, his firmer fiancée, it was the only sentiment that still subsisted in him.

He had already supported so many torments that nothing could frighten him any longer; on the contrary, the announcement of his condemnation to death was agreeable to him; it was a benefit, deliverance from all the tortures that he had endured thus far. He only regretted one thing—the amour of Françoise—and one person: Françoise.

Crassni had it easy with his victim; he could charge him and crush him entirely at his ease. Mathurin did nothing to defend himself against the unjust accusations brought against him, and the sergeant was satisfied to see his vengeance accomplished so easily.

That afternoon, he was blissfully installed on the terrace of a café in the Cours, where he was savoring his drink while following the comings and goings of the passers-by and contemplating the aspect of the busy street.

In the distance was the stout church, resembling a heavy locomotive, with its excessively short belfry and its overly compact apse. Facing him was the harbor where steamboats were moored; in the middle of the promenade, clumps of beautiful exotic plants—gigantic monkey-puzzle trees, fig-trees, agaves and palms—added a particularly vibrant note agreeable to the eyes.

Although his soul was hardly accessible to beauty, the sergeant was contemplating that spectacle when an English carriage, conducted by an elegant young woman, suddenly captured his attention.

"Françoise!" he murmured, invaded by a great disturbance. "Her! As long as she sees me . . ."

The pretty creature had slowed the pace of her horse, and her eyes were scanning the terraces of the cafés; she appeared to be looking for someone.

Crassni lifted his kepi in her direction with a very ceremonious gesture. She smiled at him and tugged the reins to stop the carriage.

The sergeant was already on the edge of the pavement extending his arm to help her down.

"Finally, it's you!" she said, with a smile, in a tone that delighted him.

"You were looking for me?"

"Yes; I thought you had forgotten me."

She was on the ground, and shook his hand in a particularly engaging fashion.

"Would you care to accept something?" he proposed.

"Gladly."

He had her sit down at the little table he was occupying alone at present, and after having inquired as to what she desired to take and given the order to the waiter, he seized her hands with a passionate excitement.

"It's my turn to say *finally*. For a long time I've desired to encounter you, and above all to have you with me. You'll recall that we had no luck the other time, for our first rendezvous."

"Indeed, but would you like to catch up?"

"Oh, yes! Right away!

"Right away—you're perhaps in too much of a hurry . . ."

"I beg you, don't make me wait any longer. You've already made me so unhappy. If you knew! So, a few days ago, I had occasion to come to Bône . . . I was counting on seeing you and I searched for you, I went to your concert hall . . . but it was impossible to find you . . ."

"Indeed; I was absent for a few days . . . a friend absolutely had to take me on an excursion with him to the ruins of Carthage . . ."

"Oh, I upset myself in consequence. Anyway, let's not think about it any longer now, since you're here beside me. But tell me quickly when I can have you even closer to me . . . I'm in haste to know the date that will mark one of the greatest joys of my existence.

"Well, listen, I share your impatience. But before then, I want to know if you have thought about the poor fellow that I asked you to take under your protection."

"Mathurin Dagorne?"

"That's right. How is he?" interrogated Françoise, with concern, trying to read Sergeant Crassni's gaze. Although she was no psychologist, she discerned a hint of embarrassment there.

The sub-officer stammered vaguely.

But cadenced footsteps resounded on the asphalt of the sidewalk. They both turned their heads at the same time. Crassni went white; Françoise stifled a cry.

It was Mathurin who was advancing, his face wan, his large-peaked kepi pulled down over his eyes, carrying under his arm a regulation blue handkerchief containing all that he possessed. His wrists chained, between two gendarmes, he was departing for Constantine.

"Oh! Mathurin! My poor Mathurin!" cried the young woman, who was no longer mistress of herself.

The sound of that beloved voice caused the former pompier to emerge from his torpor. He raised his head, and his blue eyes imprinted with resignation lit up with a last gleam of joy; he could die now. He had seen again the woman he still adored as of old, in spite of the pain she had caused him!

The gendarmes addressed an amicable smile to the sub-officer, without stopping, drawing their prisoner toward his implacable destiny.

That spectacle had upset Françoise to such a degree that she could not retain the tears that sprang from her eyes. She cursed herself, not daring to curse Tête-Rouge, and she was terribly unhappy, her throat caught in a powerful vice.

"What are they going to do to him, dragging him away like that?" she finally demanded, overcoming her chagrin. "What can he have done? This is how you protect him, then? Oh, I beg you, tell me the whole truth—perhaps there's still time to do something for him . . ."

"Listen, Françoise, I'm astonished that you're interested in that individual with a shady past!"

"You don't know what you're talking about. He's the most honest fellow one can encounter on earth. He's innocent of the sin he's purging at this moment in the military prison . . ."

"You're too good, too indulgent. He's a bad lot, believe me. I've seen him at work, and I can cite you a few examples of what he's capable of doing. Thus, I had in my company a Parisian nickname Nez-de-Coq . . ."

"Nez-de-Coq!" repeated Françoise, with a shudder. "What a rogue that one is!"

"Well, they seemed to be on bad terms together, but that didn't prevent your Mathurin from lending him a hand to escape. They knew one another in Paris at one time, it appears."

"What a lie! It's not true, I swear to you, Sergeant. Who can have told you that? If you knew the truth . . . the horrible truth!"

Crassni did not understand those last words, and he continued: "To get back to Mathurin Dagore, I made him a few observations—oh, very mildly—regarding all those events, and he raised his hand and struck me!"

"Mathurin struck you . . . you . . . him! Oh, it's not possible. He's incapable . . . or else it would be necessary for him to have changed character completely. And what is he going to get for that?"

"He's going to pass before the court martial, where he'll be condemned to death . . . this time, he won't get off!" Crassni declared, brutally.

"Condemned to death . . . Mathurin, . . . oh no, no . . . never!" stammered Françoise, with increased alarm. She clung on then to her last thread of hope and cried:

"Crassni, my dear Crassni, you alone can save the situation. Oh, do it! Do something for the poor fellow; he's greatly to be pitied, believe me!"

"But I can't do anything . . . otherwise, you can imagine that I'd like nothing better . . ."

"Try anyway; I'll be able to recompense you. I'll yield to all your caprices, provided that you save that poor fellow . . . I'll be yours, entirely yours, I'll lavish my caresses upon you, my kisses . . ."

"Go on, promise me, you also, that I'll have you tomorrow and that I can embrace you as I've wanted to do for such a long time!"

"Yes, I'll be yours, tomorrow . . . but you'll speak for my poor Mathurin, you swear to me . . ."

"I swear it."

"Thank you . . . thank you! You'll see how grateful I can be all my life for what you're going to do," she said, stifling her sobs in a handkerchief. "Mathurin is innocent, believe me . . . He doesn't belong in the prison camp . . . he's occupying the place of others . . . of, I wanted . . . if I were able to talk . . . !"

The existence of Françoise during the few months that had just gone by? Always nearly the same thing: numerous lovers in order to satisfy the demands of Tête-Rouge—for the juridical consultations that he pretended to give were only a ruse, a pretext, an alibi destined to mask the true source of his income.

As always, since she had been launched into that diabolical existence, the Bretonne had moments of insouciant gaiety in which she forgot all the ugliness of life, but when the intoxication of champagne and fine liqueurs had dissipated, how the past returned to her memory, bitter, cruel and sickening!

Mathurin was the leitmotiv; she could not think of him without a dolorous construction of the heart, a palpable remorse. And behind him there were other memories, and above all Clodomir Fargeau, the old man assassinated on Tête-Rouge's orders.

But she forgot all that now; she was no longer thinking about anything but Mathurin's salvation; she did not want him to die—through her indirect fault—and she felt herself ready for any sacrifice to stop his fall, for she would no longer have the courage to live if her fiancé disappeared. Superstitious as she was, that would presage further misfortunes in the future.

And with what joy, what sincerity, she delivered herself to Sergeant Crassni, that being she detested, but to whom she had to show a good face in order not to compromise her sole hope of salvation.

She kept her promise and showed herself delectably amorous and expert, employing all artifices and all seductions in order for him to want to render her, in return, the immense service that she expected of him.

He promised everything that she wished. It cost him so little! And they separated, he proud of his conquest, she filled with hope. But her distress was not completely appeased, and she was incapable of simulating it when Tête-Rouge said to her, point blank, that evening:

"It appears that Mathurin Dagorne has been behaving very badly; he's charged with acts of violence against the person of his superior. It's true that he's accustomed to doing that . . ."

"Oh!" she let slip. "You know full well . . ."

"Silence, imbecile! Blockhead! You're always ready to say stupid things. Watch your tongue, eh? As for the subject, his affair is settled; he won't get off; this time it's death, the stake!"

"You think so?"

"Yes, I think so; I'm sure and certain. No one in the world can prevent him from being condemned."

"No one?"

"No, no one. It's a pity, eh? You'll doubtless employ yourself for his liberation . . . well, I advise you against it; you'd do well; he's been charged with a good offence; he won't escape . . . and all thanks to the recommendation I made to Sergeant Crassni. Oh, I've made him a fine reputation, your damned Mathurin! No, but you're not going to weep because of him? You're still thinking about that rascally Breton, then?"

Françoise lowered her head like a guilty person. She understood, suddenly, that there was no longer anything to be done to save the man she loved—nothing. Crassni had lied when he said that he would undertake his defense; it had simply been a means to get what he wanted.

Oh, how base and vile she found that sub-officer! She would have liked to spit her scorn in his face, but what was the point? Mathurn was about to be condemned; he was going to die.

Condemned to death! Those words returned to her incessantly, like an anthem; they tortured her heart and she had to hide in order to conceal her distress from Tête-Rouge, for it would have attracted his anger and brutality.

Fortunately his so-called contentious occupations called him away; on the other hand, he still loved, as in the past, to grant himself amorous intervals, either in the neighborhood or in Bône. He was an indefatigable and skilful seducer, who knew how to obtain a profit from his mistresses.

His absences lasted a day or were prolonged, sometimes for a week, during which Françoise was gradually disengaged from his imperious will, recovering a little of her feeble personality. But as soon as he appeared, she became once again an inert woman whom he kneaded to all his caprices.

For several days Tête-Rouge had been prowling around the wife of a rich industrialist whose husband was in France for a few months. He had already attracted the gaze of the pretty individual to him and was only waiting for a propitious opportunity to make a new victim of his cupidity.

It happened that he attained that result the day after the meeting between Crassni and Françoise, when the latter was more anguished than ever regarding Mathurn's fate; and that night, he did not come back. She was unable to close her eyes, turning over projects in her head that she would never have had the courage to execute. However, one idea imposed itself upon her more forcefully than all the rest: to have Mathurin acquitted.

For that, only one recourse remained: to go to Constantine herself and talk, to tell everything she knew and denounce the true guilty parties. She would doubtless be thrown our, as in Paris, but she dressed as simply as possible, in order not to shock the severity of the military judges.

She was firmly decided; she would leave in the morning . . . provided that Tête-Rouge did not return before then, in order to annihilate the project.

She obtained information regarding the first train and without any preparation, but furnished with a little money, dreading that she might see Tête-Rouge surge forth, she took her place in the train that would take her to the capital.

In the meantime, Tête-Rouge made perfect love to his new mistress, without the slightest prescience of what was happening. Nevertheless, he came to call in at home during the day, and learned with astonishment that his "wife" had gone out that morning. His instinct of divination failed him for once, for he did not consider the hypothesis that she might be attempting a step in in favor of Mathurin.

After a difficult journey that lasted all day, when Françoise finally set foot on the platform in the Constantine railway station, the sun was setting and it was too late for her to go to the court martial that day. It would have to be the next day.

That delay troubled her greatly, because the Sorcerer was capable of arriving at any moment and finding her, even in a city where she was completely unknown.

She emerged from the Mansourah station, indifferent to the marvelous spectacle displayed to her eyes: the little plain that extends to the foot of the Mansourah, then Constantine with its towers, minarets and cupolas, superb and proud, a true eagle's nest on its seemingly-inaccessible rock; at its foot the ravine, a frightful precipice that traverses, in a bold curve, the bridge of El Kantara; and finally the horizon, a magnificent backcloth, the Chattaba blurring its hilly rump.

She went into the city, choosing winding side-streets, and went into a hotel at random in order to shelter and hide until the following morning.

It was another sleepless night, a night populated by nightmares and obsessive visions, a night of combat in her indecisive soul. Although absent and invisible, Tête-Rouge still terrorized her, she dreaded him. She would never dare to denounce him; she would denounce Nez-de-Coq, Gueule-d'Amour and Gros-Tas, but Tête-Rouge, the real guilty party, the *deus ex machina* of the shady affairs she would spare; it was stronger than her because she still feared him, in spite of everything, and although she had made the sacrifice of her own existence in order to save Mathurin.

XII
From Death to Liberty

In the narrow and lugubrious room of the court martial there was the same terrible spectacle. The roll was full, but the judges had rapidly expedited the various preceding affairs: a refusal of obedience, a chief who had confounded the accounts of his squadron and his own, and a few thieves arrested in military territory.

Then, in an imposing silence, the Dagorne affair had commenced. The president of the military tribunal, a colonel of zouaves, had interrogated the accused with a remarkable impartiality and a paternal mildness. But from the first responses of the disciplinary, when Crassni had deposed with his hatred and his testimony was confirmed by the depositions of the tirailleurs—from far away—regarding the fatal scene, Mathurin was doomed.

In vain, his advocate, a trainee scarcely informed of his métier, had searched for words capable of tenderizing the steely consciences of the magistrates; in vain he had refuted all the depositions, crushing for his client, whom he had depicted as a simple soul, more relevant to pathology than military justice; it had all been futile, annihilated by the former pompier's bad history, since a similar act of violence had brought him to Africa.

Once, the government commissaire had said, the judges of the fourth court martial of Paris had allowed themselves to be lenient; now, justice must be done, the law must be applied in all its force and rigor, without undue sensibility, without a humanitarian pity that would seem, in such circumstances to be a challenge to discipline and the law, ideas without which there would be no more army, and hence no more fatherland.

And, his implacable speech continued, the military magistrate demanded the pure and simple application of the law.

It was, therefore, death.

The accused was taken away while the tribunal deliberated; then the president, his long moustache whitened during distant campaigns, his hair bristling and his chest ornamented with decorations bought with his blood, rose to his feet in an impressive silence.

"Soldiers," he said, "bring in the accused."

Clad in debasing sackcloth, Mathurin was introduced, his head bowed, amorphous and atonal, vague and flaccid. Rifle-butts struck the ground, a brief command resounded and the men of the guard presented arms.

The clerk stood up and read the sentence.

"Unanimously, the disciplinary Mathurin Dagorne, number 3474 in the public works unit, has been found guilty of acts of violence against his sergeant. In consequence, the court martial sitting in Constantine condemns him to the death penalty."

The clerk sat down, and immediately, a voice rang out: "Death! My God! But he's innocent! He's innocent!"

A woman advanced, prey to an unusual distress. It was Françoise-la-Bretonne. Already a sentry was advancing in order to throw her out, believing that it was a matter of a madwoman or some curiosity-seeker manifesting her opinion too loudly.

Nonplussed, the judges, on the point of retiring, remained on their feet, hesitating. Françoise, struggling, reached the bar before the aged president.

"I must speak!" she howled. "I must tell everything . . . yes, everything. Mathurin is innocent; he has done nothing. Oh, the secret is choking me!"

And, broken by emotion, she fainted.

People hastened around her, while the tribunal, disconcerted by that abrupt interruption, deliberated.

Scarcely having come round, Françoise continued to declare, with an energy that she had never testified before: "I want to speak . . . I've had all that on my conscience for too long!"

After having consulted in low voices, the judges decided to suspend the session in order to interrogate the woman. Military justice, unlike civilian justice, never wastes its time in idle and futile argument.

Tremulously, Françoise was introduced into the office of the captain reporter.

"What do you have to say, Madame?" the officer asked. "Be brief, the situation is grave; it's a serious matter that is being judged, and there must be imperious reasons that have forced you to act in this way. Mathurin Dagorne is innocent, you say; I would have liked nothing better than to believe you if irrefutable testimony had not affirmed his culpability to me in an indubitable fashion; it is averred, in fact, that he struck or tried to strike his superior—which is absolutely similar, from the military viewpoint, the intention being equivalent to the act and punished in the same way."

"That affair doesn't matter, Monsieur, I won't dispute it; I have no proof to destroy that accusation, whereas I know that he is paying in the prison camp for a crime that others committed."

"And why have you not made these revelations sooner?"

"I tried to make them. They did not want to hear me at the court martial in Paris . . ."

"In fact, during the investigation I obtained very detailed knowledge of the file, and I found no trace of your deposition."

"I was thrown out when I asked to speak to the captain reporter . . . Monsieur Sylvain Corbigny, if I remember correctly."

"I see that you're informed of the affair. And what did you want to say to Monsieur Sylvain Corbigny?"

"I wanted to denounce the true guilty parties."

"You know them?"

"Yes. You must recall that Mathurin Dagorne was nearly accused of a murder committed on the same night as the attack of which his captain was the object."

"Perfectly."

"Well, the murderer of Monsier Clodomir Fargeau," said Françoidse, having become livid, emphasizing her words firmly, "is me."

"You?"

"Yes, it was me who killed that old man. He had been my lover for several months. He loved me a great deal, to the point that he had gradually informed me of the secrets of his house. A moment came when I required a rather large sum of money and I did not hesitate to kill my lover in order to take possession of it."

"Madame, that is the concern of civil law and cannot interest us for the moment; furthermore, I must point out to you that that does not prove to me the innocence of Mathurin Dagorne, since he was excluded from that affair."

"Yes, and yet he was mixed up in it involuntarily, for he brought a letter from his captain to Clodomir Fargeau his uncle, and came into the room at the precise moment when I finished strangling my victim. He witnessed my crime, but he loved me. He had previously been my fiancé in Bretagne; we had planned to marry one day, and although I have lived a terrible life, Mathurin had conserved a sentiment for me in the depths of his heart. He did not want to denounce me, and he ran away, maddened; he went at random, no longer in his right mind, and it was thus that he came to collapse on the glacis of the fortifications, where he was found the next morning by two policemen."

As Françoise spoke, the captain took notes. Not once did she pronounce the name of Tête-Rouge, but she spoke for a long time, giving abundant details on all the points that could enlighten the revision of the trial.

Then, when she had told everything she knew, without omitting anything, she was taken into custody, begging that Mathurin be acquitted.

Before then, an investigation was necessary.

Between two gendarmes, Françoise was taken to the civil prison of Constantine to await her appearance before civilian justice.

The Bretonne, her conscience relieved of an immense weight, was entirely resigned to her fate in advance. Whatever punishment was inflicted upon her she would accept gladly, since Mathurin's deliverance would be its consequence. Then too, she would be rid forever of the influence of the terrible Sorcerer!

She preferred the severe regime of prison to the existence she was leading. It would be the expiation of her sins—of Tête-Rouge's sins.

＊

In his cell, Mathurin was waiting for someone to come to fetch him for the execution; he no longer had any notion of time, only living materially.

A week had already gone by since the condemnation to death had rung in his ears. He only recalled very vaguely that a feminine voice had then been raised, proclaiming his innocence; not once had his poor head imagined that he might be definitively acquitted; he wanted death, annihilation, to the extent that he was capable of wanting anything—for all the events that had succeeded one another since the fatal evening had made him a body without a soul, devoid of desire and will: a human rag.

He had refused to sign an application to appeal and his advocate was no longer counting on presidential clemency

From morning until evening he remained seated in the same place, on a wooden stool chained to the wall, his elbows on his knees and his head in his hands, his eyes fixed on the floor, his eyes vague, seemingly no longer able to see,

It was necessary for the guard to shake him when he brought him his nourishment. He ate with difficulty, mechanically, like a beast, and after having remained thus all day in bottomless reveries, he went to sleep rolled up on the ground like a mass, in a dreamless slumber—the slumber of a brute, almost a sleep of death.

One afternoon, the chief warder of the prison penetrated into his cell. Mathurin did not even notice, that visit coinciding with the meal time.

"Well, Dagorne?"

He made no response. He had not heard.

The warden approached him, tapped him on the shoulder and turned his head slightly.

"Well, Dagorne?" he repeated.

The Breton stood up, and made a military salute.

"Dagorne," said the prison warden, "your innocence has been recognized. You're free."

He did not seem to understand.

"Follow me to the clerk, where you have certain formalities to fulfill . . . and then go wherever you wish, for your state of health is precarious and you must get better right away. Here are a hundred francs, which have been given with your intention by charitable persons interested in your misfortunes."

Mathurin's fixed gaze was riveted to the warden who had brought him the good news, but no glimmer of intelligence shone there. The unfortunate had still not understood.

The jailer took him by the arm and drew him away. At the door of the prison he repeated to him what he had already told him.

"Death . . . !" stammered Mathurin. "Death."

"But you're being released. Your innocence has been recognized."

"Oh," he said, simply.

The formalities of the release were rapidly expedited. Mathurin's ignominious livery was taken away, and he was obliged to put on a poor blue uniform found in a corner of the clothing store—after which, without a word of consolation or regret, and without a syllable of apology, he was set free.

He did not experience any joy when he saw the prison gate open before him; everything left him indifferent, his wretched, weak and ruined body was returned to the external world but his reason remained behind, in the Kasbah of Bône, at the thirty-three-kilometer camp and in the cell of the condemned.

His poor head empty, he went out and marched straight ahead, not knowing where he was going, with the hundred-franc bill he was holding crumpled in his hand.

✸

And like a phantom, in his vague blue uniform, Mathurin was seen wandering the streets of ancient Cirta. He was seen everywhere, in the Place de la Brèche, in the Rue Nationale, in the depths of El-Kantara, at the Rhummel; his steps took him to the Damremont column; he passed before the gendarmerie and arrived before the civilian prison.

A crowd stopped him, like a windblown feather fallen to earth when the breeze drops. Mechanically, Mathurin halted, and looked, without seeing anything.

In the middle of the multicolored crowd, where conversations in Arabic and Maltese overlapped, a few scraps of phrases reached the unfortunate's indifferent ears.

"By the Madonna, Pietro, did you see her before? She's rather pretty."

"Yes, but, poor thing, it's a pity that she has such a vile affair for which to reproach herself."

"What's that?"

"You don't know, then, wolf-child? It appears that she's a Frenchwoman from France, who came to join her lover, who was in the labor camp, after murdering an old man."

"Her affair is clear . . ."

But the conversation was suddenly interrupted. The prison door opened and Françoise came out between two gendarmes, in order to go to the instruction.

Her gaze wandered over the crowd, which was jeering stupidly, with the cowardice of the masses, and suddenly encountered Mathurin, who straightened up, seemingly returning to life.

Pushed by the gendarmes, she was lost in the host of white burnooses going to market. Mathurin understood then, vaguely, all the grandeur of her sacrifice and why he was free at present. He began to weep like an infant, still marching aimlessly. Mingling his sobs with curt, interrupted phrase:

"Françoise, my sweet . . . You, the gendarmes . . . Oh, to die . . . to die!"

XIII
The Unbreakable Chain

When Françoise-la-Bretonne learned that Mathurin had been set free, she had an explosion of joy. Finally, the innocent was delivered from all the torments he had endured. Finally, he would be able to be happy!

But what a profound disappointment she would have experienced if she had seen him, wretched and pitiful, wandering the streets of Constantine! What chagrin she would have felt if she had known that the former pégriot was no longer anything but a poor victim of dementia!

Fortunately, she did not know all that, and she was proud of the audacity with which she had testified; it was the first time in her life that she had given evidence of energy.

However, she was still thinking about Tête-Rouge; without regretting him, she wondered what he had said when he perceived her flight. He must fear being disturbed, even though she had not pronounced his name once.

The same day when Françoise heard about Mathurin's liberation, she learned that she would be sent to Paris, where the revision of the two affairs—military and civil—was to take place, and where she would be judged and condemned.

It mattered little to her; she still preferred life in prison to the existence that Tête-Rouge had made her lead; at least she would be tranquil there, no longer having remorse for the past or apprehensions for the future.

Two gendarmes collected her from the prison and were charged with taking her to the railway station, where she would travel in a carriage as far as Philippeville; there she would embark for Marseille.

On the platform of the Mansourah station, as she mounted the train, she shivered; it seemed to her that she had seen a familiar silhouette passing a few meters away.

But no, she said to herself. *It's a hallucination. Anyway, what is there to fear now?*

But when she descended at Philippeville, exhausted by a long and terrible journey, she could no longer have any doubt. She saw two violet eyes fixed upon her with an extraordinary acuity; she felt their will infiltrate her and recapture her.

Tête-Rouge was following her, at a distance.

Why? She did not know. He could not be unaware, however, that nothing was any longer possible between them.

She did not take long to comprehend, and was frightened by it.

The *Sultan* was to lift anchor at ten o'clock in the evening; it was six o'clock when Françoise set foot on the steamer that was to take her to France.

In no hurry to be enclosed between the four walls of the narrow cabin where she was about to pass long hours in the company of a gendarme, she asked to remain for a while on the deck, where she could dart one last glance at Algeria, where she had lived such cruel hours.

Modestly dressed, leaning on the rail, she watched the last preparations for the departure, resigned to her fate.

An activity that occupied her thought, an animation that distracted her gaze reigned on the quay and on the steamship.

The dockers and the sailors, their brains warmed by drunkenness, were shouting and swearing calling to one another with expressions that were as energetic as picturesque.

The steam rumbled, whistles and curt commands resounded in the midst of a rattle of chains and the grating of capstans.

Passengers and porters were arriving from all directions. Gradually, night was falling. In the distance, at the end of the jetty, a red beacon was shining, reminiscent of a large eye gazing over the black immensity of the waves. The prisoner's gaze reposed on the splendid panorama offered by the mountains, wooded all the way to the summit and bathing their forests of cork-oaks in the waves. Two fires were ignited, indicating douars; the white steeple of a minaret was outlined against the sky, which was gradually turning from intense blue to violet—transparent violet.

The gendarme to whose vigilance the Beteonne had been confided, with instructions as severe as they were precise, seeing that his prisoner was calm, had relaxed his surveillance somewhat. He had gone to join his colleague at the extremity of the walkway, and there they started to chat, uttering loud bursts of laughter from time to time.

Boats were navigating in the harbor, everything was in motion. Françoise was lost in an abyss of reflections. That part of the deck was almost deserted, all the travelers being occupied by an embarkation of sheep.

Suddenly, a familiar voice resounded.

"Françoise!"

She turned round, suddenly fearful, and saw two violet eyes that drilled into her own and dominated her.

She felt mentally annihilated, ceasing to think, to see and to feel; the two eyes had captured her and imposed a will upon her stronger than her own.

"What do you want, Tête-Rouge?" she stammered.

"Follow me," said Tête-Rouge, placing a hand on her as if to indicate that he had her once more, that again she would become a little thing in his hands, under his gaze.

"Follow me; I want it!" he repeated, and his eyes gleamed, fascinating.

Without knowing what she was doing, she traversed the steamship from the bow to the stern, in the departing crowd, and reached the tumultuous quay.

And soon, she found herself alone with him . . . free! He stopped, and looked her in the face.

"At least you didn't talk about me, imbecile?"

"No, no . . . I swear to you . . ."

"That's good; you're right. Otherwise, you know, I can always deal with clients or chicks that supply me."

Then, after a pause, during which his sparkling green pupils did not cease to drill for an instant into the Bretonne's fearful eyes, he went on:

"Well, they must have asked you questions back there at the court martial. Your Mathurin is free, it appears . . . and you're all right. Oh, listen, Françoise, you hurt me; when I think that I taught you to live and that, stupidly, you put yourself in trouble for a kind of . . . ."

"Tête-Rouge!" croaked Françoise. "You know full well that he's innocent. You remember, back there, in the Rue de Turenne . . ."

"Innocent! Innocent! No, but you're mad too, like that lunatic Dagorne . . . what, then, you wanted to go to the other side of the big cup?" And he became angry while saying that. "Oh, it's true, it goes without saying, women are all alike. Madame wanted to pay for that idiot Mathurin! Fortunately, the Sorcerer, the man who arranges things, was there and on watch. Follow me!"

"But," said Françoise, nonplussed, "I'm not going to Paris with the gendarmes, then?"

"You're really too stupid, you don't deserve that I occupy myself with you, imbecile! It's not worth the trouble I've taken traveling who knows how many kilometers by train to come and get you away from the police. I was at the Tunisian frontier organizing a purchase of cereals when a friend told me about your flight, and the Bône newspaper about your arrest. Without hesitation, I came back; here I am. Come!"

"I'd like to, but where can we go?" she said, with a renewal of energy. "Where can we flee? In a few moments the boat will leave, the gendarmes will perceive my disappearance, they'll warn the police, who will immediately mount a search and we'd soon be arrested, no matter where . . . If my affair is clear, yours isn't good . . . doomed either way I'd prefer to finish it once and for all. Get away, flee—I'll keep quiet . . . I won't talk about you."

Tête-Rouge clenched his teeth with anger, and his eyes lit up with red flames in the darkness. However, he only had one word:

"Imbecile!"

Then, he dragged her away. "Before the polichinelles have noticed that you've given them the slip, there's an Italian steamer, the *Consoli*, that will be leaving for Genoa in a few minutes, and from there to America. We're going to take passage aboard. I have money on me; let's go!"

At the moment when the gendarmes, desperate and mad with rage, perceived that their prisoner had fled, the *Sultan* delayed her departure in order to let the *Consoli* go through the passes and double the jetties.

Among her passengers, the Italian ship was carrying the reconquered Françoise and the impetuous hope of Tête-Rouge.

The progress of modern navigation has shortened distances in a considerable fashion, in such a way that it only takes a very short time today to travel from old Europe to America,

The voyage is particularly short when it is effected on one of the greyhounds of the sea of the Compagnie Transatlantique. In general, the days of the crossing go by rapidly, thanks to the organization of those floating palaces, with their luxurious cabins, their dining room with two hundred places, their conversation and music lounge, their smoking rooms and their boudoirs, life is facile and gay. People dance, gamble and flirt. The ladies find the means to change their clothes three times a day and the gentlemen to deliver themselves without reserve to the delights of baccarat and poker.

Unfortunately, the steamer was not favored by the weather. Scarcely had it crossed the strait of Gibraltar than a violent storm rose over the sea and accompanied her as far as the Azores.

A tempest does not offer, in itself, a very serious danger for those giants of the sea. Their enormous bulk and formidable weight causes the ocean to exhaust itself in vain efforts against their flanks.

However, although the transatlantic liner had nothing to dread from the storm, the enthusiasm and animation of the passengers had suffered an irreparable affliction.

Everyone locked himself in his cabin, fleeting the wind that never ceased to blow and the spray that whipped the face of the crewmen and washed the deck, the rigging and the bulwarks with a dense dew.

One could scarcely see, from time to time, a few passengers bolder or more impatient than the others, dragging themselves to the frame where the number of miles covered each day was inscribed, next to a map of the Atlantic, to which little flags were pinned indicating the precise position of the vessel on the immense liquid desert.

There were no balls, no concerts, no meetings on the first floor landing of the monumental stairway descending from the deck to the mahogany-paneled dining room.

It is on that landing, furnished with a long sofa, that the high society of the great liners is accustomed to gather at about five o'clock, in order to flirt nonchalantly while drinking cocktails. But this time, the elegant gossip-shop was deserted. The dining room, usually so cheerful and vibrant, with its numerous meals, in which French champagne runs in sparkling floods to irrigate the cosmopolitan menus, was almost abandoned.

That was because seasickness, an ordeal at once frightful and risible, felled the majority of the travelers. Only a few intrepid individuals put on a brave face and responded regularly to the steward's summons.

In that little battalion of loyal souls, two passengers resisted with an admirable strength. And while the felted footfalls of the steward brought everything that the galley could produce of the best, they chatted correctly and discreetly, without raising their voices, like people habituated moving in the best society.

The young woman seemed melancholy, and her companion said to her, suddenly: "You're not well this evening, darling; go back to your cabin; I'll go to smoke a cigar on the deck. Waiter, call the chambermaid to accompany Madame . . ."

The young woman got to her feet painfully; her feet dragging over the moquette, she descended the double-spiral staircase leading to the luxury cabins. In the small room that her companion had reserved for her, the chambermaid helped her to get into bed.

As soon as the domestic had discreetly gone away, however, after asking whether Madame needed anything else, the passenger, wringing her hands, let a flood of tears escape, prey to an immense dolor, and hid her head under the sheets in order to stifle her sobs, murmuring between two gasps:

"Mathurin! Mathurin! It's finished; I'll never see you again. Oh, life! He holds me, him . . . and I still love you, while he, the Red Sorcerer, I hate and detest! But I have him in the blood . . . forever!"

As the sobs eased, the man came back into the cabin, and, delivered from all constraint, launched joyfully;

"Good! You're not wailing, kid? Just at the moment when we're going to be tranquil, definitively honored, rid of the police, friends and the envious, that's when you lament! Think about it; with the tips I have and the fifty thousand bullets earned in Algeria, we're going to make a rapid fortune! There are affairs in quantity out there in America. I'll set up a house somewhere, no matter where . . . but you'll see, with the chicks that Pantruche sends me, that we'll quickly make a million. Then, in a few years, no one will know us, we'll be forgotten on the Quai des Orfèvres, and we'll return to Paris and live on our income. Well, do you regret existence now?"

The tears continued; the man was near the bunk and he drew closer, darting his gaze upon the woman, who, fascinated, forgot everything, extending her imploring lips toward him and drew him toward her, murmuring: "Tête-Rouge!"

The Sorcerer uttered a formidable burst of laughter and, kissing her avidly, exclaimed: "Come here, kid!"

Time has passed over people and things. Calm has settled upon souls.

In the region of Carnac, Françoise is forgotten by everyone, except for Mathurin, who sometimes thinks about her when he goes, unconscious and wretched, in rags, his eyes crazed and his gestures weary, over the heath.

Often, when dusk falls, he sits on the edge of the sea, his eyes invariably fixed on the horizon. In his rare moments of fugitive lucidity, he has the intuition that his fiancée has departed in that direction.

But immediately, his madness seizes him again, his faculties are annihilated and as darkness falls he returns to the corner of the barn that good souls have reserved for him, with a piece of brown bread and a bowl of golden cider.

He is the Innocent, the harmless village idiot, the one whose puerile exploits the children relate to their parents with a superstitious dread.[1]

By night, when the wind from the sea howls over the heath, a plaint rises up from the barn:

"Françoise!" the voice moans, in a sob. And the people who hear it, while chatting beside the fire, look at one another with a fearful dread, murmuring in low voices, in a whisper, in order not to be heard by the korrigans, the name of the man of the heath whose terrible eye cast a spell on Mathurin:

"Le Sorzour Ru! The Red Sorcerer!"

The stories of life do not often terminate as in novels; vice is not always punished or virtue recompensed.

THE END

---

1 It might well be a pure coincidence, but it is perhaps worth noting that in Jane de La Vaudère's *Les Androgynes*, André, the character who is probably based on Fabrice, is subjected to the same cruel fate as Mathurin, although he arrives there far more directly.

A PARTIAL LIST OF SNUGGLY BOOKS

MAY ARMAND BLANC *The Last Rendezvous*
G. ALBERT AURIER *Elsewhere and Other Stories*
CHARLES BARBARA *My Lunatic Asylum*
S. HENRY BERTHOUD *Misanthropic Tales*
LÉON BLOY *The Tarantulas' Parlor and Other Unkind Tales*
ÉLÉMIR BOURGES *The Twilight of the Gods*
CYRIEL BUYSSE *The Aunts*
JAMES CHAMPAGNE *Harlem Smoke*
FÉLICIEN CHAMPSAUR *The Latin Orgy*
BRENDAN CONNELL *Metrophilias*
BRENDAN CONNELL *Unofficial History of Pi Wei*
BRENDAN CONNELL (editor)
    The World in Violet: An Anthology of EnglishDecadent Poetry
RAFAELA CONTRERAS *The Turquoise Ring and Other Stories*
DANIEL CORRICK (editor)
    Ghosts and Robbers: An Anthology of German Gothic Fiction
ADOLFO COUVE *When I Think of My Missing Head*
QUENTIN S. CRISP *Aiaigasa*
LUCIE DELARUE-MARDRUS *The Last Siren and Other Stories*
LADY DILKE *The Outcast Spirit and Other Stories*
CATHERINE DOUSTEYSSIER-KHOZE *The Beauty of the Death Cap*
ÉDOUARD DUJARDIN *Hauntings*
BERIT ELLINGSEN *Now We Can See the Moon*
ERCKMANN-CHATRIAN *A Malediction*
ALPHONSE ESQUIROS *The Enchanted Castle*
ENRIQUE GÓMEZ CARRILLO *Sentimental Stories*
DELPHI FABRICE *Flowers of Ether*
DELPHI FABRICE *The Red Spider*
BENJAMIN GASTINEAU *The Reign of Satan*
EDMOND AND JULES DE GONCOURT *Manette Salomon*
REMY DE GOURMONT *From a Faraway Land*
REMY DE GOURMONT *Morose Vignettes*
GUIDO GOZZANO *Alcina and Other Stories*
GUSTAVE GUICHES *The Modesty of Sodom*
EDWARD HERON-ALLEN *The Complete Shorter Fiction*
EDWARD HERON-ALLEN *Three Ghost-Written Novels*
RHYS HUGHES *Cloud Farming in Wales*
J.-K. HUYSMANS *The Crowds of Lourdes*
J.-K. HUYSMANS *Knapsacks*
COLIN INSOLE *Valerie and Other Stories*
JUSTIN ISIS *Pleasant Tales II*

www.ingramcontent.com/pod-product-compliance
Lightning Source LLC
Chambersburg PA
CBHW050507110726
47899CB00005B/1367